AMERICAN FICTION

Volume Ten
The Best Unpublished Short Stories by Emerging Writers

Antonya Nelson and Robert Boswell, Guest Judges
Alan Davis and Michael White, Editors

New Rivers Press

1999

© 1999 by New Rivers Press. All rights reserved
First Edition
Printed in Canada
Library of Congress Catalog Card Number: 96-067816
ISBN: 0-89823-192-2
Copyedited by Anne Running
Book design and typesetting by Interface Graphics, Inc.

New Rivers Press is a nonprofit literary press dedicated to publishing the very best emerging writers in our region, nation, and world.

The publication of *American Fiction, Volume Ten* has been made possible by generous grants from the General Mills Foundation, the McKnight Foundation, the Star Tribune Foundation, and the contributing members of New Rivers Press.

New Rivers Press
420 North Fifth Street, Suite 910
Minneapolis, MN 55401

www.mtn.org/newrivpr

For my mother
Dorothy Rose Davis
(1923–1999)

Contents

ALAN DAVIS
EDITOR'S NOTE, ix

ACKNOWLEDGMENTS, xi

ANTONYA NELSON
ROBERT BOSWELL
INTRODUCTION, xiii

FIRST PRIZE
KAREN HALVORSEN SCHRECK
MODEL HOME, 1

SECOND PRIZE
SARAH MCELWAIN
BORN LUCKY, 17

THIRD PRIZE
BROCK CLARKE
THE WORLD DIRTY, LIKE A HEART, 25

THIRD PRIZE
CATHY DAY
BOSS MAN, 34

STEPHEN K. BAUER
ALL THE NIGHT COULD HOLD, 51

CATHERINE BRADY
AND THE SHIN BONE'S CONNECTED TO THE KNEE BONE, 67

RICHARD BURGIN
NOUINA'S HOUSE, 79

Annie Dawid
Boy at the Piano, 93

Lin Enger
Bones, 111

Bridget Rohan Garrity
The Holy Boys, 125

Patricia Ann McNair
The Temple of Air, 146

Ellie Mering
Still Waters, 162

Odhran O'Donovan
The Mick Sheehy Caper, 176

Tom Paine
The Mayor of Saint John, 180

Doug Rennie
Irian Jaya, 198

Jean Rysstad
Say the Word, 203

Julie Showalter
Breeding Turkeys, 211

Maya Sonenberg
Beyond Mecca, 224

Tanya Whiton
One for the Ocean, 241

Biographical Notes, 255

EDITOR'S NOTE

Alan Davis

This is the tenth volume in the American Fiction series. Our first annual anthology of the best unpublished stories by emerging writers chosen through an open competition appeared in 1987, when Ann Beattie served as judge. The following year, Ray Carver judged and chose "The Expendables" by Antonya Nelson for First Prize. Now, a decade later, Antonya Nelson, a celebrated writer herself, and her husband, writer Robert Boswell, are our judges. It is seldom in these throwaway times that a literary anthology survives long enough to come full circle in such a fashion.

In addition, *Writers Digest* this summer picked *American Fiction* as one of the top fifteen places in the United States to publish short fiction. We are grateful for their recognition; many of the writers we published years ago, like David Guterson *(Snow Falling on Cedars)* or Ursula Hegi *(Stones from the River)*, were published in our pages long before the literary world knew who they were. Herein is your chance to meet writers who in some cases have already received a good deal of favorable attention and have been notably published in their several books, and in other cases are appearing for the first time anywhere. We think that their work is dazzling; I suspect that it might do for you what it did (and does) for us—take you from your everyday frets, from the bump and warp of the daily deal, to a place where the possibility of transformation presents itself. The protagonists of many of these stories have troubles that you will recognize as realistic, but the writers' style and stance somehow rescue even the bleakest situation from the bugaboo of everydayness. The result, whether humorous or near-tragic, is an artifact that stands before us like a well-crafted item of furniture meant to last for generations: made of real wood, varnished and not stained, so that its warp and swerve are visible even to the unpracticed eye. Most of these stories, that is, are satisfying aesthetically in a way that cannot be summarized but must be experienced.

    Come inside, as Charles Baxter said of a previous volume. Wonders galore.

Acknowledgments

Some acknowledgments are in order. First, to my coeditor Michael White, whose own recent novel, *A Brother's Blood,* is a delightful example of the craftsmanship and artistry we seek in the stories we read. Associate editors Debra Marquart and David Pink, besides screening stories, are seasoned writers who have provided a great deal of useful advice and who sometimes help us as much by what they don't say as by what they do. Our assistant editors—Megan Randall, Liz Severn, and Karen Stensrud—have done yeoman duty as screeners. Thank you.

We are grateful as well to Antonya Nelson and Robert Boswell, this year's finalist judges, for writing the introduction, for choosing prizewinners, and for lending their literary reputations so that we might bring more attention to the emerging writers included herein. We thank everyone at New Rivers Press—Bill Truesdale, Phyllis Jendro, Jennifer Song, and Kelly Williams—for their support, encouragement, and hard work. Secretarial assistance has been provided by Irene Graves and Emily Gray at Springfield College and by Dee Kruger, Deb Radke, and Amanda Stegmaier at Moorhead State University, as well as by several student workers at both institutions. Both institutions also provided assistance in the form of creative activity grants, release time, or support of the kind that makes a project such as this one a pleasure instead of a burden.

We thank this year's prizewinners, Karen Halvorsen Schreck, Sarah McElwain, Brock Clarke, Cathy Day, and the other finalists for their work. Finally, and foremost, I want to thank every writer who submitted stories to us for consideration. We truly appreciate the chance to see your best work; in fact, editing *American Fiction* gives us a great deal of pleasure. We want all of you to know that we read your stories carefully and thoughtfully, and that we wish each of you the best of luck in placing your fiction before a larger public.

That's it. Amen. Grace is over, as Tobias Wolff, a previous judge, said of an earlier issue: Dig in.

Introduction

Antonya Nelson

Eleven years ago Ray Carver edited this anthology of fiction and selected my story "The Expendables" to be given First Prize in the annual contest. That designation meant the world to me, as I was in awe of Carver's fiction, the straightforwardness of his premises, the blunt desperation and hard-won enlightenment that his characters always worked toward, the nearly religious intensity of their need to be redeemed. I think Ray Carver would appreciate Karen Halvorsen Schreck's story "Model Home" for the qualities it shares with his own apparent vision of the world and its inhabitants.

Schreck's protagonist is living under the siege of forces beyond his control: the tyranny of adolescence and the stigma of his father's incarceration, the utter victimization of his sister—by father, boyfriend, culture at large—and the destruction of his childhood home. In the face of such bleak carnage, his impulse to offer his sister sanctuary, to pursue beauty by whatever means within his grasp, presents the reader with what we always seek: assurance that humanity's finer gestures will prevail, in spite of, in addition to, and possibly because of the mayhem preceding those gestures. Peter wishes to save Mary and simultaneously prays he will not defile her. He is a complicated, sympathetic character, and when he shows his sister the house he would build for her if he could—made of desire and Elmer's glue—you feel the satisfying sense of redemption and transcendence that mark all of the great stories.

Robert Boswell

"This is the saddest story I have ever heard." Ford Maddox Ford's *The Good Soldier* gets my vote for most daring opening line of any novel of consequence. Start with such a promise, and you'd better produce something pretty damn sad. Mere melancholy won't cut it. A lot of the sport in writing fiction comes from setting up a difficult challenge for yourself. Whenever the familiar tenets of fiction writing begin to sound like rules, writers find ways to bust them wide open. "Born Lucky," one of the prizewinners in this collection, opens not with the narrator's birth, but with the scheme that leads to the narrator's conception. Sarah McElwain gives herself the formidable task of writing a first-person narrative in utero. I can imagine this author hearing a creative writing professor advising against stories wherein the main character never leaves his room. "I can top that," McElwain must have thought. "I'll write a story wherein the character never leaves the *womb*." The narrative is all about pushing one's luck and still making out, and this is just what McElwain has done with the story. It's not only about a scam, it embraces the irreverent glee of the scam artist—which is not much different from the shifty pleasures of the literary artist.

Brock Clarke's "The World Dirty, Like a Heart" lives in its quirky sentences, thumbing its nose at the admonishment against writing prose that calls attention to itself. Much of the pleasure in this story is in the comic cadences of the writing. "We were both married . . . and constantly complained about our wives but only in the nicest terms, and never when they were within earshot." The reader is encouraged to fix on the lively surfaces of the prose. "I lectured him on wrong and right, on the things and strings of the heart breaking asunder." The lines are so clever they may divert the reader's attention from the actions of the characters but not at the characters' expense; rather the idiosyncratic prose serves as a kind of misdirection, the kind that literary fiction often needs. By the end of the story the narrator has been abandoned by the significant other. "I didn't even see her go," the narrator says, his attention, like the reader's, having focused on the vivid exteriors instead of on the serious business reverberating just underneath.

The reader is made to feel complicit in the character's error, which prohibits judgment unless it is self-condemning. Clarke's story is deceptively complex and aggressively mischievous. It's also way funny.

In "Boss Man," Cathy Day revs up the story engine with the very first line: "Even when it was all over—the money counted, the caravan disappeared, the carcasses rotted, the blacktop washed away in the rain—Earl Richards never spoke ill of the gypsies." This sentence makes so many promises and creates such acceleration that the reader can't help but leap into the story. At the same time, the whole narrative of "Boss Man" is contained in that first sentence, and the most important element turns out to be the least colorful part of it—that Earl never speaks ill of the gypsies. When a writer opens with such a sentence, she is demanding that the story have the tension, speed, and animation that the sentence promises. At the same time, the conclusion of the story has to be imbued with sufficient surprise and irony to provide a payoff for the ride; otherwise, the story could fall into the pejorative category of "cheap thrills." Day meets all the challenges she sets up for herself. The story ends with an ironic and heartbreaking shift in circumstances for Earl, one for which he'd been preparing himself all along.

All the stories in this collection deserve your attention. The best stories are like bad houseguests—everywhere you look you see evidence of their presence, and even after you've closed the book on them their effects linger. If the stories in this volume came to stay with you, you wouldn't be able to get a thing done. Your towels would bear muddy shoe prints, your kids' lunch money would be missing, the dog would get out, the stereo would blow a speaker, your daughter would learn the words to "I'm Henry the Eighth I Am," your cable bill would suddenly include the Playboy Channel, and your favorite easy chair would be pitted with cigarette burns. On closer inspection, you'd see the cigarette burns are O's in tic-tac-toe games scratched into the leather. They don't let you sleep, those bad guests. They don't let you take your good life for granted.

Writing fiction is an ugly business, and the young writers featured in this issue are really good at it. Celebrate them.

Model Home

Karen Halvorsen Schreck

Mary was at it again. Puking. Peter stood at the end of the dark hallway, looking down it at the little line of rosy light beneath the bathroom door. This was the fourth time this week, always while Mom was selling lingerie at Carson's and Peter was doing his homework—while Mary should have been doing hers, for she'd been held back last year; she was a freshman in high school again. Instead, she'd squat in there, hunched over the pink toilet, holding on to its furry pink cover, the cold pink tiles pressing into the balls of her feet. Or she'd kneel, her straight, dark brown hair swinging forward, sticking to her clammy forehead and flushed cheeks. Little blood vessels bursting in the shadowy circles beneath her gray eyes.

Peter turned his new bottle of Elmer's glue over and over in his hands, then pressed it into his stomach. This was how he saw Mary, now and at night when he couldn't sleep. Couldn't stop seeing her. In his mind's eye, as his sixth-grade teacher Mrs. Colson said. "Try to imagine your model home in your mind's eye, as good architects do," Mrs. Colson said. "Then you'll be able to create it." This was the day she handed out the clean, smooth, thick pieces of drawing paper on which the students were to sketch their plans. It was the richest paper that Peter had ever touched; it reminded him of the petals of the roses his father used to grow, which were all brown and broken now, and only thorns. Peter ran his hands over his sheet again and again, and could barely put his pencil to it, until he did, and then he couldn't stop making lines and angles, rooms to hide away in and windows to peek out of, a tiny scrolling lock marking every door.

Since then, Peter had been trying to develop his mind's eye. He wanted to be not just a good, but a great architect someday. He wanted to design and build beautiful, safe houses. He would make a city of them, and it would be known the world over, Peterson,

Wisconsin, U.S.A. That sounded better than just plain Peter, Wisconsin. He'd name the streets after things and people he loved: Schwinn Road, Green Bay Packer Lane, and in the moments when she smiled at him—which weren't very often—he thought he'd name the main street for Mary. In Peterson, there'd be no need for a hospital, a police station, or a prison. Psychiatrists could live in his houses, but they'd have to work elsewhere. They'd want to. In Peterson, people wouldn't need their help.

Peter kicked off his thongs because the bottoms sometimes slapped against his heels, and then he began to move quietly down the hall. He'd never actually seen Mary vomit. He'd only heard her or smelled it afterward, a tang like ammonia seeping through the cloud of rose-scented air freshener she left behind, hanging before the mirror, swirling around the flower-shaped shade of the swag lamp. He was pretty sure he had a good idea of what she looked like in there, though, based on his mind's eye.

He paused in front of the bathroom door, holding his breath. He could feel his blood thudding, the pulse in his throat and temples. Mary spat something into the toilet. She was pretty quiet about it all, actually, and getting quieter. The last time he got sick, Mom said it sounded like he was tearing his insides out. It was just after his father was taken away, almost a year ago now, and some neighbor had brought in a casserole the color of their poodle Tinker's runny yellow shit when they were giving it antibiotics for something with its ear. Peter carefully finished his dinner, excused himself, and ran from the kitchen table to the nearest receptacle—the brass umbrella stand by the front door, which held his father's golf umbrella and his father's cane—then retched into it. Mom must have taken the umbrella and the cane out and scrubbed them before she put them back, because they were still there, clean. Whenever Mom wasn't at work she did things like that, cleaned things, some that were pretty obvious—floors and such—and others Peter wouldn't think of touching. She was always dusting his father's golf trophies, for instance, until last week, when she threw them away. Things of his father's were going out with the trash these days; probably his father's umbrella and cane would go soon, too. The photographs of him that hung in the hallway with the other family pictures, those were some of the first things Mom tossed. There were blank spots on the wall where he used to be, posed in his army uniform, or wearing his tuxedo and standing by Mom in her wedding dress, or sitting with bald baby Mary on his lap. Blank spots paler than the rest of the wall, framed by rectangles of dust and dirt. They'd paint over these, Mom said, when they got the money.

Something cool and sticky dripped onto Peter's knuckles. Glue. He'd been squeezing the bottle tight, and hadn't even known. It was a full bottle, and now the orange cap was all glopped up. He bit back a sigh, then almost dropped the bottle because the bathroom faucet was running. Mary might catch him standing outside, as she had once before. She'd chased him into a corner and told him that if she ever caught him spying again, she'd make his life hell. "You tell Ma anything about my business," she said, "and I'll give away secrets about you that you didn't even know you had." She shook him and pressed him into the wall; her hair grazed his cheeks. Then she positioned her knee at his crotch. He looked down there, at a bruise that peeked out beneath the hem of her yellow shorts. Everything went still, and he stared at that bruise, until she loosened her grip and stepped back. A little dribble of blood slipped down her chin. She'd bitten her lower lip. Unconsciously, she rubbed at the blood, leaving a pink smear. "Hell. Don't you ever forget it," she said, and turned and walked away.

He'd known then what secret Mary would tell Mom. He still knew what it was: his waking up to sticky sheets, and how all these months he'd been washing them before Mom got home from work, hiding them under baskets of clean clothes when he took them down to the basement, hoping Mary wouldn't see.

Now Mary had turned off the faucet, and now the toilet was flushing, and Peter took off for the kitchen. There, he washed his hands and wiped the glue bottle until it was clean. Tinker was eyeing him from her bed by the table, so he filled her water dish and got a dog biscuit. He knelt down beside her. Her nose was warm, and she snuffled the biscuit when he put it by her mouth, then sighed, her eyes darting, worried. She wasn't the same. Peter's father had always been too busy to play catch with her, or take her for a walk, or pet her; he'd hardly even noticed Tinker. Yet she seemed to miss him. Peter scratched the tight, glossy black coils of hair behind her ears.

"Stupid mutt."

Mary's voice, huskier than usual. Peter looked up carefully. She was leaning against the doorway, glaring at the dog, then at Peter. "What?" she said. She went to the refrigerator, flung it open, pulled out a liter of Diet Coke. She unscrewed the cap and chugged from the plastic bottle, then stared into the bright light of the open refrigerator. Peter cleared his throat softly, trying to hold his voice in check. "Mom doesn't like it when—" he began, but sure enough his voice cracked on the "when," screeching up to a high soprano. His ears went hot, and Mary whirled around, grinning. Then her face darkened, and she was by him in a rush, kneeling down so close that he could see the pale freckles spattered across her nose, the gap between her two front teeth that she used to whistle sharply through, calling Tinker. He could see dried tears in the corners of her bloodshot eyes. "You know, you're lucky," she said, her breath sour under the sweet of the Coke. "You're lucky we don't live in Italy. The priests might have gotten hold of you before you got to be such a man. They'd have cut off your pecker. That's what they do there, to make men sing like women." And she was off, running down the hallway, shrieking "Volaré" at the top of her lungs. Then she slammed her bedroom door, and the house was silent.

Peter got up stiffly; his foot had fallen asleep. There was glue all over his hands again. Stupid glue. He saw now that there was a crack in the bottle. He washed up, closed the refrigerator door, walked to his bedroom, and locked himself in. He went around his bed to the three feet of space between the mattress and the wall. Hidden there, under an old sheet, was his new model home. This wasn't a school project; his school project was done. For it, he'd made a duplicate of their own house, a ranch. He didn't like it much anymore, though it had gotten an A, and Mom had put it in a place of honor, on top of the piano in the living room. Once, he'd come upon Mary standing in front of it. She was shifting the furniture around in the miniature version of her bedroom. Then she pushed the house away, and the furniture inside tumbled over. She looked up, at the mirror hanging above the fireplace. She stared into the mirror, unblinking. Peter slipped away then, and came back later to right all the pieces, the delicate chairs, tables, and beds.

That house was too familiar. Peter, Mary, Mom—they all knew too much about it. Peter lifted the sheet. This house was his own personal project, his creation. It was still a shell, two floors of plywood about two feet high, no inner walls yet, but when he lay down on his belly in front of it, his mind's eye saw a curving staircase, floors painted like marble, two fireplaces, a hot tub. He squeezed a thin line of glue next to the roof's peak, then picked up a tweezers and began to set tiny wooden shingles in place. He squinted, trying not to breathe as he nudged each one flush up against its mate. It would be perfect. Nothing would be dark or hidden. You wouldn't worry that you might come upon something that could give you nightmares.

———

Peter threw the last newspaper at the Kern's front porch; it clapped against the steps. He turned his bicycle and started home, pedaling fast. It was a gray morning, nearly seven o'clock and still no sign of sun. The trees seemed cold, the thin October drizzle a humiliation they endured. Piles of leaves stood in the gutters and he rode through them, hoping they would rise up in a swirl, but of course they were damp and only stuck to the bike's tires and spokes.

He was retracing his route, that half a subdivision that seemed like miles, after getting out of bed at five in the morning. He knew things about some of these houses: their different breakfast smells, how the women looked before their makeup, what kind of underwear the men wore. He could predict who would decorate for the holidays, and with what. The Himmels put up their graveyard yesterday. The week before Halloween, they always set up five tombstones, made of Styrofoam and painted gray, with each of their names inscribed in black, and then "Beloved father," "Beloved sister," and so on just beneath that. They draped stringy spiderwebs all around their bushes. Peter always looked the other way, driving by the Himmels' graveyard. It seemed on the edge of blasphemous, what they did. He wondered if they were atheists. He wondered if delivering to them would jinx him in all kinds of directions. Not only might they be atheists, they were also the first of his private deliveries, the ones Mom didn't know about. There were only seven total, but altogether, they gave him extra spending money, fifteen dollars more a month. Peter needed it. When his father was taken away, Mom had insisted that he hand over every penny he collected so that she could put it right into savings. For his college education, she said. She always gave him back a five-dollar bill, but she didn't know how much everything cost— computer games and food at concession stands and furniture and supplies for the model home. Mom took Mary's paychecks from Pan's Supermarket, too. Mary raged at that. She'd go to the piano and slam her fists against the keys. That was all it got played now. No more of their father's renditions of "Body and Soul," "Bridge over Troubled Water," and "Our House," which he played to wind down after selling insurance all day. No more of him playing the fast ones slow and the slow ones fast. "I can't talk and I can't listen," he'd tell anyone who tried to interrupt him, which people didn't do very often. "I'm playing." He'd grip the sheets of music with his long, agile fingers, shake the music so it rustled. *"Playing."* His thin body seemed to collapse into itself as he hunched over the keys.

Peter coasted up his driveway, braking beside the car. Mom was sitting behind the steering wheel, peering into the rearview mirror, flicking on mascara. She turned toward him and rolled down the window. She held her eyes wide so the stuff would dry. Peter knew that look. She looked frightened, like some animal that didn't want to come out of its cage. He used to think she looked like a white rabbit, when she was thinner and wore less makeup and her hair was kind of blond. But recently she'd gained weight and gotten heavy into foundation, blush, and bright eye shadows, and had dyed her hair red, and all Peter could think of now was the Inuit mask he'd seen in his social studies textbook. It was of a bear. Peter imagined that it was of a bear just before an Inuit speared it with a harpoon.

Mom fanned her hand in front of her eyes for a minute, then blinked, sighing. "Your sister's hogging the bathroom again." She leaned out the window for a kiss. A black fleck of mascara was floating in the white of one eye; now it was lost in the blue.

Peter kissed her cheek, lightly enough, but still his lips tasted powder. "Will you be home tonight?"

"Honey, you should know the routine by now." She looked in the mirror again, wiped orange lipstick from the corners of her mouth. "Monday, Wednesday, and Friday, the Credit Union and Carson's. Tuesday and Thursday, just the Union. Saturday, Carson's. Sunday, we collapse." She looked at Peter. "We don't rest on Sundays. We collapse."

Peter pressed hard against the brakes on his handlebars. "So you'll be home tonight."

"You know, for a smart boy, you're getting dumber." His mother slapped his arm playfully. "Yes. I'll be home tonight, and I'll make dinner, and we'll talk about our days, and you'll explain to me why your teacher sent you home with a detention for the first time in your life."

"I explained it to you." Peter yanked up his front wheel, and held it in the air, watching its slow spin. "I was late."

"You'll explain it again, only more clearly, and then you and Mary and I will watch a video and eat popcorn until we explode."

Peter let his front wheel drop back down on the driveway. "Right."

"*Right* right." Mom started the car, shifted into reverse, looked at him squarely. "Make sure Mary gets to the bus on time."

Peter watched her drive away, then pushed his bike into the garage and shut the door. In the dim light, he went to his father's workbench, knelt down, and peered at the cluttered shelf beneath it. He pushed aside some old cans of paint and reached back until his fingers found the toolbox. He pulled it out. Until last week, the toolbox sat on top of the workbench. Peter started looking at it about the time he began building his first model home. He'd open its battered red lid and study the contents, the smeared fingerprints on shafts of metal. He'd lift out a wrench or a screwdriver and weigh the thing in his hand, then put it back. He used glue to put his houses together, Elmer's, and also the kind that could make your fingers stick together so bad that you'd rip off the skin, pulling them apart. He didn't know how to use any of the tools.

Then last week the toolbox was gone. Peter went into a kind of frenzy, looking for it. "You pitched it, you're dead," he kept saying. Finally he found it behind the paint cans. His hands shook as he lifted the lid, but everything inside looked the same. Then the box of nails didn't rattle when he picked it up, and he opened it and found the plastic bag of pot.

The pot was still there. Untouched, he thought. He put the bag to his nose. The stuff looked like the spices Mom dumped into raw hamburger, but it smelled stale. He'd only seen joints, never what was inside them, seen the slim flash of white slipped from one hand to another behind the bleachers after basketball games. He'd never tried to smoke one, but then no one had ever asked him to.

He started to undo the tie holding the bag closed, when a car pulled into the driveway. It idled there for a moment, then someone gunned the engine and honked. Peter heard Mary open the front door. "I'll be right there," she called, her voice lilting and bright, like she could still be happy.

The engine stopped, and the car door opened, a guitar solo scrawling from its radio. Someone was walking toward the garage. Peter stuffed the pot back into its box, shoved that into the toolbox, and the toolbox back onto the shelf. He set the paint cans into place, and scuttled into a corner, crouching by a stack of papers. It was a large stack; they always forgot to put out the recycling. He tried to make himself small beside it.

The garage door swung up. The figure silhouetted against the gray sky was big enough to be a man. He walked into the garage like it was his, his hands on his hips. He opened the old white cabinet that had been Peter's grandfather's, pulled out a golf ball, then another, and slipped them into the pocket of his camouflage jacket. Then he went to the workbench, bent down, and hauled out the toolbox.

"Scott. Hey." Mary stood at the garage door for a moment, then she walked slowly toward Scott, walked toward him the way some women did on TV. She led from her hips, her short flowered skirt swaying; she gazed at Scott, not blinking, though strands of her hair curled before her eyes. It seemed like she was trying to stretch out the distance between them, not shorten it, like walking toward him was the best part. And then she was in front of him, and her hips against his. She shook back her hair, wove her fingers through Scott's shaggy blond bangs, and laughed when he slapped his hands against her rear. Then he lifted her up, and she stopped laughing, wrapping her legs around his waist. He held her there, and they kissed, tongues jabbing, then he swung around and set her down on the workbench with a thud.

"Ouch," Mary said, her voice a little girl's. She put her hand to the small of her back, but Scott was scrounging through the toolbox. She moaned a little, then slumped, kicked her heels against the bench's leg. *"Ouch,"* she said again, and looked down and saw Peter.

For a moment she didn't say anything, and Peter saw how much she took after Mom, her eyes wide and startled. No, scared, that's what she was. Something he hadn't seen Mary be for a long time. She flushed from the open neck of her blouse, up her throat to her cheeks. Her blouse was unbuttoned low, so low that the green lace of her bra showed. Too low. Peter wanted to tell her this. He raked his fingers across the zipper of his jeans, checking.

"Fuck," Mary said. "You're everywhere.

Scott wheeled around, slamming the toolbox lid down. Everything about his pale features seemed sharpened to a point, like you might cut yourself on the clean lines of his nose, chin, eyebrows, and lips. He eyed Peter, who picked up a newspaper and began folding it in thirds, as if he were about to deliver it. Scott grunted a laugh. "What are you doing, kid?"

Peter looked down and shrugged. He stared at a column on the front page, even though he tried not to read the articles when he handled the papers. Each item seemed to be filled with news about something gone wrong, people doing things to other people they shouldn't have, families, fathers and mothers. Now he read the words "alley," "night," and "crushed." Now he was staring at "punctured."

"Looks like your old man," Scott said. "Just like him in those pictures."

Mary slid off the workbench, and Peter had to look away from her stare. "Yeah," she said. "Spitting image."

"So no wonder you don't miss him, when you got Junior around."

"Yeah. No wonder."

Scott turned to the toolbox again, took out the box of nails and put it in his jacket with the golf balls. "Wish my father would get transferred. Life would be a whole lot easier."

Transferred. So that's what she told people. Peter didn't tell people anything. Telling people something would mean he'd have to come up with a story, which would mean he'd have to think about it too much.

Mary said loudly, "It's easier, all right. A whole lot."

There was a sizzle of wheels on wet pavement, and a streak of yellow. The school bus. Peter jumped up and ran down the driveway, waving his arms, shouting. But it was gone.

Mary came out and stood beside him. They looked back at Scott, who was closing the garage door.

"Is he in college?" Peter asked, and put the back of his hand to his mouth. Silence was better, Mary had taught him.

But she didn't even look at him; she'd forgotten who he was. She was smiling at Scott. "He doesn't have to go to college," she said, and then softly, "but he was high school quarterback."

Scott came up and flung his arm around her shoulder. The weight of his arm pulled down the shoulder of her shirt, and her bra strap showed, the green more startling in the daylight, against her shoulder's faded tan. Mary saw Peter looking. "Piss off," she said.

Peter looked away. "The bus—" he began, then caught his breath.

Scott was holding a portable tape deck in the hand that wasn't slipping beneath Mary's shirt. Peter's father had always kept that tape deck on a shelf in the garage. He hadn't played it much, but it had to stay there. Scott winked at Peter. Then he sauntered to his car, opened the door, tossed the tape deck in the backseat. He looked at Mary, who ran around to the other side, adjusting her shirt. "Don't worry, Junior," Scott said. "I'll drive you to kindergarten."

Peter stepped into the janitor's closet, closing the door behind him. It was dark. It could have been a cave, if Peter didn't know better, a cave to get swallowed up in. But Peter knew it was a three-foot-square closet. Approximately. The darkness made it hard to breathe, closing around him like an open mouth. For all he knew, he could scream and it would scream back, an echo. His hand found the porcelain sink, then he bumped against a pail, and one leg of his pants and a tennis shoe were soaked with cold water that reeked of ammonia. He'd reek, he was sure of it. But there was the sink, the pail, and behind it, he knew, the machine the janitor used to wax the floors, and then a solid wall.

They were charging past the door now, the guys, almost running. He could hear their different voices and laughter. They were going toward the locker room, to change and head out to gym. Today was one of the two days out of five that they played soccer, then showered. The other days, they didn't sweat so much, and didn't have to shower, naked, all of them together, snapping towels that left welts, making wisecracks. The guys who had hair under their arms stretched a lot, lathered up and let the water run over it like it was grass they were tending. Some of them had thatches of pubic hair springing up like thick lichen or moss, making their privates look to Peter more than anything like tubers or roots, things that grew in cellars. Peter tried not to catch more than a glimpse. Some of them still didn't have any hair in these places at all. Peter's own was starting to surface, fine and fair and feathering like that on a girl's legs or an old man's head. You couldn't really see it, unless you looked close.

Showering after gym a few weeks ago, he'd gotten an erection out of the blue, out of nowhere, and had to drop to the wet floor. He'd scrabbled around in the sudsy water swirling into the drain, pretending he was looking for a bar of soap.

He liked gym better last year. They didn't have uniforms last year; they stayed in their regular clothes. Hardly anyone was wearing deodorant. This year, however, everyone stank, and Peter was constantly figuring out how to get sick and sit out on the days they showered, or different excuses for why he was late, too late to get changed at all. Coach was onto him, though. Last time, he gave

Peter a detention.

So now he had to give Coach a really good excuse. Maybe he had to meet Mom out front. Maybe she'd brought the medication he'd forgotten. No, that was lame, and Peter knew it. He'd tried it once before, and Coach said that next time Peter had better bring the prescription and a note from his mother. Peter nudged the pail; the filthy water sloshed. His father. He hadn't used his father yet. He'd been trying not to. He thought for a moment, then opened the door and stepped out into harsh fluorescent light.

He found his class out on the soccer field. They were playing already, the muscular guys dashing up and down the field after the ball, kicking up clods of earth. One guy scored, and his team flung themselves on him, tumbled in a pack to the ground. On the sidelines, where Peter would have been, boys sat cross-legged on the grass, tearing up handfuls of it. Others paced, their arms folded across their chests. Two of the more hopeful were heading a ball back and forth.

Coach blew his whistle and the game started up again. He saw Peter, looked through him and away. Peter walked slowly to his side. He stood there for a moment, his hands in his pockets, head down. "Yeah?" Coach said.

"Well." Peter's voice broke, and he cleared his throat. "My dad called. I guess he's sick, real sick, and he wants me. Right now. He's going to swing by here on his way back from the doctor, so I can go home with him. He needs help."

Coach stared at the game, put the whistle to his mouth. With the whistle clamped between his teeth, he said, "That's a good one, kid. That's close enough to the truth." Then he jogged onto the field to break up a fight.

Peter knew then. He turned and ran up the hill toward the school, knowing, slipped once on a slick patch of grass, stained the knees of his pants, the palms of his hands. He ran past the school and into the streets, heading toward his model home.

Other people knew that his father was in prison. How many people, Peter didn't know yet; maybe close to everyone, maybe even Scott. Maybe they even knew why.

———

Peter was pasting small squares of flowered paper onto the master bedroom walls. He'd already papered the kitchen, the dining room, and the living room. He'd painted the upstairs bathroom green and downstairs bathroom yellow. He'd tacked up molding throughout—pieces of oak the width of chopsticks. He'd glued brown carpet to the stairs, which curved, though not as gracefully as he'd hoped. And outside, he'd attached black shutters to the white plaster walls.

He was getting a lot more done, not going to school. This was the third day he'd stayed home, not counting that afternoon after gym class. It was easy enough to pull off. He simply had to get up before his mother's alarm went off, go downstairs, pull the lint basket from the dryer, rub his nose in it, and he'd cough and sneeze for the next hour, until his mother left for work. Then he'd settle down again and work on his model home. It was ideal, really. He knew that when his mother got to the Credit Union, she called the school with his excuse, and they seemed to be buying it. He knew to repeat the whole process just before noon, when his mother called to check up on him during her lunch hour. She kept saying she was going to take him to the doctor, but she couldn't seem to get away from her desk to do it. And Mary was bringing home his homework, so he wasn't getting behind. It was only in the evenings when his mother was home that it got a little tricky, sneaking downstairs to the lint basket whenever she was occupied elsewhere. Peter wondered how long he could keep it up. He thought at least through tomorrow, which was Friday. His mother was distracted. On Saturday, she was going to see his father. Their lawyers would be there. They were going to sign some papers, something to do with the divorce.

Peter had never visited his father in prison. It had never been an option. The thought that it might become one kept Peter awake at night. Maybe Mom would get enough money to send them all to see that therapist again; they'd troop into his dimly lit office, and Peter would stare at the collection of ships in bottles, while Mom talked and cried, and Mary slumped in her seat, muttered yes and no. The therapist might send Mom and Mary out of the room, give him another ink blot test, and say that Peter had to face his father, for healing. He'd said that to the three of them once before—"You all need to find your own way to face him in order to heal"—and it was soon after that Mom ran out of money for the visits.

Now at night, Peter faced his father, whether he wanted to or not. He'd lie in bed, flat on his back, afraid to move, as if moving would get him caught—he hated bed—and stare into the shadows where he knew the ceiling was, and there, instead, he'd see his father, either standing where a ship should be in one of the therapist's bottles, or, more realistically, sitting on a straight-backed chair, in a small cement room. A naked light bulb always hung from the ceiling; water dripped down the walls. The bulb cast harsh shadows over his father's face so that his eyes seemed to have been gouged out. Peter would rub his hands over his own eyes at this vision, longing to reach the one inside his mind and crush it.

The front door banged open, and Mary stomped in. Last summer, she'd bought a pair of heavy army boots, which she wore with skirts and shorts. She seemed to like the noise they made. Something clattered against a wall in the entryway. The umbrella stand, maybe, the cane rattling in it, the cane his father used when he sprained his ankle, chasing Mary down the basement stairs that time when Peter was a little boy. His father had said they were just playing, like Mary must be now; she was laughing, and there was Scott's voice, squeaking high, like a cartoon character. Then there was a silence, the scrape of a boot. Mary shrieked and laughed some more. Now they were coming down the hallway to his room. "Here, sick boy," Mary called, and papers flew against his closed door and scattered.

Peter stuck the last bit of wallpaper on the master bedroom's wall, then he gathered up the jar of paint and his brushes, and went out into the hall, drawing his bedroom door closed behind him again. He knew how to close it without making a sound. Mary's bedroom door was closed, too. No sounds came from in there. He walked quickly past it, to the kitchen. He wanted to clean his paint brushes, and then he wanted to bike downtown and buy some furniture for his house. He turned on the faucet and held the brushes under it, and the paint colors mixed in ways they shouldn't, spilling into the sink like something vile, something that might contaminate a kitchen.

He spent all his money on miniatures: a red velvet sofa, a rocking chair with a tapestry cushion the size of a nickel, two toilets, and a bedroom set. Each piece was wrapped in tissue paper and had its own cardboard box. They would stay packed like that until tomorrow, when he could be sure that all the paint and glue had dried. He'd see then how they looked inside the house; he'd let himself enjoy it. Then he'd wrap them up and put them away again where they'd be safe and hidden. He had almost two more months to save for everything else he needed. The list was long, but he thought he could do it by Christmas.

He carried everything home in a plastic bag, balanced carefully in the basket on the handlebars. He got back safely; no one had seen him, and nothing had fallen out. He put his bike away, then went to the front door, and past it, around the side of the house, to Mary's closed window. The shade was up. He looked in.

They were doing it. What he'd seen before. Mary was naked, lying on her back on top of the bed, which was still made. Her knees were up, her feet flailing in the air, and her hair was tangled in the legs of the stuffed dog that sat on her pillow. She'd had that dog since she was a baby; its name was Nutmeg, and that was her first word. Before Peter was even born, she'd torn off its eyes and tried to eat them. It was staring blindly across the room at him now, but Mary's eyes were closed, and so were Scott's. He lunged back and forth on top of her, his shirt unbuttoned, his jeans down around the tops of his work boots. His face was twisted as if in pain. Mary's was very still.

This was how it had been with their father, too, only always late at night, never in the afternoon when the light was so bright you could see the pinkish brown of her nipples, the skin stretched tight over her ribs, the skin pulling where hands gripped her arms, now her thighs. Always late at night, when sometimes there was a moon and sometimes there wasn't, and Peter began to have trouble sleeping, though Mom never did. Sometimes Peter thought Mary was sleeping, too, that she might be like Mom, like everyone always said he was so much like Dad. "You inherited your insomnia from your father," Mom once said.

And now it was done. Scott heaved himself away, onto the single bed, pushing Mary to the edge. She slid off it and down to the floor, grabbing a tissue from the milk crate she used as a night stand, holding the tissue between her legs. Scott seemed to be asleep, one hand clenched around a clump of Mary's hair. In a few moments, his hand relaxed, and her hair fell down over her shoulder.

Mary grabbed more tissues and wiped herself again and again. Then she balled them up, wrapped the lump in clean tissues, and put it in the wastebasket. She tried to sit on the edge of the bed, but Scott wouldn't move over, so she dropped down on the floor again, smelled her hands, stared at them.

Peter realized he was cold. His nose was running and he was

shivering. He'd pressed the plastic bag into the side of the house, and the boxes inside were bent up, smashed out of shape. Tissue paper was everywhere, and there was a sofa leg poking out, the lid to a toilet. Things might be broken.

Scott was standing now, zipping himself up, buttoning his shirt. Mary looked cold, too. She'd wrapped herself in an afghan. She kept plucking at Scott's sleeve and leaning against him, but he was leaving—it was clear from the way he shook his head and muttered something too muffled for Peter to hear. Scott said something that made Mary start to cry. Scott stared at her for a moment while she did that, her face going ugly and red. Scott stared at her until she looked up, and saw his expression—blank and dull, like she was some kind of boring television show. She stopped crying at that, and he left.

Mary pulled the afghan more tightly across her breasts. Her godmother had knitted it, Peter remembered, for her thirteenth birthday. It was Mary's favorite color, turquoise, the color of the flowers on the wallpaper that Peter had put up in the master bedroom. She used to wear a turquoise ring on her right hand. Their father had given it to her. She didn't wear it now.

Mary slammed her fists against her thighs, once, then again, then she left her bedroom. Peter bolted around the side of the house, to the front door and in. He ran down the hall, toward the sound he dreaded. She was retching, gasping for breath, making no effort to be quiet. He grabbed the bathroom's doorknob, twisted it; the door opened an inch, then caught on its hook. Locked. He yanked his wallet from his pocket, pulled out his library card, and—as easily as he'd let himself imagine, but only once or twice—he slipped the card up through the crack in the door, lifted the hook from its latch. The door swung open.

She was as he'd thought, kneeling over the toilet, the afghan gathered close, trailing on the floor. Only one hand covered her mouth, hiding it. And her eyes weren't accusing as she looked at him, or flickering with anger. They were stricken blank as the heads of nails.

"Don't," he said.

Her eyes narrowed then, as if she finally recognized him—her little brother, nothing more. He pulled the door closed, stumbled down the hall, the faint rectangles of dirt on the walls flashing by. Tinker was barking now, and he was almost to his bedroom when he heard her fling the bathroom door open again and come after him, shouting, "Leave me alone."

He threw himself across the bed, and down between the mattress and the wall. He crouched by his house, blocking it from her, for she was there quicker than he could have believed, standing before him, clutching the afghan closed. "I'm sorry, I'm sorry, I'm sorry!" he screamed, his voice sounding to his own ears like the high bleating of a sheep. He kept screaming this even when he saw Mary step back. She leaned against the wall, her head drooping as if she was exhausted. Finally she held her hands to her ears, and shouted, "Stop!"

He did. His throat was raw. She lowered her hands, wrapped her arms around her ribs. "Sorry for what?" she said. "Say exactly what you're sorry for."

For being like Dad, he wanted to say. But he didn't. Instead he said, "I'm making this for you."

He stood and lifted the sheet from the house, then climbed up on the bed, out of the way so Mary could see. She squatted down, stared at it, chewing at her lower lip. There were the red marks of fingers on her upper arms, a bruise on her neck. Peter leaned over the edge of the bed and tapped one of the flowered walls of the master bedroom. "Stick your fingernail in there," he said.

"Some kind of trick?" Mary said. But then she poked at the wall.

"No," Peter said. "A little to the left."

She found it then, the thin crack in the wallpaper and the hidden door he'd made. She pried it open, and there, inside, was the little room he'd painted gold.

"It's a secret," he said.

Mary looked at him. "He'll always find me," she said flatly. But then she crouched lower and looked into the room, looked and looked into it, as if looking would take her there.

Born Lucky

Sarah McElwain

I begin as an act of greed. I'm one of my mother's get-rich-quick schemes, a business deal, a joke. My mother, Evening K. Titlebaum, believes that she is lucky. There is no evidence to support this. She does not believe, however, that luck will just fly in the window one day and find her, and so ever since she dropped out of high school her days and nights have been spent painting her nails with black or green polish and flipping through magazines and supermarket tabloids for contests to enter. She enters everything—sweepstakes that offer cars, Hawaiian vacations, costume jewelry—it doesn't matter. She just wants to win something. My mother carries a battered copy of "Turn Your Dreams into Dollars" in her backpack and consults it often. For a person who flunked out of math class, she shows a highly developed aptitude for the complicated formulae that promise to transmute the symbols in her dreams into winning lottery combinations.

If my mother believes in anything, it's in the democracy of numbers. Anyone can win, she figures. Especially someone who's lucky. My mother is fascinated by decimal points and zeros. It turns out that she's good with numbers. If she'd stayed in high school, she could have become a bookkeeper or an accountant, but to say that, is to say: if my mother was a different person. My mother plays Lotto two, three times a week. Standing in lines snaking halfway down the block, she chants, "You've got to be in it to win it." Around her, others testifying to all the good they'll do if they win. Not my mother. She just plans to take the money and run.

My mother lives with her mother, Amanda. When my mother dropped out of high school Amanda kicked her out of the bedroom, claiming it for herself. My grandmother, although only thirty-six, is very tired. She works as a nurse's aide and spends the rest of her time sleeping. Now it's my mother's turn to camp out on the hide-a-bed in front of the TV in the living room. Although my mother does not know it, she is sleeping on the exact spot of her own conception, an event that took place one night sixteen years earlier when Amanda and Frankie Titlebaum did the wild thing on this same couch, back when it was still white and new. Many shades of gray later the couch is covered with a butterscotch spread, frayed fringe trailing across tenement green carpeting murky as a swamp. Curled up in a neat fetal ball, wearing only her smiley-face underpants, my mother drifts off at dawn each night in front of the TV, wrapped in a rainbow afghan crocheted by her grandmother, Rosie Titlebaum, watching lava lamp patterns slide across the screen to a new disco version of "Brahms' Lullaby" on the Sleep Channel.

Phone sex is an easy gig. Sitting on the couch watching TV—home shopping dominates at this late hour—phone cradled on her shoulder, my mother talks dirty all night to men who call 1-900-HOTBABE. Keeping each customer on as long as possible is the trick, and my mother takes this game seriously, making lists of useful phrases in her spiral-bound notebook. Shame used to fill her every time she looked at this old journal—she stills feels horrible about what happened in English class—but this phone sex job has raised her self-esteem. It feels good to finally be good at something.

My mother quickly learns that men come in two categories. Most want to feel bigger, but some want to be made to feel smaller. The biggers are easier. They require the standard stuff. She calls it a pistol, a ramrod, an Uzi. Refers to their heavy artillery, Saturday night specials, hardware, tools, plows, or plungers. She says hosed and humped, banged and hammered. Car references are also very popular.

With smallers my mother must be careful. Smallers, she soon realizes, become hostile if not dominated or humiliated fast enough. The most important rule of all, she discovers, one that applies to both biggers and smallers, is never confuse one man's Mister Johnson with another man's Little Peter. My mother carefully notes in her journal who has Doctor Happy between his legs and who is swinging the Bishop.

When the phone rings my mother remotes the TV lower and answers it. Lorraine, the dispatcher at 1-900-HOTBABE, is on the other end.

"I've got Uncle Peepee on the line. Want to do him tonight?"

Uncle Peepee has a thin, nervous laugh, high as a girl's. Opening her notebook my mother looks at her fake gold Rolex—Frankie Titlebaum sells them from a tray in the street. Last night she kept Uncle Peepee on the line for forty-eight minutes. Tonight she's out to break that record.

Twenty minutes later my mother is just getting to the part where she finds Uncle Peepee tied up in his closet when Lorraine beeps in.

"I've got another call," she tells Peepee.

"I'll hang up," he threatens.

"If I find out you've hung up, I'll have to punish you," my mother warns.

"How?" Peepee squeals.

"You'll see," my mother promises, clicking off.

Lorraine's got Charles, the phoney Frenchman, on the other line. "Feel like doing two at a time?" she asks.

"What are you wearing tonight, mon petite?" Charles asks on the other end, in the kind of fake French accent that many men assume for this occasion.

"Black stockings . . ." my mother begins, turning up the orange on the TV until all the home shoppers look like hot dogs on a broiler.

"Seamed?" Charles asks.

Twenty minutes later, after Charles has hung up satisfied, my mother clicks back to the other line where Uncle Peepee is still waiting.

It is not her father Frankie Titlebaum who first looks at my mother and sees trouble. It is my great-grandfather Frank Titlebaum Sr. who blows the whistle on my mother. "An accident waiting to happen," is how he describes his granddaughter Evening to David Katz, his old pal from City College. This is how my mother gets her first job at Copy Katz Copy Shop, where she is introduced to the two things that will change her life forever—and begin mine—Honey Wilcox and a handheld Sharp calculator.

The fact that there's a hole in the sole of her boot, the fact that she is wearing control top pantyhose under her jeans as a result of too much caramel corn eaten the night before, the fact that David Katz is singing along to the oldies station again, and most of all the fact that my mother despises the oldies station—all contribute to the scheme that germinates in my mother's head when she looks at a 1999 calendar with a calculator in her hand. I begin as a gleam in my mother's eye when she looks at January 1, 2000, and subtracts nine months backward.

What my father sees when he looks at my mother is a crazy white girl with a bad idea. My mother's hair is green. She is wearing a vest that cost over two hundred dollars and jeans decorated with spiderwebs, roses, and daggers drawn in black Sharpie while she sits bored behind the counter. Around her neck hangs a crucifix, a peace symbol, a Jewish star, a small black-and-white yin-yang symbol and a four-leaf clover. What my father sees when he looks at my mother is a girl who's got all the major religions and superstitions covered. My father's name is Honey Wilcox. His real name is Harrington but he has always been called Honey. Blame it on my Jamaican aunties, Foxie and Marie, two women who insist on nicknaming everything they see.

"See," my mother says, pointing her pencil to March 31 on a 1999 Sierra Club Endangered Species Calendar. A bug-eyed albino tree frog, only a few hundred of which still exist in New Guinea, stares out from the picture. Flipping past the spotted cheetah and the South American eagle until she reaches the pandas nine months later, she taps her pencil meaningfully in the last square. "December 31, 1999," she says, looking at my father.

"Two thousand dollars," says my father, searching with his tongue for a gummy bear stuck between a bicuspid and a molar. "That's not shit. Especially after we split it."

"Yeah, but we'll get other stuff, too," says my mother. "Appliances and things. But that's not all. We'll be on TV."

"TV?" my father says, his eyes suddenly turning shiny with interest.

Although my mother has never been fishing in her life, she knows when she's got a live one on the end of her hook. Carefully she reels my father in. "There's going to be a movie," she whispers.

My father might look like a boy who's standing there doing nothing, but inside his mouth his tongue is performing acrobatics, forming fat pink U's up, down, left, and right—a genetic trait he's passed down to me. Fingering a dreadlock absently, he's having no trouble imagining himself in a movie. My parents have something in common. They're both ready to roll the dice and take a gamble.

My conception takes place in the Utopia Highway Motel in Flushing, Queens. My parents are the only two people in the motel that weekend having sex for the purpose of conceiving. My mother has read up on the baby business. She carries a well-thumbed copy of "Making Babies—for Fun and Profit" in her backpack these days. The twelfth day of her cycle, she's experiencing electric pinpricks in her lower abdomen and knows she'll be ovulating soon. What my parents engage in over the weekend is a common practice known as bracketing—doing it as many times as possible during the seventy-two hours spanning ovulation to increase the chances of pregnancy. Getting pregnant is not as easy as it looks. The opportunity for pregnancy is only a few short hours each month. To make this plan work, I must be born the first minute of January 1, 2000—no sooner, no later—and so, as always, much depends on timing. This is not casual sex. They go at it feverishly, fueled by greed, not by passion. The first eleven times they do it, nothing happens. It is the twelfth time, when they do it doggie style, my mother on her hands and knees, watching the Sex Channel while my father ejaculates. It will be eighty-two degrees tomorrow—this century's record high for the last day of March. One hundred forty million of my father's sperm are suddenly racing up my mother's vaginal tract trying to find her cervix. The first hundred million drown in the rough seas of acidic fluid. Forty million hardier ones begin the second, even more treacherous part of their journey up the cervical canal. If it's sperm number 39,037 that penetrates the egg, I'll inherit the Titlebaum nose and the Wilcox eyebrows, be gifted in math and science, be lactose intolerant, prone to ear infections, easily impressed by authority figures, have little to no musical ability, average reflexes, and a tendency toward acts of sadism committed against small animals. If number 39,038 wins instead then I will look like my grandfather Frankie Titlebaum, have my Aunt Foxie's red hair and a small birthmark on my neck. I will be left-handed with long, prehensile double-jointed toes and an insatiable need for attention. I will be of slightly less than average intelligence, deeply sentimental, with myopic green eyes and a lifetime of glasses. But it's number 39,039 that penetrates the egg. There's an instant fusion of cells, two nuclei fuse into one, creating that complex combination of proteins and acids that all add up to me.

Four days later the three of us are back at Copy Katz—Evening behind her cash register, Honey behind his hand truck, and me, the size of the period at the end of this sentence, inside my mother.

Four months later when the urine turns blue in the tester kit for a third time, my mother tells my father.

"Blue?" says Honey. "What's that mean?"

"Blue means yes," says my mother.

"Yes means there's a baby inside?" asks my father, looking not for the first time in the direction of Evening's stomach.

"Yes," says my mother, opening the white nurse's cardigan stolen from Amanda that she's been hiding under so that Honey can see the swelling jeans safety-pinned shut because she can no longer get the zipper up.

Neither can think of anything else to say about this subject for the moment, but more will be said later that night when Honey comes over to visit. It's the first time he's been to Evening's place. They sit on the couch watching TV. It's only July but the Millennial Countdown has already begun: 149 days, 8 hours, 10 minutes, and 6 seconds flash on the screen in green digitized numbers.

Last time this happened—Judgment Day 999—the unpaved roads of Europe were packed with peasants heading to the churches, trying to buy dispensations; a deed or wedding ring placed in the right hands here on earth could get you past Saint Peter. As the millennium grew closer and closer, people grew crazier, strapping harnesses of wings to their bodies, jumping off roofs, trying to fly directly to Heaven before the world ended. There was rioting in the streets of Rome. The Norwegians crossed the border and began grabbing the Swedes. It was chaos until the bells began to chime. Then everyone threw themselves to the ground, everyone covered their heads and began praying. Years later, most were still astonished to find that the world, in fact, hadn't ended.

At 10:30 on July 31, 1999, my mother and father do it again on the couch in front of the TV; I can hear their voices, muffled behind my mother's huge heartbeat, which speeds up slightly when Honey comes.

"Does blue mean it's a boy?" my father whispers.

It's the biggest New Year's Eve ever. My father's just returned with hamburgers. Burger King's doing a Commemorative Whopper and my mother is sitting on the couch, using the paper bag to hyperventilate into. All regularly scheduled programming has been preempted. There's nothing on but the twenty-four-hour countdown. Outside the streets have been filled since dawn with crowds of people staring up, hypnotized by the giant clocks.

My mother takes her head out of the bag and looks for the tenth time that hour at her watch. She's lost all hope that this scheme will work. My father's the only one who believes that everything will be okay. He is proud of Evening's taut, round belly. He offers her another sip of Coke and starts in on his second burger. My mother returns her head to the bag, but my father doesn't look worried.

Like many others, my parents have turned to eating for relaxation and comfort during these last few stressful days. Inside my mother I have subsisted, umbilically, mostly on the nutrients supplied by Diet Coke—the official soft drink of the Millennium—raspberry Twizzlers, and Ding Dongs, which Honey dutifully searches for in all the bodegas. At times, my mother has found herself craving strange foods like broccoli, sauerkraut, and three-bean salad.

Ten minutes later when my mother sees the water rolling down her legs into her sneakers, she taps my father on the shoulder.

At the hospital all the doctors and nurses are roaming the halls wearing children's birthday party hats and blowing into noisemakers. My father, eager to join the festivities, is wearing a gold paper crown, his dreadlocks sticking out from underneath like fat hairy sticks. In the hospital room the TV's on. High above Times Square the artist formerly known as Prince is humping the ball like a black leather spider. The roar is deafening. Everybody is wearing clothes that glitter and cutting up their credit cards for confetti.

My mother is in no mood for party hats. In the entire history of this hospital no one has ever yelled as loud as my mother. Her voice can be heard bouncing off the walls, echoing down the tiled halls. "Get out! Get out!" she screams at me.

Although it has not always been peaceful inside the womb of Evening K. Titlebaum during these last few months, I am determined to stay right where I am.

The clocks begin chiming. People are chanting, "59, 58, 57 . . ."

"Get out!" my mother screams at me with all the strength left in her body. What will be our lifetime battle of wills is now beginning. Inside, I hold on even tighter.

My mother—teeth bared, fists clenched, back arched—pushes harder. I feel myself sliding. She is winning. Outside the roar is beginning. The ball is dropping, corks are popping, and bottles are breaking, for all is not peaceful in the land on this night. In the prisons revolutions are beginning. There is much cheering and kissing. People begin singing and I am born. Although the name that appears on my birth certificate is Millennium K. Titlebaum, I will be known to one and all as Lucky. Lucky Titlebaum. Born Lucky.

THE WORLD DIRTY, LIKE A HEART

Brock Clarke

It all starts with Tull, my so-called friend. He is the real deviant in this group of two. For a while, ours was the same worn path. We were both teachers of high school history. We were both married, had been for some time, and constantly complained about our wives but only in the nicest terms, and never when they were within earshot. We were growing old but not gracefully, wearing baseball hats and jeans slung low and desperately faking youth. Like our students, Tull and I advertised our immaturity through the exaggeration of our likes and dislikes. We both were vocal in our love for cable TV, I was overly fond of my Iroc Z, and Tull denounced public transportation as something communist.

Then Tull found a girlfriend. I say "girlfriend" and not "lover," "other woman," or some other this-and-that because she was just seventeen and adulthood was still only a rumor. This was three months ago. He told me and I couldn't believe it. I still don't know what to think. It's a complicated issue. There are the not-so-tender forces of law and morality to consider. Then there is love. All I know for sure is that I don't have a seventeen-year-old girlfriend, don't really want one, and why the hell should I? What makes you so sure that I'm that kind of man, anyway?

Her name was Leslie Surprise. She was a senior and Tull said she had an eye for detail. Leslie was being courted by the community college. She had cheekbones that build and break nations. Her ankles looked sleek and thoroughbred-powerful in sheer stockings. She was an ace at long math and her voice was such that it made sarcasm sound like seduction. "Your future," the community college told her, "lies in Travel and Tourism." They promised her a free ride, bonus mileage, and the opportunity to cultivate an informed worldview.

I thought Tull was the worst kind of fool and I told him so. But he was taken. He said he was in-love serious, that he was even thinking about quitting something. Tull's first thought was alcohol, one of his dearest if most worrisome passions. "Lent," he said. "I'll give it up for Lent and that'll be it."

I reminded him that Lent had already passed and that he would have to wait a year.

"Sooner, then. Memorial Day," he said. He was all of a sudden crazy for abstinence. I could hear the creak of his mind's machine busy manufacturing other kinds of sacrifice. It was the height of bowling season. He was a fair bowler. Tull would forsake bowling for love.

"What will Judy say?" I asked him. Judy was his wife, a tough county lawyer who believes in Hammurabi and thinks due process an experiment failed.

"Bam!" Tull said. "Fireworks." He didn't seem to mind.

"How?" I wanted to know. "Where?"

"In my room during periods seven and eight. I was explaining the Louisiana Purchase. She wanted to know what we bought and how much it cost. I told her, territory by territory, and each time she said, 'Was it worth it?' Then she kissed me. Once on the cheek, then once where it counts."

"What the hell does that mean?" I was already repulsed. Every August during faculty orientation, the school administrators and psychologists and guidance counselors teach you everything you need to know about little boys and little girls, and it's all bad.

"On the lips," Tull said. "She kissed me on the lips."

"Oh," I said. Then: "What else?"

"Nothing."

"That doesn't sound like love to me," I told him. I'd been expecting much worse.

"You'd be surprised," he said.

Tull and I sat for a while. It was our spring break, noon on a Wednesday, and we were in my kitchen. My wife, Cass, was at work. She is a dental hygienist, works eight hours a day, and I wondered about the secret paths she might follow while we were apart, eight to four, Monday through Friday. I wondered what she would think about Tull and Leslie Surprise. I wondered if Cass had her own version of Leslie Surprise: someone younger than me or better looking or more articulate in his desires. I wondered if the world were split between those who acted on their desires and those who did not, and if those who did not were at the absolute mercy of those who did. I wondered just how much I knew about the world. While I was wondering I drank my beer quickly, one, then another. Tull just watched his. It sat on the table and he looked at it as if it were rotating slowly and he was checking its progress. I thought I could see it move myself after a while. It was an extraordinary display, a household miracle so small you couldn't be sure if it were actually happening or what it might mean. I drank that beer, too, and he watched me drink it, smiling. I was thinking. Tull was my friend, and I was worried about him in the same way you worry about yourself, except with less attention to detail.

After a few minutes of silence I said, "What about Ronan? Do you remember him? You remember him, don't you?"

Ronan was a business math teacher. He had been a captain of industry, and when he retired, he said he wanted to give something back to the community. That meant he longed to teach business math, and they let him until he was caught in the janitor's closet cozying up with the janitor's collection of low-rent skin magazines. Both Ronan and the janitor were promptly fired, and the school made a big production of buying new mops, buckets, cleaning solutions of all kinds.

"That's different," Tull said. "That was a disgrace. Be serious. Onanism. God's curse. Then there's me and Leslie. Two normal human beings."

"Even worse," I said. "C'mon. You've got to know that history repeats itself. You know that."

"History is a bore," he said.

"You don't know your past, you don't know your future."

"History is flat-faced, walleyed, ass-dumb to the world."

I lectured him on wrong and right, on the things and strings of the heart breaking asunder. Then I let him go. Sometimes you have to. Still, I thought about him all break. I feared that Tull, like myself, like all aging men, was a would-be victim of a world that favored youth and beauty and all things new. We were a terrorized lot, oppressed and damned like all the old Jews and Christians, and we were nothing if not vulnerable.

Sure enough, Tull returned from spring break to find himself fired. It turns out everyone knew. They read him the riot act at the school board meeting. They said his name would be forever linked with perversion. The principal promised to draft a letter to his wife personally. They all asked Tull how it felt to be a pariah, and he told them he hadn't been one long enough to have an intelligent opinion.

"Let me narrate it for you," I said afterward. "Caught. Fired. I'm sure you'll be divorced soon. That's the way it will go. Love."

"You don't understand," he said. "Let me tell you one thing. She loves the way I say Manifest Destiny."

"How do you say it?"

"What?" Tull asked. He appeared to be deep in thought. There was a lot to think about. He had a look of permanent worry.

"I said, how do you say Manifest Destiny?"

"I say it like I mean it."

I went home and told this to my wife. I'd given her daily updates of the whole situation. I am the type of fool who keeps no secrets. I tell all. The day will come and there will be none of the usual things to hold against me.

"What the hell does that mean?" Cass wanted to know. "'Like I mean it?'"

"I have no idea. Can you believe he was so stupid, though? He honestly didn't believe he would get caught. Either that or he didn't care."

"Didn't get caught?" Cass said. She couldn't believe that discovery was all I cared about. She had this furious right-and-wrong look on her face. Her eyes were menacing slots.

"Poor Judy," I said weakly. I looked straight at my wife. Even at thirty-four years of age, she has retained an astonishing degree of youth. At work, Cass wears rubber gloves and a face mask, and she says that these things help keep her young. They're supposed to protect her from the elements: from blood and saliva and the prevailing winds of bad breath. I looked at her and thought of Tull and Leslie Surprise and the offenses of love and again wondered if I too were being used and abused. The precedent, as in the court of law, had been set. I sat and looked at her, and the longer I looked the more I loved her and the less I believed she was true. I began to think of the world as a dirty, clogged heart, my clean self rejected by it as foreign.

"What is it?" she said. I had been staring at her. "Is there something on my face? There's something on my face, isn't there?"

"I've got a terrible week coming up," I told her, getting off the subject. "It's Local History week. I've got to get from Montcalm and the Battle of Ticonderoga to the Industrial Revolution in two days. Two days and two hundred years. Did you know that Little Falls produced more bicycles than any city in the U.S. between 1883 and 1887? Did you know that Ticonderoga means 'where the lake shuts itself' in Mohawk?"

"Wonderful," Cass said, taking off her stockings. She was rubbing her toes and paying no attention to me. Cass has beautiful toes, lithe like fingers. In a world of hammer toes, corns, and sweat rashes, Cass's toes are something angelic. Even then I wondered who else might be loving them.

Anyway, that's Tull and you need to know none of this except for what comes next, the party at Cass's boss's house, which is why I'm telling it. Cass and I went to the party later that same week. Every day after school, I had gone over to visit Tull. He was sitting around, drinking the same beer a sip at a time. His house was dark. It smelled like failure. Tull sat in the dark and said things like, "I'm the worst kind of man. I'm a caught man." He'd even been dropped by Leslie Surprise, who was under psychiatric supervision. Her parents had placed a restraining order on Tull. They would call his house daily and ask, "Is the Devil home?" and then hang up before he could answer.

Tull claimed Leslie was dragging him down. He said she was acquiescing to the forces of popular morality. He called her immature.

"You wouldn't understand," he said. "You've got Cass. You've got love. You've got no problem being normal, and normal has got no beef with you, either."

Those were the pressures I faced. I went to Tull's every day and received the lecher's platitudes and then I went home to Cass every night. The more normal I was, the more beautiful and detached she became.

By the party on Saturday, my heart felt like deadweight, my nerves in active revolt, the rest of my body caught somewhere in between.

It was a dentist party, hosted by Cass's boss and his wife, who was also a dentist. They had a young son, who was in charge of taking and then retrieving the guests' coats at his parents' parties. Both Cass's boss and his wife consider themselves amateur ironists. For instance, Cass's boss likes to say to me, "You know, Harold, there is no dirtier mouth than a dentist's." Then he shakes his head and says, "The world is a cruel place if you want it to be."

I always get plenty drunk when I'm around Cass's boss and his wife. That night, I had three beers before we even left our house, one in the car, a fifth of bourbon as a backup in the glove compartment. I was liquid and morose. I thought of everyone I knew. There was Leslie, Cass, dirty Tull. Who else? My parents. I remembered how they referred to each other only in pronouns. They were dead and beyond judgment, but I mourned all of their failures to be good people. I was bawling right there in the car.

"Don't embarrass me," Cass said. Not that anyone would have noticed one more weepy drunk. Cass's boss always threw knockdown parties, and this one was no exception. We walked in and there was already a fight of the man-and-wife variety going on in the dining room. It was our hosts, and Jesus, what a scene, right in the middle of their annual wingding. Whiz, their voices said. Bang. They were promising terrible things, to rend and tear and to make foolish all words of love, honor, and cherish. Their party guests were present to bear witness, just so no one could say later, after the inevitable divorce, that they never saw it coming.

It was a holy mess. The spider plants were crashed on the dining-room floor. Country music—Waylon, Willie, Hank Sr.—was playing loudly. Everyone complained about it, but no one could find a way to turn it down. In the kitchen, a man I didn't recognize was bent over the sink retching loudly. His wife, or whoever, stood next to him with her hand on his back. She was smoking a cigarette, saying, "That's right. Let it all out. You'll feel much better once it's all out where we can see it." A large crowd had gathered and no one seemed to believe her.

At some point I lost Cass but found the nitrous tank. I'd heard its sucking noises all night long and was glad I finally found it. The tank was surrounded by dentists holding brightly colored balloons. I got the feeling that they all knew each other from college, dental school, something. They all seemed to have nicknames for each other: Tree-man, Snoopy, Shoe. It occurred to me that they were doing it like they did in college, except not as well and with less joy. This put them all on edge, especially the host. He and his wife had called a momentary truce, and his low-grade shrieks told me that he wanted nothing more to do with time and loss.

"Suck," he said to the man next to him. "Dennis. You're up next. In goes the good air, out goes the bad. Don't be such a sorry old dentist. You're just a tired old fuck, aren't you?"

"Barry," his wife said, coming from behind me, "you're being seven different varieties of asshole."

Round two. More yelling. The man named Dennis dropped his glass. His eyes took on the appearance of two foggy marbles. He offered up his balloon and I took it, inhaled, stopped, and then inhaled once more. I closed my eyes. The room went away for a moment and when it returned it had assumed the texture of a plate broken and then glued back together.

"Jesus," I said to the man next to me once my head cleared. I had forgotten that dentists had access to such joy.

He agreed. "Oh boy," he said, and who knew what he was talking about? I took another hit on the balloon and looked for Cass. The room was filled with smoke and blather. When I finally found her she was in the corner talking to some smooth type wearing a seersucker suit and no shoes. He was gesturing with his beer bottle. It looked like he was lecturing on something of great importance, and he acted like he knew his shit back and front. Cass's face was red. She was rapt. My misery returned. He was good-looking, all right, a handsome young man. I took one last hit and imagined from across the room that this man could speak many languages—Romanian, Polish, Old Low Welsh—and that all of them would bring to Cass's knees a great weakness.

I felt my chances in this life drop to zero.

"Oh God," I said and turned to beg for another balloon. That's when I saw the hosts' son. He was standing off to the side. He was young—ten or eleven, I thought at the time. I found out later that he was in the seventh grade, twelve years old, and so what? That's not the point. The point is that he was young and my mind was already full of thoughts and convictions about the boundaries of age and the consequences we face in crossing them.

There was another point. The boy was drinking a beer. Did I mention that? He was drunk and weaving. Once I had assessed the whole situation, I called the father over.

"Your son," I told him, "is drunk."

"He's just tired," he said.

"Just tired? Look at him. He's got a beer right in his hand."

"He's just overtired," Barry said. "It's way past his bedtime." He smiled at his son. Then he walked away.

The boy was red-eyed and considering me from underneath his hair, which was long and had the look of sweat to it. I squatted the way baseball coaches do in front of their young sports. If there had been grass I would have plucked a blade and chewed on it until my gums bled. Here was something I could do. You're a teacher, I thought. Teach. There was beauty to be salvaged in all the ugly places.

"I remember when I was you," I told him. "I remember what it was like. I know what it is to be just yea high to this terrible old world."

"So what?" he said, pointing his beer bottle at my forehead. "You're just one more in a long line of asswipes."

Which is why I slapped him, right across the face. He didn't seem to care, the little monster, stood there like his life had always been that way and that it wasn't half bad. But his parents sure cared, nitrous oxide and the splintering of their family unit regardless. They raised a stink. Eventually, they made certain everybody knew, school board and parents included. This night, however, they just yelled murder. A crowd gathered. I was on my knees. I looked up and Cass was there with seersucker. She looked grim, and I pleaded with her in great dramatic fashion. "Where are the waters of childhood?" I asked.

Seersucker answered. He had a foreign accent, Southern maybe. His voice was resonant, like he possessed more than one throat. He said, "Sir, it looks like you've been swimming in them."

And then I hit him, too, right in the breadbasket of that smart suit, starting another ruckus with me in the middle of it, swearing, "I was wrong but I'm not sorry. I thought he was a child, but he's no child. He's old and ruined already, and I'd hit him again just like I'd beat anyone who's not what they're supposed to be. I tell you, I won't be afraid of this life!"

The school board waited until Tuesday to fire me. Cass left me the next day. She says we're not divorced, but separated. I say I'll do anything for her. I've asked her if she wants to have a baby. I insist that if that's what she wants then I want it, too. We'd be great parents, I tell her. I know that this is how marriages are saved every day, but Cass says no. She says she needs some time, is all.

I think we're divorced. I can't help but believe it's true.

Sometimes Cass still comes over on sympathy missions. She finds me on the couch with my pervert friend Tull. His wife Judy has already filed for divorce. Tull and I are starting to believe that the world is closed to us. Whatever hope we have is coming to a slow burn. We stop complaining about it only when Cass is there, just so she'll come back.

When she comes around, Cass tells us stories of the outside. Last week she came over on a Thursday. It was four in the afternoon and there were beers scattered, but she pretended not to notice. I remember how she looked coming in from the bright world. She was in her white uniform, and she had the cut and quality of lodestar. I ran over and held her hand and she let me.

"Let me tell you," she said once I had quit my fawning. "There was this guy in today. He was from Colorado. He even showed me his driver's license as proof. He told me while I was working on him that he was a cowboy, retired. I said 'Sure you are,' and he says, 'I'll prove it. I'll tell you something you don't know about us cowboys.' 'Fine,' I said. 'Tell.' Then he says, 'Do you know what we call bulls' testicles? We call 'em Rocky Mountain oysters. Did you know that? They're a delicacy. They're supposed to be an aphrodisiac, too, and I eat them all the time.' That's what he told me. I asked him what they tasted like and he said it was exactly like eating chicken. Have you ever heard of such a thing?"

I was stunned.

"He said that?" I screamed. "Where is this old bastard, talking to my wife that way? I'll kill him, I swear." I glanced over at Tull to share my outrage, but he was staring at Cass. It took me a minute to recognize his look—his eyes glassy, his brow sweaty, his face dumb with want. It was a look full of deep, long-standing, incurable desire—a look I had seen him level at Leslie Surprise—which is why I hit him, too, pow, a quick one right in the face, and he grabbed me and pulled me down and while we were wrestling on the floor Cass left. I didn't even see her go.

Boss Man

Cathy Day

Even when it was all over—the money counted, the caravan disappeared, the carcasses rotted, the blacktop washed away in the rain—Earl Richards never spoke ill of the gypsies. He had been warned, after all, the day he'd gone out to sign the papers that made him the new manager of the KOA campgrounds in Peru, Indiana. The owner, name of Altman, had run the place for twenty years and was more than ready to pass the torch to someone else. Altman showed Earl around in a campground golf cart, driving one-handed, pointing out what all needed to be looked after. The pinball machines and pool tables. The pH level of the pool. The warped and flaking picnic tables. The massive griddle for the Sunday pancake breakfasts. The goop on the maple syrup dispensers. The Frisbee golf course. The restrooms and showers. The coin-operated washers and dryers. Earl wrote down the list on the only paper handy—his pay stub from the railroad. Altman was still talking, still going strong, and Earl was running out of paycheck.

Finally, Altman turned the cart back toward his house (soon to be Earl's house), a two-story split-level a hundred yards from the KOA A-frame. "Oh. Almost forgot," Altman said, pulling his Titleist hat over his eyes. "There's the gypsies, too."

Earl nodded, clicked his ballpoint, and wrote "Gypsies" without thinking. Then he thought about it. "Gypsies?" he asked.

"There's a band of them show up every year in late summer, about a hundred of them or more. They pay cash. Tell me they travel around blacktopping and roofing. You gotta keep your eye on them, especially when they come in the store," he said, "or they'll take everything in sight." Earl's pen wavered over his check, but Altman clapped him on the back. "Don't worry about it. They pretty much take over while they're here, but they're good people, mostly. They just don't see things our way."

Earl knew the railroad paycheck in his hand wouldn't always be there; his job was slated to be cut off in a year or so. Altman's deal meant he'd be able to give his wife and son more than they'd ever had or even dreamed of having: a two-story house in the country with a fireplace, more bedrooms than they needed, an in-ground swimming pool, pinball machines, a pool table, foosball, even a Frisbee golf course. Earl figured if he saved every penny he earned over the next two or three years, he could buy Altman out. The idea of owning a franchise, of owning land, amazed him. Earl was descended from a long line of milkmen, firemen, and factory workers who'd never owned their houses outright, let alone the acreage they sat on.

The contract was waiting on Altman's dining room table. Earl signed it, shook Altman's hand, and accepted the beer offered. They clinked cans. Only three minutes had passed since Altman mentioned the gypsies, but Earl had already forgotten they even existed.

―――――

The gypsies appeared five months later, on a muggy August morning as Earl was getting ready for work. He looked out his bedroom window and through the wet mist, he saw it glittering in the distance, just like Altman had said. A train of Airstreams, Winnebagos, Chieftains, Avions, and Prowlers, thirty of them at least, coming down the road. One by one, they turned in the driveway and headed for the KOA A-frame. His wife Peggy had just left to open the store, and their fourteen-year-old son Joey had gone with her to clean the pool. By the time Earl called in sick to the railroad, changed into tennis shoes, and ran down to the A-frame, the situation was already out of hand. Women in colorful skirts pulled children into the bathrooms, and teenage boys swam in the pool fully clothed. The game room was crowded with dark-skinned men pumping quarters into the pool table and humping the pinball machines. Joey was in the camp store behind the cash register, ringing up candy and cheap KOA T-shirts like crazy. Peggy had her hand around the wrist of a little boy who had tried to walk out with a Frisbee, and a gypsy woman, the mother probably, was yelling at Peggy in a language Earl couldn't understand. He thought the gypsies would speak Spanish, like the other migrant workers who came through town around harvest time. But this wasn't Spanish.

He tapped Peggy on the shoulder. "Thank God," she said, giving up on the boy, who walked out of the store with the woman and the Frisbee. "There," she said, pointing to a fat man chalking up a cue stick in the game room. "That's him. The king or whatever. I'd better go check the bathrooms." She stuck ten rolls of toilet paper down her mop handle and marched out the door.

Earl walked into the smoke-filled game room, stuck out his hand, and introduced himself.

"Are you new Boss Man?" The king ignored Earl's hand.

Earl put his hand in his back pocket. "I guess so. I'm the manager."

"I only talk to Boss Man." The king leaned his pool cue against the wall. "We stay for three days, okay?"

"That's fine. How many sites do you need?"

"Over there. We stay over there." The king pointed out the window to the campsites by the Frisbee golf course. They were closest to the woods, the most secluded, and, on the weekends, the most popular. But this was Tuesday, and the sites were empty.

"How many sites do you need?" Earl asked, trying to count the number of campers outside the pane-glass window.

"I don't know. Other Boss Man figure it out."

Earl got a map of the campgrounds and circled off a large area. "This is twenty-five sites. Sewer, water, and electric. How many vehicles do you have?" Outside the window, a few kids zipped around on quad runners, spraying gravel from the fat tires. "And those."

"Oh, many of those."

"I need license numbers. And you can only have one vehicle per site, or you have to pay an extra five dollars each."

From his back pocket, the king took out a roll of hundreds as thick as Earl's arm, held together by a rubber band. The king wet his fingers and laid ten bills on the counter. "This how much last Boss Man charge us. When we go, I give you ten more. This okay, Boss Man?"

Earl stared at the bills on the counter. Technically, the king only owed him nine hundred dollars. Twelve bucks each for twenty-five sites for three nights. The rates were posted right over the counter, but Earl thought maybe the king couldn't read the sign. Instead, the king was offering him more than he'd made during the entire month of July, counting the Fourth. So far, Earl hadn't saved one dime toward buying the KOA; Altman's monthly profit estimates had been grossly exaggerated. At the moment, they had only one site filled, the Ramseys, an elderly couple on their way up to the Wisconsin Dells. Earl took the money.

Joey punched a one and three zeros on the cash register, and Earl placed the bills inside, trying to be nonchalant. "Checkout's Friday at noon. No later. We're full up for the weekend." Earl pointed to the stack of registration cards, every site booked in advance for Labor Day, the last big weekend of the summer. "I just need you to sign here," he said, making an X on the registration card with his pen. The king made another X right next to it. "No," Earl said, "I need your name."

The king was walking out the door, but he turned and said, "You write John Smith." Outside, he held up his arm and whistled. Instantly, the game room, bathrooms, and pool emptied themselves of gypsies. The caravan headed back to the campsites. Ten minutes later, Earl walked back to give them their three-day supply of garbage bags and found them unhitched and unpacked, campfires ablaze, like magic.

———

Earl was nineteen years old when he hired out as a clerk on the Chesapeake & Ohio Railroad. A good job, back then. Every year, the head office in West Virginia sent boxes of C&O windbreakers and baseball hats to its yard office in Peru, Indiana, one for each man, and no one, not even Earl, took more than his share. Then came the so-called prosperous 1980s. The C&O merged with the ailing Baltimore & Ohio and became the Chessie System, and from the new head office in Baltimore came boxes of coffee mugs and plastic pens. Earl stared at these gifts and knew, somehow, that hard times were at hand. He took eight mugs and stuffed thirty pens in his coat pockets.

Five years later, VTX Transportation bought the Chessie System, and all that came from the new HQ in Jacksonville were key rings and College Boys, business majors who didn't know dick about trains. For one, they didn't know that on the railroad, you call a man by his last name, not his first. College Boys wore Dockers and polo shirts, slicked their hair with styling gel, and, worst of all, drove foreign cars and never even bothered to explain why. Their job was to lay off any man with fewer than fifteen years seniority.

That's when the men at the yard office started stealing, openly and earnestly, taking whatever could be smuggled out without the College Boys noticing. Typewriters. Chairs. Lanterns. Coffee pots.

Flashlights and batteries. The old C&O logo, Chessie the Sleeping Cat, became a collector's item, and some of Earl's friends swiped Chessie calendars and clocks and sold them to nostalgic railroad buffs for a tidy profit. A memo appeared on the bulletin board: "VTX recognizes the nostalgia felt by employees of acquired systems, but urges said employees to desist from pilfering memorabilia."

Underneath, someone had written, "Translation: Quit stealing our shit. Signed, VTX."

A disgruntled brakeman named Ellis rerouted three covered grain hoppers to an abandoned siding and hired semis to come unload the corn. A drinking buddy of his, a similarly pissed-off clerk by the name of Warren, fixed the waybills and entered the cars into the computer as empties. Ellis and Warren kept their mouths shut and made thirty thousand dollars each. That is, until VTX figured out the scam and brought criminal charges against them, state and federal. Afterward, Earl realized that if Ellis had come to *him* instead of Warren, he would have done the same thing. He'd be the one in prison, and it scared him more than a little to think how easy a man can be driven to lawlessness. Earl didn't hate VTX. He simply felt no loyalty to it. Whatsoever. VTX was just three letters that sounded good together and didn't stand for anything.

The cinder-block yard office on Canal Street needed paint and new windows; the panes broken by vandals had been covered with pieces of cardboard. Broken glass, garbage, and cigarette butts were scattered along the tracks that snaked along the Wabash River. Old railroad cars sat abandoned in the crowded siding, like mammoths waiting to die. Earl knew it was only a matter of time before VTX closed the yard office and told him what they'd told the men who were already gone: move to Cincinnati or Jacksonville to keep your job or take a payoff and find some other way to make a living.

Leaving Peru. The idea began to take on the distinct, inevitable edges of fact. His mother started inviting him over for lunch on Fridays and made Earl's favorites. "Don't know how long I'll be able to make beef and noodles and rhubarb pie for my baby." Then she'd start crying and run into the bathroom, leaving Earl in the kitchen with his food and his father, who'd say, "Now look what you done." Peggy put the pressure on him, too. Her folks lived in a nursing home nearby in Kokomo, and she visited them often. If Peggy skipped three or four days, her parents told horrible stories about "the forgotten ones," the patients who didn't have family or friends stopping by. "They get bedsores, Earl. What good things they have come up missing. They cry and no one's there to hold their hand." Her worry kept them up half the night sometimes.

Peggy started putting brochures for correspondence courses and technical schools next to his La-Z-Boy. If he fixed the toaster, she told him he'd make a fine small appliance repairman. Earl went from a pack a day to two. Sometimes on the way to baseball practice, Joey pointed to the few businesses left in Peru—convenience stores, used car lots, quick-lube garages. "There, Dad," he said. "Why don't you work there?" and Earl tried to imagine himself punching a cash register, hustling cars, changing somebody's oil. He was forty-four years old.

In the end, Peggy saved them. She was the receptionist at the hospital, which was where she overheard one of the nurses, Altman's wife, say that she and her husband were looking for someone to manage their KOA. They were moving to Fort Wayne to open a Dairy Queen. Peggy acted quickly, and a week later, Earl sat with Altman in a golf cart, writing down the old man's warnings on the back of his VTX paycheck. Pool. Frisbee golf. Bathrooms. Gypsies.

The night the gypsies arrived, Earl opened the G volume of the *Encyclopedia Americana*. He'd bought the encyclopedias for Joey, although it was clear his son had hardly used them. When Earl opened the book, the spine made a pained, cracking noise. Earl read the entry for "Gypsies" at the dinner table. Periodically, he'd look up at Joey and Peggy. "They're from India originally," he said, his mouth full of hamburger. "They speak Romany. Hitler gassed a bunch of them."

Peggy nodded her head and said, "Really? That's interesting, honey."

Earl ran his finger down the page. "It's this diaspora thing. They call us 'gaje,' like Gentile to Jews."

Raising her eyebrows, Peggy said, "Oh. They're Jewish?"

"No, they're not Jewish," Earl said, shutting the encyclopedia. "They're just trying to get by, you know?" Peggy and Joey nodded and kept eating.

That night, the gypsies sang and clapped into the small hours.

Their songs blew in Earl's bedroom window, open to catch the night breeze. He got out of bed and pulled back the curtains. His own camper sat below him in the backyard, dark and abandoned, the wheels braced with two-by-fours. It was a Skamper with a small kitchenette, an oven, sink, refrigerator, bunk beds, and a bathroom stall. It smelled of cigarette smoke, mildew, and fish. When he bought it off a guy at work years ago, he told Peggy, "We can go anywhere now." He'd never seen the country. All he ever saw was the inside of the yard office and the trains passing by the window, bound for somewhere else. Once, Earl had taken them to Michigan, but that was as far as they ever got. When his vacation time rolled around for the next few years, either money was short or the bathroom tub had to be replaced or the house needed to be painted. So instead, they'd camped locally—at the KOA. At night, Earl would sit by the campfire with a beer, trying to imagine that he was somewhere else—a New Mexico desert, a Colorado mountain, a redwood forest—anywhere but where he was, which was five miles from his house in town.

Ever since they'd moved to the KOA, Peggy had been after Earl to sell the Skamper. "We live at a campgrounds, for godssake. What do we need with a camper?" she said. Earl knew she was right, but he said, "I like the idea of keeping it around," he said, "just in case we get a chance to go somewhere."

Across the field, the gypsies' campfires flickered, and he imagined his own family living that kind of life, moving north in the summer, south in the winter. In his dreams, he was in the king's Chevy Silverado, headed west with the windows down, mountains on every side. He saw a dark forest full of men swallowing flames and shiny swords, young women dancing in veils around fires, and old women in black stooped over steaming pots, cooking food filched from backyard gardens.

———

In the morning, the Ramseys came into the office to complain. "We're missing our lawn chairs and an Igloo cooler," Mr. Ramsey said. "I think we both know where they're at."

Earl remembered what Altman had said: *They pretty much take over while they're here.* Finally, Earl understood the deal struck between Altman and the king: Altman made a much-needed profit, and the gypsies got free reign of the place. Earl shrugged his shoulders at the Ramseys. "I'm sorry. There's not much I can do. I doubt they'd cough up your stuff anyway." He punched a key on the cash register, and the money drawer flew open. "Look, why don't I refund the two days you paid up for. Maybe you could head up to the Dells a little early?" Earl smiled, but he felt bad, buying them off this way. The Ramseys took the money, packed up their Winnebago, and headed for the highway.

After they left, Earl called the yard office to take a couple personal leave days. He half listened to the tongue-lashing from his supervisor, a College Boy named Jones—Travis or Trent or something like that. A few weeks earlier, College Boy had spotted boxes of VTX urinal cakes, toilet paper, and industrial cleaning supplies in the back of Earl's truck. He'd been saving on expenses this way, and College Boy knew it. "This is the last break you get, Earl," he said and hung up.

Sitting at the camp store counter, drinking his morning coffee, Earl tallied the numbers from the night before. The gypsy's thousand dollars. A bucket of quarters from the games. Sales in the camp store had doubled. Sure, a lot of merchandise walked out the door unpaid for, but the markup was high enough that he'd still come out ahead. As a sign of this blessing, a string of cars and trucks led by the king's Silverado passed by the window, shining in the pink morning light.

A few hours later, some of the trucks returned. The king, dressed in a suit and tie, walked into the office escorted by five young men in jeans and short-sleeved dress shirts, smelling of incense and cologne. "Boss Man," the king said, "where we find a pig and a sheep?"

Joey stopped refilling the candy jars, and Earl looked up from the T-shirt racks, losing his count. "Excuse me?" Earl asked.

"We christen new babies this morning. These the fathers," he said, gesturing to the men. "Every year, we come here, and then we have a feast."

Earl pointed out the store window. "There's grocery stores in town."

"We want big ones."

"You mean *alive*?" Joey said, his eyes wide.

Earl set his clipboard down on the counter. "There's farms all around here. You can ask. We just moved and I don't know any of them right well yet."

The king straightened his tie. "I understand. We be back later." He started to walk out of the store, but turned at the door. "Boss Man, you need paved driveway here. We do good job."

"Thanks, but I think everything's okay," Earl said, waving his hand.

The king shrugged and walked out the door. Children streamed into the camp store clutching quarters in their hands, clamoring for candy and pop. Earl's father usually only came out to help on Sundays with the pancake breakfasts (he was a Navy cook during World War II and could prepare a meal for fifty easier than for two). But today, Earl had assigned his father to stand guard in the middle of the store. He frowned, folded his arms sternly over his chest, and asked, "What do you want?" in a gruff voice anytime a child wandered toward the merchandise. The gypsy children fled to the game room, where Joey waited with his arms folded, trying to look as imposing as his grandfather. Peggy was on hold with the phone company. The pay phone outside the camp store was full; since the moment the gypsies had arrived, the booth had been occupied by a steady stream of gypsy women, gesturing and yelling into the silence of the enclosed glass, dropping coin after coin into the slot.

A skinny young boy ran up to Earl, who was wrapping rolls of quarters, dimes, nickels, and pennies. "Boss Man, your machine took my quarter."

The pinball machines were unreliable and acted cranky every so often; the rental company had promised to send out a serviceman who'd never showed. "There you are," Earl said, handing over a quarter from his stack. "What's your name, son?"

"Macho," the boy said, smiling a smile without many teeth.

Earl laughed. "What's his name?" he asked, pointing to another boy standing nearby.

"Fuzz. My sister is Peaches." The boy closed his hand around the quarter. "Thank you, Boss Man," he said, and ran back into the game room.

His father grunted. "Who the hell would name a boy Fuzz?"

Earl shrugged. "They keep their real names secret, for protection." Earl's father grunted again.

Thirty seconds later, Earl found himself surrounded by ten children, all of whom said the machines had taken their quarters. "Trust me for a quarter," a little girl said. "My daddy beat me if I ask for another."

Shit, Earl thought. "Joey!" he yelled, "Get in here!" The children stood with their hands out, palms up, their eyes enormously brown. "No more free games," Earl said, trying to sound stern and in charge.

"But you gave him a free game," a pudgy girl said, "and he lies. Not me, Boss Man."

Joey stepped into the camp store, his eyes small slits, his face red. "Whaddaya mean, you don't lie. I saw you in there playing just a second ago, and it was working fine."

A teenage boy in a blue T-shirt stepped up. "My sister is no liar."

Peggy hung up the phone and stood beside Earl. "If you want to play the games, you have to take the risk."

"Yeah," Joey said, looking right at the gypsy boy.

Earl raised his hands. "Okay, Joey, why don't you go on out and get the garbage. Pop," Earl said, "would you check the pool for me?" The children gave up asking for quarters and ran back into the game room. Looking out the window, Earl watched the blue-shirted gypsy boy peel out of the driveway on his quad runner. Joey followed, humming along at a fast clip in the golf cart.

Earl wanted to make sure Joey wasn't getting himself into any trouble, but his father called to him from outside. "Earl, you'd better come take a look at this." Walking around the A-frame, Earl saw the problem. The pool was packed with bobbing gypsies. A man pulled himself out of the water, his clothes shining wet and clinging to his dark skin. He yelled and did a cannonball that sent a spray of water all over the cement. The water level was down a couple of inches already. "Guess I need to put more water in the pool," Earl said.

Earl's father shook his head. "Why don't they wear bathing suits, for godssake?"

"Something about it being against their religion. Unclean. That's why they don't touch us, either."

"They're sure making the pool unclean, damn dirty Wops."

"Dad, they aren't Italian. They're from India. By way of Europe." Earl knew he'd only corrected half of what was wrong with his father's statement, but he'd given up trying to correct the other part. Earl counted himself lucky that at least he'd gotten his father to stop saying "nigger" around Joey. He said "Negro" instead.

"What's the word for somebody from India, then?"

Earl sighed. "Indian, I guess."

"If I was you, I'd tell them to hit the road. We're missing two buckets of pancake batter." In the distance, they heard a crashing sound and the whine of a motor revving too fast. "The golf cart," Earl said, already running toward the Frisbee golf course. Behind him, Earl heard the keys and change in his father's pockets jangling as he tried to keep up. When Earl trotted up to the first hole, Joey was climbing out of a ditch. Down below, the mangled golf cart sat smoking.

"Are you okay?" Earl asked, bending over, breathing hard.

"Goddammit," Joey said, "he ran me right into the woods!" A cut over Joey's eye dripped blood down his face and onto his T-shirt. Earl handed him a handkerchief from his back pocket. "The bigmouth from the store. On the quad runner. He ran me into the ditch." Then Joey looked down at the ground. "I'm sorry, Dad. I think I totaled the cart, but it wasn't my fault."

"Don't give me that shit, Joey. You were racing him."

Earl's father had finally arrived, breathing hard and pale. "It wasn't his fault," he said. "The gypsy kid didn't have to get so rough."

"He still shouldn't have been fooling around," Earl said. "Get on up to the house and have your mother look at that cut. We'll talk about this later." Holding the handkerchief to his head, Joey dragged his feet in the gravel. Earl walked to the edge of the ditch where his father now stood. "Probably should just leave it down there for the time being. Don't know how to fix it, even if I do get it out of there."

Earl's father threw a rock into the ditch. "How much one of them things run?"

"I don't know, but I'll bet they're not cheap."

"You should make them gypsies pay for part of it, at least."

In silence, Earl and his father turned and walked toward the A-frame, past the gypsy section. The campers were arranged in rings, facing into the campfires. Clotheslines, strung from every tree, sagged with wet towels and clothes. The smell of cooked meat hung in the air. The king got up from his lawn chair. "What happen, Boss Man?" the king called out.

Earl kicked the gravel. "My son ran our cart into a ditch."

"One of yours ran him into the ditch," his father said, "if the truth be told."

The king shook his head. "Oh, no. I know this boy. He good boy."

"Like hell," Earl's father said. "That golf cart was an important piece of equipment. I think you owe my son for the damage. It's only fair."

"I don't think so, Boss Man."

Earl's father stepped forward, his chest inches from the king. "I *do* think so, or do we have to call the police to come out here and have a look-see?" He spoke right into the king's face. "Understand, Cochise?"

The king lit a cigarette and reached into his back pocket. He looked at Earl's father, then at Earl. "Okay, Boss Man. You right. We pay." He peeled two hundreds from the roll and held them out.

Earl knew his earlobes were red. "Thanks," he said, taking the bills and walking away. They felt damp in his hand, and he stuffed them in his back pocket. Earl felt queasy and sluggish, as if something inside was squeezing his stomach and heart.

His dad followed. "That gypsy kid deserves a good ass-whupping, if you ask me. Joey wouldn't be getting in so much trouble if you tanned his hide once in a while." Earl remembered well how handy his father had been with a yardstick and belt. His father stopped walking and touched his arm. "Son, these people are no good. This is probably one of the only places that'll take them, and you're being more than fair just by letting them stay here. But hell, they're taking everything they can off you."

"Don't you think I know that, Dad?" Earl tried to keep his voice level. "But we're making more money this week than we would have in a whole month. We need that money, or we're going to have to move." Earl pulled out his cigarettes and lit one. Twenty years of smoking, and he still didn't like to do it in front of his father, but he needed one badly. "Just let me handle things the way I think's best." Earl knew his tone sounded disrespectful and ungrateful, but he couldn't help it.

"Maybe your mom and I should go on home."

"Maybe you should," Earl said.

"Fine. You're the boss," his father said, turning his back and walking away. A few minutes later, Earl heard his parent's Oldsmobile hustling down the driveway, rocks pinging, spraying gravel from the tires.

The next morning, Peggy and Earl got up at daybreak to clean the game room. Earl found a cigarette burn on the green felt of the pool table. A june bug buzzed around the fluorescent lights. Joey was filling the pool and dumping gallons of chlorine into the water. He walked in to tell them that the levels were way off. "It's probably not safe to swim. Should we close the pool?" he asked.

"If we did, they'd probably swim anyway," Peggy said, dropping beer bottles into the garbage with a clank. "Just make sure it's filled up and keep dumping in chlorine."

A cloud of gravel dust hung over the driveway; the gypsies came and went day and night, but through the haze, Earl saw his parents' Oldsmobile coming toward them, even though he'd expected his dad to stay home and pout all day. His mom got out with an armful of the baskets she wove in her arts-and-crafts class. "It's going to be a hot one today," she said, walking into the store. "These people will buy anything just to be buying. Thought I'd bring out my baskets and make me a little mad money." She covered a card table with a red-and-white gingham tablecloth. Off the edge of the table, she hung a sign, "Handmade Baskets, $20 Each."

"Don't you think that's a little pricey, Mom?" Earl asked.

His mom winked. "We'll see." And sure enough, when the store opened, the gypsy women hovered over her table. They tried haggling, but Earl's mom stood firm by her price. In an hour, she'd sold every one.

Later that morning, the king came into the office and asked how much Earl wanted for the Skamper. Earl's knees popped as he stood up from his crouch behind the Coke dispenser. "It's not for sale," he said.

"The sign say it for sale." The king pointed toward the Skamper parked in Earl's backyard. From a distance, he could make out the orange-and-black For Sale sign.

"It's a mistake," Earl said.

"I give you good money for it."

Peggy walked in with a large box, ignoring Earl's glare.

"I'm sorry," Earl said, his voice rising. "I'm not selling the camper." The king shrugged his shoulders and walked out of the store.

Peggy set the box on the candy counter and began tearing off bits of masking tape. The box was marked "For garage sale." Peggy kept it in their closet.

"Don't you think this has gone far enough?" Earl asked.

"Some of those boys running around are the same size as Joey."

"When did you buy the sign? That's what I'd like to know." Earl could no longer keep his voice from rising.

Peggy kept tearing tape. "Your mom had such good luck with those baskets, Earl."

"I'm going to get the garbage," Earl said. He'd risen early enough to need a jacket that morning, so he took off his C&O

windbreaker and laid it over the box. "I'm coming back for that. Don't sell it while I'm gone."

Peggy finally looked Earl in the eye. "Yes, Boss Man." He pushed the front door open with a hard shove that sent the bells ringing and shook the glass in the panes.

Earl collected garbage in the lone golf cart, slamming the lids down on the trash cans. At the gypsy camp, he saw two animal carcasses skewered on spits, turning over an open fire. The gypsy men sat in lawn chairs gathered around a small color TV placed on a picnic table. A Cubs game. Earl recognized Harry Carey's voice. The king walked up to Earl carrying an aluminum roasting pan full of steaming meat. "Boss Man, you take this. We always give to Boss Man for let us stay. Not so many are nice as you." The king gave a small bow. "You good man. You take."

"Thank you," Earl said, taking the pan from his hands. He drove slowly back to the store, trying not to spill the meat threatening to avalanche all over the inside of the golf cart. Earl set the pan on the counter. "What the hell is that?" Earl's father asked.

"Meat," Earl said. "A gift from the king."

"I wonder what they put in it?" his mom asked. Earl looked at her. "For flavor," she added.

———

On Friday morning at 11:30, Earl told the king, "You know checkout's noon, right?"

"We be gone by noon. Yes."

Earl looked around. Boys on quad runners raced around the field. Women hung laundry on the lines, and men lounged in lawn chairs, smoking and drinking beer. "But you haven't started packing up yet. Breaking camp takes a long time. I know," Earl said.

The king laughed. "When we go, we go like that," the king said, waving his hands with a magician's flourish.

Earl remembered how quickly they'd set up camp and figured the king was telling the truth. "I'll give you until one. We've got a lot of people coming in this afternoon already got these sites booked."

The king nodded. "Okay, Boss Man. We be gone by one."

At 1:30, Earl walked back to the gypsies' camp. The king said, "We fixing trucks. Have problems."

Earl noticed that the hoods of the trucks weren't open, and the gypsy women were serving lunch. "I don't see anybody working on trucks."

"My nephew go to town for parts. Can't go until he get back. Then we fix trucks."

From inside one of the campers, Earl heard a man laugh and speak a word. More laughter. Lighting a cigarette, he thought about calling the police. He knew a few guys on the force, knew they'd come out quick if he called, knew they'd laugh at him, too. He looked at the king. "Well, in any case, I guess you owe me some money."

"I was to bring you this when we go, but we not go yet." The king handed Earl a roll of bills, wrapped by a rubber band. He weighed it in his hand, thick and heavier than the first payment.

Earl said, "I've been good to you, right?"

"This Boss Man best one we have."

Earl ground out his cigarette. "You know, I know something about you people. How you've been treated and such. You might even say I'm a bit sympathetic." Earl thought the king might appreciate this, but he didn't see any reaction on the man's face. "But enough is enough. I don't want to call the police."

"Oh, you not do that. You good man, I know. How much you want for us to stay longer?"

"I don't want anything else from you people. I just want you to stick by our agreement and be on your way." Earl looked the king straight in the eye. After a few seconds, an urge to look away came over him, but he fought it and kept on staring. Finally, the king nodded his head, turned, and whistled. The gypsies left as swiftly as they'd come. In ten minutes, the first of the campers filed down the driveway, heading toward the highway, the king's Silverado in the lead. The king waved to Earl, and then they were gone.

Earl walked to the A-frame. Ringing another one and three zeros into the cash register, he took the bills from his back pocket. "I'll be goddamned," he said, fanning out the bills.

A hundred-dollar bill wrapped around fifteen singles.

———

Peggy worked graveyard shift that night, and Joey, freed from gypsy duty, escaped to a friend's house, leaving Earl alone to check in the Labor Day campers. He welcomed them with a smile and a firm handshake, glad to have the gypsies out of his hair. But near sundown, he found the animal carcasses, tiny pieces of meat still hanging on the bones, thrown near the start of the first hole of the Frisbee golf course. Flies buzzed and clung to the skeletons. In the dim twilight, Earl picked up the carcasses with his bare hands and threw them into the bed of the truck. The stink of rotten meat was all over him. He scratched his nose, smelled the carrion wedged under his fingernails. His stomach turned, but he kept it all down. After dumping the bones into the green garbage dumpster, he walked back to the house, took a hot shower, and threw his clothes away.

At nightfall, he set up a lawn chair next to the Skamper in the backyard and opened a beer. In his mind, he saw the king in his Silverado, leading his family in that long caravan. He knew where they were going. South down I-65. Indianapolis. Louisville. Bowling Green. Nashville. Birmingham. Montgomery. Mobile. The Gulf of Mexico. Sometimes at night as Peggy read her Danielle Steeles and Janet Daileys, Earl read the Rand McNally, skimming the highways with the tip of his finger, making up the plot as he traveled from town to town. But all the roads, all of his stories brought him back to the place he started. He didn't know how else to finish. The gypsies were their own home. Now, Earl saw their secret, why they were going on to the next thing, and why he was sitting in the backyard of his two-story house, watching the flicker of campfires not his own.

―――

Earl decided never to tell Peggy or Joey or his parents about the carcasses. They would take the carcasses personally, a confirmation of gypsy lowliness. Earl knew he'd never be able to explain to them that the carcasses were just part of the deal, and certainly no different than the cases of VTX toilet paper sitting in the campground storeroom. For weeks, neighbors came by to complain that the blacktop sealer the gypsies had spread over their driveways had melted and run in the first rain. The mailman delivered bills for tires, truck repairs, portable video games and televisions, and car stereos—all addressed to "John Smith c/o KOA campgrounds." Earl returned the bills, "Not at this address." Angry merchants called, trying to hold Earl accountable, but he hung up on them.

In the spring, Altman called. The Dairy Queen hadn't done well, and they were thinking about moving back to Peru, back to the KOA. He asked Earl if he was ready to buy, two years before he was even supposed to ask. Earl told him, "We've been having second thoughts. Not enough cash flow. Too far from the highway."

"It's a shame you have to move again," Altman said smoothly. "You barely just got there."

"A man's gotta be mobile," Earl said.

As it turned out, it was a good thing Earl never got rid of the Skamper. They had to move in with his parents, and since the house only had two bedrooms, Joey slept in the Skamper parked in the driveway. Then, in the fall, VTX closed the yard office and Earl, Peggy, and Joey were gone, following the rails to the next biggest railroad town, Cincinnati, the Queen City.

At the Queensgate yards, Earl asked, "Is there somewhere I can work so I can at least *see* a train?" His boss, another College Boy, rolled his eyes at Earl's request, as if trains were quite beside the point. He led Earl to a small room containing a TV, VCR, and boxes of videotapes, hours and hours of passing trains. Eight hours a day, Earl rewound and fast forwarded, writing down the numbers painted on the sides. When he tired of that, Earl was assigned to the stockroom, where he pointed a laser gun at computer bar codes so that every box was inventoried and accounted for. When Peggy asked him to bring home a case of toilet paper, he had to tell her that it was no longer possible.

Earl says there's no honor in railroading anymore. He works to pay the bills, secure his retirement, and send Joey to college. On summer nights, he likes to buy a six-pack and sit on a picnic table down at the city park and watch the barges moving up and down the Ohio River. He thinks about the quarter of a million he'll get when he retires at sixty-five, about how he and Peggy will finally see the West. They'll take the Skamper over the prairies, the desert, the mountains, all the way to the Pacific. They'll sit on the beach with beers and watch the blue ocean until the sun goes down.

All the Night Could Hold

Stephen K. Bauer

One night, as I listened to my stepfather pacing outside my bedroom door, I fell into a dream, and when I woke up, and in the days that followed, I willed myself to have that dream again. But I never did.

We were walking over a railroad trestle. Far below, glimpsed through spaces in black iron, the white and brown and green of rushing water. We had nearly reached the other side when he stumbled, and I held out my arm and caught him. He turned to me and spoke, but his words were lost in the roar of the river. From some look in his eyes, though, from my recognition of something of myself in his features, I realized I was his true son.

So many nights I lay awake. The attic door rattled, and branches scraped the roof. Did I hear him on the stairs, in the hallway, or was I imagining it? I longed for him to bring me out of my ordinary existence, and on an occasional night I heard the doorknob turn and saw the outline of his figure in the doorway.

I wished I could keep him company every time he needed help, but I didn't often have the chance. Some nights I heard him pacing in the hall, talking softly to himself, and I hoped he would ask me out for a drink. But instead the pacing ended. For a few moments I heard only the wind in the trees, and then the door closing as he returned to bed. Or my mother heard him in the hallway and went out to retrieve him. "John? Have you been drinking?" And she led him back to their bedroom. I considered his middle-of-the-night troubles heroic, and believed I would never experience anything nearly so wrenching. On the worst nights, he told me, he took his pistol from the closet shelf and sat with it at the top of the stairs. In the darkness, he removed the bullets and put them back in. He drank wine from the bottle until the light in the window facing him began to grow stronger.

On this night I heard his breathing as he paused outside my door. "David," he said. "David? Come have a drink with me."

"All right, sure." While I dressed by the light of the desk lamp he waited in the hall. I could not see him clearly, could not tell if he was watching me.

Though the floor was cold and the wind gusted outside, I felt warm as I pulled on my long underwear, then my jeans. I would walk with him stride for stride through any weather, accepting whatever hardship I faced, stoic.

I went into the dim hallway and he grasped my arm. The sweet scent of wine. Warm breath on my cheek as he leaned close. "We'll be quiet," he said. "Your mother would kill us."

Just my stepfather and I. He trusted me with our secret. We crept past the master bedroom door, past my sister's room. Down the carpeted stairs, me in front, his hands on my shoulders.

Once we were downstairs I asked, "Are we leaving now?"

"Not yet," he said.

I wanted to get out of the house with him. On one of these nights we'd spent several hours drinking at the kitchen table and he'd read to me, from *For Whom the Bell Tolls* and poems by Neruda and Robinson Jeffers. I remembered the last line of "Ocean": "It is needful to have night in one's body." But as I'd listened I learned more about those writers than about him.

As he turned on the dining-room lamp I saw our two cats stir at the edge of the light, moving away. "It sounds cold out there," he said. "Sit."

He went into the kitchen and brought back two shot glasses. Their gold rims shone against the dark wood of the table. He looked pale, unshaven, a little shaky. His dirty hair, long and gray and streaked with blond, was parted unevenly on the side. I watched him polish the glasses with the hem of his turtleneck. He held up two bottles from the top of the piano, nodded in approval when I motioned toward the Canadian Club, and poured with a roll of his wrist. In his pale blue and reddened eyes I read that his boyish energy would soon give way.

As we held up our glasses, I reminded myself to take my shot in one pull, to hold my expression steady while the drink went down. "Here's to us drinking together," he said. "Here's to always being able to get away for a few drinks. No matter where we are, no matter what happens. Here's—well, let's drink up."

We touched glasses and drank. I welcomed the whiskey's

warmth after the sting of *No matter what happens.* Was he just talking or referring to something already happening? I wouldn't ask.

"Free refills," he said. He poured, and wiped his mouth with the back of his hand. "That wind sounds cold. We need to fortify ourselves."

I knew there were some things I was choosing not to dwell on. Once I'd been taking a bath and he'd knocked on the unlocked door—none of the doors in the house had locks—and entered. He stood over me, looking down at my body. I was silent, frightened, listening to him breathe and grind his teeth. He leaned closer, hands on his knees. "I just want to see how you're coming along," he said, and abruptly his hand darted into the water and grabbed my penis hard as I gasped and turned on my side. He shook his hand in my face, not looking at me. I tried to think of something to say. "Pretty jumpy," he muttered. I felt bruised, and raised my knees. I could tell he was angry, though he had his back to me, leaning over the sink. He washed his hands and dried them. "I'll just do this once in a while to see how you're developing," he said, facing the door. He left the room, and I hurriedly scrambled to my feet.

That had happened the previous winter, nearly a year before. In the wary, fearful weeks that followed, I avoided coming home any time I thought I would find him alone. In any room, even with others around, I positioned myself in relation to him so that I couldn't be cornered. At night I slid my desk in front of the door before bed and kept the storm window up, imagining that if he managed to get in I would only have to raise one window before climbing out onto the roof. All my preparations seemed separate from the actual incident, though. I couldn't hold in my mind both his constant everyday presence and what he had done. It was as if we were on the same side, as if I was taking precautions on his behalf.

The afternoon in the bathroom still cast a shadow, and there were other shadows I did not want to dwell on. I thought of the chill that could come into the air even on the warmest summer day in Superior, the invisible chill crossing over us as the wind turned briefly off Lake Superior, turned cold for a few moments sometimes—a chill shadow though the sun burned bright—and then turned fair and warm again.

I considered, but never for long, why he sometimes turned on me. His eyes would darken, and with his jaw slung to the side, his mouth a cruel, even line, he would speak slowly and cut cruelly. Once when I was pleased with the response a teacher had written on a paper, he read the comments and said, "I'm sure there's a lot of people waiting, just waiting, a lot of people who would love to see you fall flat on your face."

The questions that pained me most concerned the severed ties in his past. My mother was his third wife. What was that saying? Why was he out of touch with the people who were the subjects of his fondest memories? Some of them lived right in the area. What was going on between him and my mother? They fought often, if no more often than usual. But she seemed to be changing, becoming fearful of leaving the house, unhappy. I sought to isolate his essence from his actions toward me or others. His occasional mistakes were only a measure of how much he'd suffered, I thought, while overall he was such a fine man, a fine father.

Still I kept wondering, and stopping. The most ominous shadow, a sign of future betrayal, was the coolness between him and his real children. There were seven of them, all older than me, the eldest one thirty-five. Some he never spoke to, others called two or three times a year. He rarely initiated contact with them. I could have asked him directly why this was so or could have found out more from my mother, but I knew it was best to not pursue the question.

―――

We drank several shots and the room became warmer, almost cozy. The color rose in his face and his eyes grew brighter as what he would need to say, his stories, continued to build. How poignant, I thought, that at two in the morning a cold wind shook the windows, that the light overhead reflected on the piano's black keys and shone through the whiskey, casting an amber glow at the base of the bottle.

Still, I was glad when he capped the Canadian Club, stretched his thin arms, and said, "Guess it's now or never." Only by leaving the house would I be able to lose perspective. Only when he talked more freely, "man to man in a barroom," would I gain the sense I cherished of being part of something larger, an ongoing history I would know through him and participate in myself, someday.

Every night was different. Every night there were signs to try to read. Would he get no further than putting on his boots, then sit on the stairs with his head on his crossed arms, inconsolable, and say he needed to go up to bed? Or would the stories flow as soon as we left the house, seeming to animate the dark streets? Tonight, judging by the set of his jaw more than by anything he'd said, he seemed on the edge of anger, of bitterness.

He went into the front hall, and I took the glasses into the kitchen. I rinsed them with hot water, dried them, and set them rim down on the top shelf. On my way back through the dining room I replaced the whiskey on its tray on the piano, turned the label facing out. I felt sentimental and talkative, but instead grew more guarded, feeling he should take the lead.

He was still dressing. A flannel shirt over his turtleneck, a corduroy suit jacket, and now a long overcoat, scarf, fur-lined leather cap with the flaps down over his ears, gloves. Finally we went outside. I caught my breath as the wind gusted. It calmed for a moment and I heard his teeth chattering.

He looked up at the sky, a quarter moon and sharp points of stars. "Your mother would never do something like this," he said. That reminded me to turn back and test the door—locked. "Oh, maybe the old Frances, but no more." He slowly made his way down the porch steps and glared back at the house, as if it represented my mother. "She's become too careful, too organized. Every minute counts to her, use it to accomplish something. Every penny must be accounted for. But goddamn it—where is the spirit in all that, where is the soul?" Move on to something else, I urged him silently. "You've still got to live, goddamn it. You understand that. You've got to feel what you feel. The passion and the pain, the horror and the joy of this life cannot be forced into a tidy schedule. You know that as I know it. You feel it in the blood. Your mother, I used to think she felt it. Now I see us understanding each other less and less. What a goddamn shame. She's changed. I only see glimpses of the woman I thought I knew."

We made it down off the porch—my stepfather pushing aside overgrown pine branches, swearing—and I thought he might be done talking about my mother. Instead he turned at the sidewalk, under the streetlight, and stared up at their darkened bedroom window. He stood staring up and kept talking about her. He didn't look at me, didn't pause for me to respond in any way as I stood beside him listening. The wind blew and needles of snow from the trees stung my face. The wind entered my chest and stayed, a thin sheet of metal, the metallic coldness radiating in rhythm with the gusts.

How he and my mother years ago sat at a Chinese restaurant through lunch, through the afternoon drinking beer, through dinner, so absorbed with each other. "That was a good time. She didn't always think I was an old man not worth listening to." How she didn't treat him as she used to, how she didn't make the space for his poetry she once had. He spit in the snow. His eyes were glistening, burning, and I braced myself for more; the coldness in my chest twisted and cut.

These were not the stories I wanted. I listened, and he seemed young and trembling, helpless. I wanted to turn away, to avoid seeing him this way, but I could not. I thought I had no choice but to listen, all the way through. He told me they'd rented a rowboat on a summer night and rowed far out onto a lake, where the boat rocked back and forth, and then they lay down under the stars and drank from a wineskin. Another story seemed to come to him, but instead, at last, he fell silent, and covered his face with his hands, while I waited.

I willed myself to believe the night could still be salvaged. I had to let my imagination go, for while he'd talked about my mother I'd viewed him with an unfamiliar harshness, as a sixty-two-year-old man reduced to getting his stepson drunk and boasting about the past, while not facing the truth of his limited and mundane present: working in a library six blocks from home, writing poetry on weekends. He didn't do much of anything anymore. He was fading out in pettiness—where had all that energy and spirit gone? Suddenly it had seemed only pathetic that he was taking me out to a bar in the middle of the night. And the town. I looked around and felt its poorness and insignificance.

Usually I felt this way only when I was totally out of touch for some reason with his perspective. Walking home tired and depressed, some afternoons, I saw only meager houses and desolate spaces. Dirty and gray. People I watched running their errands were hunched over, worried, down to their last ounce of strength. Their coats were too thin. Why had my stepfather brought us here? Through the long winters families fought; solitary people drank and watched television. The bars were full of sullen men and women steadily working on getting their lives over with.

But the desperation and sadness represented only one side of things—just as his complaining about my mother was only a fragment of the entire man—and he would encourage me to see other sides. Now that the house was far behind, his gait had begun to loosen. He was walking briskly now, hands clasped behind his back, clouds of his breath beaten down in the wind. I could imagine him upright and proud as he walked behind the plow on his uncle's farm or marched with an iron pipe in his hand in the truckers' strike in Minneapolis or crossed a battlefield in France. I walked beside him. Block after icy block slipped by; I refused to lose sight of the night's possibilities.

We were zigzagging on side streets, toward downtown. I didn't need much light to recognize the small, dark houses we passed. Tires in the backyards, broken porch steps, paint peeling on the doors. I thought the wind must blow right through the walls. But he had come from a place like this, a poor neighborhood in Minneapolis. He brought his mother up to Superior three or four times a year from a nursing home in Saint Paul, and she sat with folded hands at the kitchen table. His father had been a housepainter, unemployed half the year. From that deprivation, his mother keeping them clothed and fed on so little, from all the quarreling, his father grabbing his canvas jacket after the fighting, almost every night, slamming the door behind him as he headed for the pool hall—from all that, my stepfather had emerged. And after the war, in the early fifties, he'd lived in Superior for five years and worked organizing the steelworkers in Duluth, workers at the railroads and in the shipyards in Superior. This town hadn't always been dead. He and his drinking buddies had closed every bar along the waterfront and then headed over to Duluth, many times.

As we turned on Belknap a pickup sped past and I heard a shout as it fishtailed around the corner. He could change the way I saw the town. Even while he seemed lost in his own thoughts, I could begin to see differently. There seemed to be possibilities all around, in the clanking from the rail yards, in a train's thundering momentum, in the force of an icebreaker, the piercing blast of a ship's horn, the crashing of waterfalls, even in the constancy of the wind. People were going to the bars at night but rising again in the morning, whether to work or stand in line or dream and plan. He'd pointed out the tenacity here, the endurance. But was that his perspective tonight? We were almost downtown. He was walking at a good pace still, but he was uncharacteristically silent. I caught a glimpse of myself reflected in the side window of Globe News, saw the tension and uncertainty in my narrow face.

Tower Avenue was wider and more brightly lit. An older couple negotiating through a cut in the snowbank, laughing, drunk.

A man outside the Poodle Lounge braced against his car, searching through his pockets. "The human comedy," my stepfather muttered.

"Watch this broken glass," I said.

We passed the Elbo Room, Champions, other bars closed for the night, but further up Tower there would be some still open. I scanned the streets: rock salt glittering on the ice, the Palace Theater marquee ("The Victory Tour: Jesus Saves"), the mannequin in a black beret at Sammy's Pizza nodding slowly. What would my stepfather have me notice and what should I discard?

He seemed to lean further forward. "It's time to make my run," he said. "I can feel it." He pulled the scarf down off his face, craned his neck to free his constriction. He clapped my back a couple of times and I began to relax. "I've seen so much."

"I know you have."

"Those summers on the home farm, I always thought, 'I could be happy with a life like this, a simple life.' I loved that hard work. My muscles were like iron, and I thought I could be happy. I told you on the hottest summer afternoons, what do you think we drank?"

"Coffee."

"Hot black coffee! That's right. You remember. I loved all of it. Even those taciturn uncles of mine. You were lucky to get two words out of them a day. They figured, Why talk if there wasn't anything to talk about? I think I could have passed my whole life that way, but it wasn't to be. I got thrown into it, or I threw myself into it."

We peered into the Anchor Room. Closed. The National Bank of Commerce sign flashed 2:35.

"All the strife I've lived through. The war, of course. The strikes, the campaigns, the McCarthy years. I told you I wasn't a Trotskyite, but I thought the Trotskyites should have the right to meet like anyone else. They had nowhere to turn so they came to me to be their adviser. I agreed to do it and the gutless bastards fired me from the university! My marriages—God save me!" He laughed. "All the time I've spent in the trenches, all I've been through—and now I'm ready to get it down. I'm ready to make my run."

I was sorry I'd questioned the richness of his present life. Warmth and energy flooded through me. A car made a turn right before us and I grabbed his elbow to hold him on the curb.

"There's no more time to waste," he told me. "I know I've

worked hard, but now I've got to work even harder, get it all down, let it flow like a river. Get it started and it will flow. Poetry as I've never written it before. Poetry that takes you by the collar. Poetry that mourns and celebrates."

I wasn't sure if anything needed to be said. We were near the end of Tower now. We came upon a place that was open—black door, "High Bridge Lounge" in red letters—but he rejected it without a word and we walked on.

"Hemingway talked about this," he said. "He said you start to realize time is short. And you see people less. You realize the ties are still there but you know it's time to work as you've never worked. He thought it was a sin to do anything else at that point but to work your best. Now time is short for me and I feel I can make my run."

"You will."

"I must. Oh, it's good to get out and walk, and live a little. It's good to get some things off my chest. It's good to talk to you. I had a terrible dream about the war. I was standing with Tom in the mud, in the rain, in France. He was standing beside the jeep and he was just about to turn to me, and I didn't want him to turn, because I knew what he would say. The rain was slanting down. Smoke was coming over his shoulder, clouds of cigarette smoke, and I just knew those men had died." I saw it all. The low fields he had described often, brown and green and gray. Muddy boots and pale faces. Rain striking the hood of the jeep. His lieutenant and friend trying to keep his expression steady as he turned. Trying not to betray his judgment that my stepfather's mistake had caused those men to die.

"Your mother doesn't know what it is to live with a memory like that," he said. "To be haunted. Not too many people will listen anymore."

"And then you couldn't sleep?" I asked.

"Then came that awful period between waking and sleeping. All I saw was people on fire. My brother in the institution with burns on his chest. My uncle when the heater tipped over and his clothes caught on fire and me and three other men tried holding him down, but he was throwing us off. Then finally I came fully awake and more memories came. I was sweating and restless and all your mother told me was 'Go back to sleep.' She didn't care to hear any of it, though I listen to her whenever she wants."

He seemed to be waiting for me to react. Maybe he thought I shared his perspective on her, but I didn't know what to think. We turned on a street parallel to a row of grain elevators, standing hollow, defined vertically by lines of harsh lights. He told me he still thought often of Tom, even forty years later. He started to tell me his plans to write about that battlefield in France, but paused to stand before a bar on a corner. The Viking Lounge. A crudely cut white wooden boat was nailed over the door. "Looks like a tough place," he said, "but we'll do all right."

My stepfather pushed inside and I followed. A long room in smoky, sickly yellow light. One head turned toward us, big and bald and unshaven. The man stared at us with intense interest, almost hunger, I imagined. Another man, with greased red hair, sat resting his forehead on the edge of the bar. Though I was starting to warm already, I felt a cold draft against my legs. "Where's the barman?" my stepfather said to me. I knew he would not sit with his back to the door—an old habit from the war—and we walked the length of the bar and took two stools at the corner.

"Don't want to get too close, hey?" said the bald man. He snorted and scratched his chest, fingers spread like a rake.

"It's all right, George." A man stood from a table at the far side of the bar, lifted a section of the bar, and approached us.

"Where do you work at?" George continued. "You a professor?"

The red-haired head on the bar laughed and rocked.

"George, George," the bartender said.

"A tweed jacket, is it?"

"What'll it be?" the bartender asked my stepfather. He squinted at me as if trying to get enough light on my face, then shook his head.

"Hey, Professor. Professor 'I'm Too Good to Sit with These Others.'"

"That'll do," came a voice from the far table.

George looked down at his hands gripping a beer mug.

"Give us two boilermakers," my stepfather said. "And an extra shot."

The bartender had a gray crewcut. As he poured a beer he pulled a cigarette from behind his ear and tucked it there again. He wore a thin down jacket, hunter orange, over a T-shirt.

He slid over the beers and shots and my stepfather took out his wallet.

"It's pretty cold in here with the way that wind is whipping," my stepfather said.

I knew he was just making conversation but I also knew it was the wrong thing to say.

"Let's not hear anything from you."

"What? What's wrong?"

"This your kid? What grade are you in, the sixth?"

"He's eighteen years old."

"Whatever." The bartender departed. George turned as if about to speak.

"Christ!" my stepfather muttered. "You try to go out for a quiet drink!"

He drank some beer, put back one of the shots, and wiped his mouth on his sleeve. I was concerned for him, angry on his behalf. I didn't think he should come in for this kind of treatment, and wished I'd said or done something. But his mood had changed. Now he didn't seem upset in the least; if anything, he was delighted.

"Quite a place." He leaned close, and laughed low. "Yes sir, quite a place. You never know what you'll stumble onto in this life." He felt in his breast pockets. "Got a couple cigars here somewhere."

George seemed to have lost interest in us already; his gaze rested above the rows of bottles, somewhere on the dark, cracked wall. No one here sensed the range of experience my stepfather possessed. He came into this crummy place and just his presence made it something else.

I watched him biting off the end of his cigar, drawing out matches, and my thoughts shifted. I could feel my emotions swinging. How like a little kid he was with his cigar. He rarely smoked, and never indoors, but in this setting where he felt ill at ease, unwelcome, he was going to assert himself somehow. Detachment from him and disgust, pride in him and protectiveness—my emotions were oddly patterned and frightening. I drank my beer and tried to settle myself.

He struck a match and pulled on the cigar, turning it expertly. One slow revolution and the whole circle was burning. He summoned the bartender loudly and ordered another beer for me, beer and two more shots for himself. He asked for hard-boiled eggs or pretzels or anything else to eat.

We both drank more, and although he had at least two for every one of mine, I found that my ability to concentrate narrowed to an intense beam focused solely on him. He was telling stories, and I had stories, insights of my own, welling up inside me. Still I was unsure. I'd shared my stories occasionally and he'd listened, if sometimes impatiently, and my jokes had sometimes made him laugh. When I had a political insight of my own, I reported that I'd heard it or read it elsewhere, and he usually seemed to agree, sometimes even seemed impressed by the views I credited to others.

I would grow more confident eventually, learn when to talk, when to encourage, when I could say the first thing that came into my mind. My time wasn't here yet, but it would come. Now it was enough to be near him, to learn from him. So many possibilities: all he had experienced, all that lay ahead of me.

He drew up his collar tight, and drank, and shivered. Clouds of cigar smoke were blue and gray, drifting out of the low light. "This chill makes me remember that night in Ardennes," he said. "You remember that. You remember my stories. I wanted to stay with my men but I was so sick, high fever, terrible chills and weakness, and Tom or another officer found a small country farmhouse and insisted I stay there the night. A woman and an old man lived there. She led me up a long flight of stairs to a small unlit room and I lay down and slept. But some hours later, I heard voices down below, an argument, and I didn't know if my mind was playing tricks on me but I thought I heard German spoken. I got my pistol from under my pillow and I propped myself up and held it ready on my chest. There was silence. And then I heard footsteps coming up the stairs and I knew this was it, it was going to be me or the one coming to get me that would die. The trip up the stairs lasted so long, I can't tell you, one footfall and then another, and my head roaring, and my body soaking in sweat. And a shadow appeared in the doorway and I nearly pulled the trigger, nearly, but something held me waiting just another moment, and I made out that it was the woman carrying a blanket, and she came forward and spread it over me. Oh Christ, she didn't know how close she came."

I gripped his shoulder. "What a story. I'll never get tired of that one."

Soon he began another story, and another block of his life, another shining example, stood clear before me. He was working as a union organizer through the Iron Range and in Duluth and Superior. Crowds of shipyard workers were coming out to hear speeches on the waterfront. He was writing these speeches and writing and starring in political theater. There was one organizer, Bob Brown, he was sharing a room with at the Androy Hotel, just half a mile away from where we sat now, down Tower. Brown loved peppermint schnapps. Wherever he was staying you could reach your hand down between cushions in a sofa or feel under an armchair, and find bottles of schnapps. You could find bottles in kitchen drawers, coat pockets. At any rate, my stepfather said, after one night of drinking they got a tip that a group of thugs was on its way to the hotel. So Bob and my stepfather rushed back to the Androy, got everything together, then made a rope out of their sheets and shimmied down the back wall, laughing as a couple of bottles of schnapps slipped free and shattered in the alley. They were chased away, but just a few weeks later they came back again to organize.

His stories were laced with the advice I found invigorating. Go with the people. Choose the right side and then fight with all you've got. Save nothing. I sat there longing to be his son, longing for his blood to be my blood. But in the middle of my reverie, in the middle of listening to a familiar story and imagining what I could do someday, so that our histories and our futures could be entwined for as long as he lived, I realized he had fallen silent.

"I don't even want to go back there," he said.

"Where?" I struggled for coherence.

"Back to your mother. Do you have any idea how fucked up everything is? Christ, I shouldn't be telling you this, but everything's a fucking mess." He took a shot and rapped his glass against the bar. I tried to take this in, but could not. His face was hard and angry, the trance of the stories broken. "One more," he called.

"No, all done."

"You won't give me one more drink?"

"That's right."

"Go to hell then." He waved his arm and slipped off his stool and stood. "Let's go," he told me.

I got into my coat, embarrassed, but no one said anything, or even seemed to notice, as we walked the length of the bar. I felt completely worn out. Frightened and cold. We stood outside the door.

"You need to put your coat on," I said.

"I'm fine." He was leaning against the door, one arm bent awkwardly behind him. A car passed and he shouted "Taxi!" and laughed. His face was in shadow but I could see tears on his cheeks. Dread started to clarify in my mind, about getting him home, about what he would reveal.

"Come over here," he said. "I need you. I'm like a ship without its fucking compass." He threw his arm around my shoulder, jarring my head. He leaned on me, pressing hard against my shoulder, and I started walking us toward Tower Avenue.

Through the shaking and the fear, I held myself resolute, and carried him step by step. We were a few blocks down Tower, but still a long way from home. The physical exertion was a relief, requiring nearly all my concentration.

"Fucking bartender," he said.

I wished he would be quiet, to spare me. I wished I could feel only his weight and forget the rest.

"Fucking bartender. There's plenty more at home though, right, David? Plenty more booze, unless your mother has poured it out. Then I just buy more, right?"

He prodded me in the ribs and I said, "Right."

"Good man, good man." He laughed.

I tried to plan ahead. I would get him home, carrying him or dragging him. Then I would plead with him to keep quiet. I might even promise a drink. If I could get his boots off and manage to make him lie down on the couch I thought he would drop right off.

These nights had ended badly before. He knelt at a gutter vomiting or lay down on someone's lawn and said he wasn't going any further. At home he stood in the front hall singing "Little Man, You've Had a Busy Day" until my mother and sister came downstairs. My mother screamed at him and he fended her off at arm's length. He ordered my sister to make him a hamburger with onions and bragged that a movie should be made of his life.

All of that could always be chalked up to just drinking too much. He and I laughed about it the next day and whatever disturbed me at the time soon faded. But what I'd learned about him and my mother, and even now he was revealing more, had turned this night into a monstrous black pit. I was trying to keep myself from its bottom, but I knew I had further yet to fall.

He'd been talking and talking about my mother, recounting sentimental stories, and I hardly had the strength to listen. What could I do that I wasn't doing already? What could I say? I dragged him forward, unable to control my deep shaking, unable to control my thoughts. The wind gusted up the wide street—stayed in my chest, burned cold in my head—and gusted again.

"She wants to leave me. She's going to leave me."

"Can't we talk about something else?" I asked.

"No, we can't. She's so frightened of everything she can hardly leave the house, you know that. And she blames me, how do you figure that? What the hell did I do? I'm just trying to do the best I can by her, and it's not easy, let me tell you, not fucking easy at all. So she wants to leave me. It's fucking ridiculous. It doesn't make any sense. What's she going to do, get an apartment and stay indoors all the time? Christ, I can see it."

Another block nearly completed, six left to go.

"All right, I'm all right now," he said. "I can walk."

"No."

"Let me walk. Christ almighty!"

He pushed me forward and freed himself. "See this, see this?"

In the middle of the street he slipped and fell hard. I knelt at his side. "I'm fine," he said. "Fine."

"I'm going to help you up," I said.

"What's this?"

He raised himself on one elbow and blood dripped on the ice.

"Come on, a car's going to hit us."

"I'm bleeding."

He sat and took off a glove and pressed his hand to his forehead. Blood flowed between his fingers. I grabbed him under the arms and pulled him to the curb. Then I crouched in front of him. I knew I could do nothing, really, and felt myself growing angry at the sight of him so helpless.

"She still loves me, don't you think?" he said. "That's the worst thing about it. We still love each other."

At home he wouldn't keep quiet. I waited under the front hall lamp as his ranting continued.

"John? John? What's happening?"

A light came on at the top of the stairs and my mother appeared in her bathrobe. They shouted at each other, accusing each other. His back was turned to her, as he sat slumped on the stairs. At a lull he said, "And I've cut my head. I might have to go to the emergency room."

"What?"

I watched her come down the stairs and stand before him. They talked softly, more calmly now. I noticed my sister sitting at the top of the stairs.

I could be anybody here beside him now, I thought. It didn't matter who I was, a stranger, a friend, anyone—as long as I answered his call to drink with him and listen to his stories, as long as

I tended to him when he fell, wrapped a scarf around his head and tied it tight in back. Nothing more for me to do, nothing to keep them together.

Soon my mother was moved to pity by something my stepfather said. She came forward and cradled his head against her. His eyes closed under the line of the bloody scarf and she rocked him in her arms.

I walked past them, up the stairs past my sister sitting with her knees drawn to her chest, and down the darkened hallway to my room.

And the Shin Bone's Connected to the Knee Bone

Catherine Brady

Her brothers are always telling her that she gets her fat ass from sitting all day in her Cushman. That all meter maids have fat asses, packaged for the whole world to see in their tight, shiny polyester uniform pants. When she pulls up beside the car parked in the bus stop and steps to the pavement, Liz feels the strangeness of actually being on her feet, the tightness of the seams at her crotch and inner thighs, the unbalanced ballast of all the things clipped to her black leather belt, her transistor, her badge, her canister of mace, the heavy regulation flashlight. She feels as if she is all fat ass, with weak tendrils for arms and legs.

She presses firmly on the triple carbon sheets of her ticket pad as she writes up the blue BMW, still gleaming from a recent trip to the car wash. The vanity plate reads ULTWMN. Liz can picture this ultimate woman: a wash of blond hair, tight jeans, steep-heeled boots, one of those big sacklike purses with some designer's name printed on it, over and over. She knows what excuses the woman would make, if she came back while Liz was still writing the ticket: just running into Starbuck's for a grande no-whip mocha, only five minutes. A pleading pout, a little pucker of confusion between her eyebrows when her high little laugh and her flirting get her nowhere. Liz takes no excuses. Parking in a bus stop will cost this babe one twenty-five. Maybe she'll learn to find a parking spot like the regular plebes have to. Maybe she'll never understand that her little impulse is about more than herself. That this car in the bus stop means the next bus to arrive won't be able to pull out of traffic, and cars will clot the street behind that bus till they block the intersection. If people could only be made to understand the simple anatomy that connects one action to a chain of others. *And the shin bone's connected to the knee bone.*

Liz tucks the ticket carefully under the windshield wiper. Her tickets won't end up blowing wistfully in the gutters or drooping over sewer grates. Liz is tidy. When she chalks tires in the neighborhoods that are restricted to two-hour street parking, she thumps her rod against the tires with a steady beat—ta DA, ta DA, ta DA. Like clockwork.

She gets back onto her Cushman and pulls carefully into traffic. She is almost at the corner when she glances in her rearview mirror, sees a blond—bingo!—with a coffee cup in her hand stutter out into the street, an arm raised to call Liz back, a look of hurt on her face. As if this is personal.

Liz would have made a good cop. She has the right temperament. She doesn't get angry, she does her job. She'd wanted to join the force. But she couldn't pass the physical. Too heavy-hipped, too soft, too slow.

Liz pulls into the Tower Market parking lot to check meters. An Orowheat delivery truck is double-parked before the store's entrance. She'll give the driver another few minutes. She's fair. She tries to give a break to the delivery trucks that have to negotiate San Francisco's overcrowded streets. But every Tuesday morning for a month this Orowheat truck has been double-parked in front of the store. By the time she's slowly pulled past the cars in the metered slots, the truck is still there.

She parks behind the truck, gets out, and begins writing the ticket. Just as she is about to slap the ticket on the windshield, the driver comes running out of the store, tugging a half-full bread cart behind him.

"I'm out of here," he hollers at her. He yanks the cart over the curb and hurls it around to the back of the truck. Liz hears a bang and a crunch. The fool has just whacked into her Cushman.

She walks cautiously around the opposite side of the truck. It's a good rule of thumb to keep the vehicle between yourself and the driver. But she almost breaks out laughing when she sees the damage. Her rearview mirror has been knocked askew, and one of the bars of the bread cart has been bent at a forty-five degree angle. Loaves of bread and cellophaned packs of rolls litter the asphalt, like bodies thrown from a wreck. The driver stands panting, as if he's just run a race, arms slack and useless at his sides.

He has a fat ass, too. His own version of shiny uniform pants, the shirt with the curlicued letters of his name in red, Michael.

Sweat circles shadow his armpits.

He moves suddenly, and Liz takes a step back. But he only wants to rearrange her rearview mirror. The rod attaching the mirror snaps off in his big, clumsy hands. He drops the mirror as if it burns him, as if it can't be connected to him if he moves quickly enough. Sinking to his hands and knees, he begins scrabbling up loaves of bread and tossing them into the crumpled cart. When he strains to reach for a loaf, his shirt lifts to expose two pale ovals of soft flesh seamed at the center by his spine.

"Please don't write the ticket," he says. Without looking up at her, he says, "I know you're a nice person. I can tell by your eyes. You have honest eyes."

She has blue eyes. Pale lashes, reddish like her hair, lashes she coats lavishly with black mascara every morning, so she will not have to look out at the world from beneath their sparseness. The tickets on her pad are numbered, and she has to account for every one. "I've already written the ticket."

He looks at her now. "Can't you tear it up? Some turd in a Honda was parked in the loading zone when I pulled up. I have to make thirty-two deliveries a day."

She grins. "I've got a quota to fill by the end of the day too."

Sheepishly, he shakes his head. "They grind us under the wheel, don't they?"

She doesn't mind the ones who are nice. Liz has had people throw grocery bags, shoes, hot coffee at her, and once a driver got in his car and chased her through traffic. Things got even worse after parking control officers were moved from the jurisdiction of the police department to the Department of Parking and Traffic. You take so much abuse in this job, you're grateful for someone who treats you like a human being. On the other hand, you never can be too sure that you're not on the receiving end of a snow job.

"Oh, please," Michael says, and his mouth is a raw hook. The part in his unruly brown hair is crooked, like a kid's. Sometimes Liz thinks it's just as bad when they plead as when they throw things and curse. She feels embarrassed for people when ugliness spills from them, escapes their weak hold.

She can't stand watching him compress the yielding packages as if they are flesh, too, bruisable as fruit. She hooks her ticket pad on her belt and crouches to help him. She picks up the loaves carefully, using her hands like spatulas, and slides them back onto his cart.

"You can just toss them in," Michael says. "This stuff is all past its sell date."

She cups her hand over the butt end of the loaves to align them on his cart.

"Ah, come on," Michael says. "It doesn't matter. Go ahead, destroy them. Have a good time."

He takes a loaf of bread and squeezes it like an accordion. Then he whips it at her, and in her hands she can feel the bread swelling, trying to regain its uniform shape. The sensation makes her uneasy, squeamish. He hurls another soft package at her, and another. He grabs a package of cinnamon rolls and kneads it, crumpling it in his fists as if to encourage her to do the same. The plastic wrapping pops open, releasing the smell of cinnamon and brown sugar.

The sweet smell catches him up short, and he rocks on his heels, inhaling. He pulls out a squashed roll and bites into it, then holds out the package to her.

What tempts her to reach forward and pull a roll free from its neighbors? Carefully, she unwinds the spiral before she plucks off a piece to eat. Soon her fingers, like his, are sticky, smeared with cinnamon-colored grease.

He smiles at her. "Pretty lady, you have to let me buy you a cup of coffee to wash down that roll."

Pretty lady. She's heard that before, from pouch-bellied middle-aged men, rock-hard young guys with slicked hair who think that if they talk fast enough, she won't rip a ticket from a pad. They all think she's not pretty enough not to be susceptible to that knee-jerk compliment.

She has nothing to wipe her fingers on. She wouldn't dream of wiping them on her crisp, starched shirt. She's not going to be suckered by anybody either. "I could use some coffee," she says. "But that ticket's written."

———

They sit around the table in her parents' dining room, waiting for the kettle to boil so that Liz and her mother can bring out tea and dessert. Michael sits beside Liz chewing his nails while her father and brothers tell jokes. Her father has a store of jokes from his years as a cop. And her brothers add to this store, though none of them, as it turns out, followed their father into the force. PJ's a newly hatched lawyer, Tommy's a real estate agent, and Joe is getting on like a house on fire at the ad agency. Her father didn't think Liz needed college like the boys. They'd have to support a wife and kids one day.

"Why did the English invent whiskey?" Her father eyes each of them in turn before he answers the question. "To keep the Irish from taking over the world."

Michael doesn't laugh. The only time he's opened his mouth was when he asked if the glass of water her mother poured him came from the tap. He told her mother he couldn't drink it, the tap water was chock-full of fluoride, a poison. And Liz could see on her father's and brothers' faces what they were thinking: look what Liz dragged in. She hasn't had a boyfriend in two years, and she'd wanted to show them that at least there was somebody who was interested in her.

When the kettle screams, Liz joins her mother in the kitchen. While her mother pours boiling water into the teapot, Liz gets down the cups and saucers. She lines up the cups on the saucers so that all their handles are parallel. When she looks up, her mother is watching her anxiously. As anxiously as she peeks into all the pots on the stove before dinner, hopelessly adjusting the flames on the burners, so that just once the potatoes won't be still hard when the meat is ready.

"He seems very nice," her mother says. "Quiet."

Liz taps a cup with her fingernail. "If Joey asks him one more time where he left his sense of humor—"

"You know your brothers," her mother says.

"I'm just warning you. I'm gonna clobber the little shit if he doesn't stop."

Her mother sighs. "You've your job to thank for that foul mouth. I wish you'd let me talk to my friend at Macy's. She could get you something in the menswear department. Something more ladylike."

"For minimum wage," Liz says. She hefts the teapot. "No thank you."

Her mother follows her out to the table, carrying a big glass bowl of trifle. Her mother spoons the gooey mixture of cake, canned fruit, and custard onto plates. What looked pretty in the glass bowl looks soggy and lumpy on the plates, like all the food Liz's mother makes, her mashed potatoes, boiled cabbage, gray steak. Liz doesn't like to cook. All that effort to turn out boiled things that weep water onto the plate.

Her mother turns to Michael. "How did you and Liz meet?"

"She gave me a ticket," Michael says.

"Don't," Liz says, as soon as Joey opens his mouth to answer. Joey sings. "Lovely Rita, meter maid."

Sometimes Liz is tired of knowing what people are going to do. The way things always turn out as expected. *The shin bone's connected to the knee bone.* She knows which jokes her father will trot out in company and which he won't (the ones about Polacks and spics), exactly what her brothers will say if she puts her hair up (stick your finger in the electric socket again?). She knew beforehand that she wouldn't make the grade as a cop. She knew that Michael would sit here blinking while her father and brothers roared on around him. Knowing never seems to work to her advantage, to supply her with a good comeback when her brothers tease, to keep her from clambering hastily onto her Cushman when some double-parked guy predictably blows his top. Knowing remains inside her, a superior secret, a silent watcher, a sharp, tart observer locked inside the pillow of herself.

"Liz gave me a ticket once," PJ says. "Her own brother. She's out there saving the world from people who jeopardize the public safety by blocking fire hydrants."

"You were obstructing a handicapped ramp," Liz says. "That's unforgivable."

"My fender was maybe one inch over the line," PJ says. "What'd you do, get down on your hands and knees with measuring tape?"

"Liz, you know, you can't always go by the book," her father says. "You don't learn to let little things go, someday you're going to come up against some big guy who hauls off on you. And you'll have it coming."

PJ makes a fist. "It's still not too late for me to get even with you."

Liz laughs. She ought to thank her brothers for all the pummeling of her childhood. They helped her to develop a thick skin, to understand that if she stood still, blinking, while they hauled away, they'd never get the satisfaction they were after.

"You ought not to speak to your sister that way," Michael says.

Even Liz is surprised that Michael has finally opened his mouth.

And Michael isn't finished. "Men should learn not to rely on the trump card of physical force," he says.

Liz blushes. Sometimes she isn't sure whether Michael is too good for her or not good enough. He went to college. Berkeley. She knows enough to know that only really smart people go there.

But he dropped out. Over their first cup of coffee, he told her that he'd had a nervous breakdown. He'd been studying physics at the time. He has some kind of chemical thing wrong with him, and he's been medicated ever since. He told her that he still studied, on his own, but he couldn't go back to school. And she'd sipped at sour coffee, hot enough to burn her tongue, wondering how she could get out of there fast, away from this crazy person. But then he did little tricks for her—balanced a penny on the edge of the table where they were sitting, fooled around with a salt shaker so that it remained tilted at an angle but didn't tip over, explaining to her that it could remain tipped like that, in stable equilibrium, because its center of mass hadn't been lowered. She'd been oh so amazed by such rules, laws that could subvert themselves to make the impossible happen.

"Take it easy," PJ says. "Liz is my buddy. She knows I'm kidding."

For the rest of the evening, Michael is as good as in her brothers' pockets. They manage to find ways to insert "trump card" into their jokes, into their lazy arguments about whether real estate is worth the price it's going for. When she and Michael get their coats, PJ gives Liz a big hug at the door, whispers in her ear, "I hope you're not sleeping with this guy."

She's not. She's read the dating guidebooks. You don't give it up till the fourth date.

Driving her home, Michael is as silent as he was at dinner. And then suddenly, into the quiet, he says, "When you're so gentle with them, Liz, I don't know how they can be so rough on you."

She can give as good as she gets. "That's just how we fool around," she says. "It's not a big deal."

"What I think, you know, is that you're like a flower."

She looks at his big hands on the steering wheel, those thick fingers that can't seem to clutch even the seamed plastic, but sprawl awkward and loose. If she imagines him touching her, she can see only the clumsy way he pawed at the soft loaves of bread he spilled from his cart.

"So delicate," Michael says. "Even the way your skin is. Like if I reached over and brushed your cheek, your freckles would come off on my fingers like pollen."

She says nothing. She figures they'll be at her house in only ten minutes. Time is another thing that Liz can predict with absolute accuracy. She can always guess the hour without having to look at her watch. She rests her hand on the door latch. When they pull up at her door, she'll jump out of the car before he can lean over to her for a kiss. After this, she's not going to go out with Michael again.

Liz usually feels good at the end of the workday. She ought to feel good today. She's heading back to the Hall of Justice to return her Cushman and the day's booty collected from the meters, and her ticket pad is satisfyingly thinned out. She's bagged about thirty unfed meters, four cars parked in front of fire hydrants, three blocked crosswalks, with only one nasty argument. The fine for blocking a crosswalk has gone up to $250, a justice that pleases her. A slap on the wrist isn't going to make anyone think twice the next time.

But she knows that when she gets home, the light on her answering machine will be flashing and there will be more messages from Michael. He hasn't stopped calling her since she broke up with him. She did that over the phone. It's easier that way. Before, when she's broken up with a guy or he's broken up with her, it's never been face–to–face. None of her relationships has ever lasted more than a few months, none ever seemed to warrant more than the abrupt ugliness of a phone call, a short conversation in which nobody got mad, nobody begged or pleaded. But Michael cried when she told him over the phone, spoke to her in tear-blurred words. Now he calls two or three times a day, and all he says to the machine is that he wants to talk to her, please. Twice now she's seen him standing outside the door of her apartment building when she came home from her shift, and she's had to circle the block, eat dinner out, take in a movie, to be sure he'd give up before she finally went home. She knew all along there was something not right with him. What if he turns out to be some kind of stalker? She's been worried enough to tell PJ, her pal. He said, "You sure can pick the winners," but he promised to meet her when she came home from work for the next week or so, just in case. Only today he won't be there, because he's trying a case in Sacramento.

Liz has to brake suddenly for a guy who turns sharply in front of her to make a three-point turn. He doesn't even have the courtesy to let her go around him before he reverses into her lane to complete the turn. What else would you expect from a red Mustang convertible? When she honks at him—the Cushman's horn gives a tiny squeak—he honks back and flips her the finger. No respect for the uniform. And now that he's in front of her, he slows to a crawl, looking for a parking spot, she guesses. He'll have to look long and hard to find a legal spot on a side street along Geary. When he reaches the stop sign at Geary, he doesn't come to a complete stop but makes a sharp right turn, cutting off a driver who has the right of way.

She's not going to let that go. She can't do anything about moving violations, but she'll follow him and see what she can see. When he pulls into a parking spot, she stops a few cars back and watches him get out of the car. He doesn't even look at the meter, the bright red violation flag in its window. The rules weren't made for people like him, with his red Mustang and his soft wool suit that drapes his shoulders like silk. Maybe he got it at Macy's, from someone who should have been Liz.

She takes down his license plate number and writes up the ticket. She is approaching his car when he comes charging back.

He has a quarter in his fist. "Give me a break. I had to get change."

She is just doing her job. She slips the ticket beneath his windshield wiper.

He steps down from the curb and bats at her hand. "You saw me pull into that space." He's shouting now, humiliating himself. "You saw me!"

Let him spill his steaming guts all over the street. She'll count how many times she blinks in the next few seconds.

"Take that fucking ticket back, you ugly bitch."

When he grabs at her elbow, she swings to face him. "You want to argue?"

She brings the heavy ticket pad down hard on the hood of his car, scrapes a fingernail-thin streak of paint from the finish. "You want to argue some more?"

"Fucking crazy bitch," he says. "I'll report you."

She whacks the ticket pad against the hood again, scoring an X into the shiny red. "Back off, asshole," she says.

She raises her fist high and takes a step toward him. He takes a step back. Adrenaline surges through her like sweet sap, she can feel herself filling, swelling with that powerful syrup, till she grows so much taller than he is, till she has to look down to meet his eyes.

Retreating from her, he trips over the curb and falls backward, and for a moment his arms and legs wheel in the air as he tries to fight the gravity that plops him onto his ass.

"Nice suit," she says.

She gets back on her Cushman with deliberate slowness and pulls away. After a block, she has to pull over. Her heart squirms sickeningly in her chest, throttling her breath. What happened back there? She feels so ashamed to have let that man pull her from her perch of calm, of justice blindly dispensed. He could report her. She wants to crawl away someplace, someplace dark where she can hide from this big ugly creature that balks inside the vise of her ribs.

She drives on without knowing where she is going. She tries to talk herself back into her own self. You've got to snap sometime. All these cockroaches taking their tempers out on you. Just be careful from now on, don't let it catch you again.

She would like to talk to someone else. Someone who wouldn't believe her if she told him what she'd done. She thinks of Michael. *You're a flower.*

She's never been to his house, but she knows his address. He told her once, and she always remembers numbers. She pulls up in front of his apartment building, unhooks her helmet, and leaves it on the seat. There's no buzzer, no security gate at the entrance, so she climbs the stairs to apartment 7 and knocks on the door.

When he opens the door to her, he doesn't look at all surprised to see her. His face breaks into a wide grin. "I knew you'd come," he says.

He lets her into his living room. He urges her to have a seat, but there's nowhere to sit. The cushions have been pulled from the sofa and the one armchair, stacked on end to make a little cave in the middle of the room, with a sheet draped over it for a roof. Bits of lint and scraps of newspaper litter the floor.

He sees her staring. "Sometimes I do that," he says. "When I'm having a bad day. Make a little nest. It's not like I get crazy or anything. Don't you do things like that? Maybe soak in the tub for hours when you're in a bad mood?"

It is crazy. This whole place is crazy—the books on the shelves are stacked any old way, little towers that threaten to spill at any moment, yellow Post-it Notes are stuck on the door frame that leads to the hall, the solitary picture above the denuded, sagging sofa is crooked. Michael doesn't even know that he's poking a finger through the hole in his T-shirt, circling his finger nervously over his chest. He's pathetic.

"I just came to say I was sorry," Liz says. "I shouldn't have told you over the phone. That's all."

He stumbles against the stacked cushions, and they collapse. He tugs a cushion free and plumps it on the sofa. "Here. Sit a moment. Let's talk things over."

Her hands come up to cover her face. She just doesn't want to look at what she's looking at anymore.

He takes her hands. He pulls her to the sofa and plops her down on the one cushion. "Liz, listen to me."

But he doesn't say anything else. He snakes a hand alongside her cheek and unclips the barrette that ties back her hair, and when her hair falls down around her shoulders, he smoothes it gently back from her face. He unhooks her heavy leather belt, slides it from her hips so delicately that she hardly feels the weight leave her.

She doesn't understand. How his hands, blunt as spades, can do what they do. Slide buttons through their eyes without a catch, slip her stiff shirt free from her shoulders so that it glides over her skin like water, lift her to her feet as easily as a mother would lift a baby, so that his hands can make the starched armament of her pants glide from her body as smoothly as her shirt did.

He's clumsy again for a moment, stepping back from her to loop his T-shirt over his head and step out of his pants. The awkward angle of his elbows snaps her back to her senses, and she makes a move to get up from the sofa, to clutch her shirt.

But then he crouches before her, reaches his arms around her to unsnap her bra, to kiss her shoulders when he brushes the bra straps from them. She's never let a man undress her before. It's a rule of hers. She always sheds her clothes in a bathroom or in the dark, crawls under the covers with her lovers in a nakedness that is still, territorially, her own private possession. Now her nakedness is something he has made, inching the elastic waistband of her underpants over the flesh of her hips to complete it.

He presses his body against hers, and the sofa cushion slips to the floor with all the other cushions, bringing Liz and Michael with it. She is touching him and being touched in the shifting mass of soft rectangles, a mass made as fluid as lapping waves by some new law of Michael's physics. With his fingertip he draws a tingling line on her skin. He starts at the triangular hollow at the base of her throat, loops around her left breast, curves up to a point on her sternum, and circles his finger around her right breast, just where the skin makes a pink crease, till he comes back to that sharp point where he started. He starts again at her navel, makes a downward loop that arcs over her pubic bone and bells out again before his finger travels back to her navel. She shivers. Gently he turns her on her side and makes one last inverted heart, starting at the base of her spine and curving slowly over the twin swelling rounds of her butt.

She remembers a picture book she had as a kid, about a little boy with a piece of chalk, who could draw a window and then climb through it, draw an apple tree and then reach up to pick the fruit, draw an ocean and then quickly sketch a raft to keep himself afloat on its waves. Make the world out of the moment's wishes.

She climbs on top of Michael and her fingers drag furrows through his chest hair, through that swirling night in which his dark nipples are like reverse stars against his pale skin. She puts an ear to his belly, hears the mysterious secret mutterings of his body, feels the delicate pulse of his blood just above his navel, flickering like a tongue under the thin membrane of his skin. She moves her mouth to his hardening penis, smooth warm thing that jerks of its own will at this contact.

After a long time, a time that has no steady beat and that she cannot measure, Michael pulls her up along the length of him, kisses her, makes a path of kisses down her body to her crotch. Past his shoulder she can see her pants, tossed on the floor, the fabric swelling as if it still clings to the shape of her legs, to the shape of struggle, the pants she will have to climb back into so she can turn in the Cushman and her ticket pad at the end of her shift.

Michael raises himself on an elbow to admire her, and his gaze gives her her body: the sharp places where bones break the swells of the surface like dolphins, the perfect pendants of her breasts, veined with the flush of desire, the pout of her navel in the rippling wholeness of her belly. She studies him back, takes in the smooth winged arcs of his shoulders when he buries his face between her legs, lets her fingers discover the springy wayward life of the hair on his scalp. When he enters her, she takes a deep breath, inhaling the smell of sweat and, yes, the faint, yeasty odor of bread, the plenty it promises. Rocking her body, he draws her another window and another.

Nouina's House

Richard Burgin

There's a screaming in your head that only a woman can cause, he thought, kicking the base of the wall where he stood in front of his window looking, but not really looking, at Nouina's garden. It was like the wrong kind of music getting into your head and starting to wreak total havoc with you when you can't stop hearing it. That had happened to him, too, he remembered. There was a woman he'd gone out with after his divorce, but before getting engaged to Denise, before he'd even met Denise (a woman he'd have been better off staying with, as it turned out). She was a classical music freak and once bought him a record for his birthday of a violin and piano piece. After they broke up, he played it a couple of times. His first reaction was shock at how pretty the melody at the beginning was, but then it started to sicken him. It was like kissing your parents too long—maybe touching to do at first but if you did it too long and couldn't stop it, it would drive you mad. It was that way with the screaming he heard—after he found out about Denise—which was sometimes actual screaming, sometimes the picture of a mouth-dominated face screaming silently. Either way—when he heard the screaming or saw an anonymous face screaming silently—he knew that nothing could stop it but doing Denise and maybe, too, Peter, the man she left him for. It was not even something to debate anymore, not with that piercing sound in your ears. It was as if you had to kill in self-defense.

Nouina walked into the garden and he backed away from the window so she wouldn't see him and wave and invite him to join her. Immediately he started hearing music from the boom box she brought outside with her, as well as the squawking of her birds in their cages. It was ridiculous, he thought, kicking the floor again, how the most irritating music on earth followed her like a tail, so even when you took steps to avoid seeing her you had to hear her. To think, also, how easily he might have picked another place—

though something was wrong with every one or so he thought at the time. It was getting hard to remember. It wasn't that long ago—a month maybe—still that time was dreamlike to him now. It was funny. The thing about renting an apartment is you see a number of them, a decision faces you, and then it's as if you were always in the one you take. It enfolds you and you can't remember any other place.

But that still didn't answer why he had chosen this one. He sat down on his bed while the noises from the garden filled his room. If he couldn't remember why he was in a place, how could he function in it? It was definitely time to prove to himself that he could remember, so he began reviewing his first meeting with Nouina. She was small, dark, and looked like an Indian, though she was Lebanese. When they met she said, "I like you very much, you have a clean soul." She had a good twenty years on him, being somewhere in her fifties where a woman could make a remark like that and not appear threatening. But it gave him pause, made him think she expected to spend time with him. Moreover, there were crosses and images of Jesus all over the house—he wasn't crazy about that—and she'd also rigged up some kind of altar in the living room where she burned malodorous incense. All this could simply mean she'd have something to divert herself with and would stay off his case, but on the other hand, who knew her real motives or how deep the religious stuff really went? Since Denise had cheated on him he found himself being suspicious of people in general and women in particular. He'd thought about Nouina and her house much longer than he wanted to until he'd decided he could make her keep her distance simply by the way he'd treat her. Finally, in the middle of June he arranged to have a month off from his Xerox business, paid Nouina five hundred dollars, shut up his home in the suburbs, and moved into her house.

His first week he found himself thinking positively about the house, even making excuses when things irritated him. When he felt breathless after carrying his suitcases up three flights of stairs to his room, he concluded that the daily climb would be good for his heart. When he noticed that she was making his bed every day—violating his space as soon as he left his apartment—he thought it would be good for him to live in a neat place. It would clarify his thought process. And when he realized that she had two sources of music constantly playing whether or not she was asleep or even in the house, a radio and a stereo blaring away, plus another radio on the second floor always turned to a religious station so that every time he passed by he heard a few snatches about "Jesus Christ Our Lord and Savior," he still thought, "It's good that she has so much noise in the house, she'll never hear me."

But about the dark, steep stairways that she never kept lit, where he would stumble or brush against the weak banister, he could find no counterargument. Instead he'd curse her to himself or sometimes loud enough that she might hear him.

Then the conversations started, or more accurately, since he'd purposely say almost nothing, the monologues. She would knock on his door and invite him to eat lunch, which she'd just cooked. The first two times he refused, but how long could he keep on doing that? Or she would stop him just as he was about to leave the house on one pretext or another and he'd find himself listening to her again.

"God sent you to live in my house, Nathan," she said one day from her couch.

"Why do you say that?"

"God decides everything. It's only that we sometimes don't see the reason," she said with her dark eyes opened up wide, as if they were a kind of vagina, he thought. "It's said, 'God sees the truth but waits,'" she said smiling. She was in a small room off the living room where she had her altar and where a radio was playing show tunes. (Classical music was coming from some other source in the living room.) He was too surprised to say anything. It was like when she told him he had a clean soul—he just looked at her. But that day her eyes made him look away at the clutter of documents spilling over the low table between them—letters, photographs, bank statements, and so on. He noticed there was a fairly large hole in the orange fabric of her couch. "Why the hell doesn't Jesus make you less of a slob?" he said to himself.

She'd lived in the house for twenty-five years, she was saying, including the last ten after her divorce. She told him about her husband, who left her for a younger woman, "younger flesh," and Nathan, thinking about Peter, nodded bitterly. Then Nouina told him about her adored son, a businessman like his father, who had left the house seven years ago when he married. Why couldn't he and his wife live in the house? Perhaps her son had become too Americanized, like his wife. She'd lost her femininity by working, maybe that was why she hadn't yet been able to have a child, but she, Nouina, had never worked and had kept her femininity. She knew how to make a good home for her son.

"It's not really for money that I rent the rooms. I do it whenever God sends me special people like you. I do it to keep life in the house. Otherwise everything will wither and die. But right now, for the summer, you'll be the only tenant, so you'll have the run of the third floor. And if you want to come down here anytime to hear music or watch TV or eat any food of mine, please feel free."

He saw a picture of the labyrinth-like house even as he was sitting in part of it. It was enormous, with high ceilings and lots of stained glass windows and with a large backyard garden of roses and tulips. But it was also old, sparsely furnished, and in a lower-middle-class neighborhood of South Philadelphia—impossible to tell then what it was worth.

"I notice you leave the music on even when you're not in the house," he said.

"Does it bother you?"

He shrugged.

"This is a house that needs life. The music fills the rooms with life, don't you think?"

"Uh-huh," he said, or barely more than that.

"After my husband left it was very hard for me and then when my son moved out I found the silence extremely difficult to live with . . ."

He nodded. He was no longer listening to her. He'd been seeing an image of Denise's smile, then of her big imploring brown eyes (people sometimes said they had the same eyes and looked like brother and sister)—the look she used when she wanted something from him. The modeling she'd done as a teenager hadn't gone to waste. She'd learned how to manipulate her face to get what she wanted, he'd always known this about her but blocked it out until she'd double-crossed him. He pictured two crosses nailed together like a tic-tac-toe board through his heart. Yes, double-crossed was the right word.

Nouina was still talking, this time about her dog who died last year. "This dog, Nathan, was really extraordinary, completely unique. The warmth and love he gave me—it's not something you can get from a human being. I mean, you can't get that from a person, can you?"

"No," he said.

"Only one person could ever do that and he was the Son of God."

He looked at her again. When someone talked like that they almost compelled you to look at them. It was as if underneath whatever strong or outrageous thing they were saying they were begging for your attention. Normally he wouldn't give it because he resented that game, but this time he obliged her. She looked both fervent and comically sincere, like a woman about to come. It made him wonder what he would look like if he started talking to a stranger in a bar and suddenly said he was going to kill Denise.

"I don't believe that," he said. "I don't believe anyone died for my sins. I don't think anyone even knew I was going to be alive. My parents didn't know. I was a mistake—know what I mean?"

"You don't believe in Jesus then?"

"I don't believe anybody died for my sins. People might die because of them but not for them. I might die because of them but no one died for me."

"I will pray for you," Nouina said.

A week passed since the day he took stock of things while looking at Nouina's garden. Now he was walking out the front door thinking that he had to get out, that he'd been spending far too much time in the house. He looked back once at the lighted cross facing the street from the living-room window. It appeared to be made of something like bamboo with the wiring painted green to simulate leaves. He shook his head, took two or three steps, and stopped. He couldn't decide which diner to go to. The Melrose had slightly better food but it was harder to get a private table there and the waitresses weren't as nice, though they were better looking. It was as if because of its own TV ad campaign it was starting to take itself seriously. But the Broad Street Diner, while simultaneously friendlier and more private, didn't have a single dish he could really look forward to eating. The Melrose, which was deeper into South Philly, was a livelier but dirtier walk. That is, he'd pass by prostitutes and they might tempt him. That hadn't worked out in the past. But the walk to the Broad Street Diner, while cleaner and a bit safer, was full of funeral parlors and featured one large, depressing vacant lot. Of course he could drive to Center City, where there were many more restaurant choices, but it would be nearly impossible to find a parking space and he was too tired to walk or take the subway.

He decided to go to neither and walked into the Dolphin Tavern, instead. The Dolphin was a long dark bar with a girlie show at night. It was amazing how many excuses he could make to himself to wind up in a bar where he could watch bare-chested women dance. The problem was watching the girls made the Denise syndrome start going again even more intensely in his head. When he got that angry there really didn't seem to be anything left to do but kill himself or her, but since he couldn't do either at that moment in the bar, he'd end up drinking. That was part of the syndrome, too—the feeling of being blocked and thwarted no matter what he'd do, as with deciding about the diners. The last time he went to a bar near his home in the suburbs he had gotten really drunk and ended up taking home one of the girls who'd lap-danced with him. In his car he'd made her laugh by saying about his time with Denise, "The only thing I know for sure is she wasn't faithful to anyone else." But he was so drunk he couldn't do it, and then later the girl seemed to turn into Denise and he began yelling at her until she ran out of his house at 3:30 in the morning.

Tonight he would do things differently. He would definitely not let any of the girls dance with him. He would barely even look at them (just enough so he could remember the image later). He'd ruled out trying to have any sex with women until he finished the Denise business. It was better that way. It would help him focus and keep his edge.

He ordered a whiskey sour.

"I'll pay now," he said when the lady bartender brought him the drink. "It's all I'm having tonight."

He sneaked a peek at the brunette on the stage, took a swallow of the whiskey, and began reviewing what he *had* done so far about Denise. He'd taken a month off from his business and told his three employees that he was getting burned out and didn't want to even tempt them to get in touch with him by leaving any kind of address. They'd laughed and encouraged him. They'd completely believed him—no reason why they shouldn't. Then he'd purchased a gun through someone he'd met at a bar. Used an alias, paid for it in cash. He'd even worn dark sunglasses to the meeting, shaved his mustache, and had his sandy brown receding hair cut shorter (and dressed in black to look thinner). After that, he'd rented the place from Nouina, using a different alias, "Nathan," and paying her in cash, which luckily she'd requested anyway. Now it was just a case of learning Denise's schedule, staking the place out, and then taking care of business.

He looked up. The dancer had unusually large nipples but who knew if they were real? Cosmetic surgery was the sport of the nineties. Denise had hit him up for money for that, too. He noticed that the room was full of lighted mirrors—dark otherwise except for the spotlight on stage—so that the dancer was reflected in all of them. He watched her bend to the piped-in rock, tossing her hair like a horse.

The bartender approached him. She looked like a whore herself. "Want a refill?"

"No, I told you I'm only having one." He put a little more money on the table just to make a sound and walked out of the bar. He'd felt angry—he thought he would maybe do Denise tonight. Certainly he'd do her within three days. He walked down the block. It was almost dark out. He saw the lighted cross in Nouina's window, otherwise he would have passed by it. He heard different music coming at him in the house, but of course there was no way of knowing if she was home. On the second floor the voice on the radio was saying, "He has come that we may know Him and choose the right thing to do." He kept climbing. He noticed that his left hand was trembling. He walked into his room, found his gun, put it into his left hand and held it.

Then he heard a knocking. "Nathan, can I come in?" It was Nouina. Immediately he hid the gun, thinking it was a good thing he'd only had one drink tonight so he didn't get confused.

"What?" he said, trying to control his voice.

"My neighbor is having a barbecue next door, a lively party, and I want to invite you. Would you like to come?"

"No . . . no, thank you, I'm tired."

He walked out to face her. She looked tragically disappointed that he'd once again refused her. She was all made up herself like a Christian whore, and he was forced to notice her breasts. She was showing them off, beyond a doubt, as if proud that they were still so firm at her age. Then she turned to leave but, Columbo-like, turned back just when he thought she was out the door.

"Oh, Nathan, one more thing. Sorry to bother you, but could you help me with my dress? I need you to zip me up, please."

He felt a surge of anger. It was all he could do to not hit her. He concentrated on touching nothing but her zipper at the base of her spine. He felt like a surgeon performing an operation. Then he noticed the little dewlike remnants of perspiration on her lower back and at the beginning of her dividing line, and he walked away angry and disturbed.

———

At first he wasn't sure of it, it was just a sound among sounds. While he was mostly free of Nouina's music and radio as long as he kept his door and windows shut, there was still the TV and music (usually rap) that streamed out of the open windows from the adjoining apartment building. Then the new sound began to solidify, rising snakelike until it became distinct from the noise next door and began to dominate his room. He sat up in bed and listened more closely. It was some kind of chant coming from the garden. He walked to his central window and looked down. Nouina and some other women were holding hands at the concrete table and chanting to their Lord. Behind them in the large rectangular garden her giant roses and tulips stood up straight and phalluslike in the sharp sun.

―――

Three days later he found Peter's apartment in a two-story house on Pine Street. He'd rented a car (so Denise wouldn't recognize him), put on sunglasses, turned the radio on low, and waited two, three hours. He wore a short-sleeved shirt so he could see his muscles and feel strong. But no one came in or out, no shade or blind rippled. He thought he would lose his mind. Finally a minute before he'd decided to leave, the door opened and he saw them both wearing sunglasses themselves, walking close together down the steps until their hands joined. Peter was taller and thinner than him and had more hair. Definitely a better physical specimen. As they headed down Fifth and Pine, Peter tapped her on the bottom of her tight blue jeans.

He opened his glove compartment to get his gun but it wasn't there. He swore. He couldn't believe it. It was like reaching for a pole on the subway to get his balance and feeling air, then being forced to rattle on at high speed in the dark, feeling nothing as the train rocked through the night.

. . . He was back in his room pacing. He couldn't understand how he'd gotten back so quickly. He couldn't account for time any more than he could figure out why he hadn't taken his gun with him. The chance had been there waiting for him like a shimmering pool that he'd seen but hadn't jumped into. Christ, he could have taken out Peter at the same time. He slammed his hand again on the top of his desk. It became red from doing that, his knuckles sore. Then he started pacing, periodically looking at the empty garden.

Another week passed, maybe more. He'd called the business and said he needed more time, and, of course, they accepted it. He'd been so morose lately, they were glad to be free of him. His life in Nouina's house remained the same—Nouina bothering him all the time, sometimes calling him or sending him notes when he didn't come out from his room. Sometimes he felt like a character in a bizarre play accompanied by her hideous score. He lay on his bed mostly, hearing the crazy music and thinking more than he ever had, so much that it hurt his head. He thought about Denise and reviewed almost every memory he had of her, even his preliminary plans for the wedding. He hated himself for his inaction. It made him hate his mind so much he cut himself with his nails one day to punish himself until he decided, absolutely, to do Denise tomorrow. He'd given himself a true deadline (repeating it to himself over and over), and only then could he get up from bed and be in the present.

It was dark in his room but he couldn't bring himself to turn on a light. Then he started thinking about the diners. It seemed impossible to go to either one of them. But he kept thinking about them anyway as if they represented an imminent and momentous decision. He could feel his hunger like an organism moving through him, creating space, and he thought about Nouina's kitchen. Sometimes nice smells came from there. It seemed impossibly far away at the other end of the labyrinth, yet he thought seriously about going there (he thought there was a stairway behind the radio on the second floor that might be a shortcut) and wondered what Lebanese food tasted like. A minute later he was going down the shortcut stairway. It was as if his body decided for him—his legs that were taking him there and his stomach or the organism that was moving through his stomach.

He passed through the living room, the music room, where her phone, orange couch, and altar were. She had invited him to eat there repeatedly, he shouldn't feel criminal about it. He opened her refrigerator. There was almost nothing in it, at least not for him. Just a bowl a quarter filled with spaghetti. He saw a box of tea biscuits on the counter, ripped it open and put a few in his hands, then nearly gasped when he heard Nouina say, "Nathan, is that you?"

He was startled and aware that he looked guilty. Finally, he said, "Yes."

"Good, I'm glad you're eating. Take as much as you want, you often look so hungry to me."

He mumbled a thank-you and ate the cookies quickly.

"Nathan, I'm worried about you. Can you talk for a minute?"

"How so?"

"Would you like to talk in the music room? I could light a candle."

"Here is fine."

"I've been praying for you lately, every morning and afternoon."

"Why's that?"

"Because I feel an unhappiness in you, a great sadness that's threatening you. Am I right?"

"I'm okay."

"I've even been having my prayer group pray in unison for you in the garden."

He looked at her closely in the half-dark of the kitchen. The white refrigerator to his right gleamed like a giant snowman. She'd caught him off balance, startled him again, forced him to wonder if the chanting he heard in the garden weeks ago had been about him. "What exactly is it that I've said or done that's led you to think these things?"

"It's a feeling, a vibration I pick up. But is it so?"

"You'd have to be more specific."

"I feel you're wrestling with a big problem. Almost from the time you moved in I've felt you've been burdened with a huge decision, and if you make the wrong one you may be in terrible danger. It's because I care so much for you and know what a sensitive man and clean soul you are that I want to help you."

He stared at her. "What is it you want to do?"

"Would you pray with me at my altar?"

"No, I wouldn't feel right doing that. I don't believe."

"Could you try?"

"How is it that you even think you know me so well? I mean . . ."

"I know you. I know all about you." He felt oddly frightened then and wanted a drink.

"Please, give me your hand. I want you to take it and feel my love for Jesus pass into you."

He turned his head and looked at the refrigerator two, three times. He was thinking, my name isn't even Nathan, you don't even know my name.

"What I'd like is a drink. Do you have anything I could drink . . . wine, beer?"

"Sure, of course. Drink whatever you like. I rarely drink myself, but I keep it for my guests."

He removed a bottle of vodka from her refrigerator and began drinking from a tall glass by her sink. She was talking about holding his hand again, but he concentrated on drinking. After he finished the first glass, he gave her his left hand and poured himself a second drink with his right. It felt strange, he hadn't had his hand held since Denise left. After thirty seconds he didn't like it anymore, counted to ten, and withdrew it.

She began talking about her husband—how close she thought they'd been, what a shock it was when he left, how angry and ashamed she'd been and then how lonely. She looked at him and her eyes seemed to grow larger. He looked away. She's inventing me, he thought, just inventing me, but then he thought that with all the excuses he made for her, he'd done the same thing with Denise while she was with him.

He finished his second drink and poured himself a third. Then he remembered that he had a joint in his pocket (he'd started smoking a lot more after Denise left) and asked Nouina if he could smoke it, telling her it smelled a little like the incense she used in her living room. He thought that might shock her, but she said it was all right and added, "I'd like you to try something else, too, that will also make you feel better."

He didn't say anything—just kept his head down and smoked.

"Really, Nathan, I'm sure it will make you feel better. It's a technique I learned just after I moved into this house."

"What technique? Technique for what?"

"For massage. Just your back if you'll let me. I used to do it with my husband all the time when he was nervous about the business, and it always made him feel better. Will you let me try it on you?"

He smoked some more until he finished the joint, which was strong, then took the final swallow of his drink.

"Yeah, I'll try it," he said, as he poured himself a new drink.

"Oh Nathan, I'm so glad. It's important to be open to what other people want to give you. Here, let me have a sip of your drink. I'll share what's left with you."

She took the glass from the counter and together they finished the bottle. Then they both started laughing and soon began walking through the music room and up the short staircase. He was thinking, so this is what all the religious fanaticism was about, just another bitch in heat, but he was also high and vaguely exhilarated. He liked that it was dark and that she was so eager and thought it wouldn't matter for a night about her age and looks.

She was laughing and talking (sometimes in Lebanese) in a high-pitched voice, but so far she still hadn't touched him. Maybe she wouldn't. Maybe she merely meant to give him an actual massage and he'd misconstrued things. Or maybe, being an old-fashioned woman, she was waiting for him to touch her first, but he wouldn't do it under these circumstances. Even drunk he had too much pride for that. That was the thing about women. You were always waiting for them to make decisions no matter how decisive you both pretended you were. You were always left in a state of cold, unbearable suspense for them to release their words that could make or break you. Sometimes you didn't even know you were waiting and the words ambushed you. It was that way with Denise when she finally decided to tell him what had been going on for months. She'd told him in the morning when it was bright out but immediately he saw darkness, went into a world even darker than Nouina's house.

He took the glass back from her and had the last swallow.

"Okay, Nathan, you think you're ready now?"

He felt his heart beat in spite of himself.

"Will you take your shirt off?"

Was it the dope or was she talking to him almost like a dominatrix? That wouldn't work with him, but he took it off anyway. He must have really been stoned, so it was all right, because when he was stoned everything changed and nothing really mattered. He lay down, closed his eyes, and felt himself spinning. She began rubbing his back, speaking in a low voice so that only random words could be heard above his fan, words that seemed to have nothing to do with him.

Then he felt her weight. She was sitting on his lower back, legs out to each side of the bed, still rubbing. It felt like the weight of Denise. "Maybe this would be more comfortable in my room?" she said.

"It's comfortable right here."

He felt her move until her face was close to his and he felt her hair brush against the side of his cheek. He didn't understand the words. Possibly they were in Lebanese but it didn't matter. It was good to be free of words. She was kissing the back of his neck, then his shoulders and back. He remembered the time Denise and he had spent a weekend in Cape May. They came out of the shower together (he was incredibly erect) and she went down on him on the bed until he felt himself spin.

He heard Nouina say, "I've waited so long for you, I've wanted you for so long, always wondering if this could ever happen, if you would ever give me the chance."

He turned around and put his hands on her breasts.

"God sent you to me. I always knew. God sent you," she said.

He said nothing. When he stopped holding her she got out of her dress, then began fumbling with his zipper, talking to herself, which excited him somehow, until they both managed to get his pants off and then, finally, his shoes.

He was still free of the words. It was as if he were protected from a storm that rained all around him but not on him. His space was warm and filled with flesh and sounds but no words. Where was Denise? What was Denise? He couldn't remember her. He was in a place that was dark but also light, still spinning slightly when his eyes were closed.

Then, suddenly, Denise was back. She was underneath him. He was trying to enter her but she was closing her legs against him. She kept repeating something about condoms, and for a minute or so he didn't understand.

"I'll get it for you. I bought some a few days ago when I was still hoping for you."

The voice sounded distant like Nouina's but in the dark he couldn't tell. She was away a long time, and then she was back, whoever she was, bending over him, sucking him and trying to fit the condom on him. He thought if a light got turned on he would be able to tell who it was, but he didn't want the light on.

And then he was alone, on top in the dark and thought it was Denise again and went inside her, pushed and moved hard, but he couldn't feel himself. It was as if he were detached from it in some neutral space that he alone inhabited. He tried again, and a terrible anxiety swept through him.

"What's the matter?" she was saying—in other words, why can't you do it?—and a shock went through him. That she who stabbed him in the back and double-crossed him in the heart should ask *him* why.

He was screaming "Why" into her face, and she screamed back and tried to get up but he kept her pinned down while she was still screaming until he couldn't stand it anymore and had to stop it. He reached for her neck and shook it until she started to choke and kept shaking it because it seemed he couldn't let go.

———

He didn't know he had slept but the clock said he had. Hours had passed. It was somewhere a little past dawn. He remembered he'd heard the chanting again from the garden at first as faint as a single low whistle, then increasing until it was shrieking. It must have been a dream because no one was in the garden now, though three birds were flying in semicircular patterns above the roses.

Then he remembered Nouina, and he let out a gasp. At first he hadn't thought about her because there was no one next to him in bed, but then he remembered about the closet—how he'd put her there and thrown some clothes over her, and the pain staggered him, he nearly fell from it and had to hold on to the wall for support. It was that kind of world—you wanted to forget, but something forced you to remember. Even when you slept something forced you to remember. You were free for a millimoment of Denise and Nouina but you really weren't. Just like you thought you heard chanting but it was your dream organizer making you remember through your dream. Making you hear the chanting that was for Nouina's soul, if there was such a thing. But to his horror he suddenly knew there was, just as he knew without checking (though he would check later) that she was in the closet and that she was dead, that he had killed her (though he would check that, too, before he left). It was odd, paradoxical. You were invited to love and you killed. You were invited to live and you died. He sat on the bed shaking, covered with grief. He thought of Nouina and all the laughable things she'd said, and his eyes—his tear organizers, as he thought of them—kept releasing. If there was a soul then he had one, too, and there was nothing left to do but submit to it. But he wouldn't call the cops and do it on their terms. It was then he opened the closet door, put a hand to his face, stooped down somehow and checked the body, then turned away and stepped back.

The next thing he knew he was running into the window, crashing through it and flying like a bird himself toward the concrete chairs and table in the garden below.

Boy at the Piano

Annie Dawid

As a boy, he spent afternoons at the Steinway, a concert grand, whose erect top bollixed the sunlight that broke through the clouds hovering over Puget Sound. By sixteen, he was sure of only two things: he loved Beethoven, and he loved boys. When his fingertips pressed the ivory keys and the music he made came back up into him through the soles of his feet, he felt the one satisfaction he was to know. In college, he pinned the first girl he dated, though he might have had a thousand girlfriends, for he was kind and polite and never overeager. The pin became a diamond, the diamond a band, and by twenty-six, he was married, a father, and a doctoral student in psychology, for he had eschewed his musical studies at eighteen, declaring himself insufficiently gifted, a notion out of which every teacher tried but failed to persuade him. "I can't go on; I don't have what it takes" was his two-part refrain. In truth, Beethoven and boys had something to do with one another, and he feared their passionate linkage.

It was 1961. Robert's ménage relocated from Seattle to San Francisco, where he had his first job, resulting from his first application, as assistant professor at the University of San Francisco. Initially, Charlotte fulfilled her faculty wife duties, entertaining Robert's colleagues, keeping their child, a girl they named Beatrice after Robert's recently deceased mother, out of sight of the Friday gatherings, where the mostly male professors talked and drank for many hours while the wives listened, or murmured in the kitchen of their own concerns. Though exhausted by her maternal duties, Char began her own advanced study not long after they moved, attending classes in special education for the handicapped, as they were called in that era.

Unlike every other man in his department, Robert cooked and cleaned. The first in the office, he prepared the coffee and wiped the counters, washing the mugs his colleagues had not, leaving them scattered in the lounge for the secretary. Robert despised clutter. Actually, he preferred his own housekeeping to that of his wife, and after two years of trying and failing to parcel out their roles as other couples did, they established the pattern that would last their entire married life, with Robert doing most of the "wifely" tasks, plus working full time, always available for his students, while Char studied and attended to Beatrice, whom Robert believed he adored, yet remained strangely distant toward, as if he could never quite believe that he, too, had engendered their sturdy female child; she was a perfect miniature of her mother, down to the webbed third toe on her right foot.

His dissertation took five years to complete, for he ignored it completely until receiving a warning from his chairman to finish the project or else. Begun so long ago, it had more to do with his mentor's interests than with his own, which were rapidly falling into a category he called "existential psychology," though there was, at that date, no such topic listed in the card catalog. So he hustled his way through "Early Indications of Paranoid Schizophrenic Sociopathology in Preadolescent Males," the research all out of date, and his elderly professor vetted all 405 pages of it, then passed him, with honors, on his defense, for which he'd flown alone back to Washington. He did not alert his father or sisters of his trip, for he did not want to visit the family home, with its waiting, unplayed Steinway.

Knowing his "celebration" to be a farce, he refused invitations from his former teachers and roamed the city instead, stopping at various bars for a bourbon and water, the drink he'd come to appreciate at every department function. In his nocturnal rambling, he entered a bar occupied, he soon realized, exclusively by men. One bourbon, then another, allowed him to peruse his companions with relative security, as it was dark in the bar; he had only subconsciously remarked upon the lack of windows, the subterranean entrance to the place. Though he had permitted himself a glance, here and there, in high school and in college, a quick look at a basketball player's body in the gym or a surreptitious stare at his chess opponent's fair head of curls bent assiduously over the board, this was his virgin adult moment of freedom in an all-male setting, aided, of course, by the many drinks he had consumed that evening, though the walking had burned off some of the haze with which alcohol glazed his entire waking life.

To his left sat a man like himself, losing his hair, in jacket and tie, completely ordinary, eyes downcast. To his right, an older gentleman with a cravat, cane, and Maurice Chevalier–style hat, chatting with the bartender. He winked at Robert, then turned back to the young lifeguard type, who wore jeans, a tight white shirt, and a towel draped rakishly over his left shoulder. Other men clustered, alone or in pairs, in the dim booths, sometimes sitting nearly atop one another, as the young marrieds often did in the later hours of the Friday night psych soirees, after the bottles of bourbon and rum had emptied and no one could summon the energy to go out for more. When the bartender offered a third drink, Robert shook his head, afraid and exhilarated by where he had found himself. "This gentleman will buy it," said the bartender, and Robert turned to the smiling older man, whose elegant fingers, sporting a slim cigar, bespoke a life of leisure, a pianist's fingers. Robert was reminded of a favorite piano teacher and nodded uneasily, accepting the drink.

"My name is Wallace O'Hanlon," said the man, moving his stool closer. Robert's other neighbor gulped his beer and fled. "And yours?"

"Eugene," said Robert, using his middle name, "Beckett," he added, borrowing his favorite writer's. Sweating, he swallowed his bourbon, and the bartender provided another, which Robert Eugene promptly inhaled. When Wallace placed one delicate finger on Robert's cheek, a sudden sweet nausea arose in his gut. As he rushed for the exit, he heard the old man and the young bartender laughing at him, or thought he did.

By thirty-six, now tenured chair of the department and father of two more girls, Robert had gone completely bald. A careful dresser, though not vain, he affected a habit for hats. Berets were his specialty, and he owned six of them in a full spectrum of red-based shades and hues. After having read Camus and Sartre, in French, he found himself grievously wanting in stoical prowess and gave up on existentialism. Though the city was in full generational turmoil, men and women indistinguishable in their long hair and bell-bottoms, he and Char, now a full-time teacher in the public schools, had remained aloof from the hippies and the protesters. Too old to run barefoot through Golden Gate Park, too young to join the disapproving chorus of their older friends, they watched from their house, high on Lone Mountain, as the world metamorphosed around them. Even at his Catholic university, Robert's students showed up in psychedelic paisley fashion, and he learned to detect the woody smell of marijuana from his student conferences, during one of which a favorite sophomore, a blond boy listed as

George on the roster, who had renamed himself Geodesic, offered to share a joint. Shaking his head, Robert, while admiring the boy's disdain for decorum, reached instead for his bourbon in the lowest drawer of his filing cabinet. "This works for me," he told Geodesic, who clucked his tongue in disapproval.

"That stuff'll kill you," the boy said, his mantle of curls bobbing righteously. Then he sat up straight, looking Robert in the eyes, as if to shake off his hippie persona. "Look, I know this isn't safe, here in your office," he said in a low, more mature voice. "Why don't you meet me off campus tonight after your class, at the Grand Piano on Haight. Okay?" Then Geodesic wrapped himself and whirled off in his purple cape before Robert could refuse.

Beatrice, Lois, and Phyllis kissed him absently as he gathered his books and papers from the living room, heading off to class after an early dinner. From the kitchen, where Char was grading papers, came a tentative, "Honey? Remember we have to do our taxes? Tonight or tomorrow."

"Tomorrow," he said, regulating his breath the way he'd learned as a child at the keyboard, for sometimes Beethoven would so overwhelm him that he would forget to breathe, and an early instructor, Monsieur Forché (a dandy who insisted on the title despite the fact that he was born and bred in White Salmon, Washington; he had studied for six months at the Conservatoire in Paris), had taught him the invaluable lesson of counting his breaths. Many years later, Robert would understand this same method to be key to Eastern meditation, a technique his oldest daughter would travel to India and live in an ashram for five years to master.

Night classes were new, both to the school and to Robert. Though Char had at first objected, saying they hardly saw him as it was, Robert had prevailed, for he received a small bonus for taking on the 7:00-to-10:00 P.M. offerings, and they needed the money for the girls' orthodontia, since all three had inherited the overcrowded mouths of their mother's family. Although together they netted a more than adequate salary (one of few dual-career couples in his department, though not at all rare on her faculty), their expenses had a way of mounting beyond their means. Char had commandeered their credit card, using it rigorously at the city's many bookstores, where she would go to lose herself after school in stacks of novels and plays. Always, Robert would get excited about a new author, incorporating quotes and anecdotes into his lectures (Heidegger's "the forgetting of being" was current for several years), and Char would read all she could to keep up with him. But he never stayed focused for long, while Char's interest intensified. In the early seventies she organized a reading group among her colleagues at Galileo High School, for which she was chief scheduler, reading hungrily into the nights to determine the best works for their calendar. She also enjoyed dressing their daughters well, for she had grown up in the frugality of Seattle's Cannery Row, and consequently all three girls were treated to shopping tours on I. Magnin's children's floor.

Robert's lecture that night centered on Dr. Karen Horney, whose radical work in the 1950s made her a favorite with the rising feminist movement, which found an ally and a promoter in Robert, alone among his colleagues. For his forward-thinking ways, he was attended by a coterie of female students, some of whom, he knew, took his kind attention for flirtation. Robert neither encouraged nor discouraged their interest.

Unfortunately, someone kept giggling every time he uttered the name of the analyst, though he pronounced it "horn-eye," as his notes indicated. Two girls burst into spasms when he mentioned Horney's accomplishments, Horney's iconoclastic vision, and Horney's infamy, all in one sentence.

"What's the matter with you!" he shouted. The class hushed immediately, for he had never raised his voice before. "I'm sorry." He coughed fakely. "I'm a bit under the weather tonight." The culprit students, red-cheeked as pomegranates, mumbled apologies. Though he hadn't covered all his material, Robert dismissed them early.

Flustered, he rushed to his office before any of the usual hangers-on could stop him and, with the lights out, swallowed a shot of bourbon. His pulse finally slowed to a reasonable rate, and he watched the phosphorescent hands of his clock as the minutes passed. Geodesic would now be seated at the Grand Piano, sipping a glass of red wine, Robert imagined, rehearsing his invitation to his professor to walk with him in the park in the April night.

After the building fell silent and Robert's anxiety had dissipated somewhat, he decided to go home. But when he turned on the lights and saw the armchair reserved for students, he pictured Geodesic still sitting there, his low voice rich with desire. For him? Robert gulped. For bald Professor Moore, whose gut was beginning to droop, whose palms sweated badly before the first drink of the day? Or was it a dare, or a proposition arrived at in stoned communion with his buddies? The latter seemed unlikely, as Geodesic was always alone, never a part or appendage to any of the various cliques that formed yearly in the department. He poured another drink and, hearing footsteps, assuming it was a student with a question, composed himself. Someone knocked. "Dr. Moore?" said the low voice. "Can I come in?"

Frightened, Robert put away the bottle and glass, still full. "Enter!" His automatic pilot drive clicked on, habituated by years of morning classes, which he taught, hungover, always on time.

The young man peered around the edge of the door, as if someone might be hiding there. He wore a bleached white shirt, ironed, and brown sportscoat, no tie, with brown corduroys. Swallowing, Robert was moved by the boy's transformation, his quiet simplicity. Blond curls spilled out of the ponytail down his back, and his entire body shook as he reached for the armchair and sat. "I had a feeling you wouldn't show," he whispered, "so I came to get you."

For a moment, Robert considered calling Security. He could have the boy removed for inappropriate behavior, and that would be the end of that.

"I completely forgot!" said Robert, the lie straining the corners of his mouth. "I thought it was next week! But you know," he said, pointing to the calendar, feeling the emptiness of his chatter balloon in the still room, "it's tax day tomorrow, and, celebrated procrastinator that I am, I haven't done a thing about it." He almost added, "my wife is after me," but restrained himself for no reason he could name.

"I didn't mean to . . . make you uncomfortable today," George said, touching his fingertips to his smoothly shaven cheek. Robert followed his gesture, mouth open. "I don't ever want to make you uncomfortable," he added, pressing the tip of his middle finger to the center of his lips, as if to keep some word or words from escaping. Robert closed his mouth. "I just thought it might be nice to know you better. To know you . . ." he looked around the large room, its walls burdened with books, "in a different context. Outside your office."

Gripping the oak armrests of his chair, Robert remembered to count his breaths. "Surely you've heard of my seminar banquets," he said, managing a laugh, "so, when you're a senior—"

"But that's still student-teacher." George leaned toward him, his breath warm on Robert's hand, which toyed with a fountain pen on a pile of files. "I meant something more personal. You don't have a son, do you?"

Robert blanched. "No! But what does that have to do with anything? I am your teacher, am I not? And you, my student."

George rose. "I had a very special teacher in high school. Without him, I wouldn't be here." George checked his pockets: first his coat, right, left; breast; then shirt; then pants, front and back, finding what he was looking for in the last one. Robert watched George pat himself down with his own lips pressed tightly together. "I wanted to give you something."

"Do you need an adviser?" asked Robert, the only response he could summon.

"Don't you?" said George, smiling for the first time since he'd entered the room. "Yes. I need one. I need you."

"Who's your adviser now?" Robert knew his question was absurd.

George handed him something small wrapped in a handkerchief. "Look at it after I'm gone," he said, and left.

As soon as George shut the door, Robert pulled open his drawer and guzzled the shot he'd poured earlier. For a second he worried the boy would commit suicide, "after I'm gone" resonating in Robert's ears. Yet, after some analysis, he concluded there was nothing at all depressed in George's actions or words. He was strong; he'd come for what he wanted. He hadn't taken no, which Robert's absence from the Grand Piano would have signified. And he'd managed to get Robert to volunteer as his adviser, a task that would mean more conference time with George, alone, a prospect that elicited in Robert both anxiety and anticipation.

Promising it would be his last, Robert poured one more drink, then opened up the handkerchief. Under the dull halo of his desk lamp, an obsidian stone gleamed. It fit snugly in the center of his palm, worn smooth as if rubbed for years by warm hands or many waves. A talisman? He slipped the rock in his front pocket and was wondering what to do with the cloth when he saw something written on the white cotton, a phone number. First he threw it in the trash, then reconsidered and stuffed it in his pocket, glad that he and not Char did the laundry.

The following Tuesday, George did not attend his Introductory Abnormal Psych lecture. All weekend Robert had grazed the rock in his pocket while looking for change, or keys, or had simply felt his fingers straying there to touch it. The handkerchief he'd washed, hoping the number would vanish, but it remained perfectly legible, as if written in indelible ink. Without planning to, he had it memorized. After class and conferences and his daily schmooze with the secretary, Judy, he understood that he was disappointed George hadn't shown. He'd paid extra attention while dressing that morning, matching a geometrically patterned crimson tie with a new beret, wearing his favorite chestnut-colored jacket, which was very like George's.

A week later, Geodesic George returned to class wearing his cape, his odor of marijuana, and a pair of mirrored sunglasses. Robert had few rules about classroom fashion or behavior; he didn't mind if students came without shoes or fell asleep (as long as they didn't snore), but he would not speak to a student whose eyes were masked. In the past, he'd say, "No sunglasses indoors, please," to the general classroom, and the guilty party or parties would remove them, grateful, however, not to be singled out individually. But this time Robert remained silent. His quivering, unarticulated hopes had shriveled upon seeing Geodesic—for surely it was Geodesic who had returned, not George—slouch to the back of the room, ignoring him.

For an hour, Robert told stories of schizophrenia, a disease he knew so well he rarely referred to notes. He walked around the room, gesticulating, joking. He didn't dare travel as far back as Geodesic's desk, and when the students began their shuffling and book gathering, indicating class was about to end, Robert felt relieved. When Geodesic slithered out the back door, Robert touched the rock in his pocket, its smooth surface beside his keys and stubs of chalk, and was, for a moment, conscious of his cowardice.

On Thursday, he poured a fortifying bourbon before heading out to Introductory Abnormal Psych. But Geodesic never came back. When Robert inquired of the registrar, he was told the student had withdrawn from the university for medical reasons, though no doctor's note had been filed.

Drinking before class became a new ritual. He saw his students, his daughters, and Char floating beneath a gauzy mesh, aware at all times of their presence, but never allowing them to take on distinct identities. Ever a workaholic, he discharged the duties of the chairman's office with diligence and, with Judy's aid, maintained a busy working life for years and years. Char retreated into her books, his daughters into their burgeoning lives.

In the early eighties, gay men began to die in San Francisco, a subject to which the *Chronicle*, in the person of Randy Shilts, self-described as the only "out" reporter on a major daily, gave considerable attention. Every morning, as Robert drank his pot of coffee (he rose at six without fail) and skimmed the headlines, he pondered the word "bathhouse," which regularly graced the front page in stories about what were later known as the "bathhouse wars." He knew that gay men went to the bathhouses for sex, not baths. Yet he could never quite imagine it: a room with a claw foot bathtub? Many rooms with many bathtubs? Porcelain or PVC? Or was it a big steambath, communal, like the old Cliff House drawings, but these bathers were all naked men fornicating with one another, in front of one another? Certain health professionals argued that the bathhouses should be shut down, but the gay community, galvanized after the 1978 murder of Supervisor Harvey Milk, rejected with indignation any attempt to restrict their hard-won freedom. Robert read Shilts before anything else.

When Char joined him at 6:30, after rousing Lois and Phyllis (in 1980, after dropping out of Berkeley, Beatrice had left for India, where her guru had fled after his conviction for tax evasion), she read the headlines over his shoulder. "Those poor men," she said. "It reminds me of TB."

"You weren't around for that," he said irritably, turning the page.

"No," she agreed, taking the buttered muffin Robert had prepared for her from the toaster oven, "but my parents used to talk about it all the time. They lost people at the cannery. Long before I came along. That's all." She sat down across from him. "What is it, hon?"

"This kid," Robert said, blinking rapidly, pointing to a photograph of an intense young man with light curls. "I knew him. I mean, I know him. He was my student."

Char pulled the paper closer. "George Murphy, proponent of bathhouse closure," she read aloud. "Well, he's not your first student to show up in the *Chronicle*. Nor mine." Robert took the paper back. "One of my first kids—Ken Park. Remember him? A quadriplegic who used to get punished for racing in the hallway. Anyway, he sued one of the bathhouses to make them install ramps. And he won." She shrugged. "I hear he's sick now. With this cancer, this GRID-lock business."

"Gay-related immunodeficiency," Robert said slowly.

"Gotta go, hon," Char said, checking her watch. "Remind Phyllis of her ortho appointment, and Lois needs to pick up her prescription." Lois was on the Pill, a decision arrived at mutually between her and her mother. Working in the public schools, Char claimed she saw absolutely everything, and her method of warding off disaster with her own children was preventative medicine, from birth control to specific drug alerts. The girls responded well, speaking frankly with their mother about their lives, though they remained shy around their father. This arrangement satisfied Robert, as he preferred the relatively manageable problems of his students and office to those of his family. Robert's routine greased the wheels of his life until the heart attack, just before his fiftieth birthday.

"You don't need me to tell you to stop drinking," Dr. Finegood told him, post-op, after they'd accomplished the relatively experimental procedure of transplanting veins from the patient's thigh for use in the heart. "But I will anyway." He surveyed Robert's skinny body. "Stop drinking and start eating. Okay?"

Beatrice didn't fly home from India, though her mother cabled her immediately after it happened, a Friday afternoon during Robert's weekly roundup with Judy, a woman who, as the cliché would have it, spent more time with Robert than his wife did. Suddenly, pain pierced his body, a sharp, gouging dentist's drill kind of pain shredding his very core, and for the first time, Robert forgot how to breathe. When he regained consciousness, Char, Dr. Finegood, Lois, and Phyllis were hovering over him in the bright ward of cardiac intensive care at UC Med, where he had an extraordinary view of the ocean.

For a week he lay in his bed watching the clouds, which reminded him of the afternoon fog on Puget Sound. He remembered the gray light and the rare sun that found its way to warm him at the piano, though he hadn't needed warming as he worked his way through the symphonies. When he quit for good, he'd been struggling with Beethoven's last, the tenth, his unfinished and most beautiful composition. In this way, Robert stopped drinking, not by design or will. Miraculously, he suffered no DTs or other major trauma of withdrawal.

When he came home from the hospital, he stopped eating. "You're depressed," Char told him. He denied it. "Of course you are. You've had your whole life exactly as you wanted it until now. Isn't that true?"

Robert's colleagues and Judy visited him often, telling him how much he was missed, how they couldn't function without him. Nevertheless, a younger man was appointed temporary chair in his absence. Robert didn't care. His head ached constantly, and the spot on his thigh, from where they'd removed the veins, emitted a noxious odor he couldn't tolerate. Char swore she smelled nothing, but Robert, obsessed, spent several sessions daily swabbing the area with creams and unguents. He didn't want the smell on his penis.

Finally, a letter came from Beatrice:

> Father: While I am sorry to hear of your illness, and wish you the swiftest recovery possible, I am not surprised your heart was not functioning properly. For twenty-five years, it seemed to me you had no heart at all, so, ironically, I am glad to know you do.
>
> Please do not think me ungrateful. Compared to many, I have had an extraordinarily privileged childhood. Don't show this letter to Mom. She wouldn't understand. But I know you do.

Dr. Finegood raised his voice at their next appointment. "Jesus Christ, Robert! Am I going to have to put you on an IV feed?"

"Char can't cook," Robert mumbled.

"I don't care what you eat," the doctor said. "Pizza, Chinese, McDonald's, whatever. Look, I've seen this before: you go off booze for the first time in your life, and you don't know what hit you. That's why I want you to focus on food. Get some satisfaction somehow."

"Eating just doesn't have the same appeal."

"How are you and Char doing?" Dr. Finegood's eyebrows arched conspicuously.

"What do you mean? In bed?"

"Well, sure. That too."

"We haven't had much of a sexual relationship in a long time."

Shrugging, Dr. Finegood played with his white beard. "Maybe that's part of the problem."

"What's that supposed to mean?" Robert said sharply.

"I don't know," the doctor said, frowning. "I've seen both before a coronary—too much sex, no sex at all."

"That's insane," Robert huffed. "I'm fifty years old, I've never gotten any exercise, I drank every day—I'm surprised I didn't get sick sooner."

"And I'm surprised your liver's in such good shape, frankly. When did you start drinking?"

"College. I was a good frat boy."

"Eighteen, huh. If you only gained some weight and walked around the block every day, you'd be in pretty damn good shape. In spite of yourself."

When Robert returned from the doctor's, he received a call from his younger sister, who was crying. "Bobby," she sobbed. "Dad died this morning of a stroke. I know this must be a terrible time for you. I'm so sorry."

The estate took several lawyers several months to straighten out. The elder Mr. Moore had squirreled away enormous sums of money in numerous accounts under different names. Not only did he own the various supply ports on Puget Sound, which had prospered during the years of development, but he had invested money in scores of international corporations, and most of his hunches had been smart. To Robert and his sisters, their father's wealth, his secret life as an investor, was a revelation. They had never once seen him read the business section or pay attention to the stock market. They were sure their mother had known nothing. Except for the piano, which Mr. Moore had bought when Robert was born, they had lived careful, middle-class lives. Robert remembered his father only vaguely, for he had worked seven days a week, always out in the boat to visit his ports, and had often complained that his business was ailing.

Robert's older and younger sisters were willed the house and the boat, respectively, and, as expected, his father had given him the Steinway. Robert told Char he wanted to sell it, as there was no room for it, and, besides, he hadn't played since he was a teenager.

"We'll put it in BeeBee's room," Char announced. "And maybe *I'd* like to learn to play. Did you ever think of that?" Robert hadn't.

He was due to retire, after twenty-five years of service, and Char had been badgering him about taking up some kind of hobby, as she'd read about men who, used to a lifetime of hard work, died immediately upon retirement for lack of activity. "You could teach me," she said. "Or teach Phyllis. Remember she used to want to learn?"

"She's too old," Robert retorted. "You have to start early if you want to be any good."

"I must be way too old then." Robert didn't answer. They were watching the clouds from their living room after reading the final letter from the lawyers, informing them that they would receive a good sum of money in addition to the piano. "My family could only dream of having a piano, much less a Steinway. And you want to get rid of it." She shook her head. "I won't let you sell it. We can pass it on to our grandkids, if we ever have any." Robert knew that Char was distressed that Beatrice, now twenty-six, had never brought home a boyfriend, never discussed marriage or children, even when she'd returned from the ashram to move to a commune in Colorado, where she taught "the master's" philosophy to the lost children of America's wealthy. Though she sometimes mentioned friends with Indian names in her monthly letters to her mother, which Robert read but never responded to, these names were not identifiable as to sex, and Char did not press the subject. Robert wondered if Beatrice might be a lesbian, but he did not know how to talk to Char about his suspicions.

Lois was attending USF on his tuition waiver, studying biology, a subject that eluded both Char and Robert, and Phyllis had become an athlete, swimming, running, and biking. While he no longer drank, Robert felt no closer to his children. It was as if the alcoholic haze still lingered to cloud his view of the world, independent of his new sobriety. Although he'd felt little at the passing of his father, he was greatly moved by the obituary of George Murphy, who died the same year of pneumocystis pneumonia, a manifestation of the disease they were now calling AIDS. He remembered the boy in his purple cape and then so sweetly dressed in his chestnut corduroy; he remembered the deeply resonant voice saying, "I need you," and he wept.

During the next few months, Robert and Char fought daily about the piano, their first substantive argument in years. She wouldn't back down, as she usually did, and he recognized that the Steinway held great symbolic import for her, as if its presence in their home would verify that she'd finally arrived in the world of cultured comfort, as far removed from her life as a cannery kid as she could hope to get. Which was why he couldn't bring himself to put all his rhetorical weight behind his words, even though he desperately wanted the piano to go away.

"We could sell the house and move to an apartment in North Beach, and you could run one of those greasy used bookshops you love so much in the Tenderloin," he offered, showing his financial calculations that proved they'd need to sell the Steinway to buy a bookstore, Char's own dream for retirement.

"We could do that anyway," she insisted. "I understand that it's ultimately yours to do with what you want. Your father gave it to you." She shut her eyes. "But Robert, I've stuck with you all these years." They were, in fact, one of the few intact couples left in his department. He didn't want her to cry. He'd seen her cry only at the sickbeds of their children and, once, at his own bed, after the heart attack. "Doesn't that count for something?"

He knew that it did. He knew that she knew everything about him, though they never spoke openly of his drinking, his distance from the girls, his want of interest in sex. And because she didn't press him, he didn't bother her about the credit card bills, the debt they'd accumulated as she amassed her personal library of first editions, or about anything she did to compensate for his lack of attention to her and their children.

The piano arrived on a bright May day after his retirement was officially declared, and the movers maneuvered it delicately into Beatrice's room, which had remained literally empty since the time she'd returned from India stomach-sick for Char to nurse her and declared furniture unnecessary, selling all of it to finance her ticket back to Bombay. The piano bench was packed with neat stacks of music, all Beethoven, and the velvet interior had retained its rich, unfaded indigo. When Char riffled through the yellowing scores, she asked if he'd ever played anything else. "No Bach? No Mozart?" Her goal was to learn *The Magic Flute* before she died; she said it was her favorite music in the whole world, so full of life and humor.

She knew better than to ask him to play, and she'd given up on the teaching idea. Instead, she hired a retired music professor from USF, but it became clear to Miss McLeod and to Robert that Char had no ear whatsoever. He suffered through her diligent nightly practicing while Phyllis would indelicately put on her Walkman when her mother entered BeeBee's room after dinner. Within three months, Miss McLeod gracefully withdrew herself as Char's tutor, claiming she had to take care of her ill roommate, another retired music professor. Robert didn't believe her, but Char did, which was more important. A succession of teachers followed, none of them with the heart or guts to tell Char there was no point in her learning. Robert didn't dare.

It was 1987. Robert attended classes at the Culinary Institute and cooked intricate meals for Char and Phyllis, both of whom were indifferent to what they ate. They called him a "foodie," as if he suffered from some strange ailment, and teased him about his days spent searching for exotic ingredients in Chinatown or the Mission for whatever ethnicity of cuisine he happened to be studying. Char would retire in two more years, and though the job exhausted her, she still loved her work. Now she spent money on supplies for her classroom, since the city school budget had dried up. More than once, she thanked Robert for making her career possible, as most of her female colleagues had burned out early on from the demands of running a home in addition to the classroom. She was determined to learn *The Magic Flute*, despite her lack of appreciable progress.

One October afternoon, as Robert grated asiago cheese in the kitchen, Char arrived with the latest piano teacher in tow, a new colleague at Galileo, a man in his thirties she introduced as Steven Lovegrove. The two men exchanged handshakes before she led Steven into BeeBee's room for her lesson. Blood mingled with the flakes of golden cheese when Robert cut himself on the grater, trying to remain calm, for the man was a copy of George Murphy, a doppelganger down to the chestnut corduroy and low, rich voice, the fine blond hair spilling out from his ponytail. For the first time since the attack, with every cell in his body, Robert needed to drink.

He focused on the meal, praying Char wouldn't invite Steven Lovegrove to dinner, though he'd always encouraged her friends and those of the girls to join them, as he liked a grateful audience. Cooking was not unlike teaching, he realized; guests were always more enthusiastic than his own family members, whether about the quality of his insightful conversation or his blue cornmeal tortillas. He'd planted an herb garden in the backyard after concluding no store-bought variety would ever be any good. In the summer, he drove to Western Marin or the Peninsula for the freshest produce and eggs. In this way, he managed to make cooking dinner a project that took all day. Although Char did indeed ask Steven Lovegrove to dinner, he politely refused, saying his "partner" would be waiting for him.

At four o'clock Mondays and Thursdays, Steven arrived for Char's lesson, usually driving home from school with her, but sometimes he came separately on the bus. Robert's breathing would quicken and his hands shake when offering an iced tea or cup of coffee. Robert wanted to flee the house at those times, but Char insisted her teacher not be left alone if she was delayed by meetings or students. On the days Char was late, the two men would talk city politics or school bureaucracy or, later, cooking, as Steven said he, too, liked to putter in the kitchen, as he called it, though his partner, Doug, was the chief cook. Steven's open admission of his sexuality made Robert's infatuation more acute. In mid-conversation, he'd grow faint, his skin hot, his voice rising higher, all of it beyond his control, and he'd will Char to walk through the door to end his suffering. Other times he'd pray for Steven to boldly approach him, as George had done, and this time spirit him off somewhere. Robert resisted his desire to drink, as he felt a sort of drunkenness—there was no other word for it—in his moments alone with Steven in the kitchen. Char always invited him for dinner, and he consistently declined, except for once, when he said Doug was out of town.

If Char noticed anything unusual about Robert's behavior that evening, she said nothing. First, he broke a measuring glass, then nearly burned the crème brûlée, and refused to sit still for more than a minute at the table. "Robert's been like this since we married," Char told Steven. "Always a perfectionist. He won't even let me do dishes—I don't do them as well as he does—so don't bother to offer." Of course, Steven did offer, and though Robert refused him, Steven insisted on clearing the table of their French feast, which he had praised in all its parts, knowing, he said, how much work it required.

Steven's proximity was delicious torture to Robert, and he moved slowly about the kitchen, trying to prolong the moments, keeping his face averted as much as possible, for he was sure he was gleaming bright pink. Fortunately, Steven chattered the whole time, first about French food, then about Doug's quest for the perfect omelet pan, and Robert had to keep his hands busy for fear of doing something impulsive—he didn't know what, exactly.

When Char asked Steven to play, he said he would be honored to play for such a sumptuous supper.

For the first time, Robert allowed himself to follow Char into BeeBee's room, or the piano room, as they now called it. They sat in two kitchen chairs behind Steven, who deliberated for some time before beginning.

A breeze sent eucalyptus wafting through the room, raising the white curtains. When Steven hit the first notes of the "Pathétique Sonata," Robert felt that sweet nausea in his gut. He got up to leave, but Char pushed him back in his seat and put a finger to her lips, as if he were one of her unruly students. He listened to the music over the staccato of his heartbeat, studying Steven's back, its beautiful erect posture as he lingered over the keys. His blond curls had been recently cut above the nape, so Robert permitted himself to stare at that patch of soft skin and felt the distinct desire to kiss him, there, on his tender neck. Robert was so involved in his own body's awakening that it took him a long time to hear Char sniffling, to see her weeping, openly, by the end of the piece. He had never played for her and felt strangely jealous of Steven's ability to move her in this way. For a long time after the music had ended, Steven sat facing the piano. Darkness had fallen, and the only sound was a lone flicker at work in the adjacent yard. When Steven finally turned around, he smiled tenderly at Char, who then left the room. Robert met his gaze.

"I used to play that," he said. "But you do it better."

"You play?" Steven rose from the bench. "Please! Your turn. I didn't know."

Robert shook his head, gesturing for Steven to sit back down, which he did. "No, I don't play. When I was younger, I meant. I did play. No longer."

"You don't forget."

"I did. Honest!" Heat returned to Robert's cheeks. He gripped the seat of his chair. "Please. Play more."

"Where's Charlotte?" Steven got up to stretch, his long, thin arms reaching toward the ceiling, then dipping down to the floor. Although Steven was twenty years younger than he, their bodies were remarkably similar: long and lean and gangly. Robert imagined them naked, together, in the moonlit room with its bare floors and walls and the piano, top up, shining. His penis engorged with blood, and he leaned over to hug his knees, to hide himself.

Char returned, wiping her eyes with the heels of her palms. "To have such a gift . . ." She couldn't finish her sentence.

Steven enveloped her in his graceful arms and pulled a handkerchief from his pocket, which she refused. Robert thought of George's handkerchief, which he'd finally thrown away after it shredded in the washing machine. He traced the outline of George's obsidian through his jeans, where it had worn a small, white circle. When Robert flipped the light switch, Steven stepped backward, as if to release himself from the embrace, but Char held him tighter, her gray hair draping his shoulder. Robert fled the room and ran the three blocks to the nearest liquor store, where he bought a fifth of Wild Turkey from the old Chinese proprietor, who smiled at him and said, handing him his change, "It's nice to see you again, Professor!" He went into the alley, opened the bottle, and breathed deeply.

After rinsing his mouth with the bourbon and spitting it out, he looked at the bottle, then threw it against the brick wall, where it shattered with a satisfying cacophony.

The proprietor ran out. "Professor! What you do that for?"

Robert said nothing, for he had no answer, and left. As he walked back up Lone Mountain, he became aware of a pain slowly building in his chest, not the dentist drill pain of the coronary, but a dull burn glowing inside him like a seed, germinating. He stood outside the piano room, shivering, for he'd forgotten to take a jacket, and the fog was coming in. Now Steven was playing *The Magic Flute,* and Robert could hear Char laughing, a full-scale, full-bore laughter he hadn't heard since the kids were little, and Steven's laugh joined hers as they sang together, "Papageno, Papagena," both their voices slightly off-key. Robert stopped shivering. He imagined Beatrice, counting her breaths on her Colorado mountaintop, meditating; she would be glad of this new feeling in her father's heart, he thought, glad that the emptiness of her room had made possible this music.

Bones

Lin Enger

Six of us were crammed sweating and wind-beaten into the back of the undertaker's old white hearse. We were following after the other hearse—new, black, and air-conditioned—which, apart from the driver, my grandpa had all to himself. It was mid-April and already North Dakota was dry. A wind was blowing in from the west, giant tractors were turning the gray fields a darker gray, the ditches were greening, though palely, and the cracks and potholes were pounding away at our tires. I was on the seat facing to the rear, between my dad and my younger brother Daniel, who was trying to extract his weight-trained torso from a camel suitcoat. I helped him pull free of it. Facing us sat my aunt's three sons gazing out the cranked-down side windows. Their shaggy blond heads and beards were all roiled up, their ties flapping and whipping over their shoulders. Their blue eyes were bored.

Next to me, Dad snorted and rubbed a palm over the top of his impeccably bald skull. "You know, boys," he said, pushing his voice above the wind rushing in through the windows, "I think Karlson'd be willing to sell it back to us, as long as he did okay on the deal. He's tight." A few days ago, just before dying at ninety-five, Grandpa had sold to a neighbor the last of his land, the original one-sixty homesteaded by his father in 1883.

My oldest cousin, Tom, blinked at Dad, who had already spoken with Aunt Helen and knew she was glad for her share of the land-sale money. "Mom's not interested," said Tom.

"We are," Dad said. He motioned with his head toward Daniel and me, then reached around and gripped my shoulder, his fingers saying, *I love you,* or maybe, *You owe me.*

He knew, of course, that I was the only one in the family who could do anything about it. Daniel, just out of college, was trying to prove himself in a minor league training camp. Dad, after paying my way through grad school and then getting laid off, was broke. And me? I was twenty-eight years old, married, three years out of law school, and doing just fine in my own practice in the Minnesota town I'd grown up in. I was also sick to death of the law and of Rotary Club meetings, and terrified by the picture I kept seeing of myself at forty: standing down by the lake in a bright yellow boater's hat, manicuring the shoreline with an electric weed-whacker.

My life, you understand, was ordered and secure, the result of a decade's worth of compromise. I'd drifted so far away from what it was I wanted that I couldn't see it any longer, couldn't bring myself to talk about it with anyone other than Margaret—and even with her, my champion, I felt like an idiot, like one of the kids in her elementary school, telling what I wanted to be when I grew up. This spring, though, propelled by self-disgust and Margaret's encouragement, I'd polished up a script and sent it off to the graduate film program at UCLA. I was waiting now to hear if they wanted me. I was scared they might.

We carried Grandpa from the black hearse to the waiting grave. On one side was the pile of dirt, tidy beneath a green canvas; on the other was Grandma's stone. As the minister spoke, the wind battered us. A herd of Guernseys forty paces to the east watched, chewing. Next to me, Margaret wiped at her eyes and clutched her fingers into my arm. Next to her, my brother squeezed away at a green tennis ball with his left hand, following the advice of Rod Carew, whose book on hitting he'd memorized years ago. Dad, on my right, whispered, "That's Karlson there, in the dirty jacket. Remember him?"

I didn't, although I must have met him as a kid making the rounds with Grandpa. He was standing toward the back of the gathering, a skinny old guy with a white shirt and black tie beneath his dirty chore coat, brown hands jutting like old-time baseball mitts from his cuffs. The minister wound down toward the benediction, which was ushered in by a blast of wind that picked up half a dozen of the ladies' hats and sailed them off into the herd of Guernseys.

As Margaret and I rolled out of the cemetery and turned south toward the farm, she peered at herself in the rearview mirror and groaned. I said, "On the way home, you better crawl in back and get some sleep."

"I don't want sleep."

I shrugged and looked at her. In the harsh light of early afternoon, stripes of auburn shimmered in her black hair. Her gorgeous lips, which she'd painted a bright, unfunereal pink, sparkled. Her eyes, though, were bloody at the corners and dark as lead. "I'm sorry," I told her.

"For what?"

"Everything."

"Oh, shut up." She jammed her sunglasses on her face and looked out her window.

It was complicated. Margaret was happy with our life in Crow Point, living close to our families in a house she loved (an old Victorian she'd gone after with sandpaper and varnish) and working at the job she'd been prepared to wait years for: principal of the elementary school we'd both gone to as kids. But she knew I wasn't happy, and she wasn't going to let me pretend otherwise, for her sake.

"He asked you to help buy it back, didn't he?" Margaret said.

"Sort of. Not really."

"What did he say?" asked Margaret. Her voice was edging toward the top of her register.

I shrugged. "Just that he wants it back."

"And you said what? Nothing?"

I clamped down hard on my stomach muscles and squeezed until a white-hot pain started seeping in. "For once, Maggie, they need my help. And remember, he'll be getting half the proceeds from the land sale. We'd only have to come up with the other half."

"If you do this, Iver, you'll be stuck in that practice for the next ten years. At least."

"Is that so bad?" I asked.

Margaret plucked off her sunglasses and tossed them into the backseat. "You don't want to hear it? Fine. Go ahead, then. Turn into Billy Halvorsen. Make us both miserable." She sat back and crossed her arms in front of her, crushing her breasts. I rolled down the window and let the wind harass us.

Billy and I had been best friends growing up, then roommates in college, where he majored in theater and got the best parts in all the plays. After graduation, he went to New York on a long shot, landed some work off-Broadway and was auditioning for a small role in *Fool for Love* when his girlfriend back home called to say she was pregnant. He moved back and settled in for the life both she and his family wanted for him. Now he was one of my divorce clients: a bitter and prematurely middle-aged postal worker.

The siding needed paint and the carragana hedge was shaggy, but the place didn't look bad for being five years empty. The windows were intact, the roofline straight, and as for the outbuildings, they were all on their feet: the barn, the little brooder house, the round-roofed machine shed made of corrugated steel. Several years ago a twister had yanked the windmill off its slab and twirled it down into the soft ground next to the slough behind the barn, and now it lay there rusting, its big metal blades tangled like a bad set of teeth.

In the kitchen we sat down at the Formica-topped table, which Grandma had insisted be left behind when they moved, and drank coffee from a thermos while Dad told stories about the hard years, stories we'd heard before: grasshoppers, drought, hired men who drank anything they could lay their hands on—even rubbing alcohol—to light up their bleak lives. After half an hour Mom cut in on him, getting up from her chair, stepping behind him and placing her long-fingered hands on his shoulders and kneading. "Pete," she said, "if we're going out for a walk, we'd better do it. It's a long drive home and the kids are back at their jobs tomorrow." She bent down and gave Dad a peck on the ear. Dad colored a little. Mom was a young fifty-six then, her blonde hair still riding her shoulders, her shape well intact, and when she aimed her energy at people, they felt it. "Maybe just you men should go," she said. "I know I'm exhausted. What about you, Maggie?"

Outside, Dad told us he had to drive over to Karlson's, he'd be back in fifteen minutes. "I'm just going to float the idea, see what sort of reaction I get," he said.

He drove off, and Daniel and I crossed the yard toward the barn, then walked down the slope to where the windmill lay twisted at the edge of the slough. Some of its fan blades were bent at odd angles and others on impact had been driven into the ground.

"You going to California?" Daniel asked. He knew everything, of course. We'd stayed close into adulthood, both of us seeing in the other so much of ourselves that we appropriated each other's successes, saw them, almost, as our own. Daniel believed I'd write a great film someday; I expected him to light the rookie league on fire and work his way smoothly to the top.

"How can I? You know what this place means to Dad."

"What does Maggie think?" Daniel asked.

"That I'd be crazy not to go, if I get the chance—which I probably won't."

"She want to go out there with you?"

"I think she'd stay in Minnesota, keep her job. Let me fly back and forth."

Daniel said, "Maggie's right, you know. You're miserable. Let this go by, and you'll be out shopping for cowboy boots—the pointy-toed kind—to kick yourself with."

I shrugged and looked around the place—at the brown swamp grass at our feet, at the arthritic hackberry trees up by the house, at the line of stunted pine trees that marked the property line to the south, everything jerking in the wind. At the old, red, rusting Farm-All that Grandpa had taught me to drive when I was eight. At the red-tail hawk sitting up in the dead fir tree.

Daniel said, "Hey, it's just land."

Prompt as always, Dad drove back into the yard fifteen minutes after he'd left and came down the slope to join us at the fallen windmill. We asked him if he'd found Karlson.

"Just his wife," Dad said, "and she's mum. I'll give him a call later in the week." He bent down and followed the twisted leg of the windmill with his finger, then he looked up at us, his pale blue eyes flat on the surface but whirring away inside. He nudged at the mess of steel with the heel of his hand. "You boys remember about the buffalo, don't you? This is where we dug up the bones."

I remembered. It wasn't one of Dad's repeats, but I had the story from someplace.

Daniel said, "You never told *me* any buffalo stories."

Dad stood up straight, reaching to the small of his back to help himself along. "Let's walk," he said, and he headed diagonally toward the southeastern corner of the section. The thunderheads were higher in the sky now, and bigger, purpler. "Fifteen minutes, and then we get wet," Dad said.

"Let's hear the story," said Daniel.

Dad stopped and turned and pointed back toward the farmstead. "The water tank was right beneath the windmill," he began, "which, of course, was up behind the barn then. That's where Abel shot it. The way I heard it from Ed Sanders, the buffalo sort of ambled up one morning and took a long drink. At first Abel wasn't going to shoot it. Bison were already protected in Dakota Territory. This was 1884. But the old bull was mangy, eaten up by flies, its eyes milked over, a leg that looked like it had been chewed on by a coyote or something. And after he drank for a while, he just stood there. Made no move to leave. Abel shot him with a rifle he'd traded some potatoes for, an old fifty-caliber Sharps."

Dad took a minute to light up his pipe, then he leaned back on his heels a little, spoke past the cherry-wood stem tucked into the corner of his mouth. "Your late Uncle Halvor and I dug up the bones in '35, the summer I was ten. Like I said, it was Ed Sanders that told us the story—this was the Fourth of July picnic down by the river. The next day it was raining—probably the only day it rained all summer—and Dad took Mom into town for groceries. While they were gone, we went out and started digging. Started about six different holes, then hit the jackpot. I remember the two of us just covered in mud and jumping around like cannibals with those bones in our hands. They were sort of a yellowish brown color, same as the dirt. Dad was furious, but he didn't say much. It was just that look he had, like his heart was pounding in his eyes."

"He didn't want you digging holes?" said Daniel, "or what?"

"I have no idea. No idea." Dad looked up at the sky, which was split east from west by a greenish blue mass of clouds that looked ragged and wispy on the bottom, harder and more tightly packed higher up. A sky built for a John Ford western. "Came up faster than I thought it would, we better get going," Dad said.

We were a hundred yards from the tree line when a snap of lightning unzipped the sky, a detonation of thunder rocked us, and a squall of rain rode in on a gust from the west, the drops as big as marbles. We sprinted for the trees but were soaked through by the time we reached them. Clustered up beneath the branches of a fir, we stood panting as we watched blades of lightning, two or three at a time, stab at the country to the north.

"It was a day like this I threw a one-hitter against Jamestown," Dad said. "Have I told you boys that one?"

Daniel and I nodded. *A double in the eighth*, I thought. *Nineteen strikeouts*.

He laughed, his eyes narrowing. "They had to stop the game four times because of rain. I struck out nineteen, won it two nothing. Would've had a no-hitter, except in the eighth I got a fastball up to their number four hitter and he banged one up against the center field wall. After the game, you know what my dad said? He said, 'That mistake's going to bother you the rest of your life.'"

We were all quiet for a little while, then Dad started to laugh, little jets of air bursting from his nose. He shook his head and tried to speak but couldn't, he was laughing so hard—and coughing at the same time, wiping at his eyes with one hand and holding his gut with the other.

When he finally caught his breath, he said, "I don't know why it's so funny, but you know what? Halvor and I didn't bury those bones like Dad told us to. Or not all of them. We saved out the skull and put it up in the rafters of the barn."

"It's still up there?" I asked.

"We used spikes and fixed it good. Wouldn't be easy getting it down, though. We put it up when the mow was full of hay, and now of course, the mow floor's gone. Dad tore it out in '52 so he could store the combine in there. The skull's up on top of a truss, just below the peak."

"There's got to be a way to climb up there," said Daniel.

Dad shook his head. "A heck of a ladder, or a bucket on a crane. The peak of that roof must be forty, fifty feet high."

After the rain let up, we walked back to the farmstead and went into the barn, where Dad pointed out the spot to us, a horizontal rafter truss up near the western peak. For a long moment he stood there, rubbing his bald head with the tips of his fingers, like he does when he's feeling dubious about something. Then he shrugged, looked at his palms, turned them over, looked at the backs of his hands. "I guess I'd rather leave it be," he said.

It started with an image, as it usually does for me: a long-haired kid, seventeen or so, sitting on a horse in the middle of a treeless, weed-filled farmstead a few miles west of the Minnesota line. The buildings were bare of paint and the barn was sway-backed. I don't know if the kid lived there or just happened along on his horse, but he sat frozen, staring soberly at the sun going down orange into the prairie. Then another picture came, this one a photograph I'd seen in a book years before, a pile of buffalo bones so big it dwarfed the horse and wagon sitting in front of it. How these things work I'm not sure, but in my head the two pictures fused. It was a hundred years ago. A farm mortgaged beyond hope. And a boy, head crammed full of the West. He hatches a plan to ride west and catch on with one of the buffalo hunters he's read about in the papers. A month, two months, a summer of hunting, he figures, and then he'll come back home to settle with the banker, set up his parents for life, and prove himself worthy of the neighbor girl who's never paid him any mind.

But even before Margaret and I got back to our house in Crow Point that night, I knew it wouldn't turn out the way I'd seen it. The boy couldn't know that the buffalo herds had already been decimated. He couldn't see that his running off would strike a blow to his father's health, and that instead of winning the girl, he'd get snatched by a woman who'd make him wish he hadn't grown up so fast. This would not be the western I'd always wanted to write. This would be the one that made no concessions to the Myth.

At home that night, I drank a pot of coffee at the kitchen table and wrote in lead pencil on a yellow legal pad until four in the morning. I slept the last few hours of the night on the living-room couch, and woke to find Maggie sitting at the table reading what I'd written on the legal pad—a couple of talky scenes full of unnecessary description. Sloppy stuff. Maggie was in her peach bathrobe, freshly showered and sitting unusually straight for seven in the morning. When I came into the room she looked up, pulled her wet hair back from her eyes and said, "Promise me you'll finish this."

I sat down across from her and looked into her face, which happens to be lovely, every feature in it extravagant: her mouth wide and full, her nose just a bit too broad, her green eyes widely spaced—and at this moment serious. "Promise me."

―――

When I bought Ed Kowalski's old brick storefront, I inherited a good number of his clients, most of them elderly. So my practice was made up largely of estate work, living wills, trusts. Throw in a batch of divorces plus a few personal injury cases, and I was busy. The problem was, I disliked helping my elderly clients plan for their deaths, hated refereeing the fights among their heirs, and felt sullied every time I helped dissolve the marriage of someone I'd known growing up. I was miserable, and rather adept at hiding it. Still, I was good at what I did, conscientious, and when I snuck out the back window of my office on Wednesday, I knew I was crossing a line I wouldn't easily be able to cross back over again.

It was almost noon, and I was at my desk working on the script instead of tending to business when my secretary, Sandi Swenson, poked her face in the doorway and reminded me that she had a Tae Kwon Do lesson. "You've got an appointment in fifteen minutes," she said.

"Who is it?"

"Billy Halvorsen." She tucked in the corner of her mouth, which in this case meant Billy was a client whom I'd allowed to use up too much of my time.

She left, and before long, I heard the outside door open. Then I heard Billy bantering with someone on the sidewalk in that great actor's voice of his: "You better back that up with something!" Then, "Hey, Eddy, you think I'm made of money?" And I sat there at my desk, remembering what Billy had given up and what he'd become on account of it, and suddenly I knew I couldn't face him. I grabbed my script, ran to the window that looked out on the alley, popped the screen with my foot, tore it away, and crawled out of there. I left my car where it was and walked home, where I experienced the sort of everyday coincidence we learn early to deadpan our way through. Waiting in our mailbox was the letter from UCLA. I was in.

That night I said nothing to Maggie about the letter.

———

Next morning, I was back at the office, and at ten I took my script and walked down to the town dock, where I tried unsuccessfully to maneuver Micah, my boy hero, to the point of giving that roan horse of his a sharp kick with the heel of his boots and riding the hell out of that scraggly farmstead. It wasn't easy. His parents had logic and love on their side, while all the boy had was a lack of straight information and a splendid ache.

I was muttering my way through a scene when my dad's voice startled me. "Working hard?"

I jerked and looked around. He was crouching down beside me, elbows on knees, his blue eyes snapping as he inspected the scribbles I'd made on the legal pad. "The Swenson girl told me I'd find you down here."

"She did?"

He smiled. "I spoke to Karlson last night on the phone. He's willing to talk, but he wants me to drive out there. He's not the sort to say much over the wires."

I nodded.

"I was thinking of going out Saturday." Dad looked up from the yellow legal pad and into my eyes. "Are you going to drive out there with me?" he asked.

We didn't talk a lot during the four-hour trip. He drove. I dozed or dreamed, having stayed up late the past two nights, writing—or trying to. We reached the homestead by noon and drove past it to Karlson's place, a low, concrete-block house and a high tin barn set down on a treeless acre of dirt. Slick-eyed, mangy dogs surrounded our car, ten or twelve of them, though it was hard to tell how many because of the way they skittered around, snapping at each other, yapping and leaping up, their claws clicking at the car doors. Dad and I looked from each other to the barn-red door of Karlson's gray house, and just then it swung open and the old man came toward us in a fast, crooked lope. When he got to the edge of the pack of dogs, he clapped his hands and the animals scattered.

Inside, over coffee, Karlson was gracious and oddly articulate. He sat sober and straight in his chair, his thumbs hooked through the straps of his bib overalls. "Few years back the wife and I were sick with the flu, that variety that in*fil*trates your joints, and we found ourselves confined to bed, doctor's orders. Your grandpa"—Karlson fastened his small gray eyes on me—"he brought your grandma over to cook for us and all by himself did my chores for two days."

Karlson leaned forward then, screwed his eyes into hard little pellets, and got down to business. He understood how my dad might be upset, he said, but the sale was legal, and he had no intention of being exploited.

"How much do you want for it?" Dad asked.

Karlson held up a crooked, long, yellow-nailed finger. "I don't want to sell the whole parcel. Like to hang onto the southeast forty. That's good flat hayland, which I need. The rest, including the buildings, I'd let go for a hundred and thirty."

"That's more than what you paid for the whole thing," Dad said.

"A bit of a return, and not much, for the trouble of buying and selling," said Karlson. "Understand now, I work the land. I don't own it for its sentimental value." He lifted his cup high to swallow the last of his coffee, the long weathered creases of his neck quivering, then he turned and looked out his kitchen window. "Have to get to town now, errands and such."

Dad said, "I think we'll drive over and walk that forty you're wanting to steal from us."

We walked off the forty that Karlson wanted to keep, and all the way around it Dad was quiet. I wanted to say *Don't worry*, promise him that together we'd buy his land back, no matter what. But I couldn't. I couldn't even think it without thinking, too, of my office in Crow Point, Sandi Swenson guarding the door like a warden, my trickle of clients with their broken lives, the surge of promise I'd felt when I crawled out the window and walked home with my script stuck under my arm.

Back at the farmstead we sat down on the little slope above the fallen windmill. Behind us was the barn, whose shadow cooled the brittle grass we sat on. A flock of snow geese drifted north in a wavering V.

"Why didn't you take over the farm, Dad?" I asked. I realized—a little burst of shame warming my belly—that I'd never asked him before. He'd always been so steady, so reckonable, so fatherlike that I'd never thought to question the choices he'd made.

"That was the plan, Iver—mine, anyway. After I got out of the service and married your mom, I came back every fall to help with the harvest. Once in a while I'd ask what sort of arrangements we should make. And he'd say, 'We'll work it out, we'll talk about it later.' Then in the fall of '60 I got pneumonia and couldn't make the harvest, and Dad had to hire a man, which didn't make him too happy. When the work was done that year, Dad quit, just like that. Sold off two quarters of the land and put the other two in Federal Soil Bank on a ten-year program. All this without saying a word to me. And that was that." Dad let his head drop into his hands. I didn't know what to say.

After a minute or so, Dad said, "There's no telling. Maybe it was all the hard work, the drought, the wind, and the dust. Maybe he just never liked me. I don't know."

"He might have figured that his life didn't bear repeating," I said.

"That's a charitable theory, Iver." Dad lifted his face then and turned to look at me, and I knew this was as close to asking me for help as he was ever going to come.

From behind us came a loud, feathery pistoning and we turned to see two pigeons performing a loop beneath the prow of the barn's peak, one chasing after the other. They took a long wide circle toward the house, then made a line back toward the barn and shot in through the mow door. I could hear the pigeons flying around the old plank walls, and inside my head I followed them—swooped into that close dark sky, smelled the dust and old straw and thirsty wood, heard the soft cadence of wings, the low murmuring of nesting birds in the rafters. I said to Dad, "Let's get that skull down."

He didn't even seem to think about it. "Too high," he said bleakly. "Don't know where we'd find a ladder for that job."

"I'll drive into town for a rope," I told him.

"No," he said, but I was already on my feet and walking toward the car.

In town I bought the heaviest hemp rope they had at the hardware store, 120 feet of it, a ball of string, and a heavy steel bolt about two inches long. Back at the farmstead Dad tried halfheartedly to dissuade me, then sat down on the seat of the rusty mower and watched as I tied the end of the string to the bolt and tried to throw it up and over the truss on top of which, according to Dad, the skull was attached. It took me about twenty-five or thirty throws, but finally the bolt sailed over the truss and dropped back down, string attached. I used the string to pull the rope over the top of the truss, then I laced the other end of the rope through the loop and pulled it on through until the slipknot was fast. I gave it a couple of hard tugs, then jumped up and hung from it for a few moments, just to make sure the truss was solid. "What do you think?" I asked Dad.

"I hope it's still there, and that you can still climb. Here, you'll need this," he said, holding out a rusty claw hammer.

In grade school, one of our annual fitness tests was to see how high we could go on the heavy climbing rope that hung from the gym ceiling, which must have been nearly as high as this barn peak was. Every year I climbed that rope all the way to the top. Thinking on it now, I'm amazed our teachers let us do it; there wasn't a net to catch us if we ran out of grip halfway up.

I tucked the handle of the hammer into my belt and started up the rope. Soon I could feel small wires of heat darting through my biceps and calves. My arms started to tighten. Five feet from the bottom of the truss, I stopped to get my breath, gather my strength. With the rope tight against my cheek, I closed my eyes and saw Micah on his horse, clothes rolled into a blanket at the back of the saddle, a little .22 rifle protruding from its leather scabbard. I watched him reach back and slap that sleek roan rump and fly like a dirty, tan-skinned angel out of his parents' weedy yard toward what I knew might be his ruin.

I opened my eyes, took a deep breath, and pulled myself the last few feet up to the truss. It was a rough-hewn timber about fifteen inches square, five or six feet long, and jointed on both ends into a timber rafter. I hauled myself up on top of it and lay down to catch my breath.

"Iver?" Dad called.

The light was dim up there, the air hot and close. My heart banged against the wooden beam, to which I held with everything I had. With my cheek pressed flat to the dust-and-birdshit-coated oak, I found myself looking into a black eye that stared out through a gray, broken, triangular face. Above it jutted a single dark horn. I reached out and stroked warm, dusty bone.

"Iver?" Dad shouted.

I worked with my right hand to free the skull from the spikes my father had driven half a century before. With the rest of me I clove to the beam. It struck me that I would never learn from any written or remembered account what this chunk of bone meant to my dad's dad, why he couldn't bear to see it unearthed, what it meant to his dad before him. I would never hear what this skull could say about these men I'd known incompletely or not at all: what they dreamed of for themselves, what, if anything, they dreamed of for me.

When I'd worked it loose, I moved carefully onto my side, opened the snaps of my denim shirt and placed the upper jaw—the mandible was gone—against my bare chest. The skull reached from just below my neck all the way down to my navel. I resnapped the shirt, positioning the single horn so that it stuck out between snaps.

The climb down was fast, my arms and shoulders and calves singing with pain, my palms burning, the skull biting into my chest. At the bottom, I landed too hard and lost my balance. Dad helped me up and led me out into the sunlight, where I absorbed the pleasure of the ground under my feet, took a dozen clean lungfuls of North Dakota air, then opened my shirt and handed the skull to Dad, who held it tenderly, stroking it with the tips of his fingers. Under the sun it was an unimpressive specimen, its nose shattered, one horn gone, the other broken off at the tip. It was the yellowish brown color of dead slough grass.

Dad looked up at me, his blue eyes wide and alert, waiting.

I nodded down at the skull he held and said what wasn't easy for me to say: "It's not land, Dad. If I could help with that, I would."

Above us a lone cloud moved across the sun. Dad looked past me, scanning the landscape he probably still dreams in. When his eyes returned, they'd lost some of their intensity. He took a long, deep breath, blew it out. "I knew that, Iver," he said. Then he handed the skull back to me and spoke in a voice that from long experience I knew better than to argue with. "Here. You're the one who's going to be needing it."

The Holy Boys

Bridget Rohan Garrity

Ma sits beside me in the front seat, and the car reeks of mothballs from my suit. Ma's lost weight, and her old black dress coat comes up around her face like she's peering out of a hole. Outside snowbanks line Dot Avenue, ruined by soot now, but not melting. Murphy's said that even though the ground is still frozen they'll dig Pauly his grave, force the ground open with a jackhammer if they have to. I hear my brother's voice *Emmie, it's Pauly here* and think how even his grave won't take him. But I stop myself, *Hell no, Pauly, you're not taking me with you*, and I reach for my cigarettes.

"Off with the lead shoe already, Emmet," Ma says. "We can't afford any more funerals in this family. Not at Murphy's rates." She has a wad of Kleenex in her hands, but so far she's only used it to blot her lips.

I sigh, ease up on the pedal. The buttons on my suit coat press into me; I reach for them.

"And keep that suit coat buttoned at the wake."

"It's too damned tight."

"You had plenty of time to buy yourself a new one. A thirty-one-year-old boy should be able to buy himself a suit."

Our Chevy rattles up the Heights, past the Old Colony projects, Southie High, Flynn's On Tap, old men smoking on doorsteps. Past empty lots. When I was a kid, there were always rumors that something was coming to fill these lots: *A McDonald's is coming. A movie theater is coming. A community center is coming.* None of those things ever came. I motion to a lot littered with Coke cans and tires. "Ma. In that lot over there: The Paul Patrick O'Toole Community Skating Arena. What do you think?"

She looks injured. "What do you mean what do I think? I don't know what the hell you're talking about."

"In Pauly's memory. A rink. Maybe have some fund-raisers. Car washes, bake sales, like that."

She turns her face to the window. "I don't know what the hell you're talking about. If we're going to have any fund-raisers, it'll be to pay off this funeral. A hockey rink? For God's sake. Just the casket is a thousand dollars. A thousand dollars! For a *casket*. For that much it oughta resurrect him."

"Jesus, Ma."

"The open house, the flowers, the headstone . . . costs more to be dead than alive anymore. When I was a girl, we buried my mother in a pine box. And as far as I know, it did just what it was supposed to do. But Murphy says, 'Send him home like a prince, I'll give you a rate.' Yeah, he gave us a rate all right. What a crock. It was the same thing when your father died. We should've gone somewhere else. Your father wasn't even friends with him at the VFW, that's what burns me—"

"Ma, take a breath."

"We've got to get this car fixed before it breaks down for good and all. And that damned leak in the cellar . . ." She shakes her head. "Like my father always said—" she crosses herself.

Same old shit. Like she's reading from a script. *"It takes a lot of money to be poor."*

"Oh, you know that so well, do you? Well, you don't know it as well as you're going to know it, believe me. I pray to God every day you never know money trouble like I've known money trouble."

I exhale my drag with a loud sigh. Out on the sidewalk a kid shoves a fistful of snow down another kid's jacket. "Just an idea, Ma."

"Yeah, well, ideas are your biggest problem. Always stuck inside your head. Having dreams is nice, but you got to wake up now and again." She stops suddenly, realizes she's going too hard on me, and the excitement in her face stills. She pulls down the visor and looks in its mirror, dabs her hankie at lipstick that's bled into the wrinkles around her mouth. "No, there won't be any hockey rinks just yet, my boy. But I know your heart is in the right place. You were always a good boy to your brother." Without looking at me, she reaches for my hand, but my hand is on the wheel, so she pats the car seat.

I glance at her. Her mouth is tense, but her eyes are dry and dull, and I look away. They found Pauly in an alley off of Downtown Crossing, shot in the head. Ma said she couldn't take anymore, so I've been doing the talking with the cops. When I went to ID him, I stood there for a long time, waiting to feel something.

The back of his head was gone, but the scar above his eyebrow was still there, from the State Championship against Worcester in '81 when his mask slipped up and the puck hit him in the face. The only things they had of his were his wheelchair and his bashed-up wallet, inside one of those posed prom photos of him and Moira, a fake palm tree hanging over them. I looked hard at that photo. Pauly hadn't looked that way in a long time, not even in my mind: chin lifted, eyes fighting off a laugh. The Pauly in my mind had hard eyes and a mean set to his jaw. The kid in the photo looked more like me than him, and I can't get that out of my head.

"When did your brother Jimmy say he'd be there?" Ma asks.

"He didn't."

"I don't want you two picking at each other today, either. He's driving all night from South Carolina and I don't want trouble."

"I'm not gonna say a word."

"Did you bring the trophies?"

I feel my face harden, and turn to the window. "Yeah, I brought the trophies."

She looks at me. "What's your problem?"

"Nothing. I brought them, okay?"

She sits there scowling for a minute. Then she says, "I don't see anything wrong with wanting people to remember the old Pauly. The real Pauly. I don't want people remembering my son as a bum. My son was not a bum."

"Ma, I didn't say anything. Christ, back off already."

She sighs and a darkness moves over her face. The sidewalks are empty but for a few old people with canes, scaling the Heights to noon mass at Saint Augustine's, "cramming for finals," as Ma would say. It's only the old people who go to church anymore. In the last year, four churches have closed in Southie. Ma's always saying, 'The neighborhood ain't what it used to be,' but I've been hearing that for as long as I can remember. Sometimes I try to imagine myself in Florida or maybe out West, but nothing comes to me.

"I just thank God your father isn't here to see this," Ma says. "It would have killed him. He wouldn't have survived it. But now they're together again. And soon we'll find out who did this to our Pauly, and then we can try to find some peace."

I bear down on the pedal as we near the crest of the hill and Saint Augustine's Cemetery, chalky tombstones twisted in the snow. I remember me and Pauly running around with toy guns, hiding behind the monuments. Now with all the gangs, they keep the gates locked. No matter where I hid, Pauly always found me, came up behind me and put the barrel to my head. *Bang bang, Emmie. You're dead.*

The room fills, first with people, then with smoke. The Cookes, the O'Connells, Father Frank, old hockey buddies of Pauly's, City Councilor Kelly, neighbors and relatives and people from Southie I've never met who were fans of Pauly's on the ice. Murphy is walking around like he's looking for votes, patting people on the back, offering cigars.

At the back of the room, Jimmy sits brooding in a folding chair. He's seven years younger than I am—always the baby to me and Pauly, only five when Dad died. Still a kid when Pauly lost his legs and all the trouble started. In his face you can see what those years took from him. He joined up with the Marines right after high school, damn near showed up at LeJeune in his cap and gown. Beside him, Angela plays with the baby. She's Jimmy's high school sweetheart, but from the North End, not Southie. Behind her back Ma calls her "Jimmy's Guinea."

Ma's still fiddling with the trophy display, arranging ribbons and newspaper clippings on a card table Murphy brought up from the basement. This morning when I was grabbing awards off of Pauly's shelves, I took a good look at the MVP All-State trophy, remembered the night he won it: the sound of blades cutting the ice, Pauly flying back and forth in front of me. When they announced his name, Ma had put her hands over her face to hide her crying, and that night I'd lain in bed sleepless, replaying the look on her face. That year Pauly wrapped the trophy up and gave it to me for my fifteenth birthday. But after he lost his legs, Ma took it off my shelf and put it back on Pauly's. She never said anything about it; I just remember that one day I looked up and it was gone. When I saw it on Pauly's shelf, I put it back on mine. A couple days later, there it was on his side again. She used to come in and dust his trophies, but somewhere along the line she stopped doing that, and when I grabbed it this morning it was tarnished and dirty. Now the MVP trophy is the centerpiece of the display she's arranged. There are streaks of dust from it on her skirt.

Guests mingle, kneel at the casket. Mrs. Griffin is here from Saint Monica's, playing the organ like an ass she's trying to kick.

The Sullivans have come, Sully clean-shaven and holding Aunt Mary by the elbow. I'll always think of Sully as he was at ten, freckle-faced, foul-mouthed. He nods to me with a seriousness that makes me grin. Big man of the house.

After a while Ma tells me I should be near the casket to receive people. She goes back and stands near her little display, greeting people as they come in. The casket is closed, covered with flowers. As I take my place beside it, it occurs to me that Ma will never have seen him dead.

The line starts moving, grievers coming one after the other, until the faces and voices run together into a single echoing thing. *Our prayers are with you. We'll bring a dish by. Do they have any leads? So many sick, sick people out there. I remember when you and Pauly used to come around with penny candy and sell them for a quarter each. Southie hasn't had a goalie since who comes close. He always seemed to blame himself for what happened to the Fagan girl. Accidents happen, it's not always someone's fault. You were always a fine brother to him, but that's the kind of people you come from.*

I look out at the crowd. After the accident, everyone was there for him, visitors all the time, kids coming by. It kept him going for a while. He thought about still going to college, maybe getting a degree in sports administration. U. Mass. said they'd make good on their offer, even if he couldn't play hockey. I don't know what happened to all that.

I keep greeting people, but I can't shut out Ma's voice beside me. *We did everything we could. We didn't know what more to do than love him.* Mrs. Gannon, our neighbor, approaches Ma, her face all sad-sack. I want to remind the old bitch she's called the cops on Pauly about ten times in the last two years. Every time she saw him coming she got on the phone. Now she gives Ma a hug. "My prayers are with you, Eily. Let me know what I can do."

"God bless you, Betty," Ma says to her. "What could we do? We didn't know what more to do but love him. But now at least he's at peace."

"He's where he belongs, Eily."

She holds Mrs. Gannon's hands in her own. "We're going to find who did this, Betty. Then we can all move forward."

"You raised three boys all on your own, and you did the best you could. That's all a person can do."

When Mrs. Gannon turns toward me, I turn my back and pretend to look at the flowers. The flowers are too sweet and make my mouth water with bile. Ma's voice drones on beside me. She keeps saying the same thing over and over again, until I wonder if maybe she's delirious. But the more I watch her, the more I know she's not delirious at all: there's too much trying in her face.

I look out at the crowd. All the people from our childhood. Teachers, coaches. Grown-up faces of the kids we used to run with—Feeney, White, Tommy Harrington. In the corner, slouching behind one of the flower displays, is Rupert Meaney. He's still small, sickly looking. Pauly got suspended from Saint Monica's three different times for beating the shit out of kids who made fun of the project kids, or the ugly or stupid kids, and Rupert was one of his causes. Pauly had Dad's temper, and when he zeroed in on you, you repented damn quick. Even when he was suspended, Father Pratt still let him go on the ice. Wasn't worth losing a game over. Rupert stands with his hands in his pockets, his eyes shifting around the room. An image of Pauly comes to me, in his chair in the middle of the street, looking up at our house like a kid.

I don't allow drugs in this house. Period. I've told him time and time again.

Ma, for Christ's sake, it's cold out there. Just for tonight. I'll make up a bed for him on the couch.

I can't have that in my house. I will not have drugs in this house ever again. We're not that kind of family. Now go tell him another night, when he's clean and sober.

Ma, come on. Jesus. I can't do that.

How much do I have to take? Tell me.

I'm shocked when I see the Fagans walking toward me. Mrs. Fagan reaches for me weakly. She's tiny like Moira was, and as we hug I have the stupid notion I might hurt her. Mr. Fagan stands slightly behind her, somber-faced and silent. He shakes my hand.

"Thanks so much for coming," I say to them. "It would have meant a lot to Pauly." And it would have. He couldn't go to Moira's funeral because he was still in the hospital, so me and Ma went for him. Mrs. Fagan turned her back on Ma in the receiving line, but now she stands in front of me, weeping. When I shake Mr. Fagan's hand he shifts his eyes from me.

I watch Mrs. Fagan move to the casket and kneel, drop her head in prayer. It hurts to look at her, but I don't know it's sadness I feel. I close my eyes and press my fingers into them for a second. *I'm sorry, Pauly. Not tonight.*

Not tonight? Not tonight? What the hell does that mean, 'not tonight'? Emmie, what the Christ? It's Pauly here.

"Ma," I whisper to her as I go past, "I'm gonna get some air." I don't wait for her to answer.

On my way through the crowd, a firm grip takes my shoulder. I turn to see it's Father Frank. He's a large man with a jowl-hung face and a sad, slow voice. I've known him for as long as I can remember. Father Frank is from the neighborhood, went to grade school and high school with my dad. "Hey there, Father."

He shakes my hand solemnly. "Well, now, that's a suit, isn't it," he says.

"Maybe you remember it from my First Communion," I say, demonstrating how I can barely move my arms.

Father laughs. Then he takes my arm, lowers his voice. "You've been such a support to your mother, Emmet. You've been a pillar of strength for the whole family." His tone disappoints me. He's in prime funeral mode; I could be anybody. "I just want you to know what a fine son you've been. You make her very proud."

"I think you should go to her for a second opinion."

He laughs. "No, no, she told me herself. She doesn't know what she'd do without you. You're her saving grace."

I look down in embarrassment. "We're working on building a rink. As a tribute to Pauly."

"You don't say? That's fantastic."

"Yeah, I'm pulling together donations."

"Well, let me know what I can do." He glances at the trophy display and grins. "Oh, but I remember you two so well as boys... I'll never forget the day I heard the doorbell, and there on the stoop were two ragamuffins—'Father, we'd like to be your holy boys.' Holy boys!" His old eyes water with laughter. "And from then on, every Sunday I walked into the sacristy, there were the two altar boys, rolling around in their cassocks, wrestling for the bells."

I can't help but laugh. "Yeah, and he always got 'em. Except that time my birthday fell on a Sunday and he forfeited them to me." We used to sneak wine, too. I consider telling him, but decide against it.

"Worst enemies. And best friends, you two."

"Beat me at everything. Especially on the ice. Ma used to say he was going to go professional. We all believed."

"He was a regular song-and-dance man on the ice, wasn't he? But everyone's strength takes a turn, and you were there for him. In his victories, and defeats."

I look away, into the crowd. *Do you think it's possible, is there any chance that he ... It doesn't appear likely. No sense torturing yourself with it.*

Ma approaches and she and Father embrace. In almost a whisper, Father asks, "Any leads, Eily?"

"Oh, they'll find who did it," she says. Father pats her hand and nods. "But at least now the suffering's done. We couldn't give him what he needed, Father. But I did the best I could."

"I know you did, Eily. And God knows," he says to her.

My head is like lead and I let it drop. I feel Ma tugging at my arm.

"'Scuse us, Father." She pulls me away to the window and points out. "What the hell is all that?" she whispers. Out at the curb there's a group of what appear to be homeless guys, smoking and talking among themselves. Several cabs are parked along the street, too, the drivers in a huddle. "And is that your brother out there? Go get that boy and tell him to get his ass in here."

———

Jimmy is leaned up against a car, shivering and smoking.

"What's all this?" I ask.

"Pauly's fan club, looks like."

"Give me one of those." Jimmy hands me his pack. I feel the homeless guys and the cabbies eyeing me. The cabbies looked out for Pauly, gave him rides back to Southie now and again. I hear myself yelling, "Hey fellas, feel free to go on in and pay respects if you want." They look back at me like I've just told them to fuck off.

"Ma's gonna love that," Jimmy says under his breath.

I shrug. "I don't know. They came all the way over. And it's cold out here." I exhale my drag and rub my neck. "How's the South treating you?"

He shrugs, digs his heel into a patch of ice. "The neighborhood hasn't changed one fucking iota."

"That's not true," I say. "We got a couple new projects." I nudge him. He barely manages a grin. "Ever think about coming back?"

He snorts. "What do you think?"

"It'd mean a lot to Ma. Especially now. To have us all together again."

"Gimme a break. Ma's crying dry tears in there."

"It's a wake, Jimmy. She has to keep her head up," I say. "Besides, I don't think she has any tears left."

"Guess not," Jimmy says. "Never thought she'd run out of tears for him, though."

I say nothing. Flick my ashes toward the snow.

Finally Jimmy says, "Any more information?"

"Not to speak of. Not a hell of a lot to go on. No gun, no witnesses. They keep telling us not to hold our breath."

He squints into the light. "Pauly own a gun?"

"No. Not that I knew of, anyway."

"Probably coulda gotten one pretty easy, on the street and all that."

"What's your point?"

He shrugs. "Just thinking."

I fix my eyes on Murphy's sign. Green and gold. *Where a Stranger Is Just a Friend We've Yet to Meet.* "It was a homicide."

"Yeah, I know that. Just relax, okay? I was wondering if he was able to defend himself is all."

We stand in silence for a while, watching the homeless guys and cabbies talk and laugh. I feel their eyes on me, feel it starting to piss me off.

"Listen," I say to Jimmy, "What would you say about building a rink for Pauly? For the kids. You still know some people. We could go to the Kiwanis, the Knights, maybe have a telethon."

His scowl breaks with laughter. "A telethon? Jesus Christ, Em."

"Hey, asshole, it's possible. Think about it."

"Whatever."

"Fine. I'll do it myself."

He smirks and shakes his head. "You gotta get the hell out of Southie, Em."

"No. Not now. Ma needs a man around. It's not safe for her to be in that house alone."

"Shit." Jimmy laughs. "Em, you're the only man of the house I know who sleeps under a poster of Larry Bird."

"Hey, somebody's gotta look out for family."

"Don't give me that shit. All you are is her goddamn houseboy. Driving her around, buying her groceries." He throws his cigarette into the snow and crosses his arms. "I mean, don't you ever wonder? What the hell would you ever have done with yourself if Pauly hadn't fucked himself up?"

I look at him, stunned.

"She wears you like a crutch, Em, that's all I'm saying."

"Just shut your mouth, all right? Enough."

I shake my head and begin walking back to the funeral home. Ice cracks under my dress shoes. I feel the bums' and cabbies' eyes fixed on me again, and I feel like asking them what the fuck their problem is, but it occurs to me all of a sudden they're staring because they see Pauly in my face. I keep my head down. Without turning around I say to Jimmy that the wake liturgy is about to start and that Ma wants him in there.

Father Frank has on his purple vestments and is standing by the casket with his head bowed and his palms raised and open. Smoke hangs above the shoulder-to-shoulder crowd. Ma's at the front, gesturing to me to take the seat beside her, but I wave her off and take a spot at the back of the room. She gives me a look.

"Lord, those who die still live in your presence. And your saints rejoice in complete happiness. Listen to our prayers for Paul Patrick O'Toole, your son, who has passed from the light of this world, and bring him to the joy of eternal radiance. We ask this in the name of your son, Jesus Christ."

The crowd responds: *Forever and ever. Amen.*

"I am the Lord, I am the Way, the Truth, the Light. He who believes in me, though he be dead, shall sit beside me in the glory of everlasting life . . ."

Suddenly there's a chorus of honks, and when I look out the window I see the cabbies, laying on their horns and laughing. Then the bums start up: *Pauly! Pauly! Pauly!* Marching around like they're in a parade, laughing their asses off. I grin. I know he would have loved it. Pauly loved hoopla. Around me the mourners turn to each other, some of them chuckling, others not knowing what to do. I see Sully with his hand over his mouth, trying not to laugh. Ma looks up, stunned. Her eyes are searching for me, but I turn back to the window.

Father stops for a moment and smiles, then continues, yelling above the chants. "Out of lament for the suffering of Paul Patrick, oh Lord, we conduct today's rosary in honor of the Five Sorrowful Mysteries of your son, Jesus Christ. We begin with the mystery of Christ's agony in the garden as he awaited betrayal. Hail Mary, full of grace . . ."

Ma bows her head, her hands manacled in a rosary. The night of the wreck, when Jimmy and I walked into Pauly's hospital room, her rosary was pressed to her lips, her head resting on Pauly's chest. She turned to us with swollen eyes and asked us to give her a minute more alone with him.

For years after the accident, I'd lie in bed hearing Ma mumbling the rosary for him beyond the bedroom wall. Pauly slept downstairs on the couch—he wouldn't let anyone carry him upstairs—and sometimes I'd go over and get in his empty bed. We'd shared that room our entire lives, and every night we lay talking, staring up at the cracks in the ceiling. Going over Pauly's games play by play. Making plans. I was going to be his agent when he went pro, and when he retired we'd build a rink in Southie, The O'Toole Arena. It seems stupid to me now, but then, I believed.

Things must have been okay for a while, and as I stand there listening to Father I try to remember, but only certain images come to me. Walking into the kitchen and finding Ma in her nightgown, crying, sopping up piss with a kitchen sponge. Bandaging his arms where he'd made cuts on himself. And the sounds. Even now I can hear him screaming, not a man's scream but a shrill scream, an animal's scream, and Ma crying, begging; the cops pounding on the door. *Emmie, what the Christ? It's Pauly here.*

The noise stopped. I can't remember when, exactly; it seems sudden and unreal. Pauly was gone, and this time we didn't go looking for him. Ma took up her old life, filling her time with housework and church activities. And pretty soon we found a routine, me driving her to morning mass and on errands, eating dinner on trays in front of the TV. She spoke rarely of Pauly, and when she did, it was like he was somebody else's son. Her voice and eyes didn't change.

Now her head is bent, her expression strained. And it occurs to me as I watch her that she hasn't knelt at Pauly's casket to pay respects.

During the liturgy, a group of Pauly's friends from the streets wander in, moving huddled together, like a single person. They seem nervous and awkward, and I go over to them and shake their hands. The cold from outside comes off of them like breath. They see the trophy display and go to it, picking up the medals and ribbons, smiling and laughing. Ma looks up from her rosary, and our eyes lock for a second.

After the liturgy, Sully comes up to me and whispers, "Want some air?" His code words for a beer.

"God, yeah." I head toward Ma to let her know, but then I just turn and follow Sully out the door.

We stop at Store 24 so Sully can buy some chances. When we were kids, it was Tippy's Five and Dime. I'd go up to the counter and buy something to distract old Tippy, while Pauly stuffed his pockets with penny candy. Now I stand outside smoking, squinting into the gray light.

"Gimme a coin," Sully says when he comes out. He's got an Easy Street ticket, a five-dollar ticket. "I feel lucky today," he says. He begins to scratch. "I win, I'll buy you anything you want. You and me'll take a trip down to Daytona. No! The Bahamas. A cruise to the Bahamas."

"Let's build a rink," I say. "As a tribute to Pauly."

He stops scratching, looks at me. "That's it. That's exactly what we're supposed to do." Sully gets dramatic at times; now his expression is far off, as if he's already won. "We'll build a rink for Pauly." He starts to scratch again. "And with the money that's left, I'll take a cruise to the Bahamas."

I grin and shake my head. "Let's get up the street already. I only have time for one."

Sully scratches all the boxes but one; then he stops. "For Pauly," he says, and crosses himself. He scratches the last box, then crumples it, hurls it like a stone. "Son of a bitch."

We start heading up the street. I don't have a coat on, and the wind cuts through my suit. I curl my hands under my arms. Sully keeps his arms stiff at his sides, defying the cold. Our dress shoes click on the pavement.

Flynn's is empty but for a couple old guys nursing the midmorning shakes. When we come in, their eyes are small, almost fearful in the light that pierces the room.

Sully nods to them, then says, "Today's are on me," and pulls out his wallet. He orders a couple and lights up.

"Oh, man," he exhales. "That's the weirdest fucking wake I ever been to."

I grab a cigarette, look up at the TV. CNN—civilians being carried away in bloody sheets. Old women keening over bodies. The two old guys at the end of the bar blink drowsily up at the pictures, tap their butts against ashtrays. I think of Dad down at the VFW, me and Pauly going in there to pester him for a couple bucks. He always drank a shot with his beer, and he'd give us a sip from both. *Quiet about it. What your mother doesn't know won't hurt her.*

"All those street rats milling about," Sully laughs.

"Least he had friends out there."

"Friends?" he spits. "He had friends in Southie if he would have stuck around. Look at all the people there today. Those are his friends. Everybody loved Pauly."

Where the hell were all of them after the first few months? I think, but I keep my mouth shut.

Jackie Flynn sets our beers down. "On the house. To Pauly."

I shake Jackie's hand. "Thanks, man." I nudge Sully. "Your kind of tab."

We drink and smoke without talking for a while. Being with Sully's like being alone, and though most times it puts me in a mood, today I'm glad for it.

Between drags he asks, "How's things at Gillette?"

I shrug and take another gulp. "It's a job."

"You planning on staying there for a while?"

I nod. "Good benefits. Health, dental, the whole nine. I've been saving a little, too."

"Good for you."

One of the old guys begins hacking, a scratching, wheezing sound, and he keeps it up until I think his guts are going to come out his mouth. He keeps his eyes fixed on me, his face purple. I turn the other way. "Jesus."

"What the Christ," Sully hisses and turns to the old man. "Hey Bill, you okay over there? No dropping while I'm setting here enjoying one, okay?" The old guy nods. Jackie hands him a napkin without taking his eyes off the TV.

We drink some more—a couple beers, a couple shots. Jackie keeps setting them down in front of us.

Sully burps. Sticks the tip of his finger into his shot glass, licks. "Boston P.D. moving on the case at all?"

I shrug and blow a line of smoke in the air. "They're talking to people. It's hard when it's a situation like Pauly's. Street code and all that. No one's talking."

Sully waves the comment away. "Don't let them give you that shit. You can bet your ass if it was Weld's son or a Kennedy or somebody they'd sure as hell find who did it."

"They've been all right."

Looking into the mirror behind the bar, Sully says, "My heart goes out to your ma. Your ma's a living saint, Toolie, I've always said so."

I say nothing, grab another cigarette.

"'Member when Pauly used to hang out down by the courts? Playing coach and all that? I remember one day walking past the court at Old Colony, and there he was, sitting under the hoop in his chair, just waiting for kids to show up." Sully thinks for a minute, then shakes his head and laughs. "And he was a tough fucker, too. All these little kids heading down there for a few laughs, and here's this guy in a wheelchair on the sidelines, 'Defense, you little shit, defense!'"

We both laugh. Ma used to make me go find him and bring him a lunch. Once he settled in at a court, we damn near had to drag him home.

"What the hell happened with that?" Sully asks. "Why didn't he stick with it? I bet they would have taken him on at the high school. Especially as an assistant coach for hockey or something."

I shake my head. "I don't know, man. I don't know what happened. He got mixed up in shit, that's what happened."

Sully frowns, looks into his empty shot glass. "They never thought. . . I mean, it was never possible that he—" Then he shakes his head and wipes his mouth with the back of his hand.

"What?"

"Forget it, never mind. You need a refill? Jackie, he needs a refill."

I look at him hard, though he won't look back at me. He shifts on his stool.

I look straight ahead, into the mirror. I see Pauly's body on a steel table, the white sheet crumpled where his legs used to be. The medical examiner, the top of her head, the part in her hair like a perfect seam. *We don't think it's any other type of situation. No sense torturing yourself with it. It's not likely, judging from the wound.*

When Jackie brings me another I say to him, "Hey, we're putting together a rink in the neighborhood, in Pauly's honor. How about setting out a cup for donations?"

He gets a beer glass and sets it on the bar. Then he picks it up and sets it down in front of the old guys. They pull out their bashed-up wallets and throw in a few bucks each, and nod toward me. Then Jackie picks up the glass and sets it in front of us.

"Awesome, a rink for Pauly," Sully says and throws in a couple bucks. He pulls the money out and counts it. "Six bucks already, man. There's a doorknob for ya." When I don't laugh he says quickly, "Hey, we'll get there. Got to start somewhere, right, Jackie?"

We sit in silence for a while, watching commercials. The donation glass is right in front of me, and I stare at the six bucks inside it for a while. Then I stand, finish my drink, and stick my cigarettes in my jacket pocket.

"Where are you going?"

"Gotta get back there."

"Hold on," says Sully, collecting his cigarettes. "I'll come with."

"No. Finish your beer." I nod to Jackie and the old guys.

Sully sighs, drops back onto his stool. "Toolie! Come back here," he whines to me. "Come on, man. Let me buy you another."

Outside, the air stings, but I'm glad to feel it. I begin the walk back to Murphy's. My legs are numb, my footsteps thudding inside my head. Motors rattle past. I hear laughing, and when I look up a group of kids shove past me, fighting their way up the street.

Down the street, I stop at an empty lot surrounded by a fence. The lot is too small for a rink. But the houses behind it are ready to come down. I imagine going to their doors—making offers: *We'd like to build a community rink here, in honor of Paul O'Toole.* In the front we'll have one of those life-size statues of him, maybe a giant version of his MVP All-State trophy. Guarding the net, stick poised midair. I grip the fence and peer through. There's a lot of people who'd be willing to donate. I'd go door to door if I had to. To hell with Jimmy and Ma. I could do it on my own. If there wasn't enough money here, I could go to Boston. A lot of people still remember Pauly on the ice. He was in the papers.

His face won't come to me. I can see his figure from a distance, in the street, looking up at the house. And I can see the big gold statue of him. But for the life of me I can't see his face. What's left is his voice. *Emmie, what the Christ? It's Pauly here.* The snow inside the fence looks new, or at least a few shades whiter than the piles lining the street. When I was a kid I loved looking at the snow in the empty lots, still perfect, all the cans and wrappers hidden beneath whiteness. It always made me feel good, like there was a place safe from the rest of the world. I shove the tip of my shoe in one of the fence rungs and heave myself up. I watched Pauly climb these fences a thousand times. If he saw a spot where the snow hadn't been touched, he'd jump the fence and have his feet be the first on it, track the shit out of it. An image of him forms in my mind: parka unzipped, flapping behind him, his pants hanging out of his snow boots. I can hear his laugh. In front of me, he runs circles through the lot, kicking up snow behind him.

Leave it be, Pauly! It looks nice like that!
Come on, Emmie, jump! What the hell are you waiting for?
I balance myself against the top of the fence, the tips of its metal triangles pressing into me. My legs are shaking. I feel like I'm barely hanging on. He's wearing his old navy parka, the tear in the shoulder, the pilled polyester lining. I gave him that tear when we got in a fight on the way home from school once. He told Ma he tore it on his locker.
Come on! Are you just going to stand there like a pussy? Jump!
Stop it, Pauly! Stop it!
I watch him track through the snow, dancing almost. Then I hear his voice, not like a memory, but as if he's honest-to-God standing on the sidewalk beneath me. A sore voice, an ugly voice:
"Didn't know you had it in you, little brother."
I try to shut it out. I try to focus on the snow.
"You wouldn't let me in my own house, for Christ's sake."
What, I think, *we were supposed to just take all your shit whenever you felt like dropping by? As soon as the whole fucking world stopped revolving around you, you couldn't take it, could you?*
"You could've let me in. You know if you would have pressed it, Ma would have let me stay."
No, you're the one who fucked it all up, Pauly. You're the one who got into that car drunk and fucked it all up. A car honks as it goes past and startles me. The lot is smooth again, and as I look out at it, I imagine myself dead. I think, *I'm dead. Ma's dead. We're all dead. Forgive me,* I think, but just as quickly as I think it, it falls away, and I'm left staring out at the empty white lot. I've never felt the kind of fear I feel right then, and I know, I realize, it's not the kind of fear that will ever pass. It's the kind of fear I saw in Pauly's face, the kind of fear I see in Ma's; the kind that passes into doom. *No way. Pauly, I think, you're not taking me with you.*
Again, his voice:
"I would have let you in."
"Yeah? Well, fuck you. Fuck you, Pauly."
My feet give way. I slip down the fence and stumble onto the sidewalk, and I hear the back of my suit coat rip. When I stand I realize I'm shivering like a madman. I look up the street, wonder if anyone saw me, heard me. I brush the snow off my suit and start walking again.
I'm drunk is all. I have no idea how the hell long I've been gone, and I think of Ma. She's standing by the trophy display, holding mourners' hands. *Oh yes, we'll find who did this to our Pauly.*

She has her martyr and her villain, and after this is all over, I'll drive her to daily mass where she'll go inside and pray in adoration of one and in redemption of the other. I stumble along, feeling the wind come through the tear in my jacket. I can't stop shaking from the cold, and I break into a run.

Outside Murphy's, the bums and cabbies have left, a couple coffee cups left in the snow. The wake has emptied out but for a cluster of mourners. Murphy is chatting with Father Frank near the casket. Ma is packing up the trophies.

She sees me and continues packing. "Where the hell have you been?"

"I needed some air."

"Some Flynn's air, no doubt."

"I'm sorry."

She doesn't answer, slides a rubber band around the ribbons.

"I was at Flynn's, having some beers."

"Well, good for you. I need you to bring me by DeLuca's to pick up the party platters. And we still need some buns for the cold cuts. Is that a rip in your jacket? For heaven's sake. What are you going to wear to the funeral, then? Add that to our list."

I collapse into a chair beside her. "Where's Jimmy?"

"They had to get back."

"Get *back*?"

"It's a long drive."

"What, he couldn't stay a whole twenty-four hours? What an asshole."

"You're not exactly an example yourself, spending half the wake at Flynn's."

"Jackie put out a cup for Pauly's rink."

She huffs. "Lot of business sense you have. I can't think of a worse place to ask a man to part with his money. You won't be building any rink on nickels and dimes."

Across the room Murphy's mouth is moving; Father Frank has his arms crossed and rocks on his heels. Behind them, the casket. I reach out and pick up one of Pauly's trophies, run my finger over the little gold figure on top. "I can't remember him, Ma. I keep trying. But I can't."

She frowns but doesn't say anything.

"It's like, today I'm standing there beside my brother's casket, and the whole time I'm thinking, This could be a stranger." I look at her. "You know what I mean?"

She turns to me angrily. "Are you drunk? Because if you are,

I'm not getting in that car with you. I'll have Murphy or Father drive me home."

After a second, she continues fumbling with the trophies. She picks up the MVP All-State trophy, wipes it with her wad of Kleenex. "We have to get a move on. DeLuca's closes in forty-five minutes."

"And then I think, maybe I don't want to remember. Maybe I'm glad I can't remember."

She studies my face for a moment and then glances at Father and Murphy and whispers, "You're drunk. You're a disgrace. How am I supposed to get through all the things we've got to do today with you drunk?"

"Ma—"

"We still have a million things to do before the funeral tomorrow and we don't have time for idiocy. Did you clean the downstairs bathroom like I asked? With people in and out of there I don't want it looking like hell." She undoes the pack of ribbons, begins to shuffle through them as if counting.

"DeLuca's closes at five-thirty. And if we get a move on, maybe we'll have time to go up the street and see about a suit for you. Now start packing some of those flowers in the car. I thought Aunt Mary might like some of them. Take the roses."

I don't get up. I am dizzy, the throb of my heart beating in my ears. I watch her pack the box, her hands chapped. When we were kids, after she'd yelled at us real bad, she'd come in at night and rub our backs. I'd lay there pretending to be sleeping, dreading the moment when she'd stop and go to Pauly.

"Did you hear what I said?"

I put the trophy back down. "The truth is, I feel more relieved than sad."

She turns to Father. "Father, will you help yourself to the flowers? It's a shame for them to go to waste." She smiles and nods toward the arrangements.

"Why, thank you, Eily," Father calls back. "We could use them for the altar. A reminder of Pauly the whole week long."

"I used to feel guilty, and now I don't know if I even feel that anymore."

She raises her hand toward me slightly, whispers, "Do you want me to slap you right across the mouth in front of Father? Is that what you want?"

Across the room, Father leans over and smells the flowers.

She takes the trophy I've just set down, places it in the box.

"Do you want to go to Bremer's or Gimbel's for your suit?"

I feel my throat tighten. But I don't look at her. "Were you relieved when they said it was murder? Because when they called and said he was dead, the first thing I thought was, Pauly's gone and done it."

She turns to me, her mouth open. The ribbons in her hands scatter to the floor. For a second she stands still, looking down at them.

She kneels and begins fumbling with them, but suddenly she stands and goes behind the curtain off to the side. Murphy and Father stop chatting and look over look at me, confused. I pick the ribbons off the floor, throw them into the box, and follow her.

Behind the curtain are caskets. It's the room where we picked out Pauly's a couple days ago. Murphy went around hoisting up the lids, telling us to touch the silk lining. *So he can go to his rest comfortably. Oh no, maybe not in the literal sense, but it gives us survivors a final solace.* Ma is at the rear of the room, her back to me. I stand watching her for a moment.

"I'm sorry."

It seems like she doesn't say anything for a very long time. She looks small as a child standing there, and I feel sorry. Finally she says, in a voice that's almost a whisper, "I just don't know why you'd even say something like that. Why would you even say something like that? I don't understand—" Her voice is shaking. Her arms are clasped around her like she's cold. "Of all the days to say something like that—of all days, we should be good to each other."

I don't say anything. Instead, I just stand there, staring at her back. Around us caskets shine in the darkness.

Then she wipes her face with her wad of Kleenex, but there are no tears on her face. "Now, we just have to get through tomorrow, and then we can concentrate on finding who did this, and put it behind us. That's what Pauly would've wanted." She blows her nose and straightens herself.

Softly I say, "Pauly would've wanted a place to go. That's what he would've wanted."

"No, I won't have any of this today. DeLuca's closes in forty-five minutes and I'm not waiting around for you to sober up. I'm not going to have a house full of people and no food."

I focus on the window. Curtains mute the gray light that comes through.

"I just keep thinking, Ma. There was a time when you and me

loved him more than anybody else in the world."

"You don't know the first thing about what I felt for that boy." She dabs her temple with her tissue and starts moving toward the curtain. "Forget it. I'll have Father take me. I'll tell him my son is drunk at his own brother's funeral." She begins to move past me.

"They told me it was a possibility."

She stops moving, tilts her head up at me, but doesn't speak.

"They're not sure what happened. But they think it may not be a homicide."

"You're a liar," she says. She yanks her arm from my grip. "You're drunk and you don't know what the hell you're talking about. They said it was a homicide. They said it right to my face."

I look her straight in the eyes. "I'm sorry, Ma."

She studies my face for a moment. "Why are you saying this to me? Why would you say something like that about my Pauly?"

"Because you need to know."

She turns her back to me again. "Don't give me that. You don't know a goddamned thing. If they said that, they're liars. It's impossible."

From beyond the curtain, Murphy: "Eily? Everything okay in there?"

"Fine, Pat, fine. I'll be right out."

"Can I get you anything?"

"No, Pat," Ma snaps. Corrects her tone. "Thank you, though. I'll be right out." She is shaking, and she whispers without looking at me, "Look at what you've done. Why are you so hell-bent on shaming this family? Dragging in all those bums, spending half the wake at Flynn's, spouting off ugliness in front of Father and Murphy. You have no respect for me. And you sure as hell have no respect for your brother."

"Ma, he had nowhere to go."

"Don't give me that! What the hell was I supposed to do? He comes into my house, urinates all over everything, threatens to kill me. And a lot of help you were, I might add. If we'd had a man in the household it wouldn't have had to be that way. But you've never taken responsibility, you've always been a child—just a hateful, jealous child. That's all this is, is jealousy. You think I don't know that?"

She backs away from me, arms crossed. Her eyes shift around the room crazily, and in the stillness of the room I hear her breaths, quivering as each moves through her. Beyond the curtain there's complete quiet, as if everyone has gone. After a time, she lifts her head and looks at me. Her eyes are alive with anguish. "Emmet."

I look beyond her, to the window. Softly I say, "They didn't want to hurt you."

She stands there, waiting for me to look her in the eyes. At that moment, when I turn to look at her, I think I do believe, I tell myself I believe. "I'm sorry, Ma."

She drops her head and covers her face. "I just don't understand. They told me themselves. They looked right at me and told me themselves."

"Everything will be okay, Ma. I promise. I'll take you where you need to go, and we'll get the food and get through tomorrow and everything will be okay."

She folds into herself, shakes with sobbing. "What was I supposed to do? I prayed for him every night, every night I prayed for God to spare him."

I reach out and set my hand awkwardly on her back. "I know, Ma. I heard you. You prayed for him all the time."

"He had a place to go. But he chose what he chose." She gasps and I try to still her. "Tell me. What was I supposed to do?"

"All we knew to do was love him, Ma. We couldn't do anything else."

Her crying is high and strained. "I just can't believe—Paul never would have—I was so afraid—but I knew he had a core in him—"

"He wasn't the same near the end, Ma, you know that. He wasn't our Pauly."

It's dusk now. Beyond the window there's only darkness, and the streetlights have come on. It seems like a long time that I stand beside her, my hand on her back, and listen to her cry. Then she says quietly, "The funeral tomorrow. Father's got to know."

"No, Ma—it's not for sure."

"Even if it's a possibility, Father's got to know."

"No, Ma. Father doesn't have to know. Nobody else ever has to know. Just you and me, Ma. Nobody else."

I reach for her, and she falls into me. For a second I tell myself that God will forgive me, that Pauly would've understood. But then I realize, in a stab of grief that leaves me breathless for a second, that I don't even care. For now I hold Ma and listen to her cries, my own whisper like a stranger's, hushing her, telling her everything will be okay. It's as if the ground that's been between us is opening, taking us in.

The Temple of Air

Patricia Ann McNair

When I saw Mom sneak a pack of HiDeeHo cupcakes out from the bottom of the pan cupboard and slip them into the pocket of her sky blue bathrobe, naturally I thought they were for me. It was my birthday after all, we were supposed to do that kind of thing for each other, right? Kind of like how I'd get up every morning and start the kettle for her hot water and lemon. Like how I'd turn the shower on for her fifteen minutes before I'd shake her awake so's the whole bathroom would be steamy hot for her. Little things like that. You know. Like a candle in a cupcake. No big deal. Just enough to show she cared.

I gave her some time to get it together down the hall there in her room, sat on the old blue couch and pretended to read one of the newspapers I'd swiped from school. (Mom didn't believe in reading anymore, it weighed her down.) But when nothing happened—I mean nothing, no singing, no yelling "Surprise!" or any of that—I decided to go see what was what. And when I got to Mom's room she was already dressed, her hair still wet and streaming water down the back of her blue cotton turtleneck, and there were no cupcakes to be seen anywhere. Not on her dresser, on her night table, in her hand, or anything.

"Morning, Mom," I said quiet like she likes me to be in the morning (she's not too good at waking up). "Nice day." I stood with my back to the doorjamb, hands deep in my pockets. I tried to slide down and shrink up some because Mom was so teeny she always made me feel like some horse or something. Not like I was all that big. Just five-four and a bit over 110, pretty much average for fourteen (just turned). But Mom was one of those bitty ladies, under five feet and featherweight, doll-sized, more or less.

"Hi, Baby," she said, still looking at her own self in the mirror on the back of her closet door, working a big fat-toothed comb through the tangles in her blond hair. (Mine's dark. Like Dad's.)

"Water ready, Rennie?" she said like she always did.
"Yeah." Like it ever wasn't.
"Put me some lemon in it, 'kay?" Like it was a special request.

But I didn't smart off or anything, I never did. I was about as good a kid as you could imagine. It was just easier that way. And I strolled down the hall like everything was normal to the kitchen and poured water into her blue cup with the shining gold letters "T-o-A" on it and tried not to let the lump in my throat that swelled around my wanting to hear something like "Happy Birthday, Baby" or whatever hurt me. And then it came to me while I was pouring. She probably was setting me up. Right that minute she was probably putting that candle in that silly little sweet-sweet cake and maybe even pulling my present out of someplace at the back of her closet or the bottom of her drawer or wherever she hid things. (I only knew a couple of the places.) So I took my time, squeezed an extra slice of lemon in the mug, and another I pushed down onto the cup's rim like they do in restaurants. I put it all on a plate with a spoon, stomped around extra loud on my way back to her room, gave her time and notice enough to keep the surprise a surprise.

"I'm back," I said, just before I turned into her room, but she was right where I'd left her, on that metal folding chair that was covered with a couple of pillow cases sewn together to look like some sort of slipcovers (which of course they didn't) in front of her mirror, still combing and combing through her stupid tangly hair.

"Took you a while," she said in that way she talked mostly now, sort of dreamy and soft. Like everything that took her attention only took it part way, like something else was going on in her head that didn't really have anything to do with what she was talking about. You know. Like when you're talking to someone and they're eavesdropping on a conversation behind you? They might be answering you, keeping up their part of the conversation and all, but what's going on between you is not what's uppermost on their list at that moment.

When I stepped over to the dresser to set the mug down, I guess you'd have to say I still had my hopes up. But next to the dresser there was Mom's little trash basket she'd got at the Temple, the one the same sky blue as her mug (and chair covers and sheets and blankets and throw rugs and lampshades and pajamas and our couch and and and) with the same gold "T-o-A" stenciled on its side and inside the thing was some Kleenex and stuff, and underneath that, I could see—because there really wasn't much in there, just all jumbled up to sort of look like a lot—was the empty cupcake holder. Pushed down under the jumble, hidden away, really. Like Mom does when she's been eating stuff she's not supposed to, hiding the evidence. And when I looked at Mom in the mirror, I could see the slightest trace of crumbs on her shirt, that shiny chocolate stuff that crumbles from the HiDeeHos no matter how careful you are to try to keep them from falling apart. And at that moment I was so ticked off and hot it was like steam filled my head. "You got crumbs," I said and pointed, and she said "What? What?" all shrill like she does whenever you say something like that, something about eating. It's the only time she ever seems to pay attention to the conversation, and that's just because she has to be on her guard to get her story straight, that story about not eating anything, nothing, surviving on air, Air Only, like they tell you you can at the Temple. But only if you are worthy, truly worthy, like the floaters and the High One himself, Sky. (I kid you not, that's his name, Sky. The High One, Sky.) So most times Mom's pretending to survive just on air, and it's clear that she is doing that a good bit of the time as skinny as she is and spacey, but then there's those times she cheats, or Sins, as they call it at the Temple. "Forgive us our Sins," they say, but usually they're just talking about eating, if you could imagine. Like feeding yourself, taking nourishment could ever, *ever*, be called a sin.

And then "I'm late!" she says, still shrill and jumps up and brushes a hand over her chest that used to have boobs, not big ones, but something more than that flat plane she's got now, and grabs her purse up (sky blue vinyl, like some old-lady Easter purse), and pushes past me and down the hall. And before I have time to say "Good-bye" or "Sorry" or "Hey, haven't you forgotten something—like the day I was born, maybe?" she's at the door and yelling back "Your father's here!" And I'm fighting to not cry, it's just a birthday, for God's sake, baby birthday shit, and hoping that maybe Dad's remembered, but knowing that will never happen, it's like some miracle he's remembered it's Saturday, our day, and that he's remembered his deal with the judge to do something with me, his only kid, his flesh and blood, one day a week, that he's remembered to come here at all. And I'm hoping as I tie the laces on my Nike Airs that maybe if he doesn't remember it's my birthday, I'll be able to forget, too. And maybe then it won't hurt so bad.

———

"Where's your mom off to?" Dad asked when I stepped up into the cab of his jacked-high pickup.

"Church," I said, mostly because I was still mad and Mom hates it when I call it that. It's Temple or Service or even Worship.

"Again?" Dad said, and when I looked over in his direction I could see he hadn't shaved for a few days and his black hair wasn't combed and judging from his wrinkled-up T-shirt and sweats he might have just rolled out of bed and jumped into the truck and come right over out of a dream. He smelled like beer.

We drove for a time, neither of us saying anything. It dawned on me that I was singing in my head, "Happy Birthday to Me, Happy Birthday to Me . . ." Then Dad said something, but I couldn't hear.

"What?"

"Fucking church shit!" He said and spit out the window. "Your fucking mom and that fucking church shit!"

Well it's probably clear to you by now that that pretty much sums up how I was feeling right then, too, but you know how it goes. You can say whatever you want to about your family to whoever you want to, you know, like "My sister is such a bitch" or "My grandfather is a perv" or "My dad is nothing but a drunk," and whoever you are talking to can even nod a little along with you as long as they don't actually say anything out loud. But no one else, no one else, can talk trash about your folks. Not even your own father.

"Shut up," I said without thinking. It just slipped out while I was still singing Happy Birthday in my head. I suppose I thought that I'd said it in my head, too, but I didn't. And as soon as they hit the air in front of me, those words, I imagined myself saying them into a big balloon like they do in comics and imagined myself reaching these hands up from out of my throat (heart hands, maybe, or soul hands) and pulling the string of the balloon back inside, the whole thing deflating its way back into me, and me swallowing it all down to my gut. And that entire little scene had to play out in just a millisecond, because in the next moment Dad's hand was where the balloon had been in front of my mouth and was closing in fast and smacking me—hard—across the teeth.

"Shut you up," he hissed, and that worked, because that's just what I did, I shut up and slid tight against the door and blinked and blinked and blinked the tears back (Baby, Big Birthday Baby) and decided right then I was not going to say another word to anyone all damn day. I ran my tongue over my smarting gums. Shut me up.

Of course, Dad hated that. See, he had that quick temper, but he also had that quick remorse some guys do, you know, a spanking followed by a hug. He needed you to tell him it's okay, you understood. So he was all soft-spoken then as we drove on down the highway past the old logging road that led to the lake, past County Road G and GG.

"It's just that—" he started and put a hand out to my shoulder and I had to hold on tight to the handle of the door to keep from shrugging out from under him, "your mother gets so confused. Well, you know that. And she is so gullible." And then he chuckled a bit, quiet, like he was remembering some little gullibility of Mom's from the past.

I didn't say a word.

"Like remember how she started selling that NewTriVision junk?" And he chuckled again, no doubt thinking about when I was around five and we were still all together in that little house in town (the brown one, all earth tones inside) and Mom had the whole front room stacked with boxes of NewTriVision powdered shakes and NewTriVision lo-cal cookies and NewTriVision tuna foodstuff or whatever it was in those little cans (the three—"Tri"—staples of the NewTriVision plan). And every night Dad would come home wanting dinner, and every night Mom would try to serve him up one of those "NewTri-cious and Delicious Complete Meal Replacement Drinks." I could still remember how he laughed the first time she tried that, dressed herself up in some white short-shorts and tank top and that white NewTriVision apron with the yellow triangles on it (the one all the Tri-ologists got just for signing up) and sat on Dad's lap on the brand-new brown plaid couch and put the frosty mug of the stuff to his lips. And I can still remember how he pulled his head back, but not until his mustache was frothy with what was supposed to be vanilla shake but looked as faky yellow as banana bubblegum and, well, not at all appetizing. And when Dad said, "What's this?" and licked the goop from his mustache and made a horrible tight face but kept his hands on Mom's tiny little waist and she said "Dinner," he threw back his head and howled. And it was clear from where I was, at their feet on the braided rug tracing the yellow letters on the NewTriVision boxes over with a magenta crayon, that Mom didn't like that Dad was laughing at her, and she put her head down and her lip out, but Dad kissed her neck and pulled her close and said "Sorry, Baby. I'm sorry. It's just that that's no meal for a working man is all." And she tried to tell him it was, "what with all the vitamins and minerals in it that fulfilled a hearty part of one's suggested daily requirements as determined by highly trained NewTritionists." But Dad just laughed low while he went into the kitchen and pulled a Swanson's from the freezer and cooked it up for himself.

And as the days went on like that, and the boxes stayed in the front room and Mom spent more and more time on the phone "recruiting," she called it, and Dad started working less and less with the weather turning cold and construction jobs finishing up, and dinner never getting made unless you were willing to try one of those fishy canned things or a shake (personally, I sort of went for the chocolate ones), well, Dad wasn't laughing so much anymore. And I can still remember when the fights started in the middle of the night, Dad talking low at first and Mom's voice starting out bright and tight and cheery like it was when she recruited. And then Dad would get mad and loud and yell about money and real work and Mom would babble about the miracle of success and the slow climb up the ladder and Dad would say "Ladder? What fucking ladder? It's a pyramid, Maddie, can't you see? It's a pyramid game—only they're illegal so they're doing this—" and here I'd hear him slap or kick one of the dusty old boxes—"instead!" "But I'm on top, Ray, don't you get it?" Mom would say, her voice excited and filled with what I guess now I might call hope. But Dad would come right back with "On top? On top?! There's only a top when there's a bottom. You got nothing, Maddie. Nothing. It's just you. Good old bottomless Maddie." And sometimes in my bed in my room listening, I'd giggle at that, because Mom was getting so skinny it meant something different to me than what Dad said. "But my prospects, Ray. My prospects," and usually about this time Mom's voice would crack a little and go soft and that always quieted Dad down, too, and this quiet talk hurt me more than all the rest of it because it seemed so thick with a sadness that even then I guess I knew I'd get to feel soon enough. I was just a kid then, you've got to remember. And at this point in the arguments I'd squeeze my whole self into a little ball under my covers and stick my thumb in my mouth and rub my forefinger up and down, up and down the slope of my nose until it went numb. It wasn't long after that I'd be asleep.

We were getting close to town now, me and Dad, and my mouth didn't hurt anymore but I still hadn't said anything since he slapped me, and I could tell from the way he was squinting and working a hand over the leg of his jeans that he was getting sore.

"Remember?" he said again, and of course I did, you know, but I wasn't talking. I rolled down my window. It was one of those summer-warm days, and the sky had that gold in it that it gets come fall. At the edge of town, the dry, stripped cornfields turned to trees with patches of red and yellow in the leaves. "And remember that—what was it?—Glamorous Miss crap that came next? 'Ray,' she'd say. 'You were right about that other stuff,'" and here he was making his voice all high and singsongy like guys do when they pretend to talk like girls. I hate that voice.

But Dad was right. I even remember Mom saying that, "You were right about that other stuff," only not in the voice he was faking, but in her bright, tight, hope-filled voice. "*This* is it, Ray," she'd say. "*This* is it, Rennie," she'd say to me, too. And then she'd practice her pitch on the both of us, sell her way through the Miss Miracle Line. I'd bet she'd've been glad to sign us up, me even, a little kid who didn't have any money but what she gave me and who was too young to wear the goo Glamorous Miss had her pushing. "Maddie, don't you see?" Dad would say when she'd start to draw her business plan on the big pad and easel Glam Miss gave to all its Glamorists, a triangular stack of empty squares where she'd fill in the names of her "downline" as she "engaged" them. "Look, Maddie," Dad would say and push back his dining-room chair, knocking over a stack of crates marked GLASS FRAGILE, and Mom would gasp and put a hand over her mouth when Dad grabbed from her the complimentary pointer stick (silvery pink Glamorous Miss in cursive up its shaft) and traced the shape of her plan. "Pyramid, Maddie. PYR—" he ran the pink rubber tip up one side "A—" then down the other "*MID!*" he'd swipe the stick across the bottom of the page, ripping it. And there was no telling who would storm out of there first, but soon it would be eight-year-old me by myself at the table wondering if there might still be some of that ice cream Mom had stuffed away in the back of the freezer behind the ice pack and freezer-burned rock-solid roaster chicken. Mom had never gone back to real eating after NewTriVision introduced her to her New Thin Self, so there usually wasn't much in the house besides that. That and Dad's beer.

Dad was stepping on the brakes now that we'd passed the town limits sign and the SLOW 35 MPH posting. And as we cruised the avenue past the park, I could see the slumped shoulders of the usual kids, and Mary Ann's dyed orange head, I was pretty sure, and maybe Ricky's army jacket. But I couldn't have done anything with them anyway when I was with my Dad, birthday or no. And then we were easing across the intersection of Main and Edison where the Temple was—just a storefront in a half-block-long strip with Phil-Bert's Ice Cream Shoppe and a dentist office and a day care, and we couldn't help but see Mom's car out front. The big old Ford Fairmont—a leftover from who knows when—boxy and much too blue to go unnoticed next to the dusty pickups and wagons and compacts.

"So now it's church, huh?" Dad said sort of loud and narrowed his eyes before he pushed hard on the gas so his tires squealed. And he looked at me, raised his eyebrows up like "Well, got some insight here, smart girl?" But like I said, I wasn't talking. Only now it wasn't just out of principle, out of sticking to my secret pledge to shut me up. Now it also had to do with what I knew about the Temple of Air—Mom's church—and how it would really tick Dad off to know that this wasn't at all a different thing from those others (NewTriVision, Glamorous Miss, and the two or three more things Mom tried after he left), but instead it was painfully, horribly, exactly the same.

Like how you had to sell stuff to achieve a Higher Level. And while there was the usual junk: coffee mugs and T-shirts and bumper stickers (Air Head—I swear to God—Aboard) all sky blue and marked with the gold "T-o-A", the High One, Sky, wanted more. He had bigger ideas. He figured they could sell everything that had anything even remotely to do with air. So as you'd expect, there was air freshener and balloons and kites and wind chimes and wind socks and fans. Even some old-fashioned gliders made out of that wood that's lighter than a Popsicle stick. And then there was the other stuff: blow-dryers, vacuum cleaner bags, and, no kidding, whoopee cushions. Now to me those last things were a stretch, and (maybe it's just me) sort of, well, disrespectful.

"I hear rumors those people are supposed to be able to fly," Dad said. We were pulling into the PitStop, so I knew he was going for beer and cigarettes, which meant we'd probably go back to his place where he'd smoke and drink and jump from channel to channel with his universal remote control. Some birthday.

I looked at him.

"Hear me?" Dad asked. "I said, I hear rumors they're supposed to be flying in there."

Floating, I wanted to tell him, they call it floating. But now I was too deep into this shut-me-up stuff, so I kept it zipped.

"What, you believe this shit?" Of course I didn't. What'd he think I was, some goof? But I wasn't talking. And even if I was, I wasn't sure I'd tell him what I knew. How each member starts on the ground. Earthbound, they call it. And how by selling all that junk and bringing in new members and not eating and probably some other weird this and that, you got a little higher and higher off the ground. Mostly it's figurative, this off-the-ground thing, but supposedly, those who are truly worthy—well, like Dad said, there are rumors. But he wasn't going to hear it from me.

Dad put the truck in park and faced me. I stared at him. "Do you believe this shit? This flying shit?" He waited for me to answer, which, you already know, I wasn't doing. "Huh? Huh?"

Now I'm not a fool, I knew what was coming. But even if I started talking now, it wouldn't have made any difference. You know. So why bother? I just grabbed hold of the door handle like I did when he took me four-wheeling and held on for the ride. "You believe this shit?" And then it was like an explosion, the cab of the truck filled with his hollering. "Fine. You believe it. You just fucking believe it." And he balled up his fists on his thighs. "You and your mom. Exactly the same. Fine. How about it? Would you rather be with her right now? Want to be with her at that—that—church?" He started to sputter, and I just kept my grip on the handle and watched his whole body shake. "You want to go with her? Fly around? Do you? Do you?" His face was close to mine now, and the beer smell was right there on his skin, like he was sweating the stuff. His eyes, right up in front of my own, looked electric and shut off at the same time. How did he do that? And then he reached behind me for the handle, slapped my hands off it, and pulled it up. "Go. Get the fuck out of here. You want to fly? You fly! Fly away, chicky!" I nearly fell out of the big old truck, but I got a foot down first to right myself. I sure didn't want anyone to see me on my ass on the cracked cement of the PitStop lot. On my ass on my birthday. And then Dad was squealing tires out of the place, the door hanging open and flapping on the side of the cab until the truck turned hard back onto Main and it slammed itself closed.

Fine.

He'd be back. I wasn't worried. He always came back. But this time, I'd be gone.

I somehow ended up at the little brown house. A big hand-lettered sign stuck in the patchy front yard read "For Rent," and underneath in smaller letters, "furnished" and "like new." Around back was an alley I used to ride my bike up and down. The earth-colored couch, the one Mom and Dad and I used to sit on to watch *Family Ties* together, stood upended against the garage. The cushions, worn through so the stuffing popped out of their centers, were stacked in a sad little pile. And seeing it all there, our house empty and our furniture garbage (sure it had been three years since we lived there, and we were just renters, but still), well, it was more than I could take. I put my butt down on that little pile of pillows, sunk close to the ground, and cried.

Big Birthday Baby.

Well, you know how it goes. Crying and feeling sorry for yourself only works for a little while, and once I'd had enough of it, I had to figure out the trick of getting home. No way was I going to Dad's. I liked the idea of him rolling back into the PitStop, all slow and sorry, and not finding me there. Maybe going in and asking at the counter, maybe knocking on the ladies' room door. And then cruising the avenue, under the speed limit and watchful. Getting scared maybe. Especially when he'd pull into the park, sure that he'd find me there, and no one would've seen me. That'd teach him.

I decided to go to the Temple and wait for Mom out in the parking lot. It was just a couple of blocks, but I kept to the alleys and side streets so there'd be no chance of running into Dad.

———

"Can you see anything?"

The voice, out of the clear blue like that, made me jump. I whirled around from where I was trying to see through the Temple's front window.

"Are they flying?"

He was less than a foot from me. I don't know how he got there without my hearing, but there he was. I knew this guy. Everyone in town did. Well, knew of him, I mean. He was the homeless guy. That's what we called him. No one I knew knew his real name, and he was the only person who was homeless in town. The Homeless Guy. Only, up close, he didn't look how you'd expect a homeless guy to look. Sure his hair was long and he had a raggedy beard and jeans and a shirt all worn through in those spots that go first (knees, elbows, butt), but from where I stood he looked clean and, well, as far as I could tell, sane. Like he stood up tall and wasn't talking to himself and wasn't scratching or squinting or whatever you might expect some crazy homeless guy to be doing.

"Jim," he said and held out a hand to me. A surprisingly clean hand.

The way I saw it, I had a couple of options here. I could keep on not talking, ignore the guy. But that would be rude, and my mom didn't raise me to be rude. And I wasn't mad at this guy—heck, since I'd sat down and had that cry, I wasn't really mad much at all anymore. So it didn't seem quite right to take things out on this Jim. So, "Hi," I said, taking the second option, the talking one, "I'm Rennie." But I kept my hands to myself. I figured I was just fourteen, it was okay if I wasn't into shaking hands.

"Did you see them fly?" Jim stepped in front of me and put his eye up against the window where I'd been looking through. There was a little space between the blue curtain and the wall inside, but the angle wasn't right. All you could see was the edge of a blackboard or something. "There's a better place to watch from," he said, his head still pressed up against the glass. His words made a circle of steam on it. "Wanna see?"

I really just wanted to go home. But I was pretty much stuck. I wasn't allowed in the Temple, Mom had made that clear the last time I went with her a couple of months ago and made the mistake of asking if it would be all right to have one of the candy bars she always kept in her purse. You'd think I'd asked for a joint or a gun or something, the way the whole "congregation" gasped and tsked. Mom got so red I thought she'd pop. And so here I was stuck outside waiting for her, and the Temple was open for another hour. And Mom never, ever left Temple early.

"Sure," I said to the guy and shrugged just enough to show him how much I didn't really care. "Let's see."

And then the thing is, I was following this guy who didn't really look crazy like I said, but who I had pretty much come to believe was crazy ever since I first saw him right here, in front of the Temple, sleeping in the doorway some months ago. And even though he didn't look like what I expected (damn TV shows, give you all sorts of wrong ideas), he still wasn't anyone I knew or should trust. And at first I had all those thoughts you get, you know, He's gonna kill me, or He's gonna rape me, or He's gonna mug me—and in that order, starting with the worst and then getting less and less serious. But there was something about this guy. Something quiet. Quiet, but intense. It might have been scary, this way he was, like if you met him in some back alley or someplace dark and deserted, maybe. But as we went around the side of the building, past the day care and behind the place, in all this broad daylight, I wasn't scared at all after a while. We climbed up onto a crate, then up onto the top of a dumpster, then he reached high and grabbed hold of the wall that edged the roof and used a door frame to step up and over. He held a hand down to me and finally I got the door frame under my foot and was up and over and onto the roof next to him. Then he turned his back on me and started fast across the roof, the tails of his shirt flapping behind him. I followed, slower though, my hands deep in my pockets.

And you know what? Up high like that, I have to admit, things looked pretty good. The tops of the trees were bright with those leaves turning red, turning yellow and orange. You could see all the way down Main Street to where the highway came in, and the fields beyond town tilted up with the rise of the land. Shimmering, it looked like from up there.

"Here," Jim said waving me in. He fell to his knees and pushed his face against the roof. I kneeled next to him. He smelled like the woods around the lake. Like fresh air and damp earth. "Yup," he said and moved a little to the side so I could get a look. "There's old Sky himself." I was surprised that he knew the High One's name, but I guess it's sort of like how I knew he was the Homeless Guy. In a town this small, everyone knew everyone who wasn't one of the regulars.

I looked through the crack, just a small opening, but big enough to see through with one eye. And the place was exactly as I remembered it, pale blue and empty pretty much, except for a couple of bulletin boards and blue blackboards and the display case where they kept the smaller things they sold. The only thing different was that the chairs were out of the way, folded up and pushed off to the sides, and the floor was covered with mats. Big, lumpy mats, like they had in the wrestling room at school. Blue mats.

I saw my mom. I recognized the top of her head, although I'm not entirely sure how, since I don't know that I ever looked at it before—but I did. She sat in the middle of the mat, her legs crossed over in that way people do, swamis and stuff, the feet on top of the knees. I didn't know she could do that. And there was Sky, skinny as a reed, in front of her on the mat, sitting the same way. Even from up here I could see how tan he was, especially in his blue roby thing, and I thought like I did whenever I saw him that it was funny how he always looked sort of windswept. His bright blond hair flew back away from his face—from using the official Temple blow-dryers, no doubt. They were knees-to-knees, Mom and Sky, no one else was there. They sat absolutely still.

"Are they flying?" Jim asked. If someone else asked me this question, I'd pretty much have to think they were joking. Flying. Right. But Jim sounded really sincere. Not like he was making fun or anything. Like he really wanted to know. Like it could ever be possible.

"No," I said, keeping watch. The two beneath me didn't move. I tilted my head a little so I could use the other eye for a while. But nothing happened. They sat, and I sat watching.

I don't know how long I had my eye pressed against that crack waiting for something to happen (which never did) but when I sat back up, rolled the kinks out of my neck, and looked around, Jim was gone.

Back on solid ground again, I went into Phil-Bert's. The place was empty except for one of the old twins, Phil, I think, or maybe Bert. And in that place that never changed (tinny door chimes, eight-panel menu board, white plastic tables and chairs, red trim at the tops and bottoms of the bright white walls), I couldn't help but remember when I was five, the first time we came here, Mom, Dad, and me, on my birthday—back when Mom would still eat in public. "Whatever you want," Dad had said as he lifted me up so I could see into the big tubs. Twenty-three regular flavors and four monthly specials. Millions of possible combinations. "Whatever I want," I said to myself after I let go of the memory, and ordered the biggest thing they had: triple banana split, whipped cream, nuts, and cherries. Why shouldn't I?

At the front table by the window, I dug in. When I stopped eating long enough to get a breath, I looked up and there was Jim. Outside looking in. I waved to him, and I guess he took that to mean come on in, because that's what he did. The chimes banged on the door as he passed through, then he came over and plopped into the little white plastic chair across from me.

"Looks good," he said, "special treat?"

"Yeah," I said. I was halfway through the middle scoop (rocky road) and working my way toward the rainbow sherbet. "It's my birthday," I said. And it was sort of like letting loose a secret you've been dying to tell. Once I said it I was glad I'd said it, but a little—oh, I don't know—ashamed, I guess.

"Yeah, well, happy birthday," Jim said.

"Thanks," I said, and looked at him. He had an okay face. One of those smooth ones that makes it hard to tell how old a person is, but I figured him for twenty or so. He had bright blue eyes, kind of gold, too, like the autumn sky. Or maybe it was just a reflection. He stared at my banana split, followed the spoon from the banana boat to my mouth and back with those eyes. It got to be kind of hard to keep eating, him watching me like that, so I put the spoon down and tried to come up with something to say. I looked out the window at Mom's big blue car, then over at the plate glass front of the Temple.

"You know Sky?" I asked.

"Used to," Jim said. He kept his eyes on the ice cream.

"When was that?"

"Back as kids. Long time ago. But we parted ways." He scratched a spot on his nose and looked up. "You, uh, gonna finish that?"

Well, I wanted to. Bad. But it didn't seem quite right then, so I shook my head and pushed the banana boat across the tabletop toward him. He reached for my spoon and scooped up a mound of the stuff. I watched him for a bit. It was like there was barely time for one spoonful to melt in his mouth before he shoved another one in there.

"Parted ways how?" I asked when he stopped long enough to wipe his mouth with the back of his hand. "I mean, besides the obvious."

"Obvious?"

"Yeah, you know. The eating. You guys clearly have different ideas about eating."

"That so?" He closed his mouth around a spoon of rainbow. He went back to work on the banana split without answering my question. I tried again.

"Were you ever a member of the Temple?"

Jim just snorted. Green-and-pink sherbet spotted the edges of his mustache.

"But you know about the floating."

Jim shrugged and picked up the boat with both hands and licked the inside clean. Then he slid it aside, tilted his head slightly. Behind him I could see Phil working a towel over the counter, cleaning like he always did.

I didn't say anything for a bit, and neither did Jim. I don't think he intended to do much talking. So I went on. "Do you know how that floating stuff goes?" Jim shook his head. "I do. I've seen it."

"Yeah?"

"Yeah. Supposedly Sky is the one who can really float. You know, truly worthy and all. And a couple of the others sort of can." I figured he must know this, but he let me keep talking. "It's not floating, though," I said. "It's jumping." Jim leaned across the table, watched my mouth as I spoke. I couldn't help but lean back a bit. "Seriously. They sit like we just saw them sitting," I pointed my thumb out toward the parking lot, "and then they gather up all this energy, and jump. They keep their legs crossed, so it doesn't quite look like jumping. But that's what they're doing. Only they're so full of themselves and so dizzy from not eating they think they're levitating. A few inches off the ground and a couple feet covered. Big whip. You ask me, that's not floating."

"What about Sky?" Jim says in a polite way, like he's taking part in the conversation just to be nice, like maybe I'm not telling him anything he doesn't already know.

"Same thing. Only he's really good at it. He rises up pretty high and goes a pretty long way. To me it's like he's the champion of the cross-legged long jump. And whenever he does it—and he rarely does, you know, to keep the mystery going—everyone starts sighing and gets all quiet. Like they've just witnessed the second coming or whatever. Like it's a goddamn miracle."

Jim's staring hard at me now, his sky eyes locked with mine. I've got to look away.

"No such thing as a miracle," I say.

And that's when I hear the squeal of tires in the parking lot behind us, and I know even before I look that it's my dad. And when I do look, there's Mom, too, coming out of the Temple doorway. She sees Dad's truck first, and I can't help but notice how she reaches a hand up to her hair and smooths it down, how she puts her shoulders back and holds her head high, like she used to when she heard him come into the door of the little brown house: "Honey? I'm home!" And I notice, too, through the dusty windshield of his truck, how Dad smiles first when he sees Mom, and then how he runs a hand over his face and pulls the smile off. And how when Mom sees him do this, she frowns, too. And I know I've got to get out there before it really hits the fan, and I jump up quick and hold out a hand to Jim, which he shakes.

"See ya," I say.

"Yup," he says.

I dash to the door and pull it open, and here's where things get weird. The chimes that have been ringing in that place for as long as I can remember sound different then. Brighter and, well, sort of magical.

"Rennie," Jim says, and I turn to see him stand. Funny thing is, he's much taller than I remember, his head rising closer and closer to the ceiling. And then his feet are hovering over the tabletop, and I follow the line of his legs up past the holes in the knees of his jeans, let my eyes make their way to his.

"Happy Birthday to you, Rennie," he says. And I quick look around to see if Phil's seeing this, too, but his head is down in the freezer case, attending to some cleaning matter. And I look back toward the parking lot to see if maybe Mom and Dad—but they're standing face-to-face and talking, not yelling or anything, just talking. And I look again and Jim's still up there, floating and floating and floating. He smiles at me, and nods. "There you go," he says, and then I nod, because the way I see it, that's pretty much all there is for me to do.

And so I step out onto the sidewalk and start to cross the parking lot toward Mom and Dad, and they turn and see me, and they both get that look of relief only parents can have at those times when they know their kid is safe from whatever. And I'm thinking maybe my folks will remember now, maybe we'll go out and celebrate or something, I mean it is still my birthday, right? But then the look starts to turn a little gray on each of their faces, and I know what to expect next. I glance back over my shoulder and into Phil-Bert's, and it's just Phil in there now, clearing the table, throwing away my empty. And then up ahead I see Dad reaching for his belt and Mom's eyes go blank and spacey.

So that's when I do it. Float, I mean. I just swallow and swallow and fill up with air and close my eyes and rise. I rise up and out of this here, up and out of this now. I lift and lift, higher and higher, over the tops of their heads, over the tops of the trees starting to die, over the top of the Goddamn Temple of Air. Over and over and over it all. I'm floating, dammit. I'm floating.

Still Waters

Ellie Mering

Murderers, undoubtedly, have pressed ears against the receiver and spat words into the mouthpiece he holds intimately close. Wayne Hightower is unable to position the instrument as far from him as he'd like and still hear his sister, Emma. When she calls him Buddy, his boyhood name, nostalgia bubbles through him. Yet he's aggravated, too.

"Why can't you plain hang up the phone, jump in your old station wagon, and come get me out of this mess?" he asks her. "All you have to do is vouch for me and take me home with you."

"It's Little Willie, Buddy," she says. "The vet . . . he had to put Little Willie to sleep." Emma starts to cry, then struggling, continues in a broken voice. "I'm on pills till I get calm. P-r-o-z-a-c. Heard of it? Monday then, let's hope." Abruptly, she says goodbye.

Emma is the reason Wayne chose Arizona as a place to retire. She lived in Parker, was his only relative, and blood ran thick. At least it used to run thick, but now she's gone and mentioned her own brother in the same breath with pissing pooping fornicating Boston Bull terrier Little Willie who lusted after pant legs and would have just as soon dug up your petunias as look at you. The late Little Willie.

Wayne, sitting on a cot in the police station's holding room, resumes picking at his foot. He suspects that one tiny horn of a goat's-head burr has lodged in the tender region between his big toe and the one next to it, though without his bifocals he can't be certain. His foot is beginning to burn. Does he imagine it or is that a red line he sees? Extraordinary, how so small an annoyance as a sticker can bring down such a strapping specimen as himself.

Wayne is a big man. Once his wife Adele told him, "When I'm angry with you, Wayne, there's such an awful lot to be angry with." Then she'd returned to her peeling or scrubbing or darning—the woman's fingers never stopped. He'd not bothered to find out how he'd angered her in the first place. Adele must have been very very angry this time.

A redheaded clerk presents Wayne with a breakfast tray: Special K to be eaten from a cardboard container; orange juice, warm to the touch; a Styrofoam of pale coffee; a small carton of milk. One white plastic spoon is all the table silver he gets.

He should be out-of-his-head furious with Adele. Instead, he finds himself longing for her breakfasts. Nothing ever delivered more pure reliable pleasure than Adele's breakfasts. Sex was okay, a close second he supposes, but you could not count on sex, not even with Kitty, not the way you could count on pushing golden clumps of homemade marmalade over the peaks and valleys of Adele's thick sourdough toast. He closes his eyes and strains to imagine the special feeling against the roof of his mouth, flavors mingling, bitter and sweet, mixed with the rush from the first sip of fresh-ground, fresh-brewed coffee.

He takes a swallow of the Styrofoam stuff in front of him and grimaces. It occurs to him—never thought of it before—that he'd not once told Adele how important her breakfasts were. Not once. No question but he is a damn fool and his damn foolery has pushed him to this point and how can he save himself or is it already too late?

———

It was at breakfast in North Dakota where he'd laid down his plans. "What I'm going to do, Adele," he'd said, pulling out a chair. "Listen to this. Put down that fry pan. What I'm going to do is retire and buy us a condo down in Seeco City, Arizona." Then he babbled on about the shadows of the Santa Rita's and wall-to-wall carpets. Sounded like the damn brochure that had come the day before, when North Dakota wind was driving pea-sized sleet into his face. Felt like BB shot.

A wave of guilt floods him. That is the weirdest part, not fury at Adele, but even as his foot begins to throb, this guilt thing is trying to knock him down.

The fact is Wayne was happy in North Dakota. Even with a wind-chill factor dipping to eighty degrees below, two hundred-pound sandbags in the car trunk so's not to skid, headbolt heater on the engine. Damn happiness. Happiness is something you don't know you have until later when it's over and finished and done with. Then you get to look back and think, by golly, so that was happiness.

Well, he recognizes it now and longs for another morning in the little house on Hamline Street in Grand Hope, to lie in a tangle of Adele's sweet-smelling sheets and the old down comforter, for cooking smells rising through the registers, telling him Adele's in her kitchen, all's right with the world.

Wayne's head begins to pound. If he were a woman, he'd be boohooing and popping aspirin. At least, he's got enough pride not to call an attorney, which would only make things out to be as bad as they are, let alone the money the man would want. A small miracle he has half a cup of sense left after the hell he's been through.

―――――

Once he decided on Arizona, things happened. He'd barely put Hightower Plumbing and Supply on the market when a bright young fellow bought him out: ball cocks, flanges, float arms, and all. Went on and bought the Hightower house, too. A real go-getter. Reminded Wayne of himself, when he was young.

While passing papers at the bank, Wayne paused to wonder if he were losing every bit of his identity, but the blizzard raging outside centered him, and he signed his name with a flourish.

"We'll take this living-room stuff," he explained to Adele, once they were home again. He waved at the couch and the recliners, a sweep of his arm including the end tables and the flat-top mahogany desk. "I've lined up a moving date with Olaf over at Mayflower. That old organ of yours—we'll wait and see what it costs to move it, Lovey."

"I'd prefer to keep the organ, Wayne," said Adele, softly. "It was Mama's, and you know how I like playing my old hymns."

It was a fact that on the rare mild day when a window could be opened, he'd hear strains of "Bringing in the Sheaves" or "Rock of Ages" as he came up the sidewalk after work, but Adele's attitude mystified him. She'd never questioned his decisions.

After the movers gave their estimate, Wayne whistled.

"No way we're taking that organ," he said. "That baby weighs more than half a ton. We'll pick us up one of those CD players."

The disappointment spreading across Adele's face softened him. He said maybe they'd find something down in Arizona, but as he spoke he thought it unlikely there'd be space for an organ in a condo. Besides, it challenged a person to take up new interests;

kept you alive.

The night before the Hightowers left town the church choir, where Wayne had sung baritone for thirty-eight years, surprised them with a party. While the Ladies' Auxiliary was serving sheet cake on which colored frostings painted a cowboy lassoing a cactus under a happy sun, Adele stood up.

"I never intended to leave Grand Hope," she said. "Long friendships warm me more than winter chills me. I don't know why Wayne insists on moving."

Was this the same Adele, he wondered, who hardly spoke in front of other people, let alone a room full of them?

When the party was over and the Hightowers stood at the door hugging and shaking hands, Wayne looked over at her and saw tears, bright as dewdrops, trailing down her old powdered cheeks. Were the two of them making a colossal mistake? Then he remembered his nostrils and how the lining inside them froze up when he shoveled the walk.

The next morning Wayne slipped into his new car coat, pulled on gloves and galoshes, and headed for the garage to finish packing the blue Buick. Adele placed Bismarck, their old orange tom, in his bed on the floor of the front seat. Clothes that hadn't fit in the trunk they piled on the backseat. On top of everything, Wayne laid his greatcoat. He'd worn it so many winters that it'd become almost a second skin, and he felt light-headed seeing it off his body. For a moment, he imagined that he had died and his soul was soaring heavenward like a helium balloon, and all that remained on earth of Wayne Hightower was one gray herringbone overcoat with a fur collar and frayed cuffs. Silly thought. He wasn't near ready to die.

———

The Hightowers settled quickly into Seeco City. Wayne liked the mild weather, low taxes, and a feeling of quiet prosperity that seemed to come from carefully spent midwestern money. He liked the sidewalks, smooth and unbuckled from tree roots or hard freezes. Often he and Adele walked through the mall and beyond to a Mexican restaurant where they watched fellow pale-skinned, blue-eyed midwesterners listen solemnly to mariachis and heard them order enchiladas and tostadas, and then did the same themselves.

Sundays, they strolled to Grace Church, where Wayne had already joined the choir. Afterward, they tossed bread crusts to ducks idling in the man-made pond. A pleasant life.

At home, however, their bed was another story. After thirty-eight years on an ordinary double mattress, Wayne had recklessly donated it to the church jumble sale before they left Grand Hope. The new king-sized Posturepedic made Adele seem beyond reach. A terrible loneliness seized him.

One day, after he installed the last closet shelf, it occurred to him that nothing needed fixing. No faucet dripped, no toilet ran. He paused in front of the sliding door to the patio to glower at the No Care yard, which had sounded like a dream come true when he'd read the brochure. He paced the living room, squeezed past Adele in the kitchen, marched down the narrow hall to the bedroom, popping into bathrooms and den, idly flipping light switches, flushing toilets, peering into neat cupboards and drawers, as if searching for something he couldn't name but knew was important.

When he and Adele walked past the driving range, he pondered the hold golf had over grown men. He didn't get it. Before retirement, Wayne was constantly doing. If he wasn't at the store, he was in the warehouse, digging through bins in search of an odd-sized slip nut or a bolt cap of a certain shade or a discontinued clean-out plug. By the end of the day he was too tired to think about hobbies. Now he watched Adele jealously as she went about her routine of household chores while he sat, reflecting how swiftly the years had fled, wondering if his remaining time on earth would go as quickly, disappearing before his eyes like water rushing down a newly cleared drain.

They met on a Tuesday. He remembers, because Tuesday was trash pickup day, and he'd been in the alley behind his place, hoisting trash bags into the communal receptacle, when a woman coming through the oleander startled him. She carried her trash daintily wrapped and tied with red-and-white butcher's string.

"I suppose you'll think I'm another helpless widow, Mr. Hightower," Kitty said with a trillish laugh after they'd introduced themselves. She told him her stove didn't work, but she felt stupid calling the stove people because it might not be anything more than a fuse and could she impose just this once? He looked like the sort of man who'd know about such things.

Wayne swiftly took in Kitty. She was everything Adele wasn't: petite with an expensive scent about her, slender. What Adele would call a "helped" blond. She was Miss Crawley, fifth grade, bending over him to check his numbers, tantalizing him with hints of breasts and other dark mysteries; Lana Gumble, cheerleader, scorning his attentions; Suzanne Something in homeroom who giggled at his jokes but turned down his invitation to the prom. Unattainables who'd been living in his head all these years had melded into a single person but a few doors away.

Kitty's problem was no more than a loose fuse, though Wayne tinkered a while, feeling excitement rising in his groin as he threw circuit breakers off and on. At last he pronounced things "all set," adding, "If you'll permit it, I'll duck in next week and check those other fuses, one at a time. You get you an overload and it could spell trouble with a capital T. Don't stir. I know my way. These places are all alike."

If Adele regarded him with curiosity when he returned home a full twenty minutes after he'd left for the back alley, he doesn't recall it.

Autumn faded into winter, which felt like a North Dakota summer to Wayne, though without the flies and mosquitoes. He'd invented a Monday habit of wandering over to Kitty's place the instant Adele left for the Women's Auxiliary at Grace Church. He told himself he was only doing his Christian duty, making sure the widow lady was taken care of.

"Good morning, Mrs. Harper. Just checking to see how that washer on your kitchen sink faucet is holding up." No, he couldn't sit down.

One Wednesday he found himself counting the seconds till Adele clipped the last grocery coupon and left for the store so he might pop in and surprise Kitty. Have a second cup of coffee. A little chat. Discuss Bismarck's hairballs. What did Kitty know about hairballs?

No, looking back, it wasn't Wayne Hightower at all, but a restless stranger occupying his body, allowing him to say clever things, if he could judge from Kitty's reactions; causing him to spend more time with his grooming, splashing aftershave, snipping ear hairs; at first making sure his bifocals sparkled, then whipping them off his face altogether, as if they were entirely ornamental.

The first time Wayne appeared at the breakfast table after sprucing up his body's long-neglected nooks and crannies, Adele wrinkled her nose. "My goodness," she said, "but don't we smell pretty this morning."

When he returned home after the barber had given his gray a suggestion of brown, nothing drastic, Adele said, "Land's sakes,

Wayne, what happened to your poor head?" as though it'd gone through a windshield.

When he slipped into a brave new pink shirt and pulled on resort-bright turquoise pants, she smiled and turned her head as though she were in on a joke. Jealous, Wayne decided. He'd dared to change. Adele was hopelessly rooted in old midwestern, polyester ways.

How the hell he ended up one rainy Wednesday morning next to Kitty on satin sheets the color of seashells was anybody's guess, but there he was and that wasn't the worst of it. It happened again and again and again.

While Wayne sang lustily in Grace's choir, he felt sin gnawing at his soul, and yet he could not stop sinning. After church one Sunday, he took down the Bible and thumbed through it, fearing the lesson he'd learn would come from Sodom and Gomorrah. Instead, he found words in First Kings to cheer his weary heart. "King Solomon," it was written, "loved many strange women." It was in the Book of Job, however, where he found real comfort. Job said, "I caused the widow's heart to sing for joy." Right there in the Bible.

At dinner on Sunday, he looked across the table appreciatively. He was a happy man, delighted to have his Princess, as he thought of Adele, to come home to. She was the symbol for the kind of life of which he approved, one containing hot blueberry muffins—he broke one open, steam rising—and cold Protestant virtues. Then, to his surprise, because she popped into his head more quickly than she decently should, he remembered Kitty and he smiled. If only he could ignore his yapping conscience, his was the best of worlds.

———

A widow in the complex had invited Wayne and Adele to a party the following Saturday. At the door greeting them was Kitty Harper. She explained that their hostess had been called to the phone so she had put herself on "door duty."

"I am so pleased to make your acquaintance, Adele. Wayne has been so kind." She looked at him fondly.

This woman, who'd ripped his pants off him not three days before, was now doing all she could to strangle him. That was how it felt. He pulled at his collar. What was she up to, talking to Adele like this? Was she crazy as a loon, or crafty as a fox?

"He's been my salvation," he heard her continue. "I mean helping me out that time when my stove wouldn't work and then coming back to check my fuses. He's what I'd call a real good neighbor." Kitty reached for a carrot stick as if the subject was closed and it was time to do something nonfattening.

Adele was quiet, but then she never did talk when silence could do as good a job.

"I suspect we'd better be moseying along. What do you say, Sugar?" Wayne said.

On second thought moseying was not a great idea. For one thing, they'd only just walked in the door. Besides, if they moseyed he'd be by himself with Adele, with Sugar, and what would she say, once they were alone and away from the mercifully silencing rest of the universe?

Did he dare hope she'd not heard? A lot was going on: people talking over a Tommy Dorsey tape. Alcohol always meant noise, and there'd been a surprising amount of drinking.

For whatever reason, Adele never mentioned Kitty or her fuses. Wayne didn't, either. He just thanked the good Lord above, and then the following Monday was on his way to Kitty's as usual the minute Adele was out of the house.

Thursdays, Adele attended choir practice with Wayne. She sat in the front pew, squinting at her needlepoint beneath the dim light, while she listened to the fine old hymns. One Thursday evening the choir director greeted the group with distressing news. Over the weekend Mrs. Bodeck, the organist, had sprained her wrist. A nasty fall. Could anyone fill in? He stared gloomily at the choir.

Suddenly, Wayne saw Adele slip out of her pew and seat herself regally in front of the organ as though she had every intention of playing it. Really, Deli, he thought to himself, you don't actually think you're up to accompanying the choir?

He was still gaping at her when her fingers began to race across the keys, leaping expertly from keyboard to keyboard. Adele Hightower in jogging shoes, an old denim wraparound skirt, her old blue turtleneck lapping at the folds of her old white neck, her short gray hair every which way, was playing for his choir.

She led them as though they were children, but she was more than in charge. She had them at her mercy. In turns, she Redeemed them by the Blood of the Lamb; inquired if the Circle would be Unbroken; Gathered them all by the River; and finally left them, wretched limp rags, clinging to the Old Rugged Cross.

From portal to altar, transept to transept the little church expanded and contracted with life.

At last, when it was over, the choir rose in a body and applauded. As she stood to leave, fresh clapping exploded all around her, with Wayne sheepishly pressing his hands together in lackluster fashion, for his heart was not in it. Then he remembered the inscription under Adele's picture in their high school yearbook:

> Adele Gunderman,
> Still waters run deep.

One Friday, after Adele had left for an Auxiliary breakfast, he popped in on Kitty. She was still in her robe and for a moment, looked more puzzled than delighted, as if she were thinking, doesn't the man realize today's Friday, not Wednesday or Monday? What's he want?

But she made a pot of coffee, which they sat drinking at the breakfast counter, Kitty absently constructing a purple mountain as she pulled curlers from her hair. She looked drawn, he thought. He'd not realized she was quite so . . . well . . . quite so old. He'd never seen her this early in the day.

"Darlin'," said Kitty, putting her coffee mug down at last. "We've got to do some talking. You know it's been, let's see . . ."— long red fingernails tapping—"almost four months. I want to know just when was it you planned on asking Adele for the divorce?"

He watched her red pen busily doodling on the back of a paper napkin while she waited for his answer. Did she intend for the doodles to be fir trees? They looked to Wayne like tiny red Hiroshimas. He went numb.

She spoke again, her words coming at him louder and slower, as though he were deaf, maybe stupid. He heard impatience.

"I said, 'Darlin', when are you and Adele getting divorced?' You surely realize we cannot go on this way. Not fair to me. A girl has to make her plans, you know?" She was trying to make light of it, he saw, laughing the laugh he'd once heard as music, but which now came out hollow and hard.

Perched on a high stool, Wayne grabbed hold of the counter and clung to it as if it might possibly save him. Didn't Kitty understand that Adele was a part of him? As far as he was concerned, she could just as well have said, "Darlin', when are you going to saw off your old foot?"

Even her darlin's, he noticed, had become hollow and hard. It struck him how she gave everything the same value. His new bolo tie was darlin'. The bakery's curlicued sweet rolls were darlin'. She swept everything into one heaping unchoosy pile of darlin's. He was darlin', he realized, not because he was clever or handsome or special, but because he lived close and was a man. Had he suspected it all along?

Wayne wanted nothing more in the world than to go home, shower, put on his robe and slippers, and sit with Adele staring into the fire, although the day was balmy and the Hightowers hadn't a fireplace.

What did he say to Kitty? Looking back he isn't sure, except that his words contained some form of no, never, not Adele, not in a million years, while he held tight to the counter.

He recalls her crying softly for a minute into a corner of her napkin. "You don't understand how aching lonely widows are," she said, pushing back her stool as though her words required additional room. "The women around here, they won't hardly speak. They're scared silly I'll grab their little old wobbly husbands." She gave a tired laugh.

Wayne slipped down from the stool. His legs seemed as uncertain as if he'd spent a day on horseback. He feared they might fail him, so he felt his way cautiously along the walls until arriving at the front door. Kitty straggled behind him, pulling her robe around her. He reached for her hand, which he then shook formally, as though they were meeting after church, and hurried away.

"I'm home, my precious," he called to Adele who was already back and peeling potatoes at the sink. "Did you miss me?"

That night he slept in fits. Nearby Adele, snoring gently, appeared in harmony with the universe. The clock struck one. Then two. And three. Just after sunrise he got up and dressed. He did not want breakfast. He wanted peace of mind, some signal that Adele loved him, miserable sinner that he was, and would never leave him. Not ever, no matter what. He wanted the same expression of contentment and peace on his face that she had on hers.

He let himself out of the house and walked briskly, as though he had an appointment, the two blocks to the heart of Seeco City, memorizing as he passed them the windows of the A&P, where weekly specials were posted. Perhaps he'd become a perfect husband. Work at it, the way he'd worked at being a successful businessman. He'd start this day by reporting to Adele that chicken breasts, skinned and boned, could be had for $3.99 a pound. Was that a good price? He'd not the faintest notion.

Maybe he'd take over the grocery buying, if she'd allow it, or at the least resign himself to becoming one of those defanged old guys, tagging after a wife, pushing her cart, always alert for instructions. Once he'd had nothing but contempt for these men.

He walked past the bowling alley, through the mall, beyond Pacho's Casa, until he arrived at Grace Church. He tried the door, but found it locked.

Home again, he read directions, ground beans, plugged in the coffeepot, smelled burning, and discovered he'd forgotten to add water. He paced the living-room floor.

The second he saw Adele, he poured out his grocery buying plans. He could shop for her, or with her. Her preference. Only too happy to do it.

She thanked him, but said she'd been buying groceries for almost forty years without any help whatsoever and perhaps it was better that way. She acted as if nothing were amiss. Breakfast, lunch, supper, laundry, groceries, mending, cleaning, her needlepoint in front of the television. She maintained her routine, still attending choir practice with Wayne even after Mrs. Bodeck, to everyone's obvious disappointment, returned to play the organ.

One night Wayne and Adele were watching a television drama that concerned an affair between a husband and his secretary. Not Wayne's choice of what to see.

Out of the blue Adele muttered. "Death runs after old men." Wayne looked at her as she continued, talking more to herself than to him. "It does. They think they're safe long as their pants are down around their ankles. Ha ha." She went on with her needlepoint, but kept a stern eye on the television.

Some solace came those few hours a week when he sang with the choir, but he was never entirely at peace. Perhaps he'd see about getting Adele that organ. Hell, it could take over the living room, the whole house, for all he cared. Expense be damned.

He found himself studying Adele's every word and gesture, seeking to read in them what she knew, how she felt, what she was thinking. She seemed the same. Or did she? Was there hesitation before she laughed, after he'd repeated a joke heard at the barbershop? Was her laugh tighter, less ready than before? Were her biscuits not so frequent? hot? tender? Perhaps everything was all right. Perhaps she simply missed her friends. He did not know.

One morning Wayne saw Mayflower pull in a few doors down as he and Adele were leaving for a walk. Responding to his puzzled expression, Adele said, "Did you hear about your friend, Mrs.

Harper? She's getting married and moving to Tucson. He's that little fellow, sits at the back of the church, has a real bad squint. No accounting for taste, as the lady said when she kissed the cow. Ha ha."

Adele went on to say weren't the oleanders lovely, though she understood the leaves were just as poisonous as could be.

The relief Wayne experienced after Kitty's departure took on a physical quality. A weighty barbell had been lifted from his chest. Gratitude surged through him each time he and Adele passed Kitty's former home. He pictured a file at Hightower Plumbing and Supply marked: Harper, Kitty. Account closed.

So intense were his feelings of release that he joyfully threw himself into gardening with the same enthusiasm he once had for business. He purchased six old whiskey-barrel halves and filled them with potting soil, where he planted a brilliant assortment of petunias and vinca, added parsley, dill, and rosemary to another, and established families of climbing cherry tomatoes and China peas. He bent over them each day, thinning their ranks, suckering the tomatoes, caring for them all with newfound tenderness. From time to time he proudly harvested his herbs and vegetables for Adele.

———

July came and Wayne's sister Emma's birthday was almost upon them. He wanted to drive up to Parker and surprise her. He arranged with Mrs. Bodeck's grandson to water his garden, feed Bismarck, and keep an eye on the place.

They reached Tucson by noon, wandered the malls, keeping cool during the hottest hours. By late afternoon they left, planning to drive through the evening.

It was after the Buckeye cutoff that the air conditioner went kaput. Wayne poked and prodded and cajoled to no avail, so they opened the windows and drove into the night, stopping for a late supper. He drank a Bud while awaiting his steak and fries. Had a couple more while he ate. By now he was in a holiday mood so he drank a fourth, instead of dessert.

"Here's to us, Snuggles," he said to Adele.

By the time they'd finished and paid, it was pitch black out. The beer made Wayne sleepy, and when Adele suggested she drive, it seemed a good idea. Perhaps he'd catch a nap later. He'd enjoy just relaxing now. His life was turning around. Adele appeared content in her quiet way. She'd taken it in stride when the homeowners' group said organs were too noisy for close quarters.

After a while, the few cars on the road had disappeared. Only the Buick was left, cutting through the night. He and Adele might have been the last human beings on earth.

She put in a tape of old favorites. Slow, cheek-to-cheek music filled the car and slid easily into the night. "Someone to Watch over Me." "Moonlight and Roses." "I'll be Seeing You." Wayne slipped off his shoes and socks, wedging his bulky wallet and keys into a shoe for safekeeping. His glasses went into the glove compartment. It was a hot night, pleasant in a deserty way, but plenty hot.

Quite a meal. Not used to beer. Be more comfortable unzipped. On impulse Wayne wriggled out of his trousers. Nobody here but us chickens. Shirt off now, he sat in his Jockey briefs, feeling Adele scrutinizing him, her in-on-a-joke expression on her soft face.

Well, he could just imagine the thought behind that Mona Lisa look. "An odd getup, Christmas-colored Jockeys and not another stitch. To each his own."

The warm air was a balm to his body. He'd show Adele who was in charge here. He slipped out of his briefs. In seconds he was fast asleep.

Next, Wayne awoke with a terrific need to relieve himself and an urge to crawl into the backseat for a real nap.

"Pull over, Princess," he commanded. She stopped, and he got out of the car and stood for a minute by the side of the road, working his toes into the warm sandy soil. The desert night wrapped itself around him, a good feeling. He was a baby again, naked, fresh from his bath, washed of his sins, held in his mother's arms, safe and forgiven. Returned to a state of innocence.

"Hang on there for one second, Del. I'll be quick," he said, hearing a slur in his words. He headed for the privacy of a greasewood bush outlined against the darkness.

The next thing Wayne saw was Adele and the Buick taking off down a deserted highway, taillights ascending a small rise in the road before they melted into night. He shouted and waved an empty protest. It was then that he took a step and felt something sharp pierce his foot.

What seemed a lifetime later, though it couldn't have been more than a couple of hours, as it was still dark, a policeman searching for a missing person pulled Wayne in for questioning.

There is no doubt but what his foot is festering now. Even without his glasses, he can see a threatening line starting up his leg. The redheaded desk clerk tells him the infirmary is closed for the weekend. Does Wayne consider it an emergency?

Wayne stares up at him, wondering if the man is sarcastic or genuinely concerned. Then he feels the redness of the fellow's hair heightening the crisis within himself.

He can't recall crying since he was a boy and broke his nose roller-skating. He didn't cry, he realizes, during any of the bad times, the deaths and disappointments. It never occurred to him that tears might be waiting inside his big body, yet suddenly there they are, rushing down his cheeks, spotting his green jail coveralls, fat tears, looking like new raindrops on a sidewalk. The more he dabs, the faster they come.

"Yes," Wayne Hightower says, sobbing loudly. "Yes, yes, please help me. This is an emergency."

The Mick Sheehy Caper

Odhran O'Donovan

Once, last April, something happened to me that I doubt I will ever forget.

Let me give you the background. Being a nice, charitable person, I decided to raise money for a nationwide charity by shaving my hair until I was as bald as a coot (though I ended up looking like a sort of cactus). Everything was going fine with sponsorships and collections (I raised more than $300) when one day, while getting cards necessary for collections, I found a new lady working in the charity office. She said something that made my blood freeze.

"Have you got a legal permit?"

I was shocked. I never thought I'd need one. Here I was, something trying to improve the world, about to be arrested. I asked if it was important.

"Vital!" she said. "Crucial! I hope you haven't been collecting without it!"

I had.

So on my lunch break I walked down to the Gárda station, went in and spoke to an Officer McNulty who was at reception. I told him what my predicament was. He spoke with the confidence of someone who had lived all his life beyond sights of any city's suburbs. A bogger in common speech.

"Oh Jaze, boy, Mick Sheehy will sort you out there, so he will. He'll sort you out altogether, so he will."

"Oh great," I said, relieved to hear of such a competent person who I could rely on to keep me well away from detention centers. "Can I see him so?"

"Oh Jaze, no. Not right now, no."

"Ah . . . why?"

"He's on his lunch break. But come back at two and he'll sort you out altogether."

Wow, I thought, a cop who goes on a lunch break. He must be

real important 'cause all the crime in the city happens at lunch. Unfortunately, as I told McNulty, by two o'clock I'd be back at school. I asked:
"Um . . . right . . . I'll be back here . . . around . . . half four . . . is that okay?"
"Oh Jaze. Hang on there. Mick Sheehy finishes at half four, so he does."
Now I'm really impressed. All the crime that doesn't happen at lunchtime happens after half four. But it was clear I'd have to get Mick Sheehy to sort me out.
"Um . . . right . . . well . . . I'll try to get up early."
McNulty stared at me.
"I mean . . . up here . . . from school, like."
"Oh, fine so. You do that and Mick Sheehy will sort you out."

———

Anyhow, back I came at ten past four, and after waiting a while for a lady to get some sort of a license renewed, I met Officer McNulty again. He didn't recognize me. How he failed to recognize a boy with a head of hair like a head of cabbage is beyond me. I walked up.
"Ah . . . howya."
McNulty stared at me.
"Ah . . . I'm here to see Mick Sheehy."
"Michael Sheehy?"
"Yeah."
"Jaze, boy. Am . . . have ye got an appointment?" He was scaringly official.
"Well . . . ah . . . I was told to come back at around ten past four."
"So have ye got an appointment?"
"Yeah."
"Hang on there, I'll get someone to sort you out. Pat Burke! C'mere a second."
Ten minutes later no sign of Pat Burke.
"Um . . . C'n I just go up and see him?"
"Who?" asked McNulty.
"Mick Sheehy."
"Michael Sheehy?"
"Yeah."
"Fine so. Ye get in the lift. When ye come out turn left, turn

right. 'Tis the second door on your right."

I was pleased to abandon McNulty for a more competent policeman. I got in the lift. Got out. Turned left. Turned right, and knocked on the first door on my right.

"C'min," said someone.

I opened the door . . . and it slammed shut, the plaque reading "M. Sheehy" becoming more noticeable than ever. There was probably a reason for this, I assumed, so I waited five minutes, then knocked again.

"C'min."

I opened the door and walked in. The door slammed shut behind me. I turned and noticed a metallic instrument connecting the wall to the door so that the latter would slam shut without fail.

Mick Sheehy was sitting in a swivel chair. He was holding a pen and his desk was covered with papers, but he didn't seem to be doing anything. I spoke.

"Um . . . are you Mick Sheehy?"

"Yes."

"Well . . . um . . . I'm looking for a permit."

"Are ye havin' a raffle?" asked he, quizzically.

"Uh . . . no. It's for charity."

"Well, are ye havin' a raffle?"

"No . . . it's more . . . um . . . like a sponsorship."

"Oh. I only do raffles."

I eventually got my permit, although the workers in the appropriate department weren't sure if I needed it.

"I don't know if he needs a permit a'tall, Dolores."

"No, I think he does, Mary."

"Are ye sure?"

"No."

When I was bidding farewell to Officer McNulty, he didn't recognize me. I didn't wait around, because it was a quarter to five and after five, buses cost more (to get on). I missed my bus in the end and had to walk home. But it taught me an important lesson. It takes all kinds to make the world . . . and thank goodness I'm not one of them.

THE MAYOR OF
SAINT JOHN

Tom Paine

It was a mystery to most Saint Johnians why the newly elected governor of the Virgin Islands, Samuel Moses, had appointed a substitute history teacher at the Julius E. Sprauve Elementary School mayor of the island. For many days there was no other question, from the West Indians slapping dominoes at the Taxi Stand in Cruz Bay to the whites throwing horseshoes at Skinny Legs's Grill in Coral Bay. Only forty-two-year-old bachelor Sebastian Vye's mother, Miss Ellie Vye of John's Folly, Governor Samuel Moses, and the governor's legitimate son, the developer Victor Moses, knew Sebastian Vye was the "outside" son of the new governor.

Sebastian Vye himself, when told by his mother Miss Ellie that he was the new mayor, as he looked through his collection of artifacts on the wooden floor of their old-style West Indian home in John's Folly, was as surprised as anyone on the island. Licking a shard of a slave's pottery to test its antiquity, he told Miss Ellie in his nervous stutter that he had no interest in becoming the mayor of anything.

Miss Ellie sighed heavily as she sat in the single chair in the room. She looked up at a lizard on the rotting beams of the ceiling and listened to the soft patter of a wisp of rain on the rusted steel roof and said with a smile on her plump ebony face one word to her forty-two-year-old bachelor son: "Eustacia."

Sebastian put the shard of pottery down on the tarp and closed his eyes. Miss Ellie leaned forward in her chair with effort and said, "You de mayor, you save de donkeys. You save de donkeys, dat pretty girl you been giving the eye year by year, Eustacia January, she then your own girl."

Sebastian Vye had no idea what his mother Miss Ellie meant

about the donkeys, but he understood that as mayor he might suddenly be in a position esteemed enough to satisfy the family of Eustacia January. Her father, Liston January, was the reappointed head in the new Moses administration of WAPA, the Water and Power Authority for the three Virgin Islands. Other than the governorship, there was no more powerful position in the islands than the control of the tens of millions of federal dollars flowing through WAPA. Sebastian knew his mother had forced Governor Moses to make him the mayor, but he knew better than to ask the Saint John matriarch for the details. When his mother heaved herself from the chair and left the room, he slipped the framed photo of Eustacia January from under his pillow. He had blown the photo up ten years earlier from her graduation photo from the Sprauve School and had laid his head down on his pillow delicately every night. He found an old bent nail and a rock, and for the first time in a decade, he hung her up over their small dining-room table, openly exposing the sweet but frightened face of the former Miss Saint John Carnival 1989 to the tropical elements. Miss Ellie stuck her head back into the room as he sat looking up at Eustacia January in her carnival crown.

"I goin' say this once, Sebastian," said Miss Ellie. "But dat girl Eustacia January, she always for you, she *waitin'* for you all these years. She waitin' for you to do *somethin'*."

The red-roofed Battery sits on a small peninsula of land in Cruz Bay Harbor, the main entrance port to Saint John from Saint Thomas. Built of painstakingly squared-off brain coral by slaves in the early 1800s, it had an elaborate white iron balustrade surrounding the second-story veranda from which the mayor could survey the harbor.

Cruz Bay harbor was too small now for its moored yachts, commercial barges, and ferry traffic; the ferries wove too quickly between the dozens of yachts, some of which were the homes of sailors known as "liveaboards." Sebastian had already taken twelve complaints, in his first week in the Battery, from irate white liveaboard sailors, of near misses by the ferries. Sebastian treated each sailor with West Indian civility and sat behind his desk in jacket and tie and slacks taking down in his patient script pages of the sailors' often drunken rants, which usually quickly jumped off from the original incident and extended into a monologue on the ineffectuality of the West Indian government.

Sebastian put down his pen after the EMT and liveaboard sailor Kent Lyle left his office after complaining about a near miss of his yacht *Anchorage* at midnight by the ferry *Bomba Challenger*, shook the knots from his fingers, and sniffed the sailor's body odor crowding his office. He slipped his notes into a file labeled "Incidents in Cruz Bay Harbor" that he was preparing to show to the Department of Planning and Natural Resources on Saint Thomas. He took a handkerchief from his pocket and dabbed at the perspiration beading on his forehead. The phone rang. It was his father, Governor Moses, calling for the first time since taking office two weeks earlier.

"Dat you, Sebastian?"

Sebastian could barely hear Governor Moses over the roar of a helicopter outside the Battery.

"Sebastian," yelled Governor Moses. "You look outside, dat me in de helicopter."

Walking to the open door to his office, Sebastian waved to the thin black face staring down at him from the passenger seat of a sleek black Narcotic Strike Force helicopter hovering over Cruz Bay harbor.

"You listen now, Sebastian," said Governor Moses. "I on my way to Coral Bay for a meeting. We goin' talk hurricanes. You still there, boy?"

"I here."

"Sebastian, I ask you, what you doing about dem donkeys?"

"Dem donkeys?"

"Dem wild donkeys dat eating all de orchids."

"De orchids?"

"Don't monkey me, boy. Dat's a big problem, all dem wild donkeys. Dey eating all de orchids of dem rich whites you got over dere in Chocolate Hole. Dey complain to me, dey complain to Washington, den Washington call me with de problem. Now I calling you, Sebastian. What you doin' about dem donkeys?"

There was a spasm of static on the line, and Sebastian watched his father pass over Cruz Bay Harbor shaking a hand at Sebastian from the helicopter. The line was dead, and Sebastian cradled the heavy old receiver and walked out on the veranda of the Battery.

Just that morning, Sebastian had received an outraged letter from an old white man, Langdon Cunningham of Chocolate Hole, complete with photos of him standing among the devastated ornamental orchids around his villa. Sebastian had admired the colors of the few surviving orchids, which were not native to Saint John and could not have survived in his youth when roof-captured fresh water was at a premium and the multi-million-dollar desalination plant had not afforded the luxury of drip irrigation, and started a file he labeled "Donkeys and Ornamental Orchids." He wondered if he could obtain a few orchids from Langdon Cunningham to lay in Eustacia January's jeep someday if she left it in the parking lot near the Customs house when she took her monthly trip to visit relatives on Tortola. Sebastian Vye laughed out loud from the balcony of the Battery as he pictured the delight on the face of Eustacia January, who loved brilliant colors, always had a brilliant red hibiscus blossom in her hair, like the old-style West Indian women.

The mayor shook his head and went back into his office and returned with an antique Danish spyglass and raised it to his left eye. Sebastian instinctively avoided looking at the villas strewn upon the hillsides of the island of Saint Thomas two miles away across the sparkling aquamarine channel, and turned the spyglass, slowly searching for the deserted island of Little Saint James. Sebastian had built, in the last ten years, an elaborate vision that he and Eustacia January would marry and move out to Little Saint James and live an old-fashioned, simple West Indian life. Now, as the mayor located Little Saint James with the spyglass, he watched with disbelief as a crane on a barge lifted pallets of concrete forms onto a cleared brown swath. Sebastian turned the spyglass quickly away from the swinging pallets and ran his eye along the dark lines of a reef, into the passage between Saint John and Saint Thomas, and a cargo barge, pushing a wall of sparkling foamed sea before it, steamed into his line of vision and out again. Something on the barge caught his eye, and he swung the spyglass back, but there was nothing to see but a small wall of water pushed before what he now saw was the *P'Ti Blue* barge.

The mayor stood on the veranda of the Battery with the spyglass dangling in his hand by his side. He closed his eyes as a breeze worked through the somber heat. He remembered a day nineteen years earlier in the cool of the small rain forest at the top of Bordeaux Mountain. He was walking down from the rain forest, moving down a gut following the trickle of water among the ferns. Soon the gut dried up and he continued down the dried riverbed until his path crossed that of the Reef Bay Trail. He heard children screaming ahead of him on the trail. He ran ahead and around two bends came upon nine-year-old Eustacia January and five or six other schoolgirls in the plaid skirts and white blouses of the Sprauve School standing like small black statues in the green shadows. Ahead of them a boar snarled and kicked at the trail. Sebastian pushed his way past the girls. The boar raised its head. Sebastian Vye raised his arms at his side and involuntarily flapped them like a frigate bird and strange hooting sounds passed from his lips. He hooted and flapped and the boar stared, tilting his bristled snout from side to side, and then turned and crashed away through the bush. When Sebastian turned back to the girls, little Eustacia January threw herself into his arms. He carried her back up the trail, and she clung to him all the way back by jeep to the January home on Moorehead Point, where her mother Yolanda had to pull her away.

As forty-two-year-old Sebastian stood on the veranda of the Battery he still felt Eustacia January's nine-year-old arms around his chest. Eustacia January had grown up to be the prettiest and shyest West Indian girl on Saint John. She was elected Miss St. John Carnival 1989. During the talent portion of the carnival contest, with Saint John's entire West Indian community watching from beneath the stage built on the Sprauve School ball field, she froze and only hummed along with the sound track from the Mighty Sparrows' calypso song "We Run 'Tings," but was still awarded the crown. She went away to the University of Pennsylvania for college, but was back a month later and didn't come out of her grandmother's Moorehead Point home for three months. Then she founded the Animal Care Corps, and transported dogs and cats by ferry to Saint Thomas, where Dr. Kingston, a West Indian veterinarian, spayed them for free. Her goal was to reduce the rising population of starving wild pets left behind or lost to the bush by whites. Sebastian saw her on occasion at dawn standing at the end of the Cruz Bay ferry dock with a cat or dog in a plastic carrying case. Once she turned and smiled shyly, but Sebastian Vye's feet were lead.

The mayor opened his eyes and looked out to sea from the veranda of the Battery. The barge the *P'Ti Blue* slowed down for Gallow's Point reef at the entrance to Cruz Bay, fell back, and settled, the rush of foam lost under the bow. The barges brought jeeps and building supplies hourly to the island from Saint Thomas. Sand, bricks, cement blocks, plywood, steel, tropical hardwoods, and I-beams piled onto Saint John's small industrial dock. The barges had been beach landing craft during World War II. Marines once stormed onto beaches from the barges, then called LTVs. Now the barges were painted the colors of candy. Something was moving around on the *P'Ti Blue*'s deck. The mayor squinted and leaned forward over the iron balustrade. The deck of the *P'Ti Blue* was alive with donkeys. The *P'Ti Blue* didn't bear off to the industrial dock but headed straight for the rocky shore of the Battery. Sebastian Vye dropped the antique Danish spyglass in surprise, and it rolled under the iron balustrade, fell to the rocks below, and bounced into the shallow water. One of the donkeys looked up from the bow of the *P'Ti Blue* at the mayor and brayed loudly.

The barge *P'Ti Blue* pushed aside the stern of a small sailboat as it made its way toward Cruz Bay Beach in a narrow and shallow slot along the rocky shore of the Battery. There was just enough room for the barge to pass. Sebastian Vye ran down the stone stairs and out of the Battery, ran huffing with his tie flapping over his shoulder down Waterfront Street, past the Health Clinic, where he was followed by the curious eyes of the EMT Kent Lyle sipping a Pepsi while sitting on the bumper of the ambulance. The mayor could hear the hydraulic front gate of the *P'Ti Blue* barge lowering as he ran toward Cruz Bay Beach. He ran around the clapboard taxi stand and found the *P'Ti Blue*'s front ramp half down. The idle taxi drivers looked over from their domino game on the bandstand in Cruz Bay Park. Everett Marsh, a second cousin of Sebastian Vye, held a domino aloft. Behind the descending ramp, the donkeys were leaping to get out of the barge. A couple of shadowed faces were in the dark square pilothouse of the *P'Ti Blue*, and Sebastian waved urgently. A single donkey ran up the angled ramp and flew toward the shore, four legs flailing in the air. The donkey thrashed ashore kicking up water and looked back from the beach at the other donkeys still on the barge. Sebastian Vye stood by Miss Gertrude's safari taxi with its longhorn cattle horns mounted on the hood waving his arms at the shadows in the pilothouse. The donkeys still on the *P'Ti Blue* were all braying, and the ramp fell with a whine and clunk into the sand of the shoreline, and the donkeys raced out as one. The donkeys fell over each other up the short beach, over the stone wall, slipped between the rows of safari taxis, and charged into Cruz Bay Park.

The nearby ferry *Bomba Challenger* had recently off-loaded a few hundred tourists. There were still a dozen or so tourists in the park not yet herded on the safari buses for the ride to Trunk Bay Beach in the National Park. These tourists scattered as the donkeys charged in a circle. Heads aloft, ears pinned back, the donkeys charged as if in the center ring of a circus. One donkey leaped up on the bandstand. It crashed through the card table set up by the taxi drivers for dominoes. Sebastian Vye ran after the donkeys as they brayed and circled the park. A white woman tripped and fell, and a donkey skidded to a halt before her and raised himself up on his back feet, as if in victory.

Sebastian Vye stopped dead in his tracks when he saw Lt. Jeffreys running into the park from Sparky's T-Shirt Shack. Lt. Jeffreys had for the last ten years worked as an elite Narcotic Strike Force officer on Saint Thomas. A few weeks earlier, two real estate developers from Miami had been found executed by a single pistol shot in the back of the head in their Saint Thomas waterfront condominium. The real estate agents were in a legal wrangle over the last of the Jeffreys' family land in Charlotte Amalie. Most of downtown Charlotte Amalie, the capital and harbor of the island of Saint Thomas, had once belonged to the Jeffreys family. Lt. Jeffreys was sent to Saint John, where it was assumed he could lie low until the murders were forgotten. Instead, he spent his days stepping out of the bush on the side of Saint John's roads, flagging down whites at gunpoint, searching their cars, ticketing them for minor infractions. Now Lt. Jeffreys was in front of Sparky's T-Shirt Shack in a firing squat, his pistol trained on a donkey rearing up at one end of the park. Lt. Jeffreys fired, and the donkey fell dead, nose first, into the dirt.

Sebastian Vye saw Eustacia January running down the street toward the park and looked quickly back at Lt. Jeffreys marching in a half squat across the park, his pistol trained on a second donkey as it spun on its hind legs and kicked the air. Sebastian looked back at Eustacia January running in her bare feet, her sweet round face flushed. She was pointing to Sebastian Vye as she ran toward the donkey aimed at by Lt. Jeffreys. Sebastian Vye turned and ran toward the rearing donkey, placed himself in Lt. Jeffreys' line of fire. He heard the officer yell at him. The donkey's hooves flashed in front of his face. As he waved his arms like a frigate bird in front of the rearing donkey and started to turn back to look for Eustacia, something cracked him in the back of the head.

Sebastian Vye awoke on a gurney in the hallway of the Morris DeCastro Clinic. He was looking up at an enlarged photo of his father, Governor Moses, smiling down from behind the nurses' desk. Kent Lyle, the bearded EMT, was looking down intently into his eyes.

"How many fingers?" said Lyle.

"Fingers?" said the mayor.

Kent Lyle had no fingers out and laughed at his joke. "You're going to be okay, Mr. Vye. He got you pretty good. I had to put in ten stitches. We were out of sutures, so I used some red and green thread. Kids around here like the rasta colors. How about you?"

"Donkey kicked me?"

Kent Lyle took two steps backward in mock surprise. "The donkey? Donkey didn't get you, Mr. Vye. That coked-up cop, Lt. Jeffreys, he pistol-whipped you good when you got in the way of his shot. Surprised he didn't plug you. If you had been white, you'd be dead right now."

"Coke?" said the mayor.

Kent Lyle hopped up on the counter of the nurses' station. He said, "You sure are out of the loop for the mayor. Jeffreys is lit up day and night. He'll kill someone here, but they won't put him away till he does, and even then it's doubtful. Too many people in high places making too much money on the stuff." Lyle took out a cigarette, lit it, and pointed to Governor Moses' photo on the wall. "Like Governor Moses over there."

Sebastian Vye's head throbbed. He had never actually been a patient in the Morris DeCastro Clinic, although he knew they were always short of supplies and knew right now the only real doctor was in a psychiatric hospital in the States. He turned to Kent Lyle and said, "What about the donkeys?"

Kent took a drag on his cigarette. "Donkeys took off for Bordeaux Mountain."

Sebastian Vye waved his hand toward Kent Lyle. "No, *why* did someone bring them to Saint John?"

Kent Lyle whistled and said, "You kidding me, Mayor Vye? You don't know?"

"No," said the mayor. "I'm sorry."

The pain drummed louder in the back of his skull as the mayor shifted his head on the gurney. Kent Lyle took a deep breath and said in a single long rush, "The governor's son, Victor Moses, you know him. He's been over here every week taking out Eustacia January. But the word is he's made slow progress. And then Eustacia January heard earlier this week, like everyone else on Saint John but you, Mayor Vye, that Governor Moses plans to *do something* about the donkeys over here because all the rich white villa owners over in Chocolate Hole are losing their ornamental plants and they gave the new governor a lot of money in his campaign. Anyway, you know how crazy Eustacia January is about animals. So Victor Moses promised to save Saint John's donkeys for her, and seeing how crazy she is about the donkeys, he decided to barge some more over for her, too. So that's what he did this morning, unloaded all those donkeys from the *P'Ti Blue*. But then there was that coked-up Lt. Jeffreys to mess up his plan."

Kent Lyle took a deep breath, and said, "So that's the story, Mr. Vye." Lyle jumped off the nurses' station, came over and placed a finger on Sebastian Vye's forehead. In the midst of a now blinding headache Sebastian Vye heard Kent Lyle say, "It isn't all bad news, Mr. Vye. You got a big kiss from Eustacia January." Lyle went to the wall near the nurses' station and took a small mirror off the wall. He came back and held it over the mayor's head. There was a perfect pair of red lips painted on his black forehead. The mayor sucked in a breath. He took the mirror in his hands, stared at the perfect round lips bright on his forehead, brought the mirror closer, and the throbbing pain in his head grew smaller until it drifted away.

The mayor marched with a spark in his step out the swinging doors of the emergency entrance to the DeCastro Clinic with his fingertips beneath the kiss on his forehead. From within the clinic he heard Kent Lyle calling after him about a concussion. It was a Caribbean day of such splendor the mayor wanted to raise his arms and cry out, and spotting old Miss Hendricks, one of the tellers at the Chase Bank, walking across the Customs house parking lot he cupped his hands—as Miss Hendricks was slightly deaf—and called out, "Marvelous day, Miss Hendricks!"

Miss Hendricks's son Melvin was one of the five young crack dealers that in the last few months had taken up evening residency outside the Chase Bank in the center of Cruz Bay, and recently Melvin was found bound, beat up, and burned by cigarettes behind the Moravian Church in Coral Bay. Miss Hendricks turned and looked hard at the mayor, and Sebastian Vye slowly lowered the hand that was raised in greeting.

Sebastian Vye was checked in his ebullience only for a moment, however, and strolled toward the Post Office. He forgot about old Miss Hendricks, forgot about his natural reserve, and touched his forehead beneath the blazoned kiss gently again with two fingers. Henrietta Parsons, a transplanted New York City real estate agent, came out of the post office loaded down with packages. The mayor jogged over and took four or five off her hands, and walked with her to her car. She glanced a few times at his forehead. The mayor beamed up at the sky and said, "Isn't it a marvelous day, Miss Parsons?"

Henrietta Parsons jiggled her keys in her hands in front of her Jeep. Her lawyers had recently worked their way through a tangle of disputed West Indian family claims to a hundred acres on the East End of Saint John, and had bulldozed a road, and Parsons Real Estate was now offering waterfront half-acre lots on a gated and guarded compound for four hundred thousand dollars each, and she was preoccupied by forty million dollars. Everything had to be *perfect* if the sales were to proceed as planned, and she had heard that the local Saint John newspaper, the *Tradewinds*, was planning a front-page story on the donkey problem soon, and it was just the sort of thing that would send her stateside investors skittering off to Saint Barts or Antigua or Tortola. Henrietta Parsons jiggled her keys again as the mayor held her packages. She opened and closed her mouth a few times and then said, "Did you know you have catsup on your forehead, Mayor Vye?"

Sebastian Vye nodded as if he had been waiting for her to notice and said, "It's lipstick."

"Lipstick?"

Sebastian Vye nodded again, and decided to tell her the whole story, but as soon as the mayor said the word "donkey," Henrietta Parsons cut him off and said, "We all have been given to understand by Governor Moses you plan to do something about the donkeys, Mayor Vye."

Henrietta Parsons gave the mayor such a severe look that he forgot for a moment what he wanted to tell her, and his hand rose weakly toward his forehead.

"Do you want a tissue to wipe that off your forehead?" said Henrietta Parsons.

"No," said the mayor. "No, thank you."

Henrietta Parsons looked at him oddly for a moment, then shrugged and said, "What are you doing right now, mayor?"

The mayor shook his head. He felt a throbbing returning in his skull. He couldn't remember why he had strode so firmly out of the DeCastro Clinic. He took a quick glance at the blue sky. Henrietta Parsons waved a hand before his eyes and said, "Are you there, Mayor Vye?"

The mayor focused on Henrietta Parsons, who said as if there was to be no arguing, "I have an idea, Mayor Vye. Why don't you come with me up to Chocolate Hole? I can show you just what sort of terrific damage these donkeys are causing us."

Over Sebastian Vye's mild protestations, he was strapped firmly into the passenger seat of the Jeep by Henrietta Parsons. She squealed out of the parking lot and roared up Centerline Road. Some West Indian schoolgirls looked over from the playground of the Sprauve Elementary School. The mayor was pushed back in his seat as Henrietta gunned past a safari taxi driven by Nathan Penn around a blind corner in Estate Enighed. The Jeep bounded over the top of the hill at Jacob's Ladder, and there was Lt. Jeffreys holding his gun at his side by the edge of the road. Sebastian Vye saw Lt. Jeffreys lean over and spit on the ground as the Jeep passed him. Henrietta Parsons seemed not to see the police officer; she was beeping hard and waving furiously at a Jeep coming up toward her. She stopped in the middle of the road, and Sebastian Vye looked over at Langdon Cunningham, the old man who had written him the letter he'd read that very morning about the donkeys and his orchids.

"I've taken the mayor hostage," said Henrietta Parsons.

Langdon Cunningham looked over from beneath two heavy gray beetle brows. He seemed to be examining Sebastian Vye from his position bent over his Jeep's wheel. "I see you have indeed," said Langdon Cunningham. "Has he cut himself? What's that on his forehead?"

"Lipstick," said Henrietta Parsons. "Langdon, why don't you follow us. You can help me educate the mayor about our concerns."

Langdon Cunningham slapped his steering wheel. "He needs to eradicate them. Shoot them. Poison them. Kill them. I don't care what Vye does. Damn pests."

The mayor's headache had returned in force, along with a dizziness, and he rocked from side to side as Henrietta Parsons swerved through the newly paved roads of Chocolate Hole. Along the way she picked up Barnard Hoyt, who also agreed to come along. He followed Langdon Cunningham in his Land Rover.

The three vehicles slipped down the steep driveway to Henrietta

Parsons's villa. Flowers surrounded them in a rock garden on all sides as they passed through an electric gate. Bougainvillea, hibiscus, frangipani, and orchids blooming in disorder. Henrietta Parsons led them up through the rock garden, till they came to an area where the flowers were trampled and there was nothing but short frayed stalks close to the ground. Henrietta Parsons pointed to a fence knocked down and bent over and cupped the remaining stalks and said, "My pretty babies. Oh, my pretty babies."

She looked up at Sebastian Vye and said harshly, "Do you believe us now? Do you see, Mayor Vye? Something has got to be done."

Langdon Cunningham and Barnard Hoyt joined Henrietta Parsons in staring at Sebastian Vye, who bent over and picked up a stray orange petal. Henrietta Parsons shared a look with the two men, who both shook their heads, and led the mayor across the steep hillside. The mayor looked down at black plastic pipe snaking everywhere around his feet; he looked above and saw the concrete cistern built into the hillside to water the plants in the dry season. The water was bought from the desalination plant at Moorehead Point and trucked up once every few weeks during the dry season. Henrietta stopped and pointed down to a series of posts lying on their side, tied together by barbed wire.

"Don't touch them," said Henrietta. "The top wire still has electricity running through it."

Hoyt took off his cap, wiped his forehead and said, "Fast as we put up the fences, they just push them down."

The three of them stared at the fence, and then Henrietta led them down to the villa. It was a three-story steel and glass building. Everything within the villa was white. There was a pool built at the cliff side so the water at the edge fell over as if falling into the Caribbean Sea hundreds of feet below. Sebastian Vye had never been in one of the million-dollar villas that were slowly covering the island. He turned around, and there was Eulinda Harvey, his third cousin, in a white-and-black maid's uniform, with a platter of drinks. Henrietta Parsons took a drink from the tray and as she handed it to the mayor said, "Saint John isn't big enough for both of us anymore. The donkeys will have to go. You see that, don't you, Mayor Vye?"

"What's that smudge on your forehead, Mayor Vye?" said Hoyt.

"Lipstick," said Henrietta Parsons.

There was a thrashing sound from the villa, and Henrietta put down her drink at the edge of the pool and went inside. Sebastian

Vye looked out at the island of Little Saint James. The barge was still out there, dropping concrete forms. There was a scream from the house, and the three men ran inside. A young donkey was standing in the doorway of the villa, looking curiously from side to side. Henrietta Parsons had taken refuge behind her white counter and was waving her hands at the donkey and saying, "Shoo. Shoo. Bad donkey."

Sebastian went up to the donkey, took some nuts off a white ceramic bowl on the counter, held them out. The men were yelling behind him, asking Henrietta if she had a gun. The donkey stuck his nose in the mayor's palm, and he pulled his hand just out of reach and led the donkey out the villa's door. He led the donkey up the stone steps through the flowers, opened the gate and closed it behind the donkey, and led him down the dirt road. When he looked back once Hoyt was standing in the driveway with a shotgun held before his chest. The donkey followed him out to Gifft Hill road, where he rubbed the young donkey's nose and swatted him on the behind, sending him toward Reef Bay, and then the mayor hitched a ride back to town in the back of Herman James's empty safari taxi. Herman was playing a tape of the Saint John All-Stars in the cab, a steel pan group made up of island children. The music took Sebastian Vye back to his childhood in the late 1950s. There were only a dozen eccentric whites on the island, and they all lived at Gallow's Point and said "Good morning" and "Good evening," as was the West Indian custom. He remembered there were no cars on Saint John in those days. There was only a donkey path up and over Bordeaux Mountain to distant Coral Bay, and at the top of the mountain you were in a rain forest where it was so cold you shivered and the mist was so thick it was like standing in a cloud. Sebastian Vye had a donkey he raised named Shego, and he would ride her up to the rain forest at the top of Bordeaux Mountain and sit in the cold in a trance and listen to the orchestra of yellow and green tree frogs for hours barely breathing, for if he moved at all they stopped their ancient song.

Sebastian Vye climbed out of the safari taxi at the Chase Bank and walked down toward Cruz Bay Park. He stopped for a moment to speak to Pastor Sovingreen of the West Indian Emmaus Moravian Church. The pastor reached out with a handkerchief, and before Sebastian could argue had wiped away the smudged remains of

Eustacia January's kiss from his forehead. When Sebastian realized what the pastor had done, he felt his knees go soft. His palms flew to his forehead, and he walked off without another word.

He walked with his hands on his forehead. Some tourists passed by and snickered, and their children raised their hands to their foreheads. An island dog came toward him and stopped in the road. It was a yellow-and-black mutt, with matted hair and ribs showing. He wagged his tail weakly at Sebastian Vye and then came forward with his head bowed and sat down before the mayor. The mayor looked down at him, and he took his hands from his forehead and scratched the dog behind the ears. The dog stood up and wagged his tail. The mayor walked into Cruz Bay Park and sat down on a bench and closed his eyes. The park was empty except for the taxi drivers slapping dominoes near the bandstand. In a few minutes it would be full again, with a flood of tourists returning from Trunk Bay.

The mayor heard footsteps. He felt someone sitting next to him on the bench, smelled sweat and cologne. When he opened his eyes slightly he saw a gun being flipped around in a circle on the end of a black finger. He saw the black arm was thickly muscled. He felt goose bumps rise on his skin.

"Dis little island too small for all," said Lt. Jeffreys.

The mayor closed his eyes. After a while he heard Jeffreys sucking his teeth loudly. When the mayor opened his eyes, Lt. Jeffreys was gone. A taxi full of tourists arrived, the women in bikinis, the men pink-chested and slathered with white lotion.

The mayor sat as taxi after taxi brought hundreds of tourists into Cruz Bay Park. Some went down the street to the T-shirt shops, others milled in the park waiting for the next ferry. Sebastian Vye touched his forehead, and stood up and walked out of the park through the tourists running for the ferry. He heard something behind him and turned to see the island dog was following, wagging his tail. The mayor walked out of the town of Cruz Bay along the shoreline toward Frank Bay Beach. He climbed up a narrow road and stopped to pick some hibiscus flowers of the most delicate pink hue, and again he touched his forehead with two fingers.

He stood at the edge of Frank Bay Beach and looked out toward Moorehead Point, a short, bulbed peninsula of land. The Mooreheads had sold their half of the point for the new desalination plant. The larger portion still belonged to the January family. There were two new white government jeeps in the driveway up to the new double-floored cinder-block and shuttered home. The mayor approached the gate with the hibiscus blossoms clutched in his shaking hand. As was the old Virgin Islands custom, he called out loudly, "Inside!" from the gate, and Eustacia January's grandmother, Miss Gertrude, came to the half door and waved him up the rocky and barren dirt path. He walked up through their herd of goats.

The mayor sat in the dark living room with a glass of lemonade, and one of three little girls, Eustacia's nieces, handed him one of Miss Gertrude's homemade sugar candies. The darkness of the slat-shuttered West Indian houses struck him for a moment as backward in comparison with Henrietta Parsons's open-walled glass villa, then he was enveloped in the shadowed quiet and took a long sip of lemonade. Miss Gertrude looked at the hibiscus blossoms in Sebastian Vye's hand. After a long silence she said, "What in dis world take so long, Sebastian Vye?"

Sebastian lowered his head and looked down at the hibiscus blossoms in his hand. "She waitin' for you all these years," continued Miss Gertrude, shaking her gray-haired head. "She waitin' and waitin' for you, and Victor Moses, dat man come sniffin' 'round dis house every day now. Dat Victor Moses tell her all de time you and his fada Governor Moses got somethin' bad cooked up for de donkeys on dis island. I tell her, you crazy girl, dat Sebastian Vye, he not hurt de fly on de donkey's head."

Sebastian took a deep breath. The little girls looked from their grandmother to Sebastian. Miss Gertrude took a sip of lemonade and said, "I tell her, you wait, dat Sebastian Vye, he a good man and he come. He old-style Saint Johnian: he polite, he decent, and he care for all de little tings. I say, Eustacia, ain't no men no more on dis island like dat Sebastian Vye. All de men here, dey lose all dere sense and drink and do de drugs, or dey runnin' after de big white money like dat Victor Moses." Miss Gertrude sucked her teeth and pushed herself from her chair, came over and took Sebastian Vye's hand, and said, "She comin' back on de nine ferry from Saint Thomas. You see her, den, you tell her what you come here to say."

Miss Gertrude went into the kitchen to warm a bowl of goat soup for the mayor. When Miss Gertrude hobbled back into the living room with the bowl and a Heineken, Sebastian Vye was gone, and the little girls were each holding a handful of hibiscus blossoms, rubbing their foreheads with two fingers, and giggling.

The next morning Sebastian Vye awoke with a hangover. He had drunk a quarter of a bottle of Cruzan rum as he sat in his bed looking at his photo of Eustacia January. He had planned to drink the entire bottle, but had passed out too soon. He had gone to the Cruz Bay dock to meet the nine ferry in his Sunday suit. At the entrance to the old dock was a small red-lettered sign announcing the construction of a new two-million-dollar federally funded ferry dock for Saint John. The dock was to be built by Victor Moses Construction. Liston January, Eustacia January's father and the head of the Water and Power Authority, was listed as a member of the project's advisory board. Governor Moses' photo and enlarged signature adorned the bottom of the sign. Sebastian Vye had stood before the sign for a long time, and then turned and gone to Joe's Package and bought the bottle of Cruzan rum and walked the three miles home.

He stood up from his bed and was struck by the stillness. No thrushie was calling, no rooster was crowing, no cicadas humming in the heat. He looked out through the slats, and the sky was a dark, heavy blue. Sebastian Vye closed his eyes and felt a hurricane brewing, but by the time he arrived at the Battery, he had forgotten his premonition. He sat for a moment at his desk, went out on the balcony, and looked over at little Saint James. He could see a bulldozer scraping the tiny island. The mayor left his office and got in his white government jeep. He sped up Lind Point and then down North Shore Road through the National Park. He passed the entrance to Caneel Bay Resort without glancing at the manicured grounds, but his black hands squeezed the steering wheel. He felt faint as he passed Hawksnest Bay, the parking lot full of Suzuki rental Jeeps and safari taxis, the West Indian park employees picking garbage off the sand in the shade of the trees.

The mayor squealed up the switchbacks of Dead Man's Hill, and as he sped past Cinnamon Bay, the mayor knew his destination. He stopped at the tourist overlook at Maho Bay, got out of the jeep. He looked down at the blue-green crescent of Maho Bay. On the end of the beach near him was a small green house behind a barbed-wire fence. As he looked down he watched two white tourists walking along the beach toward the house. The mayor stared at the green house, wondered if she was home, and then from the bushes she emerged, the "mad woman of Maho," waving her machete at the tourists and screaming. The tiny old West

Indian woman remained there screaming and waving her machete long after the tourists had retreated.

   The mayor walked down the road. He caught his breath as he stood hidden behind a tree looking toward Estelle Samuels's house. Standing in the backyard next to Estelle Samuels was Eustacia January. She had one leg raised under her and was bobbing her head in imitation of a great blue heron for her great-aunt. She stood on one foot and bobbed her head, and then she suddenly turned her head and seemed to spot Sebastian Vye. She smiled in his direction, and he ran back up the road and sat in his jeep trying to think of ways to save the donkeys for Eustacia January.

———

When he raised his head from the steering wheel the sun was setting, and as the mayor drove back along the North Shore to Cruz Bay the horizon over Saint Thomas was washed by fiery red stripes. He rounded the last corner on the winding North Shore Road and looked down upon Cruz Bay from Lind Point. He drove slowly down the steep incline and came upon the first dead donkey in the road at the foot of the hill. He got out and went to the donkey, the headlights of his car made the dead donkey's eyes glow amber. The donkey was shot in the ear. From downtown Cruz Bay he heard the echo of a shot, and then another. Sebastian ran toward the shots. He heard one closer, near the ferry dock, and he ran past the post office and the Morris DeCastro Clinic. Sebastian came upon the second donkey by the phone near Cruz Bay Beach. The phone was off the hook, and it dangled near the donkey's still quivering ear. The mayor wondered what had caused the donkeys to run back into Cruz Bay from the bush. It was as if they wanted to take the ferry off the island. He heard footsteps and saw the ambulance driver Kent Lyle run up and put his hand on the dying donkey's ears. Lyle stood and ran off toward the echoing sounds of another two shots. He turned halfway across Cruz Bay Park and yelled back, "It's Lt. Jeffreys."

   The mayor ran after Kent Lyle across the park. There was a dead donkey bleeding from a gut wound onto the gravel in front of the Back Yard Bar, one shot through the eye in front of Chase Bank, and another thrashing its legs in front of Cruz Bay Realty. There were two white men bent over the donkey. One wearing a Panama hat turned, and Barnard Hoyt gave him an odd look. The mayor nodded, and Hoyt said, "Here I thought you people couldn't do anything right."

The mayor turned away and raised both hands to his forehead, looked once back at Barnard Hoyt, and started running down the road back toward the National Park. Hoyt looked after him running. The mayor ran with his hands on his forehead, and as he ran he saw a Jeep's lights coming down from Lind Point, and he raised his hands and gestured as if to push it back up the hill. His lungs burned as he saw the Jeep slow to a halt before the donkey in the road. He saw the Jeep door open as he ran, saw a figure bent over the donkey in the headlights, and as the mayor ran up and yelled, "Eustacia!" she bent and kissed the dead donkey's head. He stood gasping for breath before her, and when she raised her face to him he cried out.

Sebastian Vye was found later that night at the villa of Henrietta Parsons in Chocolate Hole. Every flower in her garden was hacked to the earth. He was lying naked and filthy with a machete by his side, rubbing a handful of flower petals to his forehead.

He is no longer the mayor of the tiny Caribbean island of Saint John.

He is obese now, and his belly lolls over the gunnel of the filthy pants cut raggedly off at his knees and held up by a length of line given by a yachtsman who said he was tired of looking at the crack of his black ass. He sports a tattered vest, and has a long feather hanging from his right ear and a sun-faded Minnesota Vikings cap backward on his shaved skull.

He doesn't talk to tourists, but will carry luggage with a shuffling gait and an obsolete smile for a dollar a bag. He buys cold Heinekens with the crumpled cash and sits in the shade under the one palm tree not torn down to build the massive new Saint John dock, and as he waits for the next ferry from Saint Thomas, he picks at the corns on his bare feet and is no more present than the panting, flea-plagued island dog by his side, until memories of Eustacia January rise like the late afternoon moon in an otherwise baby blue Caribbean sky—then his eyes flare as bright and round as those of any tourist stepping off the dock toward his tiny island.

Irian Jaya

Doug Rennie

It is dark outside and raining. A man and woman are in a kitchen. She leans against the tiled countertop while he sits at a round wooden table, writing. A small heater drones in the corner.

The woman moves some hair off her face. She is tall and cool and, wearing a peacock blue kimono, elegant. "Are you warm enough?" she says.

The man is bald and thin, his face all cheekbones and sloping planes. He nods without looking up, his focus on the spiral notebook before him.

"More coffee?" she says.

The pen continues in long, cursive strokes, until the man has finished the sentence. "Yes," he says at last. "Please."

She walks over and fills his cup. He looks up briefly, mouths *thanks*, and returns to the notebook. She touches her fingers lightly to the back of his neck. "What are you writing about tonight?"

He shuts his eyes for several seconds and runs a finger down one side of his nose. "Oh," he says. "Just the usual. The world."

"More traveling?"

"Yes."

"And today? Where are we going? Cologne? Djakarta? Fairbanks, maybe," she says, remembering some of the far-flung cities he is always talking about.

"Oh, no. No." One corner of his mouth turns up, a rough draft of a half smile. "I visited the last city a few days ago."

"Which one?"

"You tell me." He lays his pen down and looks up at her over his shoulder.

"Ah . . . Cologne. Because of the cathedral."

"Perhaps," he says. "Maybe." He lays the pen on the table, then lifts his fingertips to his eyes and circles them over closed lids.

"Oh," she says, gently massaging his head. "You're tired. Sorry about all the questions. I'll just shut up." She walks around the table.

He shakes his head. "No," he says. "I'm fine. Just a little, ah . . . a little more tired than usual, I guess. My concentration's good, though." He takes a deep breath, slowly releases it. His eyes protrude from their sockets like hard-boiled eggs. "You did remember to pick up the—"

"Yes, this afternoon." She tips her head to her right. "It's over there. On the counter." She sits down and opens a book. "So," she says, her eyes everywhere but on him. "I'll read for a while. Leave you alone. I'll just sit here and read, not bother you. Keep working. I want you to finish this."

He removes his fingertips from his eyelids, opens his eyes, looks across the table at her, then beyond, through the window, to the wall of dark trees beyond the house.

"Whose woods these are, I think I know," he begins, then stops and gives a little snort.

She says nothing.

"Anyway," he continues, picking up his pen, "thanks. Sorry if I seemed a grouch. Didn't mean to. It's just—"

"Sssshhh," she says, holding up her hand. "Just go back to where you were."

"All right." A long sigh.

Like yesterday, and the weeks' worth of days before that, the only sounds are the tick of the wall clock, the scratch of nib on paper, the occasional rustle of a turned page. As always, the silence chews away at her nerves like a hundred sets of tiny teeth.

After fifteen minutes, she can take no more. She has read the same page three or four times without comprehension. *I want to be with you*, she thinks. She closes her book. "Sam," she says, quietly, tentatively, "where are we now?"

He holds up his left index finger and keeps writing, his head nodding to the rhythm of the moving pen. He finishes the sentence, taps point to paper with a small flourish. "Irian Jaya," he says.

"That's in . . ."

"New Guinea. The whole western half of the island. The people there still live in the Stone Age. Still cannibals. Headhunters, too."

"Why there?"

He pauses, shuts his eyes, and she knows: Just that quickly, he is there, in Irian Jaya. His voice is low, as in prayer. "Hissing rains fall onto the Arafura Sea, pound down onto slick brown tidal mudflats, spongy marshlands, brackish pools. Neon-bright butterflies in blues and yellows, oranges and greens. Mangrove roots the size of small ridges. Air fat and wet, like the inside of a greenhouse, a hundred degrees at eight in the evening."

She squints, wrinkles her nose. "Hey," she says, "wait a minute. New Guinea. Isn't that"—her hand flutters—"isn't that the place where whatshisname—"

"Michael Rockefeller disappeared. Yes. In the early sixties sometime." He opens his eyes. "Seems his boat got caught in a fierce tide, capsized. Everyone else hung on to the overturned boat, but Rockefeller, for some reason, decided to swim to shore, four, five miles away. Maybe because he was a strong swimmer—and he upped his odds by concocting some kind of flotation device out of two empty jerricans." He stops talking and pushes his tongue against the inside of his cheek.

"And?"

"And they think he made it, washed up on shore. But they—well, one missionary, at least—think that he likely ran into the Karowai. From upriver. And that he—how do they put it?—'fell victim to ritual cannibalism.' Something like that."

"My God."

"Oh, yes. *God*," he says, running a thumb across his chin, his mouth twisting into a slight sneer. "Indeed." He places his elbows on the table and rests his face in his hands.

"What a horrible way to die." Her shoulders shudder. "What a horrible place."

Slowly, he moves his hands down his cheeks leaving his fingertips resting on his chin. "No," he says, "not really. Not at all." He looks at the open notebook and begins to read. "Seen from the air, the rivers are veins that gleam like silver when the sun hits them, and they meander almost drunkenly in great loops and horseshoes through every sort of shade of green. The rivers— Sungai Digul, Sungai Pulau, a half dozen others—are fed from the highlands, from glaciers on the peaks of the Penunugan Jayawijaya fifteen thousand feet high." He looks back at her with raised eyebrows. "A horrible place? Um-mm. Quite beautiful, really."

"But what about those . . . the Care-oh-eye? Is that right?" She stumbles on the syllables. "Headhunters who eat each other. How does that come out 'quite beautiful'?"

He looks up at her as if he is about to speak, but then closes his mouth and gains control of his breathing. "But they have to, don't you see?" he says after a moment. "It's as much a part of them, of what they are, of *who* they are as . . . as catechism to Catholics." He stops, once more closes his eyes. He breathes loudly, and a wheezing comes from deep in his chest. The fingers on his right hand convulse until he squeezes them with his left. When he continues, his voice is quiet, dreamy, and she knows that only his body is in the room. "The men paddle these rivers in dugout canoes the same gray-brown color as the water. The handles of their paddles are carved in the visages of ancestors' faces—dead souls all who must be avenged—and the rowers wear the lower jaws of their victims strung together on necklaces."

"And *this* is where we're going? To the mud and the heat surrounded by savages who want to eat you?"

He opens his eyes and returns to the kitchen. "You still don't understand. But, yes, I see how Irian Jaya could seem, to some, a hellish place. And it is, I suppose, in some ways." He takes another deep breath. "But it is extraordinary, too. One of the last places on Earth that hasn't changed, not really, not at all, in fifteen, twenty thousand years. Not the land, not the people. Cannibals, yes. Headhunters, yes, that, too. Savages, as you call them, by any standard. But you know what?" He looks up at her through eyes that have become watery and red.

She shakes her head.

"They still own their own lives."

His voice is weary and she stares at him sadly. *Why debate this?* she thinks. So he fly-fishes the Big Blackfoot, rafts the Kongakut, heli-skis in Bugaboos, hikes Uganda's Mountains of the Moon.

On these pages.

At this table.

A year ago, when he first found out, there was disbelief, then rage that fueled arguments, loud and vile and hurtful, and in between, silence. Long, fork-scraping silences. Then, six months ago, he woke up one morning and, just like that, decided he would . . . travel, and the fighting ceased.

She leans closer, and in the opening of his loose shirt, sees the cleft of his collarbone. His face has grown taut, each muscle twitching beneath the wrinkled skin. ("My face," he sometimes says, "looks like it needs to be ironed.") She shakes her head as she looks at him and sighs. *Skinny as a refugee, knuckles for knees.* "Is it time?" she says.

He does not answer, but sits upright and rigid, eyes closed tightly, his lower jaw quivering. She knows, as always this time of day, that he is willing himself to breathe steady and even and controlled. And, as always at this moment, she is uncertain when to intervene. She stands and begins to weave back and forth as she rocks with her arms clenched against her chest. Just under her diaphragm, her stomach flutters in silent little spasms. She looks at him, then at the clock. At him again, at the clock.

Two minutes.

Three.

Five.

The edge of his lower lip is caught between his teeth, and she moves only when she sees a tiny bead of blood form in the corner of his mouth and, seconds later, his jaw begin to tremble. She walks quickly to the counter, opens the bag, and with exaggerated delicacy removes one of several small vinyl bags. Then she moves next to his chair, to the coathanger-like apparatus from which descends a clear plastic tube. There are soft *pops* as she pulls syringes from both ends of a similar, but empty, bag and inserts them into the new one. She waits for his face to relax. She knows there will be a few moments of clarity, of lucidity, before the morphine fills his blood, fogs his brain, effaces the women and children who sit before huts set on stilts above the mud and weave bags made from orchid fibers; deletes the silty rivers, the Russell's vipers, the crocodiles and cockatoos, the feathered headdresses and skulls of ancestors. She knows, too, that for those first few moments of the descent, he will be where he wants to be, though for how many more days she cannot say. She watches his body slacken, his face sag like warm wax. Then she, too, closes her eyes, sits down and takes his hands in hers.

"Tell me," she says, her low, soft voice solemn and warm. "Tell me one more time about Irian Jaya."

Say the Word

Jean Rysstad

The boy is twelve and taller than Fran by several inches now. She has not seen much of him this summer since he is trolling with his uncle, away ten days at a time, in town for a day or two, then out, away again. Even when he is home, Fran hardly sees him because he sleeps until the phone rings or until one of the neighborhood boys hollers up at his open bedroom window. Then he is in the bathroom, at the fridge, and before she can speak with him, he is out the door, skateboard under his arm.

He used to walk but now, just this summer, he has begun to glide. He is finding a stride that is a little like his father's way of navigating the world but not so sure or sturdy. The way the boy moves down the hall or down the road toward his friends is lighter than the way Joe walks. He seems to float as if he is several inches above the ground, and Fran wonders if time on water has given him this ability.

The boy has just called from the fishing grounds, and though they have said good-bye and hung up, Fran feels as if they are still connected—it's just a time of dead air, each waiting for the other to say something that might make a difference.

How are you? Fran asked him.

Good, he said, but his voice wasn't hearty.

Where are you? Yes, at Zayus, where the blackflies are not so bad as they are at Dundas, but where on the boat, where are you now? Below? In your bunk?

I'm in the wheelhouse. Where the phone is.

She'd heard a hint of sarcasm, a hint of what would come with his changing voice.

And where is Uncle Ronnie?

He's icing fish in the hold.

And was fishing good today?

I'm not going to make as much money as last trip. We're getting lots of humpies.

What else to ask him? What piece of news would give him pleasure, something to mull over?

You got a skateboard catalog in the mail today.

What's on the cover?

Oh, Jer, she'd said, I don't know if I can find it in this mess. We're still sanding floors, you know. We're upside down.

Will you try? he'd asked.

Okay. Hold on, she'd said, rummaging through a pile of papers on the table. Jackpot, Jer. You're lucky. It's a dark blue, a nighttime sky, and there's tall white buildings, like towers or high-rises, and a big steep ramp.

You mean a half-pipe?

I don't know what it is. It's this big curved thing that's joined up to the building, and there's a boy hanging in the air on his skateboard. He's just come off the ramp, and the photographer took a picture of him hanging there in the sky.

What's on the second page?

She'd laughed, flipped the page, and told him a little about the advertising for "completes," tops, trucks, wheels and bearings, and then said maybe they'd talked enough for one night. It was good Uncle Ronnie bought that new phone that reached from the grounds to home, wasn't it? Was there anything else he wanted to say?

Will you put the catalog on my bed?

That's it? That's all? She'd encouraged him to say a little more. After all, they had privacy. Not like on a radio phone where every word you said crackled in the galleys of all the boats on the grounds.

Well, there's *something* else.

And what is that?

I'm afraid I'm going to drown. I'm afraid I'm not going to come home from this trip.

And Fran had said, Of course you will. Do you think we'd let you go fishing if we were even a little bit worried about you? But at the same time she saw the wall at the waterfront park, built with bricks, hundreds of bricks bearing the names of those who were lost at sea, life spans both long and short. Fran wishes Joe had been home. His words might make a difference. What he'd say might help the boy get through it.

Fran stood in the doorway of the boy's room, looking at the things that represented his spirit at twelve. He collected far less junk than any of them, discarded his past passions and dreams easily and often. Ninja Turtles and that pair of nunchakus he'd ordered from the back of a comic for $19.95: two heavy-duty plastic sticks attached with a chain arrived in a cardboard tube. A weapon. Where would he swing those sticks? At whom? Did they work like a boomerang? Did you swing them and let go? The boy had looked surprised. Enemies? Robbers, maybe. Killers.

Pirate ship and space station Lego sets were long gone. Now his walls were plastered with posters of Pavel and Linden, but these were tattered and droopy because the pins and staples had fallen out. They were ready for the garbage. She knew what posters came next: Smashing Pumpkins, Kurt Cobain, Hendrix, Rage Against the Machine.

She got clean sheets, made his bed, and flapped the quilt his gran had made for him from old wool coats that had belonged to the men in the family. She watched the quilt float down and settle, smoothed out the wrinkles, and sat down facing his CD player. Last summer's fishing had bought it. This icon. The machine and the neatly piled discs held his deepest self, his hopes, fears, dreams. The machine, the music, the shelf: an altar.

Above the CD shelf, he'd hung an eight-by-ten picture of himself in a deep blue hand-knit sweater and legging set. The photograph had been taken in Woolworth's on his first birthday. Fran had carried him partway through the store and then set him down, held his hand while he took head-first topple-over steps. What a beautiful boy, the grandmothers in the store had said that December day. What a beautiful boy.

Beside the portrait was a newspaper clipping of his gran and grampa taken fifty years ago on their wedding day, their heads touching, tilted in toward each other, their eyes startling in their shiny innocence. These three faces had held their places throughout the boy's changes, but this year, Fran thought, he'll take them down from the wall and put them in a shoebox. Of course he has to do this.

Fran reached behind her and turned out the light. The glow-in-the-dark stars on the boy's ceiling were dim from where she sat, and she wondered if they shone brighter when Jer lay down, thinking of the faraway future, or if they shone bright just for the next day and were faint and misty, ghostly even, when he thought of the years ahead. Did he imagine what it would be like if she died, if his father died, where he would go, what he would do? She lay down on the single bed with the skateboard magazine across her breasts.

By now he would be in his narrow upper bunk, inside his blue sleeping bag. He would have warmed his hands on the engine pipes after some last chore on deck. He'd have brushed his teeth in the tiny sink, gotten rid of the taste of diesel fuel for a moment, then turned out the light, crawled up, opened the tiny porthole, and cranked his neck around so he could see the black water and the dark gray rainy skies. No stars, no dipper, no moon.

And what would he think? Would he take his mind directly to the skateboard catalog, remember that she'd promised to put it on his bed, or would he have to take the long way to that thought, first listening to the waves elapsing like slow seconds on the sides of the wooden boat, then thinking of falling over the side, how it might happen to him the way it had happened to others. He would try not to think about the men floating in the water with their zippers open, but these dead men would knock and bump and nudge the sides of the boat. He would spend some time hating his dad for telling him about it, for making him show him how he could plant his feet solid, two feet apart, one a little ahead, think about how he hated being given a push, a playful but hard and sudden push that toppled him and proved that he wasn't planted, didn't have his sea legs yet.

And boots. New yellow-and-black Helly Hansons, size 11, the same size as his dad's and his uncle's. Last year just regular gumboots from the back of Zellers, $15.99, and now these new ones, $60 off his crew share. Buying them with his uncle in Fisherman's Supply. He's getting in deeper and deeper. And he never asked for it, except he did ask if he could fish again this summer. For the money. Now he has his own rain gear and six pairs of black gloves and a scar from when one of the hooks flew through the flesh below his thumb. Six pinpoint needle marks from the barbs on a cod. How weird and numb his whole arm went. He would think about crab bait, fish heads, his head, and then about his hand with the two big warts that won't go away even though the doctor dropped stuff on them twice this summer.

His father and his uncle had made him practice kicking his boots off. Faster, they yelled at him. See how fast you can get them off. You gotta kick hard. And even a survival suit now. For him. Uncle Ron said it was for the boat, but then why did he have to try it on in his living room? Lay it out like it's your shadow and get in as fast as you can, his dad said.

The fisherman who drowned just before they'd left on this trip.

He fell off the dock, slipped or something coming down the ramp, boards greasy with rain and oil, and fell into the harbor right beside his own boat, and no one was there to help him.

What would it be to lose him? Fran panicked, feeling as though she had fallen in herself. She kicked away from those thoughts. Did she think she could travel with the boy all his life, be his life ring? No. But she imagined she could go a long distance with him, maybe all her life, all of his, if she just floated. His dreamy way invited this kind of quiet companionship, knowing, didn't it?

This boy. He didn't use words. It wasn't his way. When he was nine, they'd been doing dishes together. He was washing. The radio was tuned into the local pop station, low, part of the air. And the air between them was easy as it mysteriously always has been—a live and let live. Lots of space and air, a sink full of water and suds. The boy liked the dishes to be clean. He didn't hurry. And she didn't say, C'mon, c'mon, speed it up, get the job done. He had pushed his hand and the dishcloth into a glass and let it fill up with water. After a bit of turning and swishing he'd held the glass up for her. His fist was crammed against the side and his thumb and finger made a kind of sad dreamy smile.

This is how I'd look if I drowned, he said.

He'd been swimming in the town pool earlier that week, he told her. The words came slowly. She'd pumped and pressed them out of him, a few at a time, as they carried on washing and drying. Shane, that bully, had held him under in the deep end. Jer dried his hands, pulled the neck of his T-shirt down onto his shoulder, and she saw the bruises on his back, his collarbone, faint blue fingerprints. She loathed that boy Shane, but kept drying and setting the dishes in the cupboard. He had struggled, but Shane had held him down harder so he stopped fighting and waited.

After that water revelation, she and Joe began to preach. You've got to get mad. Say no. Say to yourself: I will not sink. I will not go under. This will not happen to me. Find that place in your head, Fran had said. No, said Joe, find that place in your body.

Had any of these words sunk into his skin? Or did they drift through him, in one ear and out the other?

Words. He doesn't use them but Fran has noticed how the boy is drawn and held by the way she and his sister talk sometimes, as if he is warming his hands at a fire. He comes in close but he rarely adds wood. Perhaps he knows that the beach has been combed and that there is enough on the fire to keep it burning without his help. This thought makes Fran sad. How can you survive without words to keep you warm when you are shivering with cold after falling in? Still, lately, when the four of them gathered together by chance at the kitchen table, a girl and a boy, a man and a woman, they'd built some rip-roaring fires, and the laughter had leapt like cinders between them.

Before the boy left on this trip, there'd been a flare-up between Joe and Julie, some normal thing like Julie used all the hot water when Joe needed to have a shower, too. Normal and then escalated, Julie storming upstairs to her room and Joe retreating to his basement quarters. That left Fran and Jer on the middle deck. Jer headed for the television in the front room, and Fran turned on the radio in the kitchen and began to wash dishes. Vicki Gabereau was live on the Fraser River, rushing down through white water. Her squeals of fear and exhilaration rose and fell in Fran. She went to check on Jer. He was lying on the couch watching *Dumb and Dumber*, hands cupped behind his head. He paused the movie with the remote.

Do you feel sad or anything? he'd asked.

No, she'd said. And they had gazed at each other, amused, amazed. They had floated through the storm untouched, dry as a bone.

Yes, what she knows of him so far is his calm floating soul. If you don't tell me things, she'd said to him recently, I just think, Oh, Jer—his life is perfect. He'd looked at her as if she were insane. Not long ago, when the four of them were together at breakfast, Jer said he'd had a dream about falling down a deep hole and the more he tried to climb out the deeper the hole grew. And then Fran mentioned a jogger, how his wife had said he ran in his sleep and the sheets and blankets got all whipped up. Joe had talked of flying. How joyous to look at the stick-on stars and think of him soaring over Grassy Lake, flying high and tilting down into the cove where Duffy has set up his bachelor camp, watchman at the dam. Fran soared, too, circled. She saw two teenage boys, a case of beer, a canoe, a moon. The boys were laughing and then the canoe, the canoe tipped, and the boys struggled in the icy water, laughing at first and grasping for the boat. Laughing and then gasping, unable to believe what was happening.

This country has become treacherous now, Fran thought. Before kids, she'd decided that to think too much about what might happen would be to invite disaster. If your number was up, it was up. Still, on the seaplanes crossing the Hecate Strait in storms, she'd made deals with God. I'll do this if you will do this. The engine stalled on a plane Joe was on. He didn't mention any deals. He said he put his duffel bag in front of his face and chest, thinking it might cushion the blow when it came.

And the Skeena River. Ever year, sometimes twice a year, someone, sometimes families, slid in. Old cars, brand-new cars, four-wheel-drive all-terrainers, logging trucks. And lives, swallowed whole by this huge gray whale. If it wasn't the river side of the highway, it was the mountains that slid down once a year, twice a year, caving in on travelers whether they were making business deals or going to a hockey tournament with all intentions of bringing home a trophy for the town.

Now any story of survival, of how people kept their wits about them, seems important to repeat, to discuss.

Last year at the end of the summer, two boys had left their village in a canoe. They packed for an overnight adventure, intending to paddle to the far side of an island and set up camp. Their canoe tipped in the breakers as they approached what they thought was the spot they wanted, and though they made it to shore, they weren't found for three days. Their grandfather, who was aboard the rescue boat, told the crew where the boys would be, and there they were, wet, cold, and hungry. "You went the wrong way," the grandfather said.

"Well, why didn't you tell us?" the boys said. "You watched us leave. You heard us planning. Why didn't you tell us?"

"You didn't ask," said the grandpa.

Fran keeps remembering this story and telling it to her kids. Now after what happened to them, the boys will ask, she says. *Wanting* to know is so much better than being *told*. What you should know, she says to them. But she wonders: How did the grandfather keep his mouth shut? Where did he find his trust? How could he risk so much?

Fran wonders if Jeremy remembers the first lesson, the day they went out for blueberries, filling an ice cream bucket along the tracks, and then climbing higher onto the rock bluffs above the harbor, scrambling on those cliffs. They found a sheltered place to rest, and the kids had said, Let's make a fire. Okay, said Joe. But you only have one match. Pretend you are lost and you only have one match. How would you make the best of your one chance? The kids had the right instinct—they'd gathered small twigs and propped them up like a tepee—but the match didn't catch. Look under the trees, go into the bush a little, look for the driest finest smallest burnable things. Dry brown needles, anything like that.

The wind off the water was really cold when the sun disappeared. Did Jer remember that time on the bluff? Would he remember it if he needed it?

What would it be to lose him? Could she hold on to the story, the making lost into found, that the singer for the Haida dancers had explained before the dancers danced the story in the red and black, this life and that other one? How all the village mourned as they searched for a little lost girl, how in spring they saw the first salmon jump in the creek, joyful, and they knew it was their little girl, come back to them. She had heard parents say that after a while, after the passing of several seasons, they saw their lost children appear in spring, not in a fish perhaps, but in a flower, the first purple crocus raising its head through the snow.

Every mother and father goes to the place in them where the child is lost. If they do not imagine it, fall into it through events around them, through a neighbor, a friend, a relative, then it happens through the news, the falling into that empty unimaginable pit. And if they refuse to fall in waking life, then the descent comes in dreams. The child about to fall from a cliff, drown in the lake, be murdered by . . . and the hopeless grasping, stretching out to reach the hand of the child, kicking, swimming toward him, never getting there, the sheets and blankets churning. Nobody speaks of these dream deaths. Fran has never told hers to anyone but Joe, and even then, she left out details and went straight for the interpretation—"worry"—a need making itself known through dreams to make sure the boy, the girl, had survival skills.

The boy will come home. What is happening to him now is natural and good, and at twelve he must walk through it on his own. He has to learn to manage fear—waking and sleeping—to fear in dreams and wake from them, to fear before sleep, and in all the long days on the water. He needs to remember and invent survival, to imagine himself as eagle, otter, boy in a canoe, paddling to an island for a weekend adventure.

She can't do anything but wave good-bye, go with him in spirit. He will walk through it, glide through the door as he has done at the end of every trip this summer. She knows he can and will. He must. She rises, smooths the bed, and lays the magazine on his pillow.

That new boat phone. The cellular. Did it help or hinder the walking through?

Did you tell Uncle Ron you were afraid of drowning? she'd asked.

Yes, he said. I have a whistle around my neck.

Breeding Turkeys

Julie Showalter

Billie had only been in the pen with the big turkeys for five minutes when she heard a hen squawk like something was hurting her. She ran through the turkeys, some of the toms as tall as her chest, until she found the hen pinned down by a tom. He was digging his claws in her back. The hen's head lay sideways in the dirt. She had stopped squawking and had given up fighting. Billie kicked the tom, but he was heavy and she couldn't budge him. She grabbed a stick and hit him on his back. Her father came running from the other side of the pen where he had been putting out feed. He grabbed the stick and broke it across his knee. "He was hurting her," Billie said.

"Go to the house," her father said. "Talk to your mother."

Her mother said, "These new turkeys are breeding turkeys. They're not like range turkeys or brooder turkeys. This is what they're supposed to do."

"He was hurting her."

"We're getting saddles for the hens. That'll protect their backs. And don't ever hurt a turkey again. They're the way we make our living."

That night in bed, her sister Carol, who was in sixth grade, laughed at her. "They were screwing. Don't you know the F-word?"

"I hate you," Billie said. "I really hate you."

Billie was eight, the youngest in the family. Carol was twelve, and Laura was sixteen. When Billie was a baby, their mother was tired a lot so Laura was mainly the one who fed Billie and changed her diapers and played with her. Then, when Billie started school, Laura was in charge of helping with her homework. Now that Laura was going out with boys, Billie waited up to hear about her dates.

That night Laura tiptoed in with her shoes in her hand. She

smiled at Billie and held her finger to her mouth to tell her hush. Then she let Billie get into bed with her. Billie went to sleep surrounded by the smells of Wind Song perfume, hair spray, the cigarette smoke from the boy Laura had been out with.

———

They put saddles on the hens. Billie and Carol separated the hens from the toms and drove them into the pen where their dad grabbed each one and held its wings back while Laura slid the straps under the wings.

"They don't look like saddles," Billie said. She had expected more than a patch of green canvas.

"If you see one that's flipped up," her dad said, "pull it back down. These are valuable birds. We can't have them getting their backs clawed up."

———

Billie had been her father's favorite since the day she was born. He said, "I've been saving this name for a son, but I guess I'd better go ahead and use it." His name was Billy, too, but spelled differently. Billy Joe and Billie Sue—those were their names. When Billie was four, her mother went to work at the hospital switchboard. After that, Billie spent all day with her dad. She'd sit in the pickup when he went to the feed mill or the bank. She'd ride on the tractor and get down to open and close gates for him. When she was five she scooted an eighty-pound bag of turkey feed to the back of the pickup so he wouldn't have to climb up to get it. She didn't get bored and complain like Laura or talk all the time like Carol.

Laura was their mother's favorite because she was pretty and smart and because it had been just the two of them while their dad was at the war in Germany. Laura reminded their mother of herself before she had a husband and three daughters. Their mother had been a semifinalist in a beauty contest once, and she had an award for a poem she wrote in high school. She told Laura, "Don't give up on your dreams. You can have a better life than this." Carol wasn't anybody's favorite.

———

When the days started getting short, they drove all the turkeys into a special pen every night. The pen had perches, and it had lights strung up high. The lights came on at four in the morning. The hens would think it was spring if the sun came up early. Then they'd want to lay eggs.

"Are they really that stupid?" Carol asked.

"Hens?" their dad said. "If there's any animal stupider than a turkey hen, I haven't run across it."

———

Carol woke Billie up crowding against her and moaning. Half asleep, Billie poked her with her foot. "Get back on your own side." She felt something wet. "Have you peed the bed?" she asked, her voice rising. "If you wet the bed, I will never sleep with you again. I'll sleep with the sick turkeys before I'll sleep with you."

"Go get Mother," Carol said. She was crying.

When Billie followed her mother back in, she saw a red foot print on the floor where she had walked. Her mother pulled back the covers, and there was blood on the sheets. Her voice was calm. "I wish you girls didn't start so early," she said. She got a towel for Carol and helped her to the bathroom. "Get those sheets off," she told Billie. "Set them to soak in cold water."

"Does she have to go to the hospital?" Billie asked.

"No," her mother smiled. "It's just her period. You help me with this mess and I'll talk to you later."

After a while, Carol came back in a clean nightgown. Her mother helped Billie put clean sheets on the bed and settled Carol in with a heating pad. "Do you understand what this is?" she asked Carol.

"Yes. I just didn't know it would hurt."

"Well, it does sometimes." She put her hand on Carol's head and smiled. "And sometimes it doesn't. My little girls are growing up faster than I'm ready for. I'll get you your own supplies, and I'll get you a calendar so you'll know your schedule. I can't keep track of two, much less three. You'll have to know when to expect this so you won't make another mess." She pulled the covers up under Carol's chin. "I'll tell your dad you've got the flu so he won't expect you to help with chores in the morning."

"He doesn't have to know about this, does he?"

"No. He doesn't like to think about things like this. And so he doesn't find out, you'll always have to check now to make sure you don't leave any mess in the bathroom. And when you change your things don't leave them in the bathroom trash. Take them on out to the barrel."

After she left, Billie asked Carol, "What's a period?"

"It's what goes at the end of a sentence, dummy."

It was way after midnight when Laura came in. She was all giggly and fell on the bed so that her petticoats bounced up around her. "Oh, Billie," she said, "I am truly, truly in love. Truly, truly."

"With Don Randolph?"

"No," Laura rolled on her side and giggled. "This is a secret you mustn't, mustn't tell. Don just picks me up and takes me to meet Bobby Hibdon."

"But Daddy said—"

"Shush, shush, shush," Laura rolled close to her on the bed and whispered. "This is our secret. Daddy doesn't understand about love. He thinks it just stops if someone gets suspended from school. True love doesn't work like that. You'll know that when you grow up."

Billie said, "I think Carol is grown up now. Mother said so."

Laura was almost asleep, still in her pretty dress. "That's nice, Billie," she said. "Would you turn off the light?"

———

They were driving the turkeys, but one hen wouldn't move forward. She hunkered down in the dirt and shook all over. She made a rough throat noise and stuck her tail in the air. Even when Billie pushed her with her broomstick, the hen moved about two steps and then squatted down and stuck her tail up again. Their father came over and lifted the turkey with his boot over and over until she finally started walking on her own.

"What's wrong with her?" Billie asked him.

"Talk to your mother." By then Billie knew "talk to your mother" meant it was about sex.

When their dad was out of earshot, Laura said, "The hen's in heat. They get completely stupid when they're in heat."

———

The nests were like little apartment buildings for the hens. Each long nest had eight separate compartments, and each compartment had a kind of privacy door in front so that once a hen was inside another couldn't bother her until she came out. One giant lid opened the top of all eight nests. Billie was strong enough to flip the lid of the nest by herself. One of her jobs was to keep the nests lined with clean yellow straw. She imagined snuggling down in the fresh straw inside the nest with the bar across the front. If Carol ever played hide-and-seek with her again, it would be a good place to hide.

Their mother was draining a chicken thigh over the skillet when it fell off the fork. Boiling grease splashed on her arm. All the girls fell silent as she turned out the fire under the chicken, moved to the table, and collapsed with her head in her hands. "I had so many dreams," she said. Her voice was limp and soggy like a dishrag. "Everyone thought I would succeed. I was supposed to go to college. I showed promise." Laura got Unguentine for their mother's arm. Billie and Carol went back to their chores, moving carefully. They didn't want to draw attention to the difference between what their mother had been promised and what she had.

While Billie set the table, Carol filled the glasses from the wide-mouthed milk jug. She didn't spill a drop, but when she turned, wagging her eyebrows at Billie, she bumped a glass, spilling it across the table, wetting all the paper napkins.

Their mother stood up so fast she knocked her chair over. "I don't know how much more I can take," she said through clenched teeth. "Laura, you and the other two finish up. I'm going to lie down a while. Call me when supper's ready."

When the hens started to lay eggs, they were confused and dropped them under the perches at night. If they were just cracked on the outside and the tough membrane wasn't broken, their mother broke them into freezer bags and kept them for baking.

Some of the first eggs didn't even have a shell, just the membrane. You could see the yolk inside. Billie thought she would keep one warm and watch a turkey grow inside. Laura said no, it wouldn't work. So the girls played games with the soft, unformed eggs—water balloon toss, keep-away, ambush.

When Billie couldn't sleep she made up questions for Carol. "How would you rather die," she asked, "boiling or freezing?"

Carol thought a while. "Boiling would be faster. But it would hurt more."

"Which would you rather be, deaf or blind?"

"Deaf. No, blind. You wouldn't have to do chores."

"You could still wash eggs."

"Yeah. You'd probably have to wash all the eggs by yourself. And you wouldn't get to watch TV while you were doing it. Deaf."

Billie said, "Imagine watching Mother get mad and not being able to hear the words."

Carol said, "If you were with Daddy, you might not even know you were deaf."

They lay there giggling.

Everyone said Billie was just like her father. She had his smile and his eyebrows. They were both quiet, and they were shy around people they didn't know.

When her dad had to leave her in the pickup for a long time, he'd give her a puzzle. "Think of a tree for every letter of the alphabet" was one.

When he got back, she said, "I did pretty good." She read her list as he drove. "A, apple tree. B, berry tree."

He gave her a quick look. "I guess I'll allow that."

"C, cherry tree. D, dogwood. E—I don't have an E. F, fir tree. H, happy tree."

He tried to hold his mouth tight, but his smile broke out. "You got any more trees like that?"

Billy looked over her list. "I've got a sad tree and a lazy tree."

All the way home her dad would point to trees and say, "Happy or sad?" They laughed the whole time, but when they told the story and showed the list, her mother and Laura and Carol didn't know why it was funny.

One night they heard dogs barking and the next day their father found two half-eaten hens by the fence. "A hundred dollars," he said. "A hundred dollars worth of breeding hens." He bought an automatic cannon to keep the animals away. It went off every twenty minutes during the night. The first three times it exploded, they had to keep the turkeys from piling at the edge of the fence and suffocating each other. The fourth time, the turkeys stirred, gave a few quiet gobbles, ruffled their feathers, and went back to sleep.

From the house, they could still hear the dogs barking, but they were farther away now.

Laura came in from her date laughing. "Bobby nearly shit his pants. We were making out in the driveway and when the cannon went off he thought Daddy was coming after him with a shotgun." Bobby's suspension from school was over and Laura was allowed to go out with him again.

———

"Birds are the ugliest animals and turkeys are the ugliest birds because they don't have feathers on their heads," Carol said.

"Baby turkeys do."

"Yeah. But they get ugly when they lose their head feathers."

"Hens are uglier than toms, but the toms are meaner." Billie was quiet for a while. "I saw on TV that you just go to sleep in the snow. It doesn't even hurt."

———

All the farmers in the area had their names painted on their pickup doors. "Russell Heisten and Sons," "Noel Stark and Son." Laura said, "Daddy, our truck should say 'Billy Joe Stockton and Daughters.' We work harder than the Heisten boys." But when the truck was painted it said, "Stocktons' Turkey Farm." Their dad said, "It's plural. It means all of us." But Laura told Billie and Carol, "He's ashamed he has daughters."

———

Starting in December, every day when they got off the bus, Laura ran for the mailbox. She had chances for scholarships at three different schools. She told Billie, "I want to go someplace where nobody even knows what turkeys smell like. And I'll bring you up for weekends. You can visit enough so that when it's your turn you'll know what college is like and you won't be scared."

"Will Bobby go away with you?"

"No. Bobby's going to work on the night shift at the spring factory after graduation."

"Will you miss him?"

Laura bent down so she was looking Billie in the eyes. "Yes. I love Bobby. I really do. But people have to grow. I mean, can you imagine me married to someone who works at the spring factory?"

―――――

Eggs had to be gathered every three hours. The longer they stayed in the nest, the more likely that a new hen coming in would step on them. The longer they were out in the cold, the less likely they were to be fertile when they got to the hatchery.

Eggs had to have all the turkey shit and straw and yolk from broken eggs cleaned off them or they might explode in the incubator. If a dirty egg exploded, it ruined all the eggs with it. Every night after dinner, the whole family sat on low stools in front of the television with baskets of eggs. They wiped the eggs with damp cloths, stamped them with their flock number, and put them in crates.

A fertile egg was worth fifty cents. Every crate held two hundred eggs. One night when her dad moved the third case to the mudroom, Billie said, "We're going to be rich."

"How do you figure that?"

"Three hundred dollars just for today. That's a lot of money."

"That's good figuring, but a lot of them don't hatch. And we have to pay for turkey feed and electricity for the lights. And vaccinations. And nests."

"But you built the nests."

"The lumber wasn't free."

―――――

Fifty cents was ten Hershey bars or five Almond Joys or one egg that had a live baby turkey inside. The eggs were smooth and speckled. Billie thought of the baby turkey that would come out. She thought of the goose that laid the golden eggs. If they had that goose they wouldn't need the turkeys.

―――――

"Are you wearing one of those things?"
"You mean my Kotex?"
"I think it's disgusting."
"Then you think Mother's disgusting and Laura's disgusting. And you think you'll be disgusting when it happens to you."
"It's not going to happen to me. I'll be like Daddy."
"You're not like Daddy. You're one of us."

The day Laura got the letter about the scholarship, their mother stopped at the butcher shop on the way home from work and got five T-bone steaks. Billie made twice-baked potatoes. Carol rolled up napkins and tied ribbons around them so they looked like diplomas and set up the candles they kept for power outages in ashtrays. Even though they had all seen the letter, their mother, who looked almost as young as Laura in the candlelight, read it aloud. "Full tuition, room, board, and books, and living stipend. Total scholarship award over four years, $10,000." She made a toast with her iced tea, "To our oldest daughter who's made us proud."

Billie and Carol clicked their glasses. Carol said, "I get her room."

Laura looked at their dad. "How about you, Daddy? Are you proud of me?"

"You've got a chance, Laura. Not many people get a break like this. I hope you make the most of it."

"It's not just a break. I worked hard for this."

"Everyone in this family works hard."

Their mother said, "You're a special girl, Laura."

Their father pushed back his chair. "I can't see that she's any more special than the other two."

"I didn't say that. I just meant this was a special night for her."

A gust from the furnace made the candles waver and their father said, "Turn on the lights."

Billie stared at her plate. She listened to the screeches when their knives cut through the steaks to the plate. She listened to herself chew.

Their father said, "One good thing. This'll get her away from that boy."

Laura began to cry. "Why can't you be proud of me just once? Why do you ruin everything?"

Their father stood up. "Girls, help your mother clean up. Good dinner."

They heard their father and mother through the bedroom door. "You make her think smarter is better," he said. "She's not better than the rest of us."

Billie's dad could swing a basket of eggs a full circle over his head and not break a one. "Centrifugal force," he said. "It's stronger than gravity." It was a hard trick, but Billie thought of how surprised her dad would be when she showed him she could do it. He would smile and shake his head the way he did when she pushed the bag of feed to him the first time. She tried it a little at a time, first swinging the basket back and forth in a wide arc, always being careful when she changed directions so that she didn't jar the eggs. She got so the arc was as high as her head. Then, one day, she said to her sisters, "Here goes." She swung the basket up smooth and easy. When it got to the top of the circle, it hesitated. Eggs dropped to the ground. The eggs still in the basket made cracking sounds as the basket reversed direction and came back forward.

Billie looked at the eggs on the ground, the dripping basket. At least twenty eggs broken, maybe thirty.

Her sisters helped her. Even Carol's face was pale over the broken eggs. They divided up their baskets so everybody had a little less than usual. They took the broken eggs into the woods and buried them.

That night their father wrote the count for the day on the chart on the wall in the mudroom. Because Billie was good at numbers, her dad had taught her how to plot the egg production graph. She marked the dot for that day's number. With her ruler, she joined the dot to the line that started low in October, climbed through mid-November, and stayed almost level after that. The segment she drew jagged down. Her dad pursed his lips as he looked at it.

Billie wanted to say she was sorry. Instead, she asked, "Will we starve?"

Her dad smiled and put his hand on her neck. "Nope. We won't starve. Your mom's just going to have to put more oatmeal in the meatloaf for a while."

Most hens, when you flipped the lid on the nest, ran out scared. But some of them hunkered down and tried to stay on their eggs. Some of them, while you were still bent over from lifting the lid, raised up out of the nest and hissed in your face. If you reached down to push them out, they could peck you or fly up in your eye, so you poked their back with a broomstick until they left. Sometimes you had to poke a lot. They really didn't want to leave their eggs.

Laura was supposed to spend Friday night with her best friend Susan. But when their mother called Saturday morning to ask Laura to buy bread on her way home, Susan's mother said she hadn't been there. Susan said Laura hadn't been at school on Friday. Bobby's parents didn't know where he was, either. The police said to give them a few more hours.

Their mother walked from the kitchen door to the front door, back and forth. She talked about kidnapping and wrecks on deserted roads and about how Susan was probably wrong about school and maybe they'd misunderstood, that it wasn't Susan Laura was spending the night with after all, but another girl. She said, "That girl's not too big to spank." She said, "When she gets home, she's grounded until college."

Their father didn't say anything.

Laura and Bobby pulled into the driveway at noon just as Carol and Billie were coming back from gathering eggs. Their father, who had been way back at the pen a minute before, strode past them. He opened Laura's door before the car was stopped and pulled her out by her arm. "Get in the house." Bobby got out his door. "You go home now and don't come back," their father said. Bobby stood where he was, staring at the gravel in the driveway.

Laura rubbed her wrist. Her chin went up. "Where you send him, I'm going, too." She held out her left hand. "We're married now."

Their mother had come out of the house and was halfway to the car. Her hand went to her throat. "No," she said, almost in a gag.

For a moment everyone in the yard seemed frozen.

"When's it due?" their father said.

Laura's chin was still high. "Why do you always assume the worst about me?"

Bobby spoke for the first time, "I love your daughter, sir. I'm happy she's my wife."

"Wife," their father said, like the word made him spit. "I asked when's it due."

Laura stared back, angry and stubborn as he was. Bobby looked at his feet and said, "May or June."

Laura said, "Come on, Bobby. Let's get out of here." As she was getting in the car, she looked at Billie. She tried to smile and gave a little wave, but her eyes were sad and scared.

Their father walked to their mother and put his arms around her. She pushed him away, and bent at the waist like she was throwing up. When her sobs slowed, he led her into the house.

Billie and Carol were alone in the driveway.

"What does it mean?" Billie asked.

"It means Laura is going to get big and fat and ugly and have a baby. It means Laura isn't going to college. It means she's a whore. It means I get her room now."

———

Chores took a lot longer that night. Their mother was too sick to take Laura's place. When they finished driving the turkeys into their night pen, their father said, "Carol, you go to the house and heat some soup and make grilled cheese sandwiches. Billie, you gather the eggs. I'll be in as soon as I get the feed wagon loaded."

"You want me to go with you and open gates?" Billie always opened gates for her dad. "Then I can come back and gather eggs."

"No. Do what I said."

"I don't mind. It'd be a help."

"I don't want your help, Billie. Sometimes I just need to be away from all you females."

It was dark when Billie opened the lid on the last nest, and her feet were numb from being out in the cold so long. She bent over to feel for eggs and didn't see the hen that had hidden there until it raised its head and hissed right in her face, that noise that sounded like the devil coming after her in nightmares. Billie jumped back and cracked her head hard on the edge of the nest. She grabbed her broomstick. She poked at the hen, but it kept hissing. Billie started to cry, tears that came from her stomach the way her mother's had in the yard. "You stupid hen," she said. "You disgusting hen." She swung the stick and hit the hen in the head. The turkey staggered out of the nest. Billie caught it with her boot hard enough to lift it off the ground. The hen tried to get away, but Billie hit it across the back with the stick. "You're nothing but a dumb stupid bastard turkey whore." She caught the hen on the head again. And again. "Stupid hen," she said over and over. She was crying so hard she couldn't even see the turkey. When she was too tired to hit it any more, she stood there catching her breath. The hen lay with its head on the ground, looking up at her with one stupid turkey eye.

She poked the turkey. "Get up now. Get up, turkey." But the turkey didn't move.

She'd killed a turkey. This was worse than breaking the eggs, a hundred times worse. She had to hide it. Once they'd found a dead hen in a nest. If she could get this one back into the nest, no one would know. She tried to push the limp thirty-pound bird through the front of the nest, but the swinging door knocked her face down into the turkey's body. She lay there stunned for a minute, breathing in feather dust, breathing in the hen, feeling for a minute that she was the hen. She rolled over and gagged. She spit and tried to wipe the hen's germs off her face. She took deep breaths and forced the turkey air out hard.

She dragged the hen to the back of the open nest, but she couldn't get her knee under it and could only get it half as high as the top of the nest.

She thought of the turkeys the wild dogs had killed. She dragged the hen to the edge of the pen where they'd found those hens. Then she walked back scuffing up the drag marks.

Now that she was calmer, her drying sweat made her teeth chatter.

She could see the lights of the house beyond the pen. It would be warm in the house, but their mother would be crying. Laura would be gone, and Carol would be moving things into her room. With only three of them to do the work, they would wash eggs from dinner until ten o'clock and no one would talk. And tomorrow would be worse. Everyone would know she'd killed a turkey.

She looked inside the nests until she found one with fresh straw. She sat on top and swung her legs over inside, then lowered her body. It was tight, but she fit. She had to stand back up to a half-crouch to grab the lid and then duck quick when she pulled it closed. Through the slat in the privacy door she could see the outlines of the turkeys on their perches. She could hear them rustle and gobble low as they settled into sleep.

Beyond Mecca

Maya Sonenberg

Down past Mecca there is a tremendous inland sea. I know because I've seen it, the Salton Sea, stretching way across the desert valley in the morning, flat and blue. I drove there all unawares, a series of accidents—*farblondjet*, Mama would have said, *like a chicken with her head cut off*—but now I'm going back. "Meshugge," my older sister Rose said when I told her. I was on my way to visit her when I saw it first. "What do you need it for?" she said. Yes . . . but I'm on my way now, driving from the two-bedroom in Santa Monica that she wanted me to share. Something happened there, in Santa Monica, where the ocean glittered, and the palm trees were coddled and ornamental, and the crowds of young people biked and skated and bared their bellies. Or maybe something happened in the desert—before I even got to the ocean. But today, after a week of Rose insisting I live with her—"the best place in the world," she said; a week of mornings sitting on a bench, waiting for her friends to find us and chat; a week of afternoons with Rose first asking for a magazine, then a book, then the television on, then off, then the radio tuned just to one particular station and a nice hot cup of tea—I fled. I got back in the rental car and drove east, through one suburb after another, past the exit for Disneyland.

When I was in New York, my niece Phyllis called—the hysterical one—and then my nephew Danny—the doctor like his father: "Come. Your sister Rose needs you. She's been so difficult since Dad died."

"Of course I'll come," I agreed. I am alone, after all, the healthy sister, the one without any obligations, and I felt sorry for them—so many years of their mother looking after them, and now they had to look after her. I knew what that was like. And both of them busy with their own lives: the children, the work, the husband away on business for six months overseas. And I had just retired after thirty-five years of service, had been given a gold-plated pen by Mr. Jenson and a chocolate bar in the shape of a typewriter. I left my bookcases in New York, the set of Dostoyevsky I've been saving to reread, and flew to Phoenix. There, for a week I stayed with our cousin who's turned the desert into a beautiful garden just like the one she tended in New Rochelle. Beautiful roses—"They grow even better out here," she said, "as long as you water them enough." In the mornings, I always found her outside with her hose. She wanted me to stay, too. "So many people retiring here now, nice people," she said. But I remembered how I had never gardened anything, not even a window box, and I left with the promise I'd come for another visit—when, I couldn't say. In the Phoenix airport, the plane was late, not even taking off from Chicago yet, so I went to the Avis counter instead of the ticket counter. Do you see what I mean by an accident? But at that moment I just thought, a nice drive, a vacation that I deserved after all these years, and besides, by the time that plane gets here, I might already be with Rose. "Tsuris, nothing but tsuris," Rose said, "asking for trouble," when I explained, but it turned out the drive was easy, all the way to the California border. Eight o'clock, a balmy spring night. Back in New York, it's still winter, freezing rain, snow maybe, certainly cold. And on the map California looked so skinny, so easy to drive across and come to Rose's while still she was watching the *Tonight Show*. When I noticed the gas getting low, I pulled out the map again to look at. The road was short to Mecca and I could have a little break. I could stretch my legs, get a cup of coffee, and visit the ladies' room.

But Mecca was further than I thought, and the road was very dark and narrow when the highway lights disappeared. I was scared but mostly of running out of gas and then the next day, where would I be? Stranded alone in the desert. "What mishegoss!" Rose said when I told her I ended up sleeping in the car's backseat, my skirt wrapped around my knees, but what else could I do, other than wait for morning? "Like a bag lady," she said, but I hadn't thought of that. I was too busy trying not to be frightened. Before I fell asleep, I heard scurrying things outside but I knew they couldn't be people, so I locked all the car doors and hoped for the best. In the morning, I fixed hair and lipstick in the rearview mirror and headed on instead of back, which is what any sane person would have done—gone back to the main road. But I went on, looking for that gas station, because, God knows, it couldn't be far.

And you see, this is how I kissed an egret and how I ended up with Donna, but I'll get to that. The road ran between hills of sandy rock that had been made into craggy shapes—from too much scouring, I thought, like with a steel wool pad. There were a few dry squeaking trees, brown signs with no words, wheel tracks heading off into the canyons, and above a blue sky like its own river up there between the banks of the hills. I tried to tell Rose about the cool dry morning and how ahead of me were purple shadows made by strange shapes in the rocks and behind me was nothing but hot sun, but she said, "Oy, I don't understand this whole business of driving. You were supposed to fly. You know, the stewardesses tell jokes—funny ones even—while they show you how the seatbelt works." Then she said, "But you're here now," and we looked at each other, we who hadn't seen each other since after Mama died, maybe a dozen years, a long long time. "You're here now," she repeated. "We're too old for such adventures. You're seventy years old, Rachel. My *children* are too old for such things now—sleeping in a car. Even the *grandchildren* have more sense; they at least bring a tent, a sleeping bag." Between talking, she wheezed. "It's not becoming," she said, and stared at me just like she did when we were children and I did something wrong. Such a long time ago and the same look. She wanted me to stay, every day she told me. Her children wanted me to stay. I could take the other bedroom. The weather's so much better here, they said, and I would have things to do: I could let in the night nurse, do the shopping and cooking, and call the doctors for appointments. I could pick the grandchildren up from school while Rose napped and wait for them at their piano lessons. "You're so good at taking care of things," Phyllis said. When Rose dozed off, I got up and looked out her window at the ocean and the palm trees and all the people in the park above the beach exchanging pictures of their grandchildren and playing canasta. I hadn't played since I don't know how long, but I remembered it used to be fun. If I stayed, I'd have to learn again. We'd been down there earlier—me with a magazine and Rose with her oxygen canisters. Very pleasant—not too hot, the sun not too bright.

But I kept thinking about Mecca, a little nothing of a town laid out in the desert, where on Thursday morning every child in the county was coming for school—little ones in shorts and T-shirts, dragging their backpacks on the dusty ground, teenage girls in short skirts, and boys driving up fast in pickup trucks. I drove around and around, avoiding those meshuggener teenage drivers and looking for some place to have breakfast, a cup of coffee at least, but there were no restaurants. Can you imagine—a town with no restaurants! Not even around the park, a little dried-up square of brown grass where some dark men lounged in their big hats and their dogs sat in the shade with their tongues hanging three-quarters out of their mouths.

Finally on the edge of town, I found a store, clean at least, attached to the gas station. Inside, like a deli—back home we'd call it a deli—but here there were cookies, frosted pink and with a look like packed sand, and a glass case full of some type of sandwich wrapped in bright yellow paper where there should have been bagels and cream cheese. I bought a cup of coffee and a big cookie with sprinkles and pointed to one of the sandwiches in the case. "Burrito?" the girl behind the counter asked, and I got through the rest of the transaction with sign language, lots of nodding, and a *gracias*, though I was worried—was I pronouncing it properly? I tried to remember my high school Spanish but nothing. I tried to remember what Spanish I'd learned on the streets of New York, but every phrase made me blush. When I handed over my money, she said "Thank you" in perfect English. What had I been thinking? California, I needed to keep reminding myself, not Mexico! Now I laugh at my foolishness. I walked around the town, what there was of it. Like a tourist! When I had seen the stucco houses, the gas station, and the little drugstore—a *farmacia*—then I stood by the school fence, eating my burrito and watching all the little ones getting off the buses, because where else could I go in that poor ugly town? What would those men have said—very nice men, I'm sure—about an older Jewish lady sitting down under their tree with them to eat? No, I couldn't do that. "Oy, Rachel, such chozzerai," Rose said when I told her about my breakfast. "A burrito is full of lard. Terrible for the heart, my Danny says." But, I said, the coffee tasted of cinnamon. Maybe they would have talked to me, would have let me rub the dogs' bellies with a stick.

Later in the day, again Rose started in, between complaining about the wait at her doctor's and about the friends who would be coming for cards. "You'll be staying," she said again, like an order more than a question. "I don't need much. Just someone here to make sure I don't stop breathing. I'll just stay in my room, and the whole apartment will be yours."

I said, "I'm here, Rosie. Don't worry."

"And why, Rachel, why did you keep driving? Why didn't you stop earlier? Why not stay in a motel a second night, you can afford this, no? Still I don't understand."

"What's to understand?" I said. "I thought I would be here faster," but she waved her hand at me as if something smelled bad, because already she understood, before I did even, that I would be leaving.

In Mecca I stared at the dingy Chamber of Commerce sign: "Eastern Gateway to the Salton Sea," it read. "Largest Body of Water in California." And I picked up a brochure. The lake was formed, it said, in 1905 when an irrigation canal failed. The flooding lasted sixteen months, until boxcars filled with rocks were used to dam the flow. Sixteen months of water flowing into a valley that used to be under water. It was flowing back toward its home. Largest body of water? It was—forty-five miles long and twenty-five miles wide—but I'd never heard of it. Rose never said.

At the gas station, I asked the quickest way to Route 10 and Los Angeles, and the man pointed me north, not back the way I came. "Are you sure?" I asked.

"Sí, up through Indio. Takes you right there."

And there, another little mistake, following his advice—shorter maybe, but the road took me so that I could glimpse this Salton Sea. Maybe my sister was right—what normal person would drive around in the heat, in the desert, already the asphalt shimmering, prickly things and gray bushes piled up against fences? I drove alongside a railway track on which freight cars rumbled. Then the road turned right, and there it was, a pale blue lake so long I couldn't see its southern end, a mechiaeh—like a turquoise in a ring. Really, it was pretty, and I skipped my turn-off. Again crazy instead of sane. The road drove through green fields of something growing but I didn't know what, then desert again, then groves of oranges and palm trees. When I told Rose I'd seen orange groves, she said, "Oranges I can get you here, as big as your head nearly, nothing like those hard green balls we got in Brooklyn as kids. And remember how Mama always made us eat them with a glass of milk. The acid wasn't good for our stomachs, she said. Well I've learned since then, it's just not so. For once, Mama was wrong."

When I told her I'd walked through groves of date palms, she sighed again. "Palms, schmalms," she said. "There are palms here," and she lifted her hand above her head. We were outside as usual in the early morning, in the park, and there were palm trees all around, sprinkling us with their shade. "And dates . . . here I can buy you dates all the way from Arabia, you want dates." She tapped my knee.

"You'd like it, Rosie, so much to look at. Maybe we could go back there for a visit. You know, just like Israel, they turn the desert into a garden. Then there's a fence, the water stops, and boom—desert again. So strange . . ."

"Yes, irrigation. I know about irrigation, Rachel."

"And it's so bright . . . ," I said, but then I remembered—her conversion. My sister had raised her children by the backyard pool, but since her best friend got skin cancer fifteen years ago, she has not left the house between ten in the morning and four in the afternoon. Similar to her conversion from Reform to Conservative that happened when David, her husband, died.

She said, "So what do you need with that? You know how terrible sun is for the skin. And you especially, someone who spent her whole life indoors. Besides," she said, "there's plenty light here, just open the curtains. And here, it's so close to the hospital, just in case—God forbid—anything should happen. And what would you do there? Here, there's the library for books, and a synagogue. Here you can hear the symphony at the Hollywood Bowl. I can't go—the walk from the bus, it's all uphill, and besides, the seats there are so hard, three cushions you need to schlepp. But you, Rachel, you're younger." I didn't understand how with each sentence I felt older, not younger, until, finally, I felt my age. The fog came in off the ocean and I felt the arthritis in my fingers. The sun went down and I couldn't see. I woke in the middle of the night and couldn't sleep, so hobbled around the apartment, afraid I would trip and fall and break a hip. I kept thinking, the life here *is* better than Mama's in the home in New York where she couldn't go outside all winter, not even up on the roof because of the ice. But when Phyllis came the next morning, my favorite niece, I didn't want to talk to her. At breakfast, I complained the orange juice was pulpy, the lox cut too thick, and the coffee too strong. Already, I too was a kvetch.

And then at the sign for Salton City, I turned off the main road. I kept driving because once I saw the water, I wanted to get closer. "Water," I thought, "lunch. I might as well." Streets ran off, with a neat sign at each corner: Tilapia Avenue, Paradise Lane, Oleander Drive. And there really were pink flowering bushes—oleanders?—growing, and down one street, a tank truck even, watering them, but hardly any houses anywhere. The streets were waiting for them to be built. Closer to the water, there were signs with the price of a lot, the price of a house, and then some houses—just one here, one there, along all those streets—all the blinds drawn, some cactus in the yard, a scrawny tree, and a boat pulled up to the top of the driveway.

And the man I met at the dock, in his greasy garage coveralls, kinky hair gone gray, skin a nice mahogany color but dusty—Rose would think that was crazy, too, just talking to him. And why did I, anyway? Rose would have tossed her head the way she did in high school when a boy she didn't like came to speak with her: she'd toss and walk away. And from riding the subway all these years I have made my own way to fend off strangers: I clutch my handbag to my stomach and look right through them. But this time I didn't. I saw him fishing, then I went and stood behind him. In a white plastic bucket, I could hear something thumping. Finally he said, "Pretty lucky today," without turning around, and I crouched down and watched him fish. It was hot, dry like an oven, so I fanned myself with a map from my purse to make a little breeze and watched the little blue waves lapping all along the treeless shore and the sun move around and hit the mountains, brown like corrugated boxes, on the eastern side of the lake, pretty even, so long as you didn't breathe through the nose—it didn't smell very nice. To tell the truth, the whole place smelled fetid, like sulfur and salt and dead things. I could see there were dead fish floating near the shore. And it was hotter and hotter. When I could feel the perspiration run down my chest and my stockings stick to my legs, I remembered suddenly that Rosie wouldn't approve. I had to get going, and I stood to walk away.

"Don't go yet. Dontcha want to see me catch something?" he chuckled, and goodness knows why, I stayed to see, though my head kept telling me, "Rosie will be worrying about you. Already it will be dark by the time you reach her." But maybe I got sunstroke or some other sickness out there. Or maybe the ugly smell from the lake was some sort of a drug, because I stayed and stayed. Finally he reeled one in, a gray and scaly fish, the size of his two dark hands. He unhooked it and held it out to me, still flopping and flapping. "Whoa," he said, and grabbed it tighter. "That's Tilapia. That's some good eating. Pretty much the only fish that'll stay alive in here." He waved it at me, smiling, and I stood up so fast, I got dizzy. "Take it. Take it," he said, "come on now. But don't kill it till you get home." When he saw me shrinking back, he laughed, put it in a plastic bag with some water. "Now come on, take it," he said and laughed some more and patted me on the arm with a slimy, fishy hand, until I had to take it, just to make him stop. What do you do with a live fish when you don't have a knife to kill it with or a kitchen or even a bucket to keep it alive in? I thought of slipping it back into the lake. But I didn't want to hurt his feelings, either. I was embarrassed to think of him watching me put his catch back in the water, so I just thanked him and started to walk away.

"If you're not from around here, you can take that to Johnson's Landing and Donna'll cook it up for you," he called after me. "It's about the only restaurant around, just around that bend."

Well, okay, I thought, it was past lunch time anyway. "Now you're eating poisoned fish!" my sister said when I told her. "And when there's a new deli here that, I swear, makes kreplach like you haven't tasted since Mama died."

My mouth began to water. Mama would spend a whole day in the kitchen and come out dusted with flour. To the table, she would bring the bowls of chicken soup and kreplach, chewy dough filled with ground meat, onions, chicken fat. On special occasions—on Purim or to break the fast on Yom Kippur—she drew hopeful messages, Hebrew letters, into the dough so that Rose and I and our brother Itzhak would swallow God's blessings. "She's in a better place," I said, remembering her last years in the nursing home that you had to check every day were they bathing her and changing her clothes when she soiled them. She lived to ninety-five, but she could recognize me, thank goodness, at least enough to know I was the one to complain to. Rose visited once every year, the same time she came to visit Papa's grave. I always got to the home early that day, made sure Mama was clean and dressed in her best, wearing the latest piece of jewelry Rose had sent that otherwise I kept at home, or her roommate, an even older lady but cunning, would steal it.

I stumbled along the shore, wishing I'd changed into some other shoes, until I saw it—a white shack on salt-crusted pilings out over the water with a big red sign and flowering cactuses all along the front. It was right in the sun, but inside the air conditioning was on and it was cool and dark. There were some canned goods on shelves, a soda machine, a bar, two covered pool tables with, in the middle of each, a vase of flowers. A young woman bent over the counter, her long dark hair falling and covering her face. She was reading a magazine, and when she looked up, I saw she was Japanese. Maybe I was in the wrong place. In the background, I heard a television going. Then I realized I was holding the fish in its bag in front of me like something dirty. "Oy, how silly," I said, waving the bag. "Are you Donna?" I asked, unsure.

"Who else?" She smiled at me. "Did Vick give that to you from the lake? Ugly, isn't it? I don't eat those—I hear the water's full of chemicals from all the farming round here. Do you want it for your lunch?"

"Oh no, thank you. I don't think so," I said.

"Well, here, give it to me." She held out her hand for the bag. "I'll have the kids take it back to the lake when their show's over. I can't drag them away from it. They're home sick from school today. I'll put it in the sink for now." Then she came back with her order pad, and I noticed she was looking me up and down, leaning over the counter, even, to see my bottom half—my skirt all wrinkled from sleeping, my heels all coated with mud. "You're not from around here, are you?" and before I could answer, she asked, "You're not lost?"

"Oh no, I have a map," I said. "I'm going to visit my sister in Santa Monica, but I got off the highway to . . . well, it's too long a story. Now I see I might as well drive to San Diego and then north. I need to start again soon."

"Well, San Diego's pretty nice. Least that's what the kids tell me. Their dad lives there."

"Oh," I said and looked down at her order pad. Her hand was still poised to write. Her fingernails were painted pale pink, the color of carnations. "I'll have a turkey sandwich." I watched her paint mayonnaise onto the bread slices. I'd never seen someone make a sandwich so slowly. It would take forever and when would I get back on the road? "My, I'm hungry," I said, but she didn't fix the sandwich any more quickly. "Well, it's nice and cool in here, anyway, isn't it?"

"Deadly out there. I keep the lights low, too. That helps."

When she brought the sandwich over, she had a sad look, and she kept looking at me as I started to eat. "I'm sorry," I said.

"Sorry?"

"About your husband," I said.

"My ex? He's okay. He sends money when he can. And he's good to the girls, takes them for a couple weeks every summer, takes them to Disneyland at Christmas, too. He's a trucker, so even if we were still together, they'd hardly see him. It just didn't work out with us is all. He never even yelled that I can remember."

She took it all so smoothly. "Oh," was all I could think to say.

"Maybe that was it," she said, thoughtfully. "Someone *not* yelling can be terrible, can't it?"

We laughed together, and I ate the sandwich. Soon her children came into the dining room and climbed up on two stools at the end of the counter—two girls about eight and twelve. Both with her mouth and eyes, but with freckles, too, and brown hair done up in braids that looked as though they'd been slept on. They didn't look a bit sick.

"What have you been watching?" I asked.

"Mole People," the one closer to me said, the littler one. "It's really neat. There're these people who live underground. They're all white and these other guys find them, sort of by mistake, I think. They're evil—the mole people, I mean—but the other guys get them with this big flashlight."

When she paused for breath, her mother said, "I think that's enough, Sue. We barely know what you're talking about."

"But Mom, she asked."

"Why don't you do something for me? Get out of the house for a few minutes and take this fish back to the lake, will you?"

"Aw, it's so hot out there," the older girl complained, but she slid off her stool and pulled her sister after her. They took the fish in its plastic bag, but they lingered, kicking the screen door open and letting it slam shut. Their mother went over, put her hands on their shoulders. "Hey, you're letting all the hot air in." She gave them a little shove out the door. "You can have ice cream when you come back," she called after them.

"What nice girls," I said.

She wiped her hands on a towel. "Sometimes I just let them stay home," she said. "They keep me from talking to the radio. It's not too busy round here, you can see. Sometimes I get a crowd on the weekend when the fishing's good and sometimes a couple people want to stick around late playing pool but otherwise . . ." She'd been there for over ten years, she said, first with her husband and now alone. Still, she wasn't really thinking of leaving. "Some fools—me included—thought this could be a second Palm Springs! You know, lots of rich white people on vacation, spending money!"

"But it's so quiet here," I said. "Wouldn't people come just for that?"

"You've got to be kidding," she said and laughed. "It's hot. It's smelly. And it's miles from nowhere. My parents won't even come visit from LA. They say the desert reminds them of the camps."

"The camps?" The word is a curse, involuntary cringing.

"You know. They were in Oklahoma during the war," she said, "before I was born."

When the girls came back in, they got up on the stools again, waved their hands wildly in front of their faces. "It's hot out there, Mom. Where's that ice cream?" the older one said.

The younger one came over and stood in front of me silently, rubbing her damp hair out of her face. "Do you know how to make braids?" she asked. "These are a mess."

"Leave the lady alone now," Donna said. "She needs to leave soon," but the girl didn't move. She just stood in front of me, tugging on the ends of her braids.

"Of course I know how to make braids," I said. I held my arms out to her, and she turned around and stood between my knees. While I struggled with the tangles, Donna turned the radio on to a country station. It was foreign-sounding music to me but it certainly had a beat. When the song changed, she grabbed her daughters. "This is it," she said, "the song I've been telling you about. Come on Sue, Misha, I'll teach you that dance." They stomped and kicked and twirled across the floor, the girls giggling every time they got the steps wrong, their mother yelling, "That's it, that's it," every time they got it right.

I sat uncomfortable on my stool at the counter, watching them dance, waiting to pay my check. "I never had children," I thought suddenly, and it was as if someone pulled a plug and tears came to my eyes. "Of course, you didn't," I thought. "How could you with no husband? And working all the time. And besides, there were Itzhak's kids, those three beautiful babies who ended up with no father. And then later Rose's kids came east for school and stayed with you summer vacations while they worked in the city. Remember how you liked to take Phyllis shopping for her winter college clothes at Gimbel's and how you liked it when Danny took you out to dinner, just the two of you like a mother and son on a date. And now, all the grandnieces and grandnephews," I thought and started to list their names in my head. The tears disappeared again, and by the time the song was over, I was fine, just fine. "Let me finish those braids," I said. And when a waltz came on the radio, I said, "Would you like me to teach you?" and Sue nodded her head vigorously, and I was happy to show her and her sister the fundamentals of the waltz. Rose and I had often practiced the waltz and the fox-trot together, and the tango, too, when Mama wasn't looking. We dreamed of reincarnation as the dancing Levine sisters.

When the news came on, Donna turned the radio off. "Well, you girls need to call up and find out what your homework is. I'm not letting you stay home another day," she said. "And I've got to get to those books. It's almost tax time, and it always takes me forever 'cause I never really know what I'm doing, even after all these years."

"And I need to go to my sister," I said.

Donna walked me to the door. Outside, the sun had gone down. Can you believe it? I'd spent that much time without even noticing. The sky in the west was turning pink. To the east, the lake and the Chocolate Mountains behind it were all one creamy brown-pink smear, like a Necco wafer. When I pulled the car keys from my purse, Donna said, "It'll be getting dark soon, you know. You don't really want to be driving all that way in the dark, do you?"

And that was that. That's how I came to stay with her. One night, I thought, but then I started to help with her taxes and stayed three days. After helping Mr. Jenson with his books twenty years, the skills came in helpful, helpful to someone who really needed some help, not just useful to someone, Mr. Jenson, who could afford to pay someone to do this work. When we put the finished forms in the mail, Donna gave me a big hug. I shrank back, but she said, "You don't know what a help you've been. Now, tell me what I can do for you."

―――

"Where have you been?" my sister insisted when I finally arrived at her apartment Monday noon, in time for the first seder. "We've been waiting and waiting."

"Ah, our missing person," Danny joked when he came from the kitchen holding a glass of something dark over ice.

"We even called the police we were so worried," my niece said, "but they wouldn't start looking for another day."

I reminded them I'd called—I did call and say I would be delayed. I explained it was an accident, a series of little accidents all piling up, and everything else—really, I myself didn't know how it had taken me so long to reach her, but Rose sighed with exasperation. "Like a crazy child," she said. "Just like you always were, Rachel," she said. "You remember Aunt Mildred? How she used to go to the store in her slippers and come back with only a box of cookies, not even kosher? Listen, Rachel, you stay here and Danny will help."

I remembered we laughed at Mildred, but now I think maybe that was all she wanted, a box of Mallomars.

Rose's voice was the same as I remembered, coarser but still reedy like an oboe is reedy, musical, that is. And my head, as I stood in her living room, it was still full of the sound of the typewriter bell when it hit the end of the carriage and the buzzing of the computer when it saved a file. It was full of sirens and subway trains and the garbled voices that come over the loudspeakers in the subway stations, especially Union Square. *Beware of the moving platform* . . . I could still hear the voices of all my nieces and nephews, too, at all different ages—the babies when they clamored for something sweet, the older ones with their stories of parties and classes. And Mr. Jenson wishing me good morning and then his friendly bellow: "Oh Rachel, oh Rachel, you're needed here." So many noises inside my skull. Why wouldn't they go away?

I have only one thing left to tell you, really, and that is how I kissed the egret. Sunday, Donna took us for a drive. "Come on," she said, "Margolita's here to watch the place. Let me show you around." We got in her car and drove south along the lake's western shore, past green growing fields and orange and grapefruit groves with the fruit shining between the leaves like Christmas decorations, the girls in the backseat.

Desert passed by with little dry bushes growing in sand. Then when water glistened in ditches, there were brilliant green fields. "That's alfalfa, I think," Donna said. Then another field.

"That's onions!" I said.

"More onions!" Sue and Misha cried.

I saw row after row of green onion stalks, and in the dirt I could see the white onions, almost like eggs or bones. The car filled with the smell of onions, as if you had just cut one in half to grate for latkes. "This soil must be very good," I said, looking at all the growing things.

"Only because they irrigate," Donna said. "Only because of all that stuff they pour into it, fertilizers and I don't know what else."

"And all the water's stolen from the Colorado River," Misha

added. "It used to run into the gulf and it's not supposed to be here at all. They built about six dams, though, so now all the water comes here to grow things and to LA so all the movie stars have water to drink. Now it's just a swamp where the river used to go into the gulf."

When the road curved, we drove through a town that was nothing but shacks, tin warehouses, garages, fertilizer stores, and one dusty motel—even uglier than Mecca, even less than Salton City. Then we turned again and headed to the lake, now from the south. In the distance, there were some buildings with concrete domes, clouds of white steam coming from them. "What are those?" I asked.

"Geothermal plants," Donna said. "The Magma Energy Company—isn't that a goofy name? The kids got to go to one for a field trip but I had to stay with the store. Misha, you explained it to me. How does it work again?"

"There's hot water, really hot, deep down in the ground, and they . . . do you really want to hear about this?"

"Yes." I turned around to see her. "Tell me how it works."

"They pump the hot water up, and when it hits the air, it turns into steam, and the steam turns the turbines. All the heat gets turned into electricity—somehow. I don't remember that part so well. People used to think it was a really clean way to get energy but it makes air pollution, too. And noise. And when they put the cold water back into the ground, it can make earthquakes happen."

We kept driving, and I realized I was in a very strange place, where things did not go together in the way I was used to, ugly and pretty at the same time so I couldn't figure out should I smile or not, where Japanese mothers danced some country music jig, where you needed a shmatte bobby-pinned on to keep the hot wind from blowing your hair, where you brought the smell of living vegetables and dead, salty fish into the house with you every time. "Where are you taking me?" I asked.

"Just around. You'll see," was all Donna said.

"I know where," Sue said. "It's a surprise."

We were driving on smaller and smaller roads until we pulled up at a bird sanctuary. "This is one of my favorite places," Donna said. We walked along a marsh—Donna lent me gym shoes this time—scaring rabbits, lizards, and roadrunners out of the underbrush, then the grasses split and there was the lake. White pelicans swooped overhead and avocets dipped with the black and white stripes along their backs and grebes swam and sandpipers poked along in the mud. I looked them all up busily in a pamphlet I'd picked up. The girls ran around in circles. At the foot of a hill, we saw a burrowing owl sitting calmly on a post. It eyed us but didn't move until I pulled my camera out. Already I wanted a photo to prove to Rose there was more here than dust. Then we all sat on a bench near the water, and a cool breeze blew. It seemed thousands of ducks were floating on the lake—a convention, a conference, all headed in the same direction. Even the girls were quiet. Then out of the sky, a great white bird came sweeping, wings spread wide wide wide. It landed near us on long skinny legs and ruffled the long plumes on its back, and we sat so still it didn't fly away. Sue held my arm tight. Donna leaned close. "An egret," she whispered in my ear. Slowly, I held out my hand—I don't know why. My hand was empty, no fish to entice it, but the bird came closer, until it looked right up at my face with that quick pecking birdie look that even sparrows in Central Park have. It looked at me like my nieces and nephews used to look at me when I baby-sat, when they wanted something and neither of us could figure out what it was. I moved my hand but the egret stayed. I remember Mama wanting a hat with egret plumes, a blue hat so it looked like a bird on water, but she could never afford it. And I learned later almost all these birds died to make such hats. I touched the bird's neck, its crest, but it didn't startle. It actually stepped closer and tipped its beak up. If it had opened its mouth and spoken, I wouldn't have been surprised, but it didn't. It just stood there, so I bent down and kissed it, kissed the spot right above the beak. The feathers were soft—of course they were—and I smelled fish and salt and a completely new smell that must be the smell of live birds. I heard Donna gasp and the girls gasp, so I gasped, too—what *was* I doing? "Feh!" Rose would say, "dirty." And then the egret hopped back and flew off, disappearing into a great flock of other egrets wheeling above, as if it had never been there in front of us.

Monday noon I arrived in Santa Monica, and six days later, I called the family together in Rose's living room. "I've decided," I said. "I'll come visit, but I won't stay. This time, I am the one to leave." My voice was shaking, and I needed to sit down in the middle of my speech.

"All these years," Rose said. "So you were upset that I left. Who would know? But Rachel, you were the baby, you were always the favorite, that's why I left."

Her children were silent. They looked at their hands.

"Me, the favorite?"

"Yes, it was true. Mama always made a dish special for you. Papa gave you books. Me, he gave something little he didn't care about, a hair clip, a sewing kit. Ah, enough of that. This place you've found, I don't understand, but if you like it . . . And you know you're always welcome here."

———

On the dock, I sit, just sit, happy to be back. Happy? What is that? I don't know that. The lake is blue and the waves make little lapping sounds—otherwise silence. As usual the water smells bad. The dead fish float but maybe not so many as last week. I sit on the dock anyway, where Vick baits hooks and spills gasoline for his boat, where birds have relieved themselves. Just a few days ago, I came here in my nylons and could barely think to crouch. Now I have an old black cotton skirt, the one I used to wear only for housecleaning, and no shoes, and I'm sitting right on this smelly dock. Up above, the sky is pale yellowish blue like always just after sunset, and the Chocolate Mountains fade pink into the lake. Overhead there are the silver glints of jets flying from the Naval Air Station in San Diego ("Don't go driving off onto the bomb range, now," Donna told me when I was heading for Indio to get us some groceries). I wish I could say it was all very nice, but this place isn't like that, not right off like this. It will take a long time for all the noises in my head to go quiet, all the people talking to me and all the machines I've heard clanging and banging and whining and whistling, all the radio programs and television programs; it will take many days of reading, walking, and continuing the dancing lessons with Sue and Misha. The sky turns orange, then pink, then violet, and the colors reflect in the lake's water like flowers, like double flowers. I am like them—an accident, a switch being turned in the brain by mistake, water pushing through a levee, like a medication that pushes the cells apart, like blooming. On the way back from seeing the egret we stopped at a date grove, and seventy feet up, I saw a man working, with his hands buried in a cluster of bright yellow flowers. "He's pollinating," Donna said. He tied the male flowers into the female and placed a net bag over all, no good relying on wind to do the job. I thought, the man's hands must get filthy, coated with golden pollen.

Suddenly Daniel, I have never told anyone about Daniel, our decade-long Thursday afternoons affair, Daniel with the limp that kept him from the war, but he made me open, like the brightness here—everything tight loosening up. My legs spread wider and wider, my hands grasped the headboard. Why would I remember that now? I'm afraid even Donna might find it sordid, the hotel room with a window opening on the airshaft, my dream that never happened of one time spending a whole night with him in one of the big rooms overlooking Gramercy Park. Sometimes it would be his child's birthday and he would come with a present, a big box wrapped up in paper. He'd try to hide it from me, to spare my feelings, and that made me almost cry, almost as nice as if the present were for me (though what would I have needed with a doll or a toy railroad, I don't know). Still, once we were undressed, once we were in bed . . . And now forty years without it, my goodness, forty years! The other day, when Donna touched my wrist—that's the feeling I had. Oh, not as strong of course, not really the same of course, but still it was skin on skin. Ah, all that was years, no, decades ago, and now gone with the others—Itzhak; our parents; Itzhak's daughter to leukemia; my best friend from high school, Leah, who died trying to get rid of a baby; Rose's husband David; and Rose soon, too. She sounds sharp to me, but Phyllis says how difficult it is for her to breathe (how could she have stopped sunning but not smoking!). "No use crying," Papa always said and snapped his *New York Times* out full width to read. But some things are worth crying over, I think, and I remember his bald head, all freckled. I see a silver glint high up, another jet. Here, they practice bombing things, they suck energy up from the ground and let chemicals seep down into it and into the water so things can grow, they pay people nothing nearly to pick those fruits, which is terrible, but still, there is a space to breathe. It's almost dark now, just an orange glow up there, up above. A few tears, and then suddenly, absurd, I realize I'm filled with some feeling I don't know. Each cell pulses. They move fast. I can't imagine how they stay together in this one body. The world tastes sweet and there's so little time. Breathless, I think, stunned, "This is joy!"

One for the Ocean

Tanya Whiton

The night Big Ely hauled the *Bessie Marie* across town to our house, I slept outside on the porch, a musty quilt wadded up over my legs. "Ellen, honey, come inside," my husband, Ely Jr., said, standing in the doorway in his boxer shorts. His sparrow-colored hair stood up all over his head.

"I'm staying right here," I said, shifting my hips on the swing bench. Cats slept all around me, in the corners, on the railing. Mojo, the newest one, wove around Ely's ankles. The shadow of the old lobster boat loomed over the porch, blocking any light from Chipmans next door. It was cold, still mud season, with fog drifting over, but I didn't care. "I'm not playing nurse to that son-of-a-bitch," I said, and turned over.

I heard him pad back up the stairs to our room, the boards groaning underneath him. "You could have asked twice," I muttered. In the dark back room of our house, Big Ely coughed, a raw, phlegmy sound.

I hate boats. I even think about getting on a boat and my stomach flips over. Five years back, when we first got married, I'd gone out with Ely and his father on a short afternoon run—back when I still cared whether or not Big Ely liked me. I took two Dramamine in the morning and stuffed a bunch in my bag, along with some sandwiches, a big bottle of soda, and a bag of chips. "It ain't a picnic we're goin' on here," Big Ely said when he saw the canvas tote, although he ate two sandwiches and most of the chips.

I was fine till we got out past Grant's Island and one of Corey Stringer's shrimping boats sent a big wake our way. I'd been up in the bow, clutching the only spot that wasn't smeared with seagull shit and bait. The *Bessie Marie* hit the first ripple and I puked all over the wheelhouse floor. After that, I couldn't stop. I threw up everything I'd eaten for two days, and then, just when I'd think it was over, a wave of seaweed and dead fish smell would creep up my nose and I'd dry heave over the side. Big Ely had to leave the traps unchecked, and as he steered back into the harbor, his cold blue eyes looking right at the sun, he said, "Don't look like she's cut out to be a fisherman's wife."

"Dad," Ely said, "I'm not a fisherman."

A year ago Big Ely came back to Sully's Harbor to die. He won't admit it, of course. He had a perfectly decent trailer out in back of Jack and Lenny's and a place to store that junker of a boat. It's as many colors as a money cat and Jesus, it stinks. But Big Ely claims he moved back because his younger sons are a *disappointment* to him, what with their odd jobs and drinking; he says the reason he left was *pure frustration*.

"I can't watch those two sittin' round the yard when the damn house is fallin' apart. They wouldn't mind if it was raining right through the roof onto their heads." Now his battered traps are piling up against the side of our shed.

———

I'd been smoothing up the new wallpaper when I saw my husband's beige wagon pull in. Out climbed the old man, plastic waders still on, one of his smelly caps pulled down over those glittery eyes. "Barely recognize the place," he'd grumbled, setting two brown suitcases on the floor.

He had cancer blooming out all over his body, but the stoic old bastard marched around like a soldier. The only change in him was a yellow color to his skin, like a bird claw. He surveyed the living room and dining room, all redecorated, pulled a cigarette from the mashed pack of Winstons in his flannel pocket, and lit up. I hate smoking, don't even allow it in the house, he knows that. But it used to be his house—the house he raised his *children* in, he reminds me, as though the fact I can't have any makes me cold-hearted.

"Ely, d'you know your mother put up that wallpaper?" Big Ely said, as if I wasn't in the room. I'd put a nice floral over the old colonial stuff: curling-up strips of soldiers firing cannons at redcoats, brown horses galloping all over the place. It gave me a headache.

"Time for a change," I said brightly, and stomped back into the kitchen. A cat sniffed at Big Ely's bags and raked a claw over the fake leather.

The whole town knew Big Ely and I didn't get along. They'd been there when he passed out at our wedding reception—a man who rarely drank. It had been outside at Lowry's Point, and he got right down in the sand and fell asleep with the tide trickling in around him. And they'd been there for Bessie Marie's funeral, which I was not invited to. "Ely's girlfriend?" Big Ely'd said to old Alice Chipman. "She thinks she's somethin'. And she's barren as a rock farm." One of the little Chipmans let that fly the day we moved in, swarming around their dooryard to get a look at me. I felt as big as a barn in my wedding suit, a pale pink with lavender lapels and, for Christ's sake, shoulder pads.

I wasn't born and raised up here, that's a black spot on me. I'm from inland Augusta, spent the first twenty-two years of my life in a spick-and-span white house on downtown Boe Street, till the day I went to nursing school. "Takes a while for people to warm up to ya," Ely said. He'd been engaged to the eldest Chipman daughter, Eileen, since he was sixteen. Eileen was married now to Ely's best childhood friend, Blake Stevens, and had three daughters, all of 'em screaming, tow-headed little Chipmans, but she still held a grudge against Ely—couldn't forgive him for breaking it off. We didn't meet till Ely was twenty-eight years old, so I could hardly see any reason for the whole damn town to call me *"Missiz Carter,"* in that way, like I'd stolen something.

"They're just bein' formal with ya, that's all," Ely said. But I knew they all agreed with Big Ely. My father was a state representative, and my mother and sisters all work for charity and run things—bridge clubs and church groups and other people's lives. I'm the black sheep, the only one who's ever worn a uniform to work. They've come up twice to visit in the past five years, and both times my mother asked, "Does he drag home every stray thing he finds?"

The morning after the *Bessie Marie* went up on blocks, with a whole lot of grunting and shouting and carrying on, Tammy Chipman cracked about me sleeping on the porch, while she was dragging my groceries over the checkout sensor at Sully's IGA.

"Wade come home last night, said he thought there was a bear on your porch," Tammy said, with a high-pitched little laugh. Her blond hair was just permed, and when she laughed, yellow ringlets joggled back and forth.

"Maybe if Wade didn't drink so much he could see straight," I said, shoving my packages of food into a paper sack.

Tammy was only a few years younger than me, but strutting around the IGA in her acid-washed jeans she always made me feel like some middle-aged summer lady. "She's mighty forward," was all Ely Jr. had to offer up on the subject. He'd never give me the satisfaction of agreeing when the Chipmans got me wound up, although anybody could see what a gang of white trash they were. Somehow Tammy Chipman knew every bit of everybody's business in Sully's Harbor and half of Grant's Harbor as well. I'd no doubt she could quote my and Ely's conversation from the night before. I pushed on the in door to get out and nearly took it off the hinges.

Tammy was on to the next customer, Blane Edwards, a pimply-faced kid who worked cutting bait at Stringer's Tackle Shop. "Somebody's a little ugly today," she said.

She had some nerve, that girl. All she and her scumbag boyfriend Wade ever did was ride around in his rusted Monte Carlo, smoking pot and drinking coffee brandy—that's when they weren't making out or squabbling in Sully's parking lot or the Chipmans' dooryard. It made me uncomfortable, watching them squirm all over each other in public. But Tammy could do whatever she wanted—steal another woman's man right out of the marriage bed, even. Wade's wife and two kids drove by like shadows every now and then, staring out the car window at the circus the Chipmans call home. Wade's wife is a pretty French-Canadian girl raised up by a widowed mother who still barely speaks any English.

Tammy, on the other hand, is related to half the town. She's known Big Ely since she was a little girl. She grew up running through the woods in back of the Carters' house, came to cookouts and saw Bessie Marie in her funny apron with the lobster claws on it. Bessie Marie and Alice Chipman used to shuck twenty ears of corn, pile up plates of steamers and lobster salad, and everybody would eat and carry on till the kids got tired catching fireflies and the men got stumbling drunk. Then they'd all go down to the rocky beach at Tinker's Cove and shock the booze out of their heads in the icy water. I'd heard all about it, the good old days. The family doesn't come around much—Ely says everybody got too absorbed with their own selves. "Ma knew how to bring people together," he likes to say.

"Well, I guess I never knew that Bessie Marie," I tell him, and we go into one of those long silences. Because we both know that when Big Ely looks at me he remembers his beloved wife, shrunk up and pale. He thinks I let her go, that I wasn't doing my job. "I've got a ward full of people who could go at any minute," I'd said to Ely once. "I'm supposed to see into the future?"

I was third-shift nurse on the floor where Bessie Marie Carter spent her last days. I was on duty the night she died. That last stroke curled her up like a leaf, and I found her, frozen up in her bed; she hadn't tried to press the help button, or made any sound at all. I looked in on her every hour, patrolling the wing from midnight to eight, my white shoes squishing down the linoleum hallways. She was the last room on my round, and for three months I'd given Bessie Marie her breakfast every morning, then sat watching the winter sky turn gray, then pink and orange. And three nights a week, Ely Jr. sat by her side, leaving at four to drive home, sleep for two hours, and go to work at Thibodeau's Hardware. It was February, and snow piled high up on the first-floor windows, but he still came, Thursday, Friday, and Saturday, right at eleven-thirty, and drank a cup of hospital coffee in the cafeteria before going to room 102, always with something for her, a piece of blueberry pie or an old family photograph.

I couldn't get over it, the sight of that big man holding his mother's wrinkled-up hand. His face is his mother's face, sweet, apple cheeks and freckles. I started wearing makeup on my shift and dawdling at the red plastic tables in the cafeteria, reading a magazine or going through my pocketbook. I bought a new bra, brought my white polyester shirt down a couple of buttons. "I think I got one," I'd tell my sisters on the phone, listening to the racket in the background of televisions, kids, men talking.

The day nurses told me about Big Ely, hunched up in a waiting room chair, scowling suspiciously at the nurses' station. He didn't trust doctors, didn't trust hospitals. "He smells like fish," Roberta Jenkins, the second shift supervisor told me. It had gotten around that I had a crush on Bessie Marie's boy, and now everybody passed on whatever information or opinions they had. "The Carter fella was askin' after you," Loey Hillman from the flower shop reported. "The nice one." Jack and Lenny would come every now and then, and slouch around the room, hats pulled down low. They were narrow built and dark, like Big Ely had been before his hair went gray.

"It happened all in one winter," Bessie Marie told me one morning, spooning awkwardly at a soft-boiled egg. "Catch was so bad we had to heat the house with pallets from the boatyard." I imagined that, a winter spent eating potatoes and macaroni, worrying over bills and wearing holey boots, your whole fate controlled by weather and tides. "I think Ely Jr. remembers that winter, even though he was just four years old," she said. "He's never been one for the ocean. Fished with his father all through high school, but I could tell he didn't much like it."

She must have seen something in my expression, because as I went to clear her tray, she looked intently at me, with her hazel-spotted eyes that looked so much like her son's, and I knew she knew. "He's bighearted," she said, a one-sided smile hitching on her face. "He's my best one."

———

Two sights greeted me on weekday mornings when I drove past Tinker's Cove to our shingled cape with the porch tacked on: the boat, yawing back and forth on its blocks and rusty jack stands, and Big Ely, parked on my swing bench, crushing out butts in a clamshell with the cats clustered all around him. I could hear his breath rattling in his chest from the yard. My Ely's projects were sunk in the pine needle dirt all around me: an old Chevelle with a cracked engine block, lawnmowers with tripped innards and oil-gunked pull strings, rings and washers and tires and hoses tossed like a horseshoe game all around them. The cats rose up in a chorus when I came up the steps. "Hello there, Mr. Carter," I said each day with bullet-proof hospital cheer. "Erghum," he said back, every time, with a draw on his cigarette and a single, ragged hack. Then I'd march past him into the house and bang things around in the kitchen while the cats butted their furry chins against cabinets, door frames, and my shins, rumbling like motors past their empty bowls until I filled them. I'd sleep till five, when Ely came home, and then we'd do battle for his attention.

"No needles or pills for me, missy," Big Ely announced one night, after Ely and I'd been to the oncology specialist to talk about his condition. He was losing weight, and his coughing kept Ely awake at night, like somebody was operating a power saw in the spare bedroom.

I cut my T-bone into tiny, square pieces. "I don't believe I offered you any," I said. Ely looked at the both of us, and lumped more mashed potatoes onto Big Ely's plate. "Ellen knows what she's doing, Pop. She'll make you feel better."

"I feel fine," the old man barked. The steak was leathery—Ely'd gotten distracted with some piece of machinery and let it shrink up on the grill. I dumped some more gravy over it and reached for the corn and peas. A yellow cat stalked along the back of the couch, readying itself for a jump in Big Ely's direction. "Mr. Carter," I said in my best bedside voice, "you don't have to do anything you don't want to do."

"Well, I know that," he said, poking at the brown hunk of meat on his plate. "Them goddamn city doctors'll do anything to ya for a dollar, and you don't come up none the better for it." He looked at me, and for a second we locked eyes like two toms.

"Strawberry shortcake," Ely said, scooping up the yellow cat and grabbing his plate. "Who's in the mood for some?"

"Well, I ain't even done with this," Big Ely said, although we all knew he couldn't eat more than a few bites of anything. Every night, the same thing, Big Ely jabbing at his food for an hour and a half. If Ely cooked, the old man gnawed determinedly. If I cooked, he just sat there, looking offended. He lived on cigarette smoke, I swear it. We'd had it out one night over some American chop suey, and I stormed right out of the house and huffed up and down the road a few times. I'd been in the kitchen getting seconds for me and Ely when I heard the old man whisper, "It's *her* cooking that's killing me, son. Honest to god I can't eat a bite of it." The worst part was Ely just tried to please the both of us, never taking a side, never raising his voice. I would've dropped dead if the man showed any passion at all.

"I'd love some strawberry shortcake," I said, still frozen in my seat. He had no idea what he was in for. I could see him grit his teeth against the pain every now and then. You can't scare pain down, can't bully it away. "Sure," Big Ely said. He ripped another paper towel off the roll and tucked it into his shirt collar. Ely set three bowls of strawberries down and loaded them with Cool Whip, looking at us both. I dug in, scooping determinedly at the stale biscuit and tart berries.

"Soon as you get the boat fixed up, we'll be out on the water," Big Ely said to his son, and Ely smiled, his hazel-brown eyes seeking mine across the Formica table.

We hadn't discussed the boat since that first night. I'd resigned myself to its decorating the yard till the old man died, if he ever did. I could tell by Ely's expression that he'd meant to say something himself, but the old man had beat him to it.

"Don't you already have a full-time job?" I said, mashing my shortcake with a spoon.

"You can't call that a job," Big Ely said. "Slingin' parts in Alex Thibodeau's junk shop."

"It's not a junk shop, Mr. Carter," I said loudly. "It's a decent, dependable way to make a living." I felt my face go bright red.

"I don't have to take that kind of talk," Big Ely said, shoving back his chair. His fingers fumbled for a cigarette. "I made this house with my own two hands. I wasn't off taking a nap when—"

"Dad!" Ely said.

Big Ely lit up, glaring at me with narrow eyes, inhaled, and let a cloud of smoke drift over the table. "I've always been where I was supposed to be when I was supposed to be there," he said, and stalked out of the room. The screen door banged behind him. Ely stood, his arms half raised like he was trying to catch something.

Ely said quietly. "I'll work on her weekends—it'll just be weekends." He'd cleared all the plates and started the water for dishes by the time Big Ely came back in. We settled into opposite chairs in front of the TV and looked straight ahead, a heavy silence hanging over us. I glanced at my father-in-law's nicked and swollen hands and thought of the stories—men disappeared, not found for months, because they'd gotten their sleeves caught in a winch or been knocked off balance by a wake while taking a leak off the side. My stomach felt off even thinking about it. Christ, just last year Jason Bickford went down with a line around his ankle, and they didn't find him till the baitboy pulled a jawbone out of a ground fishing net. That was all that was left.

―――

In my sleep the ocean rolled over the shore and filled the streets of town, surrounding our house with its slushy sounds and mysterious stinks. The boat battered up against the front door, cats scrabbling up its sides, and Bessie Marie herself appeared in our kitchen, an apron pinned to her dress, her fleshy hands holding something submerged in the sink.

I woke up with that feeling of swimming in a mucky lake, when the underwater plants wrap around you like arms. I looked at Ely snoring gently in the darkness, his broad boy's face more familiar than my own, and fear bunched up in my chest.

Banging and sawing, sanding and scraping. By the time I woke up Ely was under the hull, a belt sander hooked up to the porch outlet, making so much racket he couldn't hear me till I got right behind him. He'd put together a makeshift scaffold with sawhorses and planks, and lay back on the narrow board, flecks of paint and old fiberglass raining down on him. "For God's sake, Ely, he'll be in the hospital before you get it patched up," I said over the whine of the machine. "You oughtta at least wear some goggles." The smell of seaweed and old bait fermented in the sun like low tide on a hot day.

He clicked off the sander and looked at me, hot red streaks showing through his freckles. He didn't say anything for a good long minute. Then, he shook his head slowly, like a bug was in his ear. "I'm gonna fix this boat, Ellen," he said, as if it could be left at that.

I remembered how Saturday mornings had been: Ely and I laying in our big saggy bed till noon if we felt like it, or going up to Ronnie's for pancakes and sausage. We'd walk a safe distance from the shore out to Lowry's Point and look back at the glitter of water rushing toward Tinker's Cove. Ely'd never been much of a talker—I knew that. It never bothered me before. I liked the idea of a man who was more at ease with something in his hands than with words. My people put too much value on talking—they could talk you right to death. But what if Ely really didn't have anything to say? Zzzhhhht. Nothing.

"All I'm saying," I said in a loud voice, "is it's too much work. You know as well as I do he doesn't have that much time. The doctor said he'd be hospitalized by fall if he didn't take any cure."

"He ain't gonna go to the hospital, honey. You know he won't."

"Well, having a boat isn't gonna do him much good, hospital or no hospital." Ely clicked the belt sander back on, and I stood there for a minute, looking hard at him. He turned it off.

"It's the only thing he's got to pass on, Ellen."

I felt myself softening up, just like I did every time he brought home some broken or damaged thing. He'd bottle-fed a litter of kittens left in a box at the town dump, brought home abused farm animals to foster, hauled every piece of half-busted machinery left at the shop or by the side of the road right into our backyard. He had a sweetness to him most men couldn't even approach.

"I don't like the idea much myself," he said, surveying the scarred underside of the boat.

"What idea?" I demanded.

"Well, I'm not fixing her up so she can sit in the yard," he said. Then he put a hand on mine. "It's not gonna be forever."

"It's been forever already," I snapped, and snatched my hand out of his, just as Big Ely came out of the house in his overalls, a mug of instant coffee in his hand.

―――

The doctor hadn't meant hospitalized, he'd meant *dead*—and Ely knew I hadn't taken it as exactly bad news. I'd do my duties, give Big Ely painkiller if he'd take it. At work, I patrolled the hallways, turning patients in their beds, talking softly to the withered faces that glowed in the lights of IV machines and lamps left on to fight the darkness. I couldn't stand to see a person suffer—I did everything in my power to ease it. I'd tried to coax the stiffness out of Bessie Marie Carter's permanently cupped hands, and I'd done the same for hundreds of others.

But sickness has its place, and it was not in our house. Each day I could hear the cancer cutting its path through Big Ely's lungs and throat. I could see it in his eyes, with their yellow-green tinge. He mumbled and sputtered to himself in the night, unable to sleep—the whole place felt restless and sick. And when I went to work, I saw Big Ely's hard cold eyes and curled-up lip in the dear faces on the ward, and I felt compassion leaking out of me.

―――

Jack and Lenny came over from time to time to put in their two cents about the improvement of the *Bessie Marie*. They tromped all through the house with their muddy boots from the clam flats, helped themselves to the fridge, and took up posts on the front porch steps, cussing at the cats to shoo them into the yard. I made a sign for the front door that said "BOOTS OFF" and a hiding place for beer and snacks I didn't want them to take. They felt more at ease in my house than I did. A lot of talk about the "good old days" started up, and handprints appeared on the white doors and window frames. The place reeked of chemicals and the thick black mud that Jack and Lenny tracked in. Cans of thinner and paint, jugs of bilge cleaner and coolant potted themselves around my front steps like plants.

Ely set a launch date for the boat.

"Only on weekends," he promised me. "We'll just do a few runs on the weekend, to keep Dad happy. He's got nothing to do but—"

"WRECK MY HOUSE!" I said at the top of my lungs. Because it was my house. I'd helped pay off the mortgage, I'd put in new floors and shingles and paint and plaster. I'd fixed all the damage from the salt air and soggy weather. And they were taking it back. Big Ely's smell of smoke and decay mingled with the rank smells of the yard and sank into the walls of my clean house, my safe place, the home where Ely and I were going to make our lives together. I hated him. I hated it all.

———

"Fuu-uck you!" I heard Wade Gibbons yelling in the darkness. I sat up, squeaking the new twin bed. "Fuu-uck you, Tammy, you fuckin' slut! You bitch!" Tammy screamed something back, and I heard breaking glass. Ely snored lightly in his own new bed. My idea. I'd been hoping to punish him when I suggested it, to make clear that the distance between us was growing dangerously. He'd said, "That's probably a good idea, my back's been hurting," and continued fixing a broken trap.

I punched him on the arm. "Moon's full, Ely," I said, and he shook his head, eyes still locked shut. "Ely, do you think you ought to go over there?" The moon sent Wade off the deep end every couple of months, and if Tammy sensed it coming she locked all the doors, spirited his keys out of the car while he sat at Ronnie's, and holed up in the attic till it passed. Sometimes it lasted a couple of days, sometimes longer.

"Let me in the fuckin' house, woman, or I'm gonna break every goddamn window!" Ely finally sat up, and we both plunked heavy feet on the floor and went for the door. "What the hell's goin' on?"

Big Ely said from the downstairs hallway. The three of us went out on the porch and watched Wade leaping and kicking in the yard like a crazy man, a string of words coming out of his mouth. "Fuckin' slut!" His voice broke on the last words, and he sounded like a twelve-year-old boy.

"That ain't right," Big Ely said, and started off the porch in his long johns. The cats all crouched in anticipation, their eyes glowing yellow and green. "Dad, no," Ely Jr. said, moving to follow the old man. "Stay right there," Big Ely barked, and bowlegged his way through the bushes and over onto the Chipmans' property. "He shouldn't go over there," I said, and Ely didn't reply. Four generations of Chipmans lived in the house, and none of them would tangle with Wade when he was like this, although if it got bad enough, someone would fire a shotgun in the air.

Big Ely stepped into the ring of moonlight Wade occupied, and when Wade turned around, I sucked in my breath. Ely started out into the yard, both big hands curled into soft fists. "Young fella," Big Ely said, "no cause makin' such a scene of yourself over a woman."

"This ain't your property," Wade snarled, "and it ain't none of your business what I do."

"All I'm tellin' you is you look downright comical over here, jumpin' up and down like a rooster."

Wade rose up a fist in the air, and Ely Jr. started to run, just as Big Ely swung a quick right and took Wade out clean across the jaw. He crumpled on the dew-soaked grass, one hand swiping clumsily at the air. "Wade!" Tammy yelled from the attic window. "Wade!" Lights flipped on all over the house, and suddenly at least ten Chipmans crowded the yard, led by Tammy with a man's robe wrapped around her skinny body, blond hair hanging in her eyes.

"Christ Jesus, Tamara, he's gonna live," Alice Chipman said, inspecting Wade's face. Big Ely shook out his right hand, and nodded to Alice. "Hello there, Ely," she said, herding the small Chipmans back inside. Tammy swept her hands across Wade's face, gathered herself up, and walked slowly across the yard, glaring over her shoulder at my husband and his father. She stopped when Big Ely started to cough.

It sounded like metal grinding against metal, and Ely and I stepped forward to support him. Down he went on all fours, the coughing spasming his whole body. A thin stream of yellow spittle mixed with blood came out of his mouth. "Dad!" Ely said, going down on the grass beside him. "Ellen, can't you do something?" I stared at the three of them, Wade drunk and unconscious, the old fisherman with his insides twisting, and the man I'd loved. The man I thought would make me a better woman.

Big Ely looked at me, hatred and fear leaking into his blue eyes. "Yeah, we've all heard what a great nurse you are," Tammy said, her voice aiming for sarcasm but sounding girlish and scared. She ran toward the Chipmans' tarpaper house, calling for Alice to come out. I considered the three of them without an ounce of feeling.

"Ellen, please," Ely said, reaching for my hand. A quick sharp stab of pain made my eyes well. And I turned. I turned my back and walked beneath the shadow of the big lobster boat up the steps of the house, past the cats arching up and resettling themselves, and fetched the box with its needles and pills neat in their wrappings.

I'd had dreams often enough to know how this would all end: with me in the bow of a boat, retching my guts out over dark water, while white birds screamed and circled my head.

There were lines clanging against masts in the stiff wind cutting across Tinker's Cove. The sound made me feel watched, together with the creaks of boats in their slips, the balloon sounds of rubber fenders butting against the dock. And the dock itself was alive and murmuring—between planks I could make out the inky water slapping at pilings. I found my feet carefully, walking a zigzag over the gaps.

The *Bessie Marie* was third in from the end, her bow cocked right at Grant's Island, like she already knew where to go. The new white lettering stood out in the darkness, bobbing up and down like a passing ghost. I reached the slip, and looked back down the long dock to the landing. I'd called in sick to the hospital, put on my uniform, and driven around for hours. Nobody here. I put my hands on the boat's side and she shifted—my heart jumped, and I stepped back a minute, breathing hard. All around me the black water rippled.

Her lines were looped in a tidy circle. The new rope felt like a living thing when I picked it up. I looked on board at the power-washed deck, the fresh gray paint that had Ely reeling in the yard like a drunkard.

He'd built a new bench in the wheelhouse and put a vinyl

cushion on it. "I ain't never seen nothin' so fancy," Big Ely said gruffly, but you could see he was pleased. Since that episode at Chipmans he'd set up a bed on the porch, where he lay under a mound of musty blankets, too tired even to smoke. I unwound a line, kneeling down next to the cleat to undo it. My fingers wrestled against the rope, and I felt the water tugging at it.

Tide ran out past Grant's Island, whirled treacherously in the bay, then went straight for the open sea. That much I knew from newspaper stories about lost boats and lost men—I felt tears jamming my throat and filling my eyes. I put my white nurse's shoe against the side and shoved as hard as I could, gasping as the boat slid out, nearly losing my balance. She'd carry me with her if she could—I felt the strong pull of will, the will that had almost unraveled my house and my marriage. That old man's face, his hateful, bitter face. I ran to the bow, yanked the line free and pushed again. The *Bessie Marie* swung for a moment in the water, her nose clearing the urchin boat ahead, and then the ocean tugged her forward, coaxing her out into the fast-running tide.

Biographical Notes

Editors

Alan Davis has published an acclaimed collection of short stories, *Rumors from the Lost World* (New Rivers Press, 1993). His fiction and nonfiction appear in such newspapers as the *Chicago Sun-Times*, the *Cleveland Plain Dealer*, the *New York Times*, and the *San Francisco Chronicle*, and in such journals as *Ascent*, the *Hudson Review*, *Quarterly*, and *South Dakota Review*. He has received a Loft-McKnight Award of Distinction in Creative Prose, two Fulbrights, and a Minnesota State Arts Board Fellowship. He teaches at Moorhead State University in Minnesota, where he chairs the Department of English and codirects the creative writing program.

Michael White is the author of *A Brother's Blood*, published by HarperCollins (1996) in the United States and Viking/Penguin in Great Britain (1997). HarperCollins will be publishing his most recent novel, tentatively entitled *Redemption*. His fiction appears in numerous magazines and journals, ranging from *Redbook* and *American Way* to *Nebraska Review* and *New Letters*. He teaches at Springfield College in Massachusetts.

Associate Editors

Debra Marquart's work has received numerous prizes, among them the Dorothy Churchill Cappon Essay Award from *New Letters* (twice) and the Guy Owen Poetry Prize from *Southern Poetry Review*. Her first book, *Everything's a Verb* (New Rivers Press), won the Minnesota Voices Project and is now in its second printing. She teaches creative writing at Iowa State University and sings and writes for the Bone People, who have released two CDs.

David Pink has published fiction, nonfiction, and poetry in many magazines, including *American Literary Review*, the *North*

American Review, Salmagundi, and *Nimrod.* He has received grants and awards from the Loft-McKnight Foundation, the Edelstein-Keller Fund, and the North Dakota Humanities Council.

Judges

Antonya Nelson received First Prize in 1988 in the first *American Fiction* collection from judge Raymond Carver for her story "The Expendables." The collection from which the story is taken won the Flannery O'Connor Prize. *In the Land of Men,* her second collection, has been followed by two widely acclaimed novels, *Talking in Bed* and, most recently, *Nobody's Girl.*

Robert Boswell has written four novels: *American-Owned Love, Mystery Ride, The Geography of Desire,* and *Crooked Hearts,* which was made into a movie. He has also published two collections of stories: *Living to Be a Hundred* and *Dancing in the Movies,* which won the Iowa Award.

Work by Nelson and Boswell has appeared in the *New Yorker, Esquire, The Best American Short Stories,* and *The O. Henry Awards: Prize Stories.* They are married with children and divide their time between Las Cruces, New Mexico, and Telluride, Colorado.

Contributors

Stephen K. Bauer holds an M.F.A. from Vermont College and teaches writing at Babson College. He has written two novels and published stories in the *Louisville Review, Prairie Schooner,* and *Sewanee Review.* One of his essays was cited as a Notable Essay in *The Best American Essays 1997.*

Catherine Brady's stories have appeared in *Redbook,* the *Missouri Review,* the *Kenyon Review,* and numerous anthologies, including *American Fiction, Volume Eight.* Her collection of short stories, *The End of the Class War,* is forthcoming from Calyx Press in June 1999.

Richard Burgin is the author of three short story collections: *Man without Memory, Private Fame,* and *Fear of Blue Skies.* He is also the editor of *Boulevard,* a literary quarterly.

Brock Clarke has appeared in *Mississippi Review,* where he was one of the finalists in the 1997 *Mississippi Review* Prize for Fiction. In 1997, he received New York's North Country Award for Fiction, a fellowship from the New York State Writers' Institute, and a scholarship to the Bread Loaf Writers' Conference. He has a Ph.D. from the University of Rochester.

Annie Dawid won second prize in *American Fiction, Volume Five* in 1993. Her novel *York Ferry* is now in its second printing, and her essays have appeared in *Women on Women II*, *Rage before Pardon: Poets of the World Bearing Witness to Holocaust*, and *AIDS: The Literary Response*.

Cathy Day's stories have appeared in *Story, Quarterly West*, the *Gettysburg Review*, and the *Florida Review*. She received an M.F.A. from the University of Alabama.

Lin Enger's work has appeared in *Glimmer Train* and other periodicals. He received an M.F.A. at the University of Iowa Writers' Workshop, where he was a Michener Fellow. In collaboration with his brother Leif under the name L. L. Enger, he has published five mystery novels, one of which was a finalist for the Edgar Award.

Bridget Rohan Garrity has been a Teaching Fellow at the University of Iowa Writers' Workshop and a Wallace Stegner Fellow at Stanford University. This is her first publication.

Sarah McElwain is a graphic designer who lives and works in New York City. Her book reviews appear regularly in the literary supplement of the *Valley Advocate*, and she has been a student at the Writer's Studio since 1995. This is her first published story.

Patricia Ann McNair received an M.F.A. from Columbia College Chicago, where she now teaches. She has also served as a lead artist for Chicago's Gallery 37 arts apprenticeship program. Her work has appeared in a number of magazines and journals, most recently *Fish Stories* and *Sport Literate*.

Ellie Mering lives in Tucson, Arizona, and believes that the titles "grandmother" and "emerging writer" are not incompatible.

Odhran O'Donovan is an American living in Ireland who

attended KISS (Kerry International Summer School of Irish and American Authors) in 1998.

Tom Paine is a graduate of Princeton University, the M.F.A. program at Columbia University, and the U.S. Marines. His short stories have been published in the *New Yorker, Harper's Magazine, Playboy, Zoetrope, Boston Review, Story,* and the *Oxford American,* and anthologized in *The O. Henry Awards: Prize Stories 1996, The 1997 Pushcart Prize XXI, The 1998 Pushcart Prize XXII, The Best New Stories from the South 1996,* and elsewhere. With Francis Ford Coppola, Touchstone Pictures will be turning his story about Bosnia, "War Crimes," into a screenplay. He has been a finalist for the National Magazine Award for fiction and was recently awarded fellowships from Yaddo and the Mellon Foundation. He teaches creative writing at Middlebury College.

Doug Rennie has published fiction in the *Quarterly, American Way, Chicago Tribune Magazine, Cream City Review,* and several dozen other publications. He lives in Portland, Oregon, and is currently completing a collection entitled *Stories My Wife Never Saw.*

Jean Rysstad has published two collections of fiction, most recently *Home Fires.* Her work has also appeared in many Canadian and U.S. anthologies, in Canadian literary magazines, and in *Prairie Schooner.*

Karen Halvorsen Schreck's work has appeared in *Other Voices, Private Arts, Quarter after Eight,* and *Literal Latté,* where she won the 1995 national short story competition. She was a winner of the 1997 Pushcart Prize for Fiction and in 1998 received an Illinois Arts Council Fellowship in Prose.

Julie Showalter's work has appeared in *New England Review, Calyx, Other Voices,* and elsewhere. She is a winner of the 1998 Pushcart Prize for Fiction. She lives near Chicago with her husband and two sons.

Maya Sonenberg won the Drue Heinz Literature Prize in 1998 from the University of Pittsburgh Press for her collection *Cartographies.* More recent fiction has appeared in *American Short Fiction, Gargoyle,* and *Santa Monica Press.* She lives in Seattle and teaches at the University of Washington.

Tanya Whiton is a fiction writer and poet based in Portland, Maine. "One for the Ocean" is her first published story and is one in a series of interrelated stories set in a rural fishing village in Down East Maine.

NORMANDALE COMMUNITY COLLEGE
LIBRARY
9700 FRANCE AVENUE SOUTH
BLOOMINGTON, MN 55431-4399